DREAM
TO ME

DREAM TO ME

MEGAN PAASCH

FEIWEL AND FRIENDS
NEW YORK

A Feiwel and Friends Book
An imprint of Macmillan Publishing Group, LLC
120 Broadway, New York, NY 10271 • fiercereads.com

Our books may be purchased in bulk for promotional, educational, or business use.
Please contact your local bookseller or the Macmillan Corporate and Premium
Sales Department at (800) 221-7945 ext. 5442 or by email at
MacmillanSpecialMarkets@macmillan.com.

Library of Congress Cataloging-in-Publication Data
Names: Paasch, Megan, author.
Title: Dream to me / Megan Paasch.
Description: First edition. | New York : Feiwel and Friends, 2023. | Summary:
After moving cross-country with her sister, Eva Sylvan begins having dreams with
devasting real-life effects on the already hostile town people; to stop these dreams
and save the town, Eva must investigate her family's magic-filled history and
confront her guilt over her father's death.
Identifiers: LCCN 2022036834 | ISBN 9781250817051 (hardcover)
Subjects: CYAC: Magic—Fiction. | Dreams—Fiction. | Grief—Fiction. |
Sisters—Fiction. | Fantasy. | LCGFT: Fantasy fiction. | Novels.
Classification: LCC PZ7.1.P15 Dr 2023 | DDC [Fic]—dc23
LC record available at https://lccn.loc.gov/2022036834

First edition, 2023
Book design by Maithili Joshi and Michelle Gengaro-Kokmen
Feiwel and Friends logo designed by Filomena Tuosto
Printed in the United States of America

ISBN 978-1-250-81705-1
1 3 5 7 9 10 8 6 4 2

For Dad.
I wish you could see this,
but I'm sure, somewhere out there,
you know.

CHAPTER 1

Daylight is fading to twilight in that slow, creeping way of summer evenings. Here under the shadow of the trees—so many trees, tall as the skyscrapers back home—it's already night. My sister and I left New York for the fabled land of man buns, flannel, and old-school grunge, and I can see how the look would have come about in a place like this. I wouldn't be surprised if everyone was a lumberjack in their spare time.

"Eva, put your feet down."

I ignore my sister, the Cranberries lulling me to sleep through my earbuds. Dolores O'Riordan's haunting voice tells me I'm a dream to her as I drift off against the dark blur of forest sliding past my window.

My feet remain on the dashboard.

It's an uneasy kind of sleep. The kind where I'm still half-aware of my surroundings but the details are shifting. Next to me, Rhonda's presence is overtaken by a heavier, deeper feel as my dream-addled mind rearranges her form into Dad's. In a moment, I've slipped into the back seat, my tiny feet pressed against the vinyl pocket in front of me. A younger, less somber Rhonda sits beside me again, staring contentedly at a dog-eared paperback. Dad, eyes shining, looks over his shoulder at me. His image is hazy, backlit by the sun.

How you doin' back there, Bug? Excited for the beach? His voice isn't quite right. It's close, I think, but the precise depth, the way he forms his words . . . I've already lost them.

We hit a pothole, and my eyes fly open.

"What?" I ask, a little too loudly, startled into wakefulness.

"Feet," Rhonda says. "Down. Help me find the turn."

I sit up properly, removing my earbuds. My hand instinctively reaches into my pocket and wraps around the smooth oblong of Dad's Swiss Army knife. Rubbing my thumb along the bumps of the corkscrew, I take a few breaths, gathering myself, tucking the ever-present ache safely into the background where it belongs.

"What's the street again?"

"Fay Road," Rhonda says.

As I watch out my window for street signs, the forest turns to brush, fields, a smattering of buildings. A carved wooden sign marks our approach to Madrona, Washington: population 723. According to my great-aunt Miriam's estate lawyer, a madrona is a type of tree. Of *course* the town is named after a tree.

"Damnit." Rhonda cranks the wheel and pulls into a rundown gas station. "We must have missed it. Go in and ask for directions while I fill up, please?"

Her tone is short, and I know she's tired. So am I.

"You're the one driving. Shouldn't you ask?"

She shoots me a look.

"I'll fill up," I offer.

"Evange*line*." She tilts her head toward the gas station's minimart.

"Eva," I mutter under my breath, unclipping my seat belt.

Rhonda points out a handwritten sign taped to the geriatric pump. "Looks like we have to pay inside, too."

I sigh and grab Rhonda's wallet as I exit the car. The gas station is practically dead right now, despite it only being 9:00 P.M. Small towns aren't open 24/7 like New York, but knowing this doesn't help with the creep factor. I eye the mini-mart's neon beer ads and grime-streaked bait-and-tackle sign with suspicion. The only trace of life besides Rhonda and me is an old blue pickup truck parked at an angle up front.

The bell on the door jangles against the glass as I push my way inside. Glancing over his magazine, the grizzled attendant catches my eye from behind the cash register. His brows twitch inhospitably. I hesitate, then make a beeline for the refrigerator cases in the back. It'll take Rhonda a few minutes to fill up, and I could use something sugary and caffeinated. Or maybe I'm procrastinating.

Just go and ask him, I hear Dad's indistinct voice in the back of my mind. Snatching at the essence of the words—ones spoken to me many times over the years—I try to squeeze out the exact tonality and cadence. Again, I'm unsuccessful.

As I pass the snack aisle, the store's only other customer—a tall, blond-haired, country-looking boy—glances up from a display of potato chips. His clear blue eyes lock with mine for a split second before I duck my head and hasten my step.

Again, Dad's voice runs through my head. *You need to work on being more assertive.* A frequent criticism from him, especially when I was younger, coaxing me to approach the counter and order my own food, or return something at the store. *I won't always be around to do it for you.*

3

I never dreamed it would be so soon. It's not that I'm shy or anything. I just need to prepare myself before interacting with people I don't know. Some days I need more time than others. Especially lately, with everything still so raw. I continue to repeat Dad's advice over in my head as I hurry to the refrigerator cases. His voice was deep, but how deep? I no longer know.

I've been thinking a lot about this lately. Impermanence. The speed at which things slip away. How something can be there one day, and a fraction of a second later, it's gone. Pop. Like that. And how some things, smaller things, dissolve gradually, less noticeably, until you wonder if they were ever even there to begin with.

Shake it off, Eva. Get your soda, ask for directions, and go. Right.

When I reach the back of the store, I see the boy again, distorted in the corner surveillance mirror. Caught staring, he jerks his chin down and continues his examination of the potato chips. The corners of my lips quirk up involuntarily. Did I just catch him checking me out? I have to admit, he's kinda cute.

It takes a hefty yank against the refrigerator's suction to get the soda case open. I reach for an energy drink, then reconsider and go for a Coke instead. I just want to wake up a little, not run a marathon.

On my way to the counter, I risk another glance toward the boy. He doesn't look back at me this time, fully absorbed in decision-making. Who knew choosing a potato chip flavor could be such a life-defining event?

"Evening." The station attendant's voice is low and gravelly. He smells like stale cigarettes. My eyes slide from his weathered face to the neatly embroidered *Rob* on the pocket of his polo shirt.

"Hi, uh . . ." Leaning back on my heels, I check which pump Rhonda's using through the glass doors. "Pump four, please. Oh, and this." I set my Coke can on the counter.

"That'll be forty sixty-three."

I fish Rhonda's credit card out of her wallet and place it on the counter next to my Coke. "Oh, and could you, um, please tell me how to get to, uh . . . to Fay Road from here?" I cringe inwardly as I stumble over the words.

He juts his chin so far back, it disappears into his neck. "Fay Road?"

"Yeah, it . . . it exists, right?"

"Sure, it exists. Barely. Are you sure that's the road you're looking for? Nothin' up that way but the old Sylvan place." Before I can assure him I'm aware, he narrows his eyes and grumbles, "You're not planning on meeting your friends up there, are you? Damn kids," he adds, more to himself than to me. "It's dangerous running around up there. Especially at night."

"Dangerous?" My great-aunt's house? Though . . . it *has* been vacant for a while. I feel a twinge in my gut. I hope these "kids" he's talking about haven't been breaking in. I hope it isn't trashed.

"You and your friends stay away from that place. You'll get tetanus, or worse. Oh, and cash only," he adds. "Card reader's broke."

Fumbling, I fish out two twenties and a five. "You don't understand. We're just lost." I fork over the last of Rhonda's cash. "The road's not showing up on GPS, and—"

His hand slaps down on the credit card before I can take it, startling me. Rhonda's wallet slips from my fingers and hits the floor; dimes and quarters scatter, rolling and spinning with a chorus of metallic ringing.

"Holy shhhhh . . ." He stares at the card, his voice a strange whisper. "You're a—a Sylvan?" For the first time, he takes a good look at my face. I can feel my cheeks burn under the scrutiny as he slowly shakes his head. "It can't be. You look so much like—" He stops himself, then gives Rhonda's credit card a hard push, sliding it across the counter to me. "You need to go."

I stop the card from flying off the edge in the nick of time. I'm shaking, and so is he. What just happened? "I—" My voice is small. "I still need my change."

After an impossibly long second, he reaches over and opens the register. Mouth set in a hard line, he roughly swipes four one-dollar bills out of the change drawer. "Good or bad, doesn't matter," he mutters to himself as he scrapes the rest of my change out of the drawer. "There'll be trouble either way."

"Trouble? We—we're not—" I squat down, frantically gathering the coins that escaped Rhonda's wallet. I've probably missed a few, but I don't care. "We just want directions."

"No," he says, firm, as I stand up. "I don't know why you're here, but I'm warning you, you need to leave."

Without further protest, I scoop my change off the counter and hurry for the door. "It's dangerous," he repeats as I yank it open and rush outside.

The bells on the door clatter angrily behind me as I march across the rainbow-greased pavement. My pulse pounds in my ears, and my breath catches in my throat. What the hell was that about? Why does he care that I'm a Sylvan? Or that I look like . . . who? My great-aunt Miriam? Some other relative? I've never met any of them, so I wouldn't know.

I'm halfway to the car when the door jingles again and I hear a voice call out, "Wait!"

The boy from the snack aisle sprints over to me, holding my Coke. "You forgot this."

"Thanks," I manage as he hands it over. My heart's still beating a mile a minute.

"Sorry about Rob back there," he says. "He's . . . well, he's . . ." He shakes his head, then holds out his hand. "I'm Cal."

I transfer my Coke to my left hand and am wiping the condensation off my right when my sister leans her head out the car window. "Eva! Did you get directions?"

"Just a second," I yell back. Maybe Cal can tell us where to go.

His hands shoot to his pockets. "Why are you looking for the Sylvan place?"

"We're moving in." I watch him carefully, studying his reaction.

"*Really?*" His eyes widen. I can't help noticing how bright they are, even in the dimming light. But his surprise, though somewhat expected, sets my nerves off and running again. What could possibly be so wrong with this house?

"That guy"—I gesture toward the mini-mart—"he said it's dangerous. How so?"

"Well, it's, uh." He thinks for a moment. "It's old."

Old? Every apartment I've ever lived in has been old, but I wouldn't have called them dangerous. "So, a fixer-upper?"

He nods.

"Okay." Good to know, I guess. "Can you tell us how to get there?"

"Not really," he says.

My jaw tightens. Not him, too.

"I suck at giving directions." His face reddens. "But I can show you. Follow me."

I let out a slow breath as he sprints over to his truck.

"What was that all about? Did you get directions?" Rhonda asks while I climb into the passenger seat.

"Sort of," I say. "Follow that truck."

CHAPTER 2

"Everything okay?" Rhonda glances sideways at me. The red glow of Cal's taillights illuminates the circles under her eyes, deepens her worry lines, giving away the stress she tries so hard to hide. I wonder what it's revealing about my own face.

"Yup."

"You sure?"

I'm half here, half replaying the interaction with Rob on a loop, trying to understand it.

"Well—"

"Where the hell's he going?" Rhonda leans forward and peers out the windshield, searching the side of the road.

Cal's clicked his left blinker on, but there's nowhere to go that we can see. He turns anyway, straight into the brush, and keeps going, the cab of his truck just visible over the weeds and wild grasses. As we approach the same spot, we find there really is an opening here—a gap barely wide enough for a single vehicle, marked by a pair of ruts. There's no sign to tell us this is Fay Road. No wonder we'd missed it before.

I grab the oh-shit handle above the car door to brace myself as we make the turn. The rough road jars my teeth, and the stiff grass scrapes against the car's sides and undercarriage, making any further conversation impossible.

Knots form in my stomach. What kind of person was my late great-aunt Miriam to live in a place as secluded as this? What have we gotten ourselves into? I reach for my soda but think better of it before cracking it open. This road's probably turned It into the perfect fizz bomb by now. I grip my seat belt. Dad's Swiss Army knife presses against my thigh in my pocket, providing some comfort.

Maybe it's better if I don't tell Rhonda what happened at the gas station. She's stressed enough already, and besides, it won't change anything. We've come all this way. No matter what we find at the end of this road, we're not turning around.

This is home now. We can't afford to live in the city anymore, especially now that it's just the two of us. Even before, with Dad's income as a paramedic, things were getting tight. And as for Dad's life insurance policy, well, we're still waiting on that. So, when Rhonda discovered Great-Aunt Miriam's will among the mess of paperwork in Dad's desk, she pounced on it. *It's a free house, Eva. In the town where Dad grew up. It's the perfect opportunity for us. There might even be family there.*

Family Dad never talked about. He'd had that will for at least a year and hadn't mentioned it to us once. Guilt pricks at me as I remember the shadow that passed over Rhonda's eyes when she examined it further and realized she wasn't mentioned anywhere. Miriam had even bypassed Dad, inexplicably leaving the house to me, a minor, with Dad as trustee until I turn eighteen. Rhonda's the trustee now, since she's my legal guardian per *Dad's* will, but it serves as a stark reminder that Rhonda, though Sylvan by name, is not Sylvan by blood. We're half sisters through our mom. Dad still considered Rhonda as much his daughter as

I am, but I guess Miriam had other ideas. Maybe that's why Dad kept her will hidden away.

Cal's truck banks upward, then disappears down the other side of a hill. In a moment, we do the same.

I suck in my breath.

Up ahead is the bushiest, most imposing wall of greenery I've ever seen. I'm sure it was a hedge once. Now it's a wild, monster thicket. Just over the top, the shadow of a peaked roof rises. Behind it, dark forest stretches into oblivion.

Rhonda's jaw is set, her knuckles white on the steering wheel. I don't know what either of us expected, but it certainly wasn't this.

We roll up next to Cal's truck in front of the hedge and park. Silence overwhelms us. No distant cars, no crickets, not even a breeze rustling the leaves.

Cal's truck door slams and his shoes crunch on the gravel, breaking the stillness. Rhonda and I get out to greet him.

"Rhonda, this is Cal," I say. "Cal, my sister, Rhonda."

"Thanks so much for your help." Rhonda holds out her hand to shake. "We really—"

She stops, whipping her head around at the sound of something rattling. There's a long hiss, then laughter from beyond the hedge. We're not alone.

My feet stay rooted to the ground as Rhonda squares her shoulders and marches over to the wrought-iron gate embedded within a gap in the hedge. The laughter and that strange hissing continue over her crunching footsteps, oblivious to the impending storm that is Rhonda after a long day.

"Hey!" she shouts. More laughter. More hissing. "I said, hey! What the *fuck* are you doing?"

11

Silence. I look to Cal, my heart pounding in my chest. But whether I'm more nervous for Rhonda or for whoever's behind that hedge, I'm not sure. Cal returns my look. We take a few tentative steps in Rhonda's direction until she holds up her finger, telling us to stay where we are.

"You lost or something?" says a voice, young, slurred.

"Who the hell are you?" asks another.

"Who the hell am *I*?" Uh-oh. I know that tone. "I live here. Who the hell are *you*?"

"Oh . . . shit." Without warning, two shadowy figures come barreling out of the gate. If Rhonda hadn't stepped to the side, she'd be flat on her back. They're past us before I can get a good look at their faces, but as they stumble up the hill, one of them yells, "I told you she could still hex us, I told you, we're hexed, we're hexed!" The other yells at him to shut up and hurry up as they disappear over the other side.

If I wasn't so bewildered, I'd laugh. *Hexed? What?*

Cal and I jog over to join Rhonda at the open gate. The scene that greets me brings hot anger to my cheeks. It's almost fully night now, but not too dark to make out the sorry state of the imposing Victorian before me—rotting porch steps, missing shingles, shutters hanging askew around the weathered plywood boarding up the ground-floor windows. Empty beer bottles and discarded spray cans litter the overgrown front walk. The smell of chemicals lingers in the air.

But none of that bothers me nearly as much as the message those boys left behind. Freshly sprayed across the entire front of the house, in gruesome red letters, is the word *WITCH*.

The visceral effect it has shocks me. All apprehension about moving to a strange house in a strange town is washed away by a wave of pure rage. How dare they? I've never met Miriam; I know nothing about her, but she was family, and she left this house to *me*. And those boys are calling my great-aunt—the woman who *raised my dad*—a witch. This will take forever to clean off. We'll have to repaint this . . . this falling-apart wreck. *This* is what she left me? *This* is where we're supposed to live? And now I'm angry about that. I'm angry that Dad isn't here to deal with this. I'm angry and angry and tired and angry and—footsteps crunch behind me. I'm unable to disguise my expression as I spin around to face Cal.

"Who were those guys? Do you know them?" It's a small town, right? Everyone knows everyone in a small town.

"I—" His words catch as he, too, scans the front of the house.

I turn to look again, and only then do I notice the rest of the message. Smaller words flank the main one, harder to make out in the near dark, but when put together, I recognize them: *Ding-dong, the WITCH is DEAD.*

I hear the phrase in my head, sung in the high-pitched voices of the munchkins from *The Wizard of Oz*, picture them dancing and skipping in all their Technicolor glory. But there are no ruby slippers here. No clicking of heels to carry me home. *This* is my home now. *This*. It takes every ounce of effort I have left not to sit down, right here in the weeds, and cry.

Rhonda takes a breath, lifts her chin, then marches down the path and up the front steps, kicking a paint canister aside along the way. I hang back behind the gate and watch as she wrestles with the key in the lock. She peers through the doorway and reaches inside, feeling around for the light switch. When no light comes on, her shoulders arch, then drop in a heavy sigh. She closes the door, struggles to lock it again, and returns to where Cal and I are standing.

"Back to the car," she says. She looks paler than usual, even in the moonlight. "We're not staying here tonight." She pulls out her phone, scowls at it, then holds it up in the air. "*Damnit.* No signal." Sagging ever so slightly, she turns to Cal. "Are there any motels nearby? Preferably something cheap?"

He thinks for a moment. "There's the Roadhouse. My friend's mom runs it. Mrs. Lieu. I'll show you."

"I'm sure we can find it if you give us directions. Unless it's down another road like this," she adds, and I can't tell if she's being sarcastic or truly thinks it's possible. Could be either, after the evening we've had.

Cal shifts on his feet. "But, I mean, I'm going that way anyway. I have this . . . thing, where I have a hard time with—it'll be easier if I show you."

Rhonda's forehead wrinkles. "All right. We'll follow your truck again. Thanks."

He is visibly relieved, but when he looks to me from Rhonda, he tenses again. His eyes shoot down to the ground, and nodding, he turns on his heels and hurries back into his truck.

I check myself. I think maybe I was staring. There's something familiar about him I can't place. It's similar to a feeling I get from time to time, that something's missing. That there's a hole in me like the gap in a window frame letting the chill seep in, but

14

I can't pinpoint which window needs patching up. I give myself a mental shake to clear it. *He must remind me of someone back home*, I decide as I climb into the passenger seat. *That's all.*

"Well, he seems nice." Rhonda shoots me a meaningful look as she starts the engine. "And kinda cute."

I click my seat belt. "And kinda weird." But yes, also kind of cute. *And familiar. Why so familiar?*

"Yeah, he's a little awkward." She shrugs. "But *nice*. I think he likes you."

I groan and pop my earbuds back in. The ending refrain of "Dreams" fades out and "Sunday" begins as we pull out of the weeds onto the highway.

CHAPTER 3

In my mind, the term "Roadhouse" conjures images of antlers and cowboy boots, dark wood, and a jukebox playing country music. But this place has a more retro-fifties-diner-meets-British-manor-house look, which sounds like an odd combination, but somehow, it works. Dark green vinyl booths and chrome-backed dining chairs are mixed with floral wallpaper and oak trimmings. It's dark, but in a cozy, inviting way.

It's also super crowded tonight.

The owner, Mrs. Lieu, offers us a friendly but distracted smile, telling us she'll be with us in a minute as she punches in a customer's credit card. She hisses under her breath as she mistypes, cancels the transaction, and tries again.

"There," she says to herself, setting the card aside and directing her full attention on us. "Welcome to the Roadhouse." She glances at our suitcases. "Booking a room?"

We confirm we are, and she darts around behind the counter gathering our paperwork, wisps of graying black hair falling from her loose bun. Her eyes widen then narrow as she looks over Rhonda's driver's license, and I hold my breath, preparing myself for another gas-station incident. But she blinks, recovers, and plasters on another smile as she hands it back.

"I have the perfect room for you," she says. "Bethany!" she calls to a girl bustling past with a tray of dishes.

"Yeah?" The girl stops and glances over at Rhonda and me with interest. A silver charm bracelet dangles from her wrist below the tray, catching the light. I can't make out the charms from here, but I think the black typewriter X on her T-shirt is from an old sci-fi show.

"While you're back there, tell your dad to come out and cover for me while I show these guests to their room, all right?"

"Holy shit, we actually have guests?"

"Bethany—" Mrs. Lieu's eyes dart toward us.

"I mean welcome to the Roadhouse. I hope you enjoy your stay." Bethany shoots me a mischievous smile, forcing me to stifle a laugh.

"I also need you to take this back to table five," Mrs. Lieu tells her, tearing a receipt off the printer and sticking it in a vinyl billfold with the credit card from earlier.

Bethany's smile fades as she slides the billfold in her pocket. "Um, Mom?" She lowers her voice. "Table five is that asshole I was telling you about. He's making me uncomfortable."

"Language," Mrs. Lieu scolds, then nods in agreement. "Have your dad handle it."

"Thanks." Bethany gives Rhonda and me another curious look, then hurries off to the kitchen.

"My daughter," Mrs. Lieu sighs as she gathers the check-in paperwork and files it away below the counter. "She's at that age. About your age, actually," she says to me. "You're in high school, yes? She'll be a junior this fall."

"Me too," I tell her.

"Maybe you'll have some classes together," Rhonda suggests with a cheerful lilt.

"Oh. Are you staying long, then?" There's something about Mrs. Lieu's tone that I can't quite put my finger on, but it sounds like more than idle curiosity. Almost . . . guarded.

"We're moving here, actually, but the, um . . . our house isn't quite . . . ready for us yet," Rhonda says.

Understatement of the year.

"Oh! Well then, welcome to Madrona," Mrs. Lieu says, turning before I can get a good read on her expression. Her words sound friendly enough, but there's that guarded undertone again that makes my stomach knot the way it did when she was looking over Rhonda's driver's license.

Keys jangling from her hip, she leads us past the kitchen, where I catch a glimpse of Bethany popping an errant french fry in her mouth as the chef has his back turned. I'm guessing that's Mr. Lieu, since there isn't anyone else in there.

"Sorry about the noise," Mrs. Lieu tells us over her shoulder as she leads us outside. "Fridays are karaoke night." Then she gives us a quick history of the building as we follow her out the back door into the parking lot.

According to Mrs. Lieu, our room used to be one of several apartments on the top floor of the Roadhouse, which dates to 1911. "One of the oldest original buildings in Madrona," she tells us proudly as we round the corner and head down a narrow alley to a set of wood stairs. "Watch your step."

I wouldn't call our room fancy, but it's much nicer than any of the rooms we've stayed in on our drive out here. There's a kitchenette with a sink, a mini fridge, and a coffee maker, but no stove. A small table and a pair of spindle chairs are tucked into the corner. Opposite the kitchenette, two quilt-covered beds are separated by a nightstand, and at the room's farthest end, a door leads to the bathroom. Simple, but inviting to our road-weary souls.

Rhonda crashes soon after Mrs. Lieu leaves, then spends the rest of the night snoring. But despite my exhaustion, I'm wide awake. I fiddle with my phone for a bit, frustrated by the slow Wi-Fi, until half-loaded, pixilated pictures of my friend—ex-friend?—Riley on her summer vacation show up in my feed. Guilt pricks at me.

Riley was my rock when it came to simple, everyday problems. And I was hers. Crushes, bullies, parental arguments—we always turned to each other for support. But all that changed when Dad died. Things got awkward very quickly. Maybe she wasn't perfect at knowing how to help this time, but she was my best friend—I could have at least let her try. Instead, I pushed her away until finally she just . . . stopped checking on me.

My thumb jerks down on the power button before Riley's pictures can finish loading. I don't need to see what she's up to right now. How my summer would have been if everything had stayed the same.

Night has always been my favorite and least favorite time of day. Thoughts and emotions become tangible, living things at night. Sometimes I welcome them, wrap my arms around them, and pull them in close. But now, in these last few months since Dad died, I find myself desperately trying to ward them off as they chase after me, hunting me down.

Tonight, I feel a mixture of both, my mind a swirling dance of contradictions. Coming to Madrona, in a way, should bring me closer to a part of my dad I never knew much about. At the same time, it feels like a betrayal. He refused to talk about his childhood here, no matter how much I pressed him, until I finally learned to stop asking. This piece of his past was private, buried, and now Rhonda and I are here, about to pry open the casket. There's obviously a reason that casket was sealed. I've already had two blaring indications we might not like what we find inside.

Things will probably look better in the morning, I tell myself. *They usually do.* If only I could fall asleep.

Karaoke night isn't helping.

I stare at the glowing red numbers of the bedside clock, willing them to hypnotize me to sleep: 12:09 changes to 12:10 and still, the music below continues. I miss my bed back home. I miss my room. I even miss the traffic noise outside my window. I could sleep through that. It was more of a constant, background thing, whereas the music downstairs is rhythmic, changing, vibrating up through the floorboards. No matter how hard I try, I can't tune it out.

I miss Dad.

I miss him so much, it physically hurts.

Resigned, I give up trying to sleep and scoot out from under the covers. My hands feel around in the pitch black, knocking against a table leg, brushing a corduroy chair cushion, until they finally find the familiar, coarse nylon of my backpack. Slowly working the zipper so as not to disturb Rhonda—I'm not sure why, since she's sleeping through everything else—I open it just enough to root around for my journal and pen. I bring them back into bed with me and pull the covers over my head like a tent, using my charging cell phone as a flashlight.

Dear Dad, I write, then pause, my pen hovering over the page.

My therapist suggested I start keeping a journal a few months ago, right after Dad died, and all my entries begin like this. Sometimes, it makes him feel more alive. Other times, it knocks into me that he's gone forever. I'll never get another chance to hug him. Or tell him I love him. Or that I'm sorry. No matter how much I write it in here, he'll never know. But tonight, I'm too tired, too out of my element to feel anything either way. Tonight, I feel numb.

I'm finally in your hometown, Dad. We just got in, so I haven't been here long. But I'm already getting an idea of why you left.

Scenes from this evening flash through my head.

Ding-dong, the WITCH is DEAD.

You're a Sylvan?

There'll be trouble either way.

You need to leave.

My fingers loosen. The pen drops.

It was seeing our last name on Rhonda's credit card that set that guy off. I close my eyes and rest my head on the open pages.

He was bothered by our last name, Sylvan. Why?

The old Sylvan place.

It's dangerous.

WITCH.

I can hear laughter, distant, over the Roadhouse's rumble of activity. Distant, yet strangely clear. I lift my head off the journal to listen. Children? Laughing . . . taunting . . . calling . . .

I don't remember getting out of bed, but in a moment, I'm outside our room on the porch. The laughter is coming from somewhere down the alleyway, but I don't think it's from the Roadhouse. Curious, I tread down the steps, my chunky-soled boots—*when did I put those on?*—clomping against the wood boards in rhythm with the karaoke beat. Despite my heavy footfalls, I feel light and floaty.

The laughs turn strange—echoey—the farther I glide down the alley, no longer walking, yet somehow still moving toward the sound. Drawn as if by an invisible rope tied around my middle. Maybe I should be concerned, but it doesn't feel strange in this moment.

Now I'm in front of a building, facing a door. It's glass, but I can't see much through it besides blobs amid bright lights. This is where the laughter's coming from.

"Hey! Kids! Take your disagreement somewhere else," booms a gruff voice from the other side.

More laughter. Nasty, teasing laughter.

"I mean it. Take it outside or I'm calling the cops."

The laughter stops dead. So does my pulse. Open the door. *Don't open it.* Open it.

Now I'm inside the mini-mart.

It's the same one I was kicked out of earlier this evening, except for a few small differences. Some things have moved, and the letters on the signs and product labels are blurry; they keep shifting around among the flickering yellow lights.

Three boys are here, faces blurred, like the signs. Two are

at a standoff with the third, and though I can't make out their expressions, I can see and feel their emotions as tangible things. The emotions of the third boy, the one standing alone, are especially strong, roiling off him like hot steam off the sea. It bends and curls in thin, shadowy wisps, and the longer I watch, the more I can't help but feel its draw. The draw of its . . . what is it? Anger? No, not quite. It's focused inward. *Like guilt.* Yes, I know that feeling. I understand it. It's what I've felt since Dad died, deep down inside. I sense myself leaning forward, leaning into it. I *am* that feeling.

That's when the boy with the wisps finally notices me. I still can't make out his features, but I can feel his eyes lock onto me like a tracking device.

Shaken out of my trance, I take an involuntary step back toward the door . . . that I never actually opened or walked through. I thought about it, and then I appeared here. Or did here appear around me?

The other two don't seem to notice me at all. I don't think they even see the curling shadows like I do. If they did, they'd be afraid, *very* afraid, but they're not. I can feel the chill of their smirks without seeing their lips.

"You."

I swivel toward the voice—the same voice I'd heard from outside—to face . . . what was his name again? Rob. That's right. It's embroidered on his shirt. Strangely, I can see his features clearly, unlike the boys. He's wearing the exact same expression as he was when he told me to leave mere hours ago, but I sense something more behind it. He's holding something back. Something dark.

"Get out of here."

Is he talking to me or the boys? I point a finger to my chest, questioning him with my eyes, but he's looking past me, so he must be talking to the boys. Except when I look again, the two harassers are gone. Only the small angry one remains, growing murky and indistinct like the smoky cloud surrounding him. Like a shadow. The hairs rise on the back of my neck. Is it even still him, or is it someone—some*thing*—else?

The shadowy figure grows and grows, mixing with the cloud and spreading out, darkening the store, swallowing it up in gulps. Sparks fly as each light goes out, one by one, accompanied by pops and bursts, like fireworks. I can even smell it—that acrid, lingering scent of cordite that permeates the air on New Year's Eve and the Fourth of July.

Am I drawing it to me somehow? Bracing myself against its strange, emotional pull, I risk a peek over my shoulder at Rob.

"It's happening," he says, backing into the cigarette case behind the counter. "Go. Please, you have to go."

I wish I could, but my legs are frozen in place.

"I was afraid this would happen!" he shouts to me over the pop of the lights. "You're just like her. That's why you *need* to *go.* Get out of here! Hurry!"

The shadow advances faster, licking up the walls like storm waves crashing against a breaker. It's almost here.

"Go!" Rob yells as it surrounds him. "Now!"

CHAPTER 4

I blink.

My eyelashes brush against something rough. Paper. It's hot and stuffy and dark. With a groan, I lift myself up on my arms, slipping the blanket off of my head, then blink again at the journal entry I've been using as a pillow. I've drooled on it, smearing the word "Dad."

There's a flush, then water splashing in the sink. When the bathroom door opens, the room fills with light, bringing my unfinished journal entry into full relief. I stare at the smudge that used to be my father. It's like pressing against a bruise to see if it's still tender. It is.

I flip the book shut and shove it hard under my pillow as Rhonda exits the bathroom.

"Oh, good, you woke up on your own. I didn't want to bother you when you were sleeping so peacefully for once."

"Peacefully?" I prop myself up on my elbow and wrinkle my nose. I was dreaming about something—I can't remember what—but I don't feel peaceful right now. There's an uneasy feeling in the pit of my stomach. Maybe I need breakfast.

Rhonda comes and sits on my bed, sweeping a sweaty strand of hair off my forehead, like Mom used to do. "You look like a little kid again when you're sleeping. It's sweet."

"I was under the blankets," I retort.

Her attempt at a smile falters. She moves over to the dinette and opens her ancient laptop. "Well, the lump of blankets looked at least five years younger," she says, then mutters, "Seattle power company" as she types it into the search bar.

There she goes again, acting like a middle-aged parent instead of my twenty-two-year-old sister. "Will you stop?"

The loading circle turns and spins on her screen as the Roadhouse's crappy Wi-Fi struggles to make a connection.

"Stop what?" she asks.

"Stop always trying to make up for Mom."

I regret it as soon as I've said it.

The laptop slams shut. She doesn't turn to look at me, but I can see her back go rigid.

"I'm doing the best I can right now, okay?" she says. "It's not like you've been making it easy."

The necessary apology catches in my throat. Her shoulders roll forward as she rests her forehead on her palm, and I think maybe it would be better to give her a minute. To give us both a minute. I drag myself out of bed and shuffle into the bathroom to take my turn in the shower.

I didn't mean it. I know how much she's given up since Dad died. Her job, her friends, the premed degree she was working toward. All to keep me out of foster homes when Mom, true to form, never bothered to show up. If our mom even knew what had happened. She left when I was eleven, favoring her addictions and the new boyfriend who helped supply them over her own family. Maybe she thought she was doing us all a favor. Or maybe she just didn't care. Rhonda was seventeen when Mom left and is the closest thing I've had to a mom ever since. It's no wonder she acts so much older than she is. And while I at least still have Rhonda to look up to, who has Rhonda had besides Dad? Now he's gone, too.

I should apologize.

I step into the shower and let the hot water wash over me, let the sound of it beating against the tile drown out my mental self-flagellation. If I close my eyes and breathe in the herbal aroma of Rhonda's favorite shampoo, I can almost imagine I'm back home. Until the showerhead splutters and the temperature drops as someone else in the building dips into the hot water supply.

Also like home.

Our hair dryer shorted out on day three of our trip, so after toweling off, I wring out my locks, then twist them into a topknot. If I don't and allow my hair to air-dry loose, I'll have a halo of flyaways within an hour. My look, if you can call it that, is complete with a pair of artfully torn jeans and a Doors tee—also full of holes, but these aren't intentional. It's just well loved. Dad introduced me to the Doors; he was always listening to old music. It was kind of our thing. He got me this shirt for my birthday a couple years ago from a vintage place near the fire station where he was based. It's getting a little small for me now, but I don't care.

I emerge from the bathroom feeling slightly better, an apology ready on my lips. But Rhonda's on the phone now and sounds like she might be a while.

"I called to have it turned on last week." Pause. "Uh-huh.

You sure about that?" Another pause. "Is there someone higher up I can speak to?" Her tone is sharp, and I think maybe it would be better if I got out of her way.

I catch her eye to let her know I'm heading out, then slip from the room before she can stop me. I don't even bother lacing up my boots until I'm already out the door, sitting on the top steps of the long wooden staircase leading to the alley. As I peer down them, I'm hit by an uneasy wave of déjà vu. *Clomping down steps to the sound of drumbeats. But it was night. Wasn't it? And there were dark clouds . . . smoke?*

A whiff of something burning—food, I think—tickles my nose, jolting me out of . . . whatever this is. A dream. Yes, I was dreaming last night about smoke. I peek through the cracks between the steps and spy a head of silky black waves. Mrs. Lieu's daughter, Bethany, leans against the wall below the porch, one knee jutting out with a black apron draped across it. A gray haze wafts from the door propped open next to her.

As if sensing my stare, her face turns up. "Hey."

I hurry to tie my other boot, then clomp down the steps. Clomp, clomp . . . there's that déjà vu again.

"You're one of those chicks Cal brought by last night, right? Rhonda? No, you don't look like a Rhonda. You must be . . . Angela?" She reaches up to scratch an itch on her nose, her bracelet jingling. This time, I'm able to catch sight of an alien charm and another I think might be the TARDIS from *Doctor Who* before she crosses her arms again, tucking the bracelet out of sight.

I repress a sigh. I get Angela a lot. "It's Evangeline, but you can call me Eva."

"Ah, sorry. Eva. At least I was close, right? I'm Bethany."

"I remember."

She points to my shirt. "You're into the Doors, huh? Cool. So is my dad."

I feel myself blushing awkwardly as I look down at the logo. "Yeah, they're pretty great."

"You see that old movie about them? With that guy who was a hottie back in the nineties, what's his face . . ."

"Val Kilmer?"

"Yeah, Val Kilmer." She draws his name out dreamily and waggles her eyebrows at me. "Seen it?"

It makes me laugh, melting away my self-consciousness. "If Val Kilmer's in it, believe me, I've seen it."

"I knew I was gonna like you." The skin around her eyes crinkles as she grins and pushes off from the wall. "I could tell by your boots. Totally retro. Love it. Though I'm more into retro horror myself. Or just, well, anything spooky or sci-fi. Or both. Both is good. I heard you're moving here."

I nod, trying to keep up with the abrupt change in the conversation.

"Fuck yeah. That means you'll be around for my first annual Spooky Sci-Fi and/or Horror Film Fest this October. I'm . . . still workshopping the name. But you have to come!"

I blink. "Um, sure. I mean, I'll try. I don't know what my schedule's going to be like three months from now, but . . ."

"Oh, I can tell you that. School and absofuckinglutely nothing," she laughs. "This town's the most boring place on the planet." She makes a face as her phone buzzes in her apron pocket. "Shit. Break's over. I gotta get back in there. You and your friend—"

"Sister."

"Sister? Wow, you two look nothing alike. You guys coming down to eat? Continental breakfast's free with the room."

It's true we look nothing alike. Rhonda takes after her biological dad, or so she's been told, tall with soft, delicate features and dark brown hair, thick with curls. I take more after *my* dad, short and all sharp angles, exacerbated by my stick-straight sandy-blah hair. Neither of us takes after our mom. Not even a little.

I shrug, glancing toward the porch. I wonder how Rhonda's doing with her phone call. "Maybe later. Thinking I'll go explore the town and stuff."

She snorts. "Well, that shouldn't take you long. Breakfast goes until ten thirty in case you get hungry or bored."

"I'll probably see you soon, then."

"Most likely." She grins at me again. "See you around, Eva."

I watch her disappear into the Roadhouse kitchen, then I head down the alley to the sidewalk that runs along Main Street. She seems nice. Sweary, but nice. Maybe that Rob guy at the gas station was a fluke.

And those boys who vandalized Miriam's house.

Then again, maybe Bethany and Cal are the flukes. At first, I don't notice the strange looks as I make my way down Main Street. I'm more interested in checking out the shopwindows, trying to get a feel for what there is to do around here, which, as Bethany warned, isn't much. But there's a used bookstore and a library. Cheap books and free books. Not a bad deal. Rhonda, especially, will be happy about that. I check the hours posted on the door and spot a strange symbol etched into the wood. It's a spiral with a cross over the top—very small—and I can tell it's been there for a long time, barely visible from the buildup of paint settled into the lines.

As I continue my walk, I notice it near the doors and windows of more buildings. Always the same symbol. Seems someone went on a carving spree at some point in the past. I wonder what it means . . . and why it makes me feel so uneasy.

As I approach the local coffee shop, the pleasant aroma of espresso lifts my spirits again. I don't drink coffee, but that warm, earthy scent has always been comforting. My stomach growls. *I wish I had some cash on me. Then I'd go in and get a muffin or something,* I think as the door opens, exposing the shrill grind of an espresso machine, and an elderly couple emerges. I smile at them automatically.

They freeze.

At first, I think the woman is having a heart attack because she gasps, clutching her chest. I take a step forward to help, but the man, hunched over his cane, thrusts his free arm protectively in front of her. He nudges his wife back toward the building side of the walkway, and the two huddle together in front of the coffee shop's picture window, eyeing me with suspicion.

Inside, a woman sitting by the window looks up from her laptop and stares at me through the glass, brows crinkling then eyes widening as if something has just now dawned on her and it isn't pleasant. I check behind me for some unknown threat.

That's when I notice the other reactions I'm getting.

A man behind the steering wheel of his parked car, hand paused on the ignition, looks quickly away. A mom pushing a toddler in a stroller rushes along the other side of the street, darting wary glances at me until she's safely around the corner. And when I turn back toward the coffee shop, the woman inside returns her eyes to her screen, face flushed. The elderly couple, however, continues to stare.

Hairs rise on the nape of my neck. "Excuse me," I mutter as I hurry past them.

I continue to feel their eyes on me as I reach the end of the block, and when I finally risk a glance back, they're standing in the same spot, still watching. Scowling. Another wave of discomfort washes over me. I slip inside the nearest shop, barely registering the sign above the door: PETERSEN'S GIFTS. Gift shops aren't my thing, but it doesn't matter as long as it gets me away from those accusing eyes. Accusing me of what, I have no idea.

The heady smell of potpourri immediately makes my throat itch as I find myself surrounded by displays of postcards, key chains, figurines, and other tchotchkes. A sign advertises framing services in the back, and another promotes personalized invitations for weddings and baby showers.

Two women stand at the counter in the center of the store—one behind the register, one in front. They immediately stop chatting and turn to look at me. I tense, expecting more weird stares, but they simply nod in acknowledgment before resuming their conversation in low murmurs. I think I'll hang out for a few minutes—give that creepy old couple some time to move on.

Biding my time, I browse the postcards—mostly pastoral scenes and forested waterfalls. Some Seattle skylines have been thrown into the mix for good measure, despite Seattle being at least an hour's drive away. Maybe I'll get one of those to send to Riley. She'd probably appreciate it more than a picture of a barn.

I told myself I'd call her when I got here, thinking maybe with some time and distance—miles and miles of distance—I'd be ready to explain. To tell her I'm sorry and I needed space to grieve. But I doubt she'd answer. A postcard might be easier. Acknowledgment without expectations; a peace offering she can take or leave. I pull out a picture of a full moon over the Space Needle—*Wish you were here!*—then stuff it back into the rack.

Thinking about Riley, about home, makes my chest hurt, so I abandon the postcards to explore deeper into the store. As I wander the aisles and kiosks, grimacing at porcelain cherubs and Americana quilt puzzles, I manage to catch snippets of the conversation happening at the counter.

"Last night," the woman behind the register says.

". . . He's sure?" the other lady replies, shocked.

Now and then, I sense their eyes on me. I'm getting that prickle on my neck again, like at the coffee shop. I suppose with my grubby Doors tee and combat boots, I'm not this place's typical customer. They're probably worried I'm going to steal something. It's fine—I'm sure it's been long enough for that creepy couple to have moved on. Rhonda's probably wondering where I am by now, anyway. I reach into my pocket for my phone and come up empty. *Crap.* I must have left it charging on the nightstand. I should head back before Rhonda starts to worry.

But before I can leave, the door opens and a police officer walks in. He has his hat in his hand, and his face—the expression on his face is one that's been burned into my mind from the night my dad died. I stop cold, Rhonda and my phone forgotten. One of these ladies is about to receive bad news.

"Did you find him?" The woman behind the counter's voice wavers.

The officer nods.

My heart flutters against my rib cage. This is private. I should leave. But I can't get my feet to move. *Eva*, I hear in my head. *I'm sorry.* It echoes over and over again, blocking out everything else. *I'm sorry . . . shot . . . critical condition . . . I'm sorry . . . I'm sorry . . .*

Gradually, I become aware of the glares focused in my direction. With some effort, I unglue my feet from the floor.

"I'm sorry," I blurt out. Ears pounding, I find my way to the door and fumble through it, back out to the sidewalk.

Gotta walk.

Fresh air.

Clear my head.

I recall what my therapist told me: *Some things will trigger memories, images. You may relive the event in your mind. This is all perfectly normal. It's the brain's way of processing trauma.*

But it's not like I saw my dad get shot, I'd told her. *How can I keep picturing something I never saw?* I'm even seeing it now: the flashing lights, the crumpled pileup, Dad working to stabilize a passenger while the panicked, disoriented, and very drunk driver pulls out a gun and . . .

Because brains are geniuses at filling in the blanks, even when we don't want them to. And also? Because brains are jerks, she'd added, forcing a morbid chuckle out of me.

Brains are jerks, I repeat to myself as I walk past the parked police car. My eyes dart away from it. *Brains are jerks.*

CHAPTER 5

I'm not sure why my jerky brain has led me to a cemetery tucked into the far corner of a neighborhood, but that's where I've ended up. The houses along the way look old, but not as old as the buildings on Main Street. They must be from the seventies or eighties—split-levels with rough wood siding and black window frames, exactly like every other neighborhood from that time. Except for the symbols. They're the same as the ones I saw on Main Street. Not on every house, but on enough that I'm actively looking for them now. Some are carved into the wood, and some are even painted on doors or porch railings. Not recently—they're chipped and faded—but it can't have been as long ago as I'd first thought. I don't like them. They give me the creeps.

It seems counterintuitive, but once I'm in the cemetery, I feel a little better. The atmosphere here is welcoming and peaceful, like a park. A barrier of old fir and oak trees surrounds it, providing a natural separation between the housing for the living and the dead. No gate. Just an opening in the trees. I breathe in, breathe out, merging my breaths with the breeze rustling through the leaves. It's helping. Maybe my brain knew what it was doing bringing me here after all.

The sun filters through the branches, speckling the freshly mowed grass with light and shadow. Tall, worn gravestones and monuments poke out of the grass, spreading from the middle to the back and far corners. Smaller, more modern headstones, some vertical, most flat, fill the rest.

I wonder where the Sylvans are. Miriam must be in here somewhere at the very least. We were told she only died a year or so ago, so she'd have a modern stone, I guess. But if there's a family plot, she could be with them in the older section.

Family. Dad's family. And Dad's not here with them.

My pulse quickens. Would he have wanted to be here? Or is he happy to be far away, even in death? Are his parents here? My grandparents? I don't even know. All I know is Dad never met his father and his mom died when he was young. My head swims a little as I turn in place, scanning the cemetery.

I take it back. This was a stupid place to visit. Yet, here I am, and I don't know what's gotten into me, but now I can't leave until I've found Miriam. Since I can't see my dad, the least I can do is find *her* and pay my respects. She left me her house. She'd never even met me, and she left me—*specifically* me, not Dad—her *house*.

Why? I've been asking this question since the day we found the will, and I've yet to come up with a satisfactory answer. Why me? And why did Dad keep it from me? Keep *her* from me?

I wander with my arms crossed, hugging myself, as I peruse the names on the graves. I recognize a surname from the sign of a store I passed this morning: McMurray's Hardware. Here's a section of Burkes, there's a section of McNamaras, a few Petersens—like the gift shop. The whole town must have ancestors here. But I can't find any Sylvans.

Maybe there's another cemetery somewhere. Or maybe they

were all cremated—the entire lot of them—and are kept in urns on a shelf somewhere. I shiver, picturing a display of jars filled with dead people in the rickety house with *WITCH* painted across the front, like a horror movie.

Stop that, I tell my brain, and keep looking. I shouldn't stay much longer—Rhonda's probably getting worried—but now I'm obsessed. They've *got* to be here. Somewhere. At least one or two?

A small cough off in the distance tells me I'm no longer alone.

I step out from behind an obelisk, then duck behind it again—I'm not sure why—when I recognize Cal. After a brief moment, I risk peeking around the edge. I don't think he saw me. His head is bowed, his shoulders hunched; he's carrying a small paper bag, the top rolled in his fist like a lunch sack. But I doubt he's here for a picnic.

He trudges over to the newer section and stops in front of a bare space in the grass left by a flat gravestone. He stays there a moment, his lips moving silently, then tips the bag upside down, dumping its contents out over the grave. Then, without a second glance back, he leaves, crunching the emptied bag into a ball in his fist and tossing it into a trash bin on his way out.

I wait until he's disappeared through the trees and into the neighborhood beyond before leaving my hiding place. A pair of crows swoop down to the ground and peck at Cal's offering.

Curiosity gets the better of me. I give up looking for the Sylvans for now and weave my way through gravestones and monuments to where Cal had been. The crows caw and scatter as I approach, abandoning their feast.

Popcorn.

I bend down and pick up a kernel. Freshly popped, too, with a hint of butter according to the greasiness on my fingers and the warm, inviting scent. I let the kernel drop and examine the gravestone.

"Graham David Yeats," I murmur. Born six months before me. And died—damn, he died when he was only twelve? Could he be Cal's brother? I don't know Cal's exact age or last name, so it's possible. Whoever he was, they must have been close. My throat feels tight. I shouldn't have come here. It's time for me to go.

As I emerge from the trees separating the graveyard from the neighborhood, I look around for Cal but see no sign of him. Then, after about a block, I round the corner and there he is . . . talking to a police officer about a block away. My chest thumps as I realize it's the same police officer from the gift shop. His cruiser is parked along the curb a few feet away. I consider doubling back to look for a different route, but it's too late. I've already been spotted.

"Excuse me," the police officer calls out. "Can I have a word with you?"

I freeze again, like in the gift shop. Turning, Cal shoots me a curious look, then nods to the officer, shoving his hands in his pockets. He remains where he is, waiting, as the officer saunters up the street to where I'm standing. Wrinkling my brow in confusion, I catch Cal's eye. He shrugs, then feigns interest in a crack in the sidewalk.

The officer hooks his thumbs in his belt loops. "I'm Marcus Burke, chief of police." He must notice how tense I am, because he then adds, lightening, "You're not in trouble. I'd just like to ask you a few questions."

Rather than reassuring me, this makes me tense even more. If I'm not in trouble, why do I feel like I am? Though I have no idea why I would be. I haven't done anything besides get triggered in a gift shop after being stared at by a bunch of strangers.

When I don't respond, Chief Burke smiles and gestures at the curb. "Let's have a seat."

He eases himself down, sighing as he stretches his legs out, then pats the space next to him for me to come sit, too. As I hesitate, readjusting my assessment of the situation, he waits patiently, pulling his knees back in and casually resting his arms on them until I finally relax—only a little—and settle onto the curb beside him.

"There we go," he says. "So, may I ask how you're connected to Rhonda Sylvan?"

Why is he asking about Rhonda? Did something happen? My heart flips at the thought. "She's my sister. Is she okay?"

"Oh! Yes, she's fine. As far as I know."

I let out a sigh of relief.

"Sorry, didn't mean to give you a heart attack there." He winces apologetically. "Evangeline, is it?"

"Eva," I correct. "What's going on?"

"Well," he says. "There was a bit of an incident at the gas station last night that I think you might know about. I ran your sister's plates—that's where I got her name—and I've been cruising around looking for the two of you—well, mostly you—all morning. Could have kicked myself after I took too long to recognize you in Diane's shop this morning. But someone said

40

they saw you heading up this way, and, well, imagine my luck to have found the other person I wanted to talk to along the way."

He indicates Cal, who is now occupying himself—or, I suspect, *pretending* to occupy himself—with his phone. Chief Burke pauses again as if waiting to see what my reaction's going to be.

"Okay." I take a steadying breath. The gas station. Did it get robbed or something after we left?

"According to surveillance footage, both of your vehicles were at the gas station last night. It appeared as if there was some kind of kerfuffle between you and the attendant in the mini-mart. Then you hopped back in your sister's car and Cal over there hopped back in his truck, and you all drove off at the same time. Not long after, the attendant shut down the mart early and sped off as well. Any idea why?"

That déjà vu feeling from earlier washes over me again as the image of the mini-mart, taken over by shadow, flashes through my mind. I catch a whiff of something burning. Like fireworks. Strange. I shake my head as if to erase it, but the chief seems to interpret that as a no, which is fine by me. I have the right to remain silent, don't I? I'm not saying anything until I know what he's getting at. He must also have been able to tell through the security cameras that I did nothing wrong. That Rob guy obviously started it.

"So, you wanna tell me what the altercation between you and the attendant was all about?" Chief Burke asks. "Or if it might have had anything to do with why he closed up shop so early?"

Every muscle in my body has gone rigid. Altercation? I wouldn't go so far as to call it that. He said I wasn't in trouble, but it sounds very much like I am. "What's going on? Did something happen to him?"

"That's what I'm trying to figure out." Chief Burke goes silent for a moment, looking off across the street at the houses and front yards.

"Your father . . ." He pauses, gathering his words. "So, uh, when I ran your New York plates and saw your sister's last name, it prompted me to do some more looking. I just want to say I'm—"

"That guy at the gas station kicked me out because of our last name," I blurt out before he can finish.

Rob's gravelly voice sounds in the back of my head—*You're just like her. That's why you* need *to* go. But that's not exactly what he'd said, was it? He'd simply said I needed to go, without any explanation. *Just like her* . . . That was from a different time. It was . . . it was from that dream. Last night. That's where the déjà vu is coming from. There was a cloud of something . . . smoke? Curling up the walls, coming for me. Or was it coming for Rob? *Has something happened to him?*

"Because of your last name?"

"Yeah." My words sound vague and distant to my own ears as the dream plays itself out in the back of my mind. "It was weird."

The dream was weird. It didn't feel like a normal dream. It was too . . . tangible. I blink and collect myself. "I—I don't know why he freaked out about it, but he did, so when he told me to go, I left. Nothing else happened. Then Cal showed us how to get to my great-aunt Miriam's house because Rob wouldn't tell me. He didn't have anything to do with it." *Whatever "it" is.*

"Rob?" Chief Burke cocks his head. "I don't believe I told you the station attendant's name."

"It was on his shirt."

Chief Burke's eyes twinkle approvingly. "You'd make a good detective."

"Did he die or something? What's going on?"

"No, no, he's not dead," Chief Burke assures me. "I'm just, uh, trying to piece some things together, that's all."

Still not an answer. Frustrated, I stand and brush off my shorts. "Can I ask *you* a question?"

He stands, too. "Shoot."

"What's wrong with my last name? Was Miriam, like . . . an awful person or something?"

His shoulders tense a bit as he tucks one hand in his pocket. "Oh, well, I, uhhhh, I'm probably not the best person to ask."

"Why not?"

"I just, uh—well . . ."

I don't get it. Why is he being so cagey? I glance over again at Cal, who immediately shoots his eyes down to his phone. I'm positive he's been trying to listen, though I'm not sure how much he could have caught from where he's standing.

Fine. "So, I'm not in trouble?"

"Not a bit."

"Can I go, then?"

"Yup, that's all I needed. But before you go . . ." Chief Burke rests a hand on my shoulder, stooping to look me straight in the eyes. It makes me feel prickly like I'm under a magnifying glass in the sun. I break eye contact, looking down and away.

"Before you go," he says again, "I need *you* to know that

if you or your sister need anything—anything at all—you can come to me, okay?"

Sure, because you've been super forthcoming so far.

"Your dad was a friend," he continues. "We went to school together . . . a long time ago. And this town can be, well, just know you can come to me. Got it?"

I risk a glance up at him, then quickly look away again. My eyes are burning, and I don't want him to see it. I nod, jaw clenched.

He gives my shoulder a reassuring squeeze before letting go. "All right, then. Thanks for your help in clearing things up."

Cal tucks his phone in his pocket as Chief Burke strolls back to where he's been waiting—or should I say eavesdropping—patiently. After a brief exchange of words, Cal hurries over to join me as we watch Chief Burke drive away.

CHAPTER 6

Cal and I stand several feet apart, regarding each other.
"Did you, um . . . did you hear any of that?" I gesture
vaguely at the curb where Chief Burke and I were sitting.

"Nope," he says.

"Cool." I don't believe him, but I appreciate the discretion.

"So, were you just in the . . . coming from the . . . you
know . . . ?"

"The cemetery?" I finish for him.

"I didn't realize there was anyone else there."

"Yeah. Sorry."

He shakes his head. "No worries."

Again, I don't believe him. It's obvious I caught him unaware
in what he thought was a private moment. "All right, well, I'd
better get back. I guess I'll see you around?"

"Yeah," he says. "I guess, probably. Yeah."

I hesitate, then with an awkward smile, I start walking. And
so does he. And it just so happens we're both heading in the
same direction. He returns my awkward smile and shrugs.

As we fall into step, his arm accidentally brushes against
mine, ever so slightly. I continue to feel the tickle of it even
after he corrects and widens the gap between us, just enough
to not bump shoulders, but he's still close. Normally, this would

bother me. Personal bubble and all that. But somehow it doesn't with Cal. It does feel weird walking together in silence, though. Like back in the graveyard, his demeanor is somber.

"Was he your brother?" I ask, both the silence and my curiosity getting the better of me.

His step falters. "Who?"

I cringe inwardly. Too personal. I should have let it go. "Back at that grave you were visiting. In the cemetery."

There's a heavy pause. Then, "No. A friend."

"He was so young. How'd he die?" *Oh my God, Eva, shut* up.

"He, uh. He fell." His voice is quiet, and I know I've definitely overstepped.

"Sorry."

"It's fine."

It doesn't sound fine. And I, of all people, should know better. Time to change the subject. "So, what do you think was up with that police interrogation? Was the station robbed last night or something?" It's bothering me that Chief Burke asked me so many questions without ever fully answering mine. I should have kept my mouth shut. But then he started talking about Dad, and . . .

"Rob didn't show up for work this morning," Cal says. "They found him in a coma."

Now *my* steps falter as the image of that dark cloud flashes across my mind again, lights flickering out, one by one.

"A coma?"

"Yup."

A cloud made of shadows. And there were kids, too. Or was it just one kid?

"So, the chief wanted to question us because we were the last people to interact with him? Why didn't he just tell me that?"

Take it outside or I'm calling the cops, I hear in Rob's voice. I remember now. The shadow came from the kid. The kid *was* the shadow.

"Don't know. Maybe because he doesn't know you."

"He sure acted like he did," I snort, pushing the dream to the back of my mind. Because that's all it was. A dream.

"If it helps, he didn't tell me much, either. I heard about the coma thing from . . . *Shit*," Cal mutters under his breath. Two boys are messing around on skateboards a few blocks down. One hops onto the curb, flips his board up, and catches it while the other shoves his to start it going without him, then jumps on while it's already moving.

"Who are they?"

"Nobody," Cal says. "Come on."

He taps my arm and indicates that we should go left, steering me around the corner, rather than crossing the street. I struggle to keep up as he trudges up the hill, the two of us hurrying away from some perceived threat. Clearly, those guys aren't "nobody."

The skateboards rumble closer behind us.

"Hey!" one boy calls out. I resist the urge to look over my shoulder as Cal keeps walking.

"I said, hey! Who's your girlfriend?"

Cal's face reddens. He quickens his pace. Heat rises to my cheeks, too.

"That's not his girlfriend." I hear the other guy laugh. "Gotta be a cousin or somethin'. Hey, Cal, you gonna introduce us?"

The muscle at the back of Cal's jaw pops. Staring hard ahead, he gives his head a slight shake, advising me not to respond.

"Naw, naw, wait, dude," the first voice says, a little slower, a little quieter. "I think I know who that is. Remember?" And then, barely audible, "*Last night*, dude."

The second voice, not catching on to his change in tone, laughs. "Dude, I was way too wasted last—Ow! What the fuck, dude?"

A stinging chill flushes the heat from my cheeks, down through my chest. My mind flashes back to the sharp, red letters painted across Miriam's house, cuts etched into its shingled skin. It's them—the boys who yelled about hexes as, terrified, they stumbled off into the night. These images swirl together with the strange looks people gave me as I walked down Main Street. Small town, tight-knit community—word must travel at lightning speed whenever someone new comes to town. But it feels like there's more to it than that.

Ding-dong, the WITCH is DEAD.

We're at the top of the hill now. Cal grabs my hand and pulls me around another corner. But the voices have stopped, and the skateboards, too.

I gently untangle my fingers from his sweaty palm and wipe them on my shorts—discreetly, my heart pounding. His jaw is still clenched as he beckons me across a driveway, past his blue pickup truck. We stop and lean against the far side of it, our shoulders touching, nerves heightened. Hidden and waiting.

"Who are they?" I whisper to him again.

"Assholes," he whispers back, breath tickling the stray hairs on my forehead. He peers around his truck cab and relaxes, then looks from me to the house, then to me again.

"Uh." His Adam's apple bobs up, then plunges down. "Wanna come in? I guess? My sister's been whining all morning for, um . . ." He snaps his fingers, trying to get a word off the tip of his tongue. "Baked goods, round—chocolate chip . . . *you* know."

I blink at him. "You mean . . . cookies?"

"Yeah." His cheeks flush. "My mom's probably broken down and made some by now."

I pause as I process this abrupt turnaround. Laughter bubbles to the surface. I can't help it. I snort in a futile attempt to hold it in, then it bursts forth in a full roll.

The flush deepens, spreading down to his neck. He steps away. "Sometimes I have trouble getting words out."

"No! I'm sorry," I gasp as I work to rein in the laughter. That's not what I meant at all. "I'm so sorry, it's not that. But we just ran away from some skaters, and now you're inviting me in for cookies? What are we, twelve?" I want to take it back as soon as I've said it, but the whole situation suddenly feels so absurd.

"You don't—you don't like cookies?"

"No, I like cookies," I'm quick to add, sobering.

"Then come have some cookies."

"You sure that's a good idea?" A knot forms in my stomach. He's inviting me over, is what he's doing. I'm not sure how I feel about it. I just got here and I barely know him, and I'd need to call Rhonda somehow to check in, which I have a feeling wouldn't go well after my disappearing act this morning. And besides, is he *sure* he wants to hang out with me? "Those guys back there left us alone pretty fast once they figured out who I am."

He stares at me.

"Probably doesn't look so good to be hanging out with the witch's niece," I mumble.

"No!" He recoils slightly, then swallows again. "I mean yes. I mean . . . I thought you seem, um, kind of cool, I guess, and we're here . . . and there might be cookies. You—you don't have to . . . um, you don't—"

"Sorry," I cut him off, cringing. *Now, who's the asshole?* I berate myself while simultaneously latching onto the fact that *he thinks I'm kind of cool.* "Cookies sound great. But—"

He waits.

I think about it, then sigh. "I kind of just took off this morning. And I forgot my phone, so Rhonda's probably gonna be pissed if I don't check in soon. You saw last night what an angry Rhonda's like."

He nods. "Yeah, makes sense. You should go let her know you're okay. Maybe we can, you know, hang out some other time? If . . . you want."

"Yeah, maybe. Yes," I decide. "I'd like that."

I'm keenly aware of his eyes on me as I stumble on my way down the driveway. Blushing, I look over my shoulder to see if he caught my clumsiness, but he's already going inside.

Okay, so maybe Rhonda was right. I still think Cal's a little weird, but he's *nice*. And, I remind myself as I head back to the

Roadhouse, a fresh bounce in my step, so was Bethany this morning. And Chief Burke—they were nice, I mean. Not weird. Well . . . Chief Burke was a *little* weird. And maybe *too* nice. But he says he has my back, I guess, and that's something. Maybe things aren't so bad here after all.

CHAPTER 7

"This is bad. This is really bad."

"Hey." I scoot into one of the Roadhouse's vinyl booths across the table from Rhonda. "What's bad?"

Startled, she looks up from the papers she's muttering at over her untouched salad. "Oh. *There* you are. Could you please make sure you have your phone the next time you decide to take off without telling me where you're going?"

"Sorry."

"Where on earth have you been?"

"Around. Walking." Probably best not to go into the details when she's in this kind of mood. "What's bad?" I ask again, leaning forward to check out the papers she's examining.

She takes a long, deep breath, and I brace myself. "Well, while you've been out, apparently *just walking* all morning, I've actually been looking into our situation here, and we have a problem." She pauses to take a bite of salad, then slides the papers across the table to me. "I went by the post office to set up mail forwarding and found out they've been holding on to these."

I scan the first page. It's from a bank, and there are dates and dollar amounts, and below that, *NOTICE OF DEFAULT*. That does sound bad.

"What's this for?" The words blur as I read over the rest, my eyes skipping from one line to the next while Rhonda clarifies the legalese.

"Miriam had a loan out on the property. And everything was fine as, I think, Dad was keeping up with the payments, but then, well . . ."

I flip to the second page. It's similar to the first but harsher, with more bolded lettering and the words *URGENT: FINAL NOTICE* at the top. It's from about three weeks ago. I flip back to the first paper. It's from a month before that.

My mouth goes dry. "But then he died."

"So now we're behind a few payments, and if we don't do something about it by the end of the week, it'll go into foreclosure, and we could lose the house."

"The end of the *week*? But we just got here."

"Would have been frickin' nice if the estate lawyer had mentioned this before we blew through our bank account driving all the way across the country. We could use Dad's life insurance money right about now, too, if it ever actually shows up."

"We can't go back there." My eyes are stinging.

She puts her fork down and stares. "All you've been saying the entire drive out here is that you want to go home, and now you don't?"

"I don't . . ." I pause to catch my breath. I can feel the anxiety bubbling in my stomach. "I don't know what I want. Nothing feels right anymore."

"Well, even if we did want to go back, we can't afford to now, so it doesn't matter."

Tears threaten to fall. I press my teeth against my bottom lip to hold them back. It's not so much the house. I'm sure there are other options. Other houses . . . and apartments—rentals. Other places we can live. It's the fact that Miriam's house is the only thing left of our family besides ourselves. It's the fact that Dad grew up there. I don't want to lose that—*can't* lose that—even though it's covered with graffiti and practically falling down. It's the only thing left of *Dad.*

"Eva?" Rhonda's voice has softened. "Hey, let's not panic yet." I get the feeling she's trying to calm herself down about it as much as me. "I'll go talk to the bank in person. Maybe if I can explain our situation face-to-face with someone, I can get us an extension or something. I don't know how these things work, but I'm sure they'll understand. They have to have seen this kind of situation before, right?"

"Yeah." I nod, though I'm not so sure myself. "Okay."

"With any luck, Dad's insurance will come through soon, and we can get this all settled before the end of the summer, okay? Oh, shit, we need to get you registered for school here, too . . ." She trails off, making checklists in her head.

Guilt gnaws at me as I remember our disagreement this morning. I don't know how she stays so . . . so solid. Always the one left to pick up the pieces, to kiss the hurts, to make things right. Even after I took off, she was working to get us all settled in. And I was out . . . walking.

"How did your call with the electric company go? Was that who you were on the phone with this morning?"

"Ugh." She puts her fork down, allowing her frustration to show again. "For over an *hour.* They kept *insisting* they'd turned the electricity back on already. I told them it definitely wasn't on when we were there last night. And then they tried to tell me it was a burned-out bulb. Like I'm that clueless."

I nod along. No need for her to know I was about to suggest the same thing.

"I mean, there were three switches next to each other, and I tried them all. It's not a bulb. Then they said a fuse probably blew. Like, from a surge or something when they turned the power back on. They told me that can sometimes happen with old houses. It's a nightmare."

With a series of short jabs, she stacks her fork with the perfect ratio of lettuce to toppings.

"We'll have to hire an electrician." *Jab, jab.* "Which we can't afford. Especially now. I mean, do *you* know how to replace a fuse?" She gestures at me with her loaded fork. "Because I sure as hell don't."

"I do," replies a voice next to us.

I jerk and fold up the bank papers as Bethany, paying more attention to her phone than to my documents, scoots into the booth next to me. I glance at Rhonda, expecting her to be annoyed by the intrusion, but she looks more bemused than anything.

"Quick, before my mom notices." Bethany checks over the back of the booth while handing me the phone. "The last three pics," she says, then slumps down into her seat, hunching so the top of her head is out of sight from the check-in counter.

I scroll through a trio of mock-up movie posters, but instead of film titles, they have *Spooky Horror Film Fest, Saturday, Oct. 29th. Be there, or be SCARE.*

"The pun's shit, I know, and I'm *still* working on the name, but what do you think? If you had to pick one, which one would you go with?"

"Hmm." I scroll through again. "They're all great," I say truthfully. "But I think I like the one with the aliens best."

"I was hoping you'd say that!" Bethany takes her phone back. "Thanks!" She risks another peek toward the check-in counter, then starts to slide out of the booth, when Rhonda stops her.

"Wait. What were you saying before? You know how to change a fuse?"

"Oh, uh . . . yeah." Bethany scoots back in. "Haven't had to since we finally upgraded to a breaker system a few years ago, thank God. Industrial kitchen appliances draw a shit ton of power, so it was like we were constantly blowing fuses. Such a pain in the ass. Especially when you're trying to run a business. But I still remember how—it's easier than you'd think."

"Can I find them at the hardware store, or will I have to special order some?" Rhonda asks. "I don't even know what kind to get."

"I think it depends on how old the setup is." Bethany pauses, mulling something over in her head. "Is . . . this for the old Sylvan place? Mom said you're moving here, but your place isn't ready . . . and your last name's Sylvan, right?"

My chest thumps. Here we go. "Yeah," I mumble.

Bethany leans forward, eyes shining. "Holy. Shit. What's it like? Inside, I mean?"

"I wouldn't know. I've only ever seen the lovely artwork on the outside," I mumble.

Rhonda gives me a Look, but I don't think Bethany, now distracted by something out the window, even noticed what I said.

I follow her gaze in time to see a lanky boy leapfrog over the short fence enclosing the patio dining area. Upon landing, he swipes his wavy dark hair out of his eyes. His brows knit when he sees me, then his attention swivels to my sister and his expression neutralizes. It gives me an uneasy feeling in the pit of my stomach, like I'm being accused of something, but I have no idea what. He's probably figured out who I am already, like those skaters and the people at the coffee shop earlier. Or maybe my morning's experiences have made me paranoid.

When he sees Bethany, he grins impishly and winks as he strolls past our window toward the restaurant's patio door.

Bethany's gaze flutters down, then back to me as if nothing happened, but her cheeks have taken on a rosy hue. "So, um . . . fuses. Right. I'll have to double-check, but I think we *might* have some in storage still."

"Oh," Rhonda says. "I couldn't—I mean, I'll pay you for them, of course. But it might, well, it might be a while." She glances at the bank paperwork, still folded on the table next to me.

Bethany shakes her head. "Oh, don't worry. I'm not just giving them to you for *nothing*. You're gonna have to bring me along. I've been dying to see the inside of that place. Do we have a deal?" Bethany looks eagerly from Rhonda, to me, back to Rhonda.

I clench my jaw, not trusting myself to answer. This morning, Bethany seemed different than everyone else—well, everyone besides Cal. But I should have known her interest in my sister and me was more than just friendliness. Rhonda and I must be the most exciting thing to happen in this tiny town for years. Decades, even.

As for Rhonda, she *hates* accepting unsolicited help, and she especially hates feeling like she's in anyone's debt. But like she said, we can't afford an electrician, and Bethany's offer to help, though costing Rhonda some dignity, is, in all other ways, free. I can practically see the gears turning in her head as she weighs one option over the other, until finally she says, "Sure. I mean, deal. Thank you."

"Fuck yeah." Bethany hops out of the booth, then remembers afterward to make sure her mom didn't see. Fortunately, the coast is still clear. "You guys are, like, the only ones here, but I technically don't get off for another few hours, so when I get a minute, I'll double-check the storage closet and let you know."

"Sounds great," Rhonda says.

As Bethany heads back toward the kitchen, she's accosted, playfully, along the way by the boy who we watched hop the fence a moment ago. He puts his arm around her shoulders, and she ducks out from under it, tilting her head meaningfully toward the back. I risk a peek over the booth to find her mother has finally reappeared and is shooting them a disapproving look from behind the counter.

Before disappearing down the hall, the boy turns and sweeps a last glance around the room—empty of customers now besides Rhonda and me. His brows knit again as his eyes breeze past me, then both he and Bethany are gone. I slide back down into my seat. Why does he keep looking at me like that? And why do I feel like I have something to apologize for?

I hand the bank paperwork back to Rhonda. "I'm not feeling awesome."

"Have you eaten anything today? Maybe you need food."

"No, I just—" I glance at the stack of torn envelopes.

Rhonda catches it. "Eva, seriously. We can still afford to eat."

"It's not that. I didn't sleep well and"—I indicate the bank notices—"then there's all this, and . . . this morning's been kind of a roller coaster."

Her gaze turns inward. "It's weird being here, right? Why don't you go get some rest? I've got this."

I feel another pang of guilt. By going back to the room, I'm abandoning her to do all the responsible stuff without me again. But she senses my hesitation and insists, "Really. I'll be fine. Keeping busy helps me."

With some relief, I head up to our room and flop onto the bed, leaving her to deal with the bank in the way only Rhonda can. And before I know it, my eyes are drooping, then closing. My restless night has caught up with me.

CHAPTER 8

No weird dreams this time. Just pure sleep. I guess I needed it. I probably would have kept on sleeping through the rest of the afternoon if not for the knocking.

Groggy, it takes me a second to realize what's going on. There's another triple knock and a muffled voice. "I don't think she's in there."

"She has to be." Then louder, "Hey, Eva, it's Bethany. From downstairs? You in?"

I fumble for my phone. It's three P.M. already, and I have several missed texts, a missed call, and a voice mail. All from my sister. Crap.

"Coming." Smoothing my hair, I trudge to the door and open it to find Bethany and that guy from lunch. He's carrying a Monster Energy drink in one hand and a plastic take-out bag in the other. Up close, I'm struck by his eyes—startlingly green and full of mischief. I swallow down the immediate urge to apologize. What am I sorry for? Him shooting me weird looks at the restaurant? He's not now, and it's possible I imagined it. I'm feeling off-kilter from last night's bad sleep and taking a nap. I always feel off after naps.

"Hey," I say. "What's up?"

"Fuses," Bethany announces as her companion lifts the plastic bag into the air like he's presenting me with a prize.

"For your house! Cal's gonna drive us there, since your sister can't," Bethany continues. She points down the stairs, and I lean out the doorway to see.

Cal waves up at me from the open driver's side window. I duck back inside.

"Now? Why can't my sister drive us? Hold on." I pull out my phone and scroll through Rhonda's texts.

Bank's a no go. Are you awake?

Arrrgh!!! Car won't start. At the mechanic.

Are you awake yet??

Not sure if texts are going through & you're not answering your phone. Call me.

Sending Bethany up. Check your voicemail.

The sleep-rusted cogs in my brain take their sweet time getting up to speed. I rub my eyes. "Rhonda's at the mechanic? Why didn't she come and wake me up first?"

"Don't know," Bethany says. "Maybe she thought you needed your sleep? We were going to help her with the fuse box, but her car wouldn't start. And then she got really quiet and looked like she was gonna cry? So . . ."

It couldn't have been that Rhonda didn't want to wake me up—if that was the case, she wouldn't have tried to call me. She knew I was already upset about the letters from the bank, and she didn't want me to see her frazzled. Much easier to mask that over the phone. She must have been *really* frazzled if she was on the verge of tears. Rhonda doesn't cry in front of people. Ever. I sigh internally. Poor Rhonda. Always trying to be the strong one. And here I've been sleeping through my phone, going for walks around town, basically leaving her to take care of everything on her own when she could have used some support, whether she knew it or not.

I turn to Bethany's boyfriend—I assume. "I take it you're coming, too, then?" *I'll bet he's also just* itching *to check out the house of the town freak.* A surprisingly bitter thought, even for me.

He answers with a noncommittal shrug.

"Oh yeah, this is Daniel." Bethany pokes him with her elbow.

"For what it's worth, I told her this wasn't a good idea," he says.

He thrusts the bag out for me to take. Our fingers touch as the plastic loops transfer from his hand to mine, and for the briefest moment, there's an odd sensation in my chest—like familiarity, but not quite. At the same time, he gets that look on his face again—the one he kept giving me at the restaurant. Lines form between his brows like he's trying to figure something out. And again, I have the urge to apologize for I don't know what. Existing?

"You guys coming?" Cal calls from below, and as quickly as it arose, the odd feeling is gone. Bethany signals Cal to hold on.

"Okay, so, confession," she says to me. "Dan's dad's the police chief."

Chief Burke? I groan inwardly. Dan looks off to the side, then twists to look behind him as if searching for an escape route.

"And," Bethany continues, "he overheard some stuff." She pauses, choosing her words. My chest tightens because I know what's coming.

"I'm really sorry about your dad." *There it is.* "I can't even imagine how awful that must be. So, we thought maybe, you know, after what you've been through and everything, you and your sister could use some help and stuff. You know, some friends."

"This town's full of assholes," Daniel adds. "With a name like Sylvan, you're gonna need some allies."

My fingers dig into my palms. They think they're being helpful, but they're not. They're being intrusive. Sorry about my dad? They've never met my dad. They've barely met *me*.

They've barely met me, and yet they're here, reaching out. So, what if they *are* just curious about the house? So am I. For different reasons, sure, but . . . *It's okay to let people help you.* Riley told me that before I pushed her away. Before I told her she couldn't possibly understand.

Bethany and Daniel exchange uncomfortable looks. They couldn't possibly understand, either. But does that matter?

Cal calls up from his car again, an undertone of warning in his voice. "Hey, guys? Maybe we should get going."

I'll bet *he* could understand. Head bowed over a gravestone, popcorn sprinkled over the ground. Smart enough not to ask questions after pretending not to listen to my conversation with Chief Burke. Jogging out of the gas station with my abandoned can of Coke.

"All right." I step out from my safe space behind the door-frame. "Let's go."

Bethany's face splits into a grin before she bounds down the steps to join Cal, stopping short at the end of the alley as she barely avoids a collision with two skateboarders. They slow long enough to pound on the hood of Cal's truck and give him the middle finger before speeding off, laughing and jeering. I can feel my face heating up again. It's those same two who were teasing Cal this morning. The same ones we caught vandalizing Miriam's house last night. I'm positive.

"Fuck off!" Bethany yells after them, but I doubt they hear her over their own laughter, or even care if they do.

Daniel shrugs at me again, resigned. "Welcome to Madrona."

"Forget about those assholes," Bethany tells Cal as we pile into his truck. "They're not worth your time. All right?"

Cal nods, his grip on the steering wheel loosening as he lets out a breath.

It takes some squeezing and maneuvering to fit everyone along the bench seat. I end up scrunched between Cal and Daniel with Bethany perched on Daniel's lap. Cal mutters an apology each time he turns the wheel and jostles me with his elbow, which is partly my own fault, since I'm leaning his way to avoid rubbing shoulders with Daniel—a fruitless effort. Daniel smells like cologne with a vague undercurrent of boy sweat. Cal, however, smells like cookies . . . and also a vague undercurrent of boy sweat. I hope I don't smell like sweat, too. It *is* July after all, and the truck doesn't have air-conditioning.

I lean even closer so Cal can hear me over the air rushing past the open window. "Did your mom make cookies?"

"What?"

"Did your mom make cookies?"

"Oh! Yes." He perks up. "Hey, Bethany, check the, uh, the . . . the compartment thingy."

"What?" she yells from the other side of the truck.

I press my back into the seat as Cal reaches across me, the sleeve of his T-shirt tightening around his biceps as he pushes the button to pop open the glove box.

"Sorry," he says as he bumps me with his arm while straightening back up.

"It's okay," I tell him, but it comes out quiet, so I don't think he hears me over the wind.

"Niiiiice." Bethany pulls a zip-top bag out of the glove box, fishes out a cookie, and passes the bag down the line. By the time we've reached Fay Road, we're all a little sugar high. Me, especially, since these are the only things I've eaten all day. They're good, too. Cal's mom makes a mean cookie.

We dip into the gully, and my sugary giddiness ebbs as the massive hedge looms ahead: a fortress wall rising from a moat of tall grass. It's even more imposing in daylight than it was in the shadow of night. Silence overtakes us as the truck eases to a stop. Daniel opens the passenger side door for Bethany to climb out, then hops out after her.

The vinyl scrunches beneath Cal as he leans toward me, his soft voice tickling my ear. "You don't have to do this, you know."

"Do what?"

"Let them in there. Before you've had a chance to go in yourself."

My ears burn as I remember how he witnessed my reaction upon first seeing the house last night. I must have looked pretty freaked out, exhausted as I was and near tears.

"It's cool," I tell him while, internally, I'm feeling anything but. "I'm as curious as the rest of you."

Daniel ducks into the truck cab. "Hey. You two coming, or do you need some alone time or something?" Bethany smacks him on the back of the head, then he bumps it for real on the doorframe as he turns around to protest.

My ears are on fire as I hurry to scoot away from Cal and out of the truck. When Cal comes around the other side, he's holding up two flashlights. "Just in case." Daniel plucks one out of his hand, but as I go to take the other, Cal keeps his hold on it. He glances at Bethany and Daniel as they're walking away, then locks his clear blue eyes on mine, and I swear, everything around us becomes a little more distant.

"I mean it," he says.

I hold his gaze, my hand tightening around the flashlight as my inner chain mail clinks protectively around me. "Why'd you agree to drive us out here if you think this is such a terrible idea?"

I tug the flashlight out of his grasp, then jog to catch up with the others before I have a chance to think too much about the way Cal's shoulders dropped as I turned away.

"Whoa." Bethany's mouth falls open when she reaches the gap in the hedge. "*Assholes.*"

"Troy was here," Daniel says. "See? His tag." He points out a scribbled symbol in the middle of the front door. "And if Troy was here, you know Chris was, too. Follows him everywhere like a freakin' shadow."

My stomach flips as I remember those skateboarders and their middle fingers this afternoon, and the mad dash up the hill to Cal's house this morning to get away. Troy and Chris. I file their names away for later.

"Why would they paint that?" I ask. "Was Miriam the local mean old lady or something?"

Bethany and Daniel exchange startled looks.

"Oh, I—I never really met her in person," Bethany says.

"Barely anyone really met her in person," Daniel says.

"So, she was a recluse?"

"Yeeeah. Kinda," Bethany says.

Makes sense . . . I guess. But I feel there's something more they're not telling me.

The gate shrieks as I throw it open and hold my arm out, welcoming the others through. First Bethany, then Daniel . . . but no Cal. I turn to find him staring passively at a massive, rotted-out tree stump a few feet away from the hedge. Something about his demeanor reminds me of his visit to the graveyard this morning.

We've both lost someone close to us, which means we have something in common. Which is probably why I'm so curious about it. But I don't want to pry any more than I already have. I don't think it would be welcome. Regret jabs at me. I don't know why I got so prickly back there. He was only trying to help. *Let people help you. Jerk.*

"Coming?" I ask him.

"After you," he says quietly. "It's your house."

Right. I suppose I deserve that cool response. With a sigh, I turn and start down the path to the front steps when a new realization hits me. If Cal isn't too irritated with me already, he's going to be *really* irritated now. I can't believe I didn't think to ask this before we left.

"Hey, guys?"

Daniel pokes Bethany, who's peering through the darkened windows on either side of the front door—the only windows on the ground floor that haven't been boarded up. Bethany spins around and stands at attention.

"Did Rhonda remember to give either of you the key?" I ask.

Bethany shakes her head and Daniel tries the doorknob, but I know it won't open because I remember watching Rhonda struggle to lock it last night.

"Let's look for a broken window or something," Daniel suggests.

"Uh, where?" Bethany throws her arms out toward the lengths of plywood where panes of glass should be. "On the top floor?"

He shrugs. Shrugging must be his signature move. "Might be one in the back."

I get the impression he's not beyond creating one himself. Then again, his dad's the police chief, so maybe not.

Then *again* again, Riley's dad was also a police officer, and if she were here, she'd already be looking around for the perfect rock to chuck. Personally, I'd rather not add one more thing to fix to our growing laundry list of expenses we can't afford to deal with. And I'd definitely prefer not to have to shimmy up that splintered, rotting porch post in a dubious attempt to reach one of the windows on the second floor. I'd probably fall right through the shingles, if I even made it to the top.

"Cal, you don't happen to have more tools where those flashlights came from, do you?" I ask. "Any electric screwdrivers or a crowbar or something hanging around in your truck?" These boards are going to have to come off eventually, anyway. Maybe one of the windows behind them is unlocked.

But Cal says he doesn't have any of those things, so we pick our way through the shaggy yard around the side of the house to check the back, only to find more plywood. But there's also another door, and this one's lock looks pretty flimsy.

"Right." I take a breath. "Fine." I pull out Dad's Swiss Army knife.

"Whoa," Daniel says, and backs away, hands in the air.

I ignore him and head up the concrete steps leading to the back door.

"What's she doing?" Bethany whispers loudly as I slip the tweezers out of the end of the knife base and use my teeth to bend one of the tines to a ninety-degree angle.

"She's gonna try and pick the lock," Daniel answers.

"Not try," I mutter to myself, examining my handiwork. "Do."

At least, I hope. It's been a while. I pull the toothpick out of the other end of the knife and return the enameled base to my pocket. *Thanks, Dad*, I think as I feel its weight against me once again.

Sure enough, the doorknob looks like it hasn't been replaced for decades. Good. Because I'm not exactly an expert. I've only ever done this on our apartment door back home . . . and Riley's father's liquor cabinet. Just the once. But once was enough to mess up everything. We got caught, and my dad was never a fan of Riley after that.

I slip my bent tweezer tine into the lock, then proceed to rake the pins on the inside with the toothpick. How different would things have been if I hadn't done it? Would he have allowed me to go to Riley's that . . . night? Would I still have said the things I said? The rush of guilt the memory conjures is replaced by a rush of satisfaction when the doorknob finally turns without resistance.

"Ta-da!" I lift my hands in the air and turn to find a trio of shocked faces.

"Holy shit, you just broke into a house," Bethany says.

"Better than scaling the drainpipes and breaking a window," Cal points out.

"I think it's okay since it's technically my house," I add, bolstered by Cal's defense. Though he may have meant it more as a dig at Daniel.

Daniel eyes me suspiciously. "Did you pick a lot of locks in New York?" I doubt he's serious, but I can feel myself flushing in shame anyway. What is it about this guy that constantly makes me think I've screwed up? It's annoying.

"Daniel," Bethany hisses.

"I was just wondering," he says with an impish smirk. "My dad's the one with the badge, not me."

Cal shoves his hands in his pockets and rocks onto his heels. And again, I can't read him. Is he reacting to Daniel, or did my lockpicking make him uncomfortable? He probably thinks I'm some kind of petty criminal now. Awesome.

I do a shoddy job of unbending my tweezers so I can stick them back in the base. I'm too flustered to get them flush, which turns to frustration, which isn't helped by the fact that my mouth has decided now's the perfect time to vent that frustration through sarcasm. "Everyone in New York can pick locks. We learn it in kindergarten. You guys don't learn that here?"

Bethany laughs, thank goodness. So does Daniel, which relieves the tension somewhat. I still can't read Cal, but at least this once, my sarcasm has worked in my favor. And besides, I'm not about to go into the real reason why I know how to pick a lock.

When I was younger, our building superintendent, Mr. Hodges, got sick of having to come let me into my apartment whenever I locked myself out, which happened frequently for a while after Mom left. "Your brain ran right off with her, didn't it, kid?" he'd grumble at me, then soften it with a ruffle of my hair. Eventually, he brought me down to his office and showed me how to let myself back in using his array of hobby locks and lockpicking tools. I think it was his gruff way of giving me something new to focus on.

"Ready?" I ask, more for myself than the others.

The handle turns, but the door sticks. I try again, this time

71

adding a shove with my shoulder. When the door gives way, I stumble inside, choking on the smell that immediately engulfs my lungs.

"What *is* that?" Bethany coughs out behind me.

I give my eyes a second to adjust in the dim light leaking in from the outside. "It's the kitchen."

My words are muffled behind my palm. My first inclination is to hunt for the light switch so I can see better and discover the source of the smell. Then I remember the reason we're here and click on Cal's flashlight instead.

Its beam bounces off the metal of a toaster, the smooth white surface of a refrigerator, the worn earpiece of an old rotary phone mounted on the wall.

"Rotting food?" Cal guesses.

"I don't think it's just food," I say.

Daniel also shines his flashlight around the room, but it's pointed toward the floor. "It smells like a corpse."

"How would you know, Mulder?" Cal asks him.

"Shut up, Scully," he throws back.

Bethany snorts involuntarily.

"I think Daniel's right." I've smelled this before, unfortunately.

I get to work sliding open drawers and checking behind cupboard doors. Daniel does the same—the cop's kid and the paramedic's kid wading in to do the dirty work while the other two, flashlight-less, hover in the doorway. Not that I blame them. I'm having a hard time keeping my gag reflex in check as I try not to suffocate on the stench.

"Gah!" Daniel jumps and drops his flashlight, causing the

rest of us to jump as well. Stomach knotted, I fix my own light on the drawer he's opened, edging my way over to see if my suspicions are correct. I spy fur. Using the tip of the flashlight, I open the drawer a little more. Sure enough, nestled among some chewed-up cracker boxes is an extremely well-fed, extremely dead mouse.

Trying not to vomit, I nudge Daniel to the side, remove the drawer completely, and rush it to the door. Cal and Bethany bolt down the steps and out of my way as I run to the edge of what I think used to be an herb or vegetable garden, now overgrown and riddled with weeds. Swinging the drawer like a catapult, I fling the mouse and cracker boxes as far into the hinterland of weed-dom as possible, then prop the drawer against the side of the house to let it air out. Poor mouse. At least it died happy.

When I look up, everyone's staring at me again.

"Dude. You're a badass," Daniel declares with approval.

"Hardly." I bow my head and march past the three, up the steps. "And don't *any* of you dare tell Rhonda about this. She has a phobia."

More a phobia of rats—big New York sewer rats. This was nothing like that, but still a rodent and therefore close enough, so I guess it's a good thing Rhonda couldn't drive us after all. Not sure if she'd ever come back here if she knew. There better not be any more.

CHAPTER 9

We gingerly make our way through the kitchen to the dining room, where Daniel suggests we split up. "We'll cover more ground that way," he says, handing me one of two boxes of fuses. Since there's no cell signal here, Cal suggests we flip light switches on as we go, so we'll each know if the other group finds it first when all the rooms light up at once.

"Okay, but what if I find it first? I still don't know how to change a fuse," I point out.

"It's like changing a light bulb," Bethany says. "You might need to test a few to figure out which ones are burned out. Oh, and heads-up, these are fifteen-amp ones, but I double-checked with Dad, and he says they should still fit even if this house is wired for thirty. Do it the other way around, though, and you risk a fire."

"Right. Okay." Fire? I hope Bethany knows what she's talking about as much as she sounds like she does. She and Daniel pair up and go off together one way, because of course they do, and I find myself alone with Cal again. It's the perfect start to every horror movie.

"Where do you think this fuse box is gonna be?" I ask.

Somewhere off in the other direction, I hear Daniel go "Wooooo," followed by Bethany's giggles.

"Hmm." Cal pauses in the archway leading from the dining room to whatever room lies in the dim light beyond.

His eyes flutter down to the floor for a second. He swallows. "Maybe the basement?"

I don't think he wants to go into the basement. Neither do I. It's creepy enough up here on the ground floor. Even creepier when I remind myself that Miriam *died* in this house. I knew this—the estate lawyer told us she died at home in her sleep—but it only truly hits me now, standing in the semidark, surrounded by dust and stillness. Suddenly every tiny sound, every shuffle and creak gives me goose bumps. Does Miriam still roam the halls as she did when she was alive? Did she ever stand in this very spot, listening to her old house creaking, wondering the same about those who came before her?

"Basement," I say. "Makes sense. Let's look for one."

Stepping past Cal into the next room, my eyes are drawn to the archway on the other end. That must lead to the entryway and its un-boarded windows due to the faint gray light bleeding in from beyond—not enough to light the rest of this room, though.

Hovering just inside, the darkness pressing around me, I make a shaky sweep of the area with the flashlight. I'm not sure what I'm expecting—cobwebbed skeletons in the corner? Bats on the ceiling? Fortunately, there's nothing like that. All I see is furniture—a well-worn sofa, two wingback chairs, and a standing lamp with ratty fringe trimming along the bottom of the shade. I take another step and nearly blind myself as the light bounces off the glass front of a curio cabinet. Flinching, I swivel to the side and bump against the end of the mantel above the fireplace. A series of frames in all shapes and sizes stretches down its length.

"What is it?" Cal asks.

"Pictures." It comes out as a whisper. The photos on this end of the mantel are tilted toward the center, so they're facing away. It's too dark to get a clear view of the ones on the other end, but these could be relatives. They must be. Who else would you place above your fireplace? If only my legs would cooperate so I can get a better look.

I'm possibly about to be presented with the faces of people whose blood I share but have never ever seen before—not once in my life. I've never even seen pictures of my dad as a kid. Will there be any here? I—I don't know if I'm ready for that.

"May I?" Cal gently removes the flashlight from my frozen hand and uses it to navigate to where he can take a look, since I'm not doing it. I feel the darkness pressing up against my back, exposed here in the doorway to the dining room, as the light moves farther away from me. And still, I can't move.

As Cal shines the flashlight down the line, a strange expression crosses his face. He steps closer, peering at each photograph, then squinting at me in the dark, then back again.

"I think . . . these . . ." He does another check back and forth. "I think these are all you."

"What?" A nervous laugh escapes my throat. *That can't be.*

Finally, my feet unstick from the floor, and I rush over to see for myself. And he's right. There's me running track in middle school. There's me graduating kindergarten. There's me standing next to my project at the fifth-grade science fair. And there I am at the beach. I think I was about seven. I'm beaming next to a sandcastle decorated with sea kelp, driftwood, and sand dollars. I remember that sandcastle. I was really proud of it.

I look to Cal, as if he'd have any explanation for this bizarre gallery of my life, but one photo in particular has grabbed his attention. He picks it up, holds it, stares at it like nothing else exists. I lean over his shoulder to see which one it is, and my heart drops into my stomach.

I'm eleven in this picture. My hair is in two braids, my favorite way to wear it at the time. I'm sitting, grinning, perched on the back of Dad's ambulance, nearly swallowed up by his pullover fleece, the caduceus patch displayed prominently on the front. I was so happy, so innocent, so blissfully unaware of what the future held. I was going to be a paramedic, too. Rhonda was going to be a doctor—and would have been well on her way now if our circumstances hadn't changed so dramatically.

"This . . . this is *you*?" he mutters.

"Yeah." I slide the frame out of his grasp and lay it facedown on the mantel. "That's me." I turn away from the photographs and from Cal, to hide my face. "Let's keep searching," I say, eyes watering as I head toward the archway at the other end of the room.

"Hold up." The flashlight beam bounces around me as Cal hurries after me. He puts a hand on my shoulder. "Are you okay?"

I resist my natural impulse to dart away. His hand is warm, and the warmth stays with me after he removes it on his own.

"You were right," I tell him. "It would have been better for me to come here privately. Let's just find this fuse thing so we can get out of here."

Since Cal has the flashlight now, he goes first, though it's light enough in the entryway that we don't need it. Happy to have his back to me, I hang behind for a moment to collect myself. But as he leaves this room and enters the next, I feel the skin prickling on my arms and neck again, and hurry to rejoin him. I don't want to be left alone with the shadows of old memories.

The entryway is larger than I expected. More like a foyer. Afternoon light filters through the leaded glass windows framing the front door, creating fractured patterns across the worn parquet. A grand staircase curves up to a balcony on the second floor, with a beadboard wall below it.

"Wow." I pause in the middle of the foyer, taking it all in.

"Wow," Cal repeats. "Your aunt was loaded."

I doubt it. Miriam left me everything, and everything is this. But the Sylvans must have been well off at some point. I crane my neck to look up at a cobwebbed crystal chandelier. It makes me dizzy. If it really is crystal, it alone might pay off the mortgage. I'm not sure how we'd manage to get it down without shattering it, though. Besides, with my luck, it's probably glass.

"Look, there's a door." Cal points the flashlight toward the beadboard under the stairs, and sure enough, a thin line traces the shape of a small door in the middle. A metal loop hangs in place of a doorknob, like a trapdoor turned on its side. Placed before it, as if an attempt to hide it further, is an ornately carved bench.

"Do you think that goes to the basement?" I ask.

"Might. Or a closet. Or . . ." He raises his eyebrows at me. ". . . a secret passage."

A smile creeps onto my face. "Or a dungeon."

"Or a mad scientist's laboratory."

78

"Or the entrance to Narnia," I laugh. But despite the jokes, something about that door is making my skin prickle.

Cal tucks the flashlight under his arm; we each take an end of the bench and lift. It's heavy, but we manage to shift it just far enough to access the door. Cal looks to me, then tugs on the metal ring. The door creaks open. Cold, stale air hits our faces as the flashlight illuminates cobwebs and a concrete staircase leading down, down to pure darkness.

"You go first," I tell him.

"It's your house. You go first."

"How gentlemanly of you."

"I was kidding," he says, but he still doesn't move.

Swallowing the lump in my throat, I take the flashlight from him, duck through the opening, and immediately regret it as claustrophobia kicks in. My lungs tighten as my heart thumps against my sternum as if it, too, has a need for more space. But I can't turn back now—not without looking like a coward. I carefully pick my way down the steps, feeling more and more resistance the farther I go. Why do I feel so much like I'm going somewhere I'm not supposed to? This is my house now. Nowhere should be off-limits.

I'm about a third of the way down with Cal close behind me, when the lights turn on, catching me off guard. I stumble and flail at the wall for support, banging my elbow against the railing instead. The flashlight slips from my grip, clattering down the steps, and my heart leaps into my throat as my foot shoots out from under me. I'm bracing myself for more pain—or worse— when my shirt goes tight around my chest, arresting my fall. Cal's arm reaches around my middle, and we both ease down to sitting—Cal one step above, me just below, locked tight between his knees.

Silence.

Deep exhales from both of us.

"Thank you." My voice shakes.

Eyes now adjusted to the light, I stare at the concrete landing ten or so steps below us. The flashlight is there, popped open, its batteries several inches away. That could have been my head.

At the end of the landing, there's another ominous-looking door. Something about it gives me a strange buzzy feeling in my head. Or maybe that's the adrenaline. What's beyond it? What things might I find hidden away in the basement of this strange, spooky house? I have the disconcerting feeling that, somewhere in the furthest recesses of my mind, I already know but shouldn't. Like there's a barrier in my brain, which is silly because I've never been here, so there's *no way* I could know what's in there. Still, I think I'd rather leave it for another day. The flashlight is welcome to stay down there for now, too. With the lights on, we don't need it.

Gripping the railing, I try to pull myself back to my feet, but I'm stuck. It's my shirt—my shirt is stopping me. I reach over my shoulder and work my trembling fingers between Cal's fist and the fabric still bunched within it until he loosens his grip and I can turn around to look at him. Face blanched, pupils wide, he's staring past me, at nothing.

"Hey," I say.

His eyes recenter on my face, but he's still not *looking* looking. His mind has gone somewhere else. He looks exactly how

I feel sometimes. How I feel when my brain's being a jerk. *What happened?* I want to ask, but I know better. *What's happened to make your brain be a jerk to you, too?*

I soften my voice and try to keep it steady. "It's okay. We're okay, see?"

He refocuses, then flushes and looks away. "Sorry." It comes out as a breath.

"It's okay. I get it." I ease myself to standing, then reach down and give him my hand, which he uses to pull himself up, too.

"So, I guess they found the fuse box." I try to sound light, but it sounds singsongy and fake. "Let's find the others."

As we trudge back up the stairs, I focus on Cal's shoes and mine, making sure to place each foot squarely onto each step. The worn concrete reminds me of the gravestones I walked among this morning, tugging at my heart as I piece it together. His friend. The one whose gravestone I saw him visiting. This morning, he told me his friend "fell." Was Cal there when it happened? Is that why his brain's being a jerk? Because I almost fell just now, too.

I pause for half a step, gripping the railing, and look down over my shoulder again. If Cal hadn't been right behind me . . .

Nope, now I'm dizzy. I turn around and follow Cal's shoes the rest of the way out.

The house is transformed with the lights on, though not any less spooky. While there are fewer shadowy corners for monsters to hide in, there's a disconcerting clash between the appearance of lived-in-ness and the unshakeable emptiness of death and abandonment. Knowing everything is as Miriam left

81

it—*she* hung that coat on the hook by the door, *she* tossed that moth-eaten blanket along the back of the sofa—makes it even more eerie. The lights also showcase the amount of fixing and cleaning Rhonda and I will have to do, and it's a *lot*. I make note of the peeling wallpaper, cracked ceiling plaster, tattered drapes, cobwebs. So many cobwebs. The spiders have claimed this place as their own, and I'm not looking forward to evicting them.

My steps falter as we pass the fireplace; I strain to keep my eyes forward, avoiding the images of my life spread out before me. It feels like a shrine, and a depressing one at that. Here was a woman who apparently cared about me enough to keep up with my life, yet in all that time, I never knew she existed. Why hadn't Dad told me about her? Is it the same reason he'd never talked about this town? Clearly, he'd kept in contact. Clearly, he thought Miriam ought to know about me. Why, then, wasn't I meant to know about her?

"There you guys are," Bethany calls out from her spot at the head of the dining room table as I pass through the archway. Feet crossed at the ankles on the table, she tips her chair precariously on its back legs. Daniel sits next to her, face scrunched comically between his hands as he props himself up with his elbows.

"We had a near disaster on the basement staircase." I glance over my shoulder to gauge Cal's reaction, but I'm not sure he heard, as he's just now strolling into the room, still looking shaken. "So, where'd you find it?"

"In the laundry room," Daniel says between his scrunched

cheeks. "It's around the other side of the kitchen. Almost didn't see the door."

"There's still laundry in there," Bethany says, widening her eyes. "Like, *in* the washer. Reeks as bad as the kitchen. We had to come out a few times for fresh air. That's why it took us so long."

"Nasty." I shudder. That'll be fun to clean out. The fridge, too, probably.

I'm already thinking ahead, making plans of action. I know our funds won't hold out much longer if we keep having to pay for a hotel room, and who knows how much fixing the car will cost, so the faster we can make this place livable, the better. And yet, I'm not exactly looking forward to moving in. It's creepy enough during the day, even with the lights on—what about at night? Out in the middle of nowhere, flanked on three sides by acres of dark forest . . . Are there bears out here? Wolves? Bigfoot? But we don't have much choice now. *And besides,* I remind myself, *Dad lived here, and he was fine.* Maybe it will help me understand him a little more.

"Right." Bethany slides her feet off the table, leaving a trail in the dust, and stands up. "Mission accomplished. Let's get out of here."

"I thought you wanted to explore," Daniel teases.

"I did! And I still do! But I never expected it to reek like this." She turns to me. "No offense."

"None taken."

She grins. "Please, please, please invite me back when you've aired the place out a bit, though, okay?"

"Hey, you fixed my electricity. Of course you're invited b—"

There's a pop from down the hall, and we're plunged again into darkness. A faint smell of burning drifts into the room, then dissipates.

"Well," says Bethany. "Shit."

CHAPTER 10

The enticing aroma of pepperoni makes my stomach growl, reminding me I've eaten nothing but cookies all day. It's no wonder I'm shaky. I shut the hotel room door behind me and make a beeline for the kitchenette, where the remnants of a lukewarm pizza await me. Rhonda, stretched out on her bed, looks up from the well-loved paperback she's reading: *Dune*, by Frank Herbert. One of Dad's favorites. Where Dad and I bonded over music, their thing was books. Especially fantasy and science fiction.

"You get the lights back on?" she asks.

"Yup," I mumble, mouth full. "For a few minutes."

"What do you mean a few minutes?"

I swallow and lean against the tiny sink. "I don't know. Bethany got it to work, and then something made the main fuse blow. She didn't want to mess with that one. She said it looked older than the one they used to have here at the Roadhouse, and it wasn't insulated. So, basically . . ." I cringe. "We do need to hire an electrician."

Rhonda's eyes roll up into her head as she closes them. She lets her book flop. "Okay," she mutters to herself. "Okay, okay, okay."

I wolf down the rest of my slice. "And the car?" I ask as I grab another. "What was up with that?"

"Don't know yet. It's still in the shop. But at least the loaner we get to drive in the meantime is free."

"That's good, at least." I consider telling her about the mouse but stick with my earlier decision that it would be better for her not to know. Not right now, anyway.

Still chewing, I head over to my suitcase and rummage around for my pj's. It's not that late, but I'm done for the day. And it's probably my imagination, but over the smell of grease and cheese, I'm detecting this faint whiff of mustiness mixed with dead mouse. It must be coming from my clothes.

"What was it like in there?" Rhonda asks. "What are we dealing with?"

I swallow. "*Lots* of cleaning."

She pauses, then asks, "Any, um . . . you didn't see any evidence of rats or anything, did you?"

Crap. Pj's found, I straighten up, letting the suitcase lid flop. "No . . . no evidence of rats." Not a lie, because technically, it was a mouse. But rat, mouse—it's just semantics to Rhonda. I send a silent plea to the universe that we don't find any more of either when we return.

Rhonda visibly relaxes. "Good. I was worried about that, so at least something's gone right. I don't want to have to pay for an exterminator on top of everything else. The tow this afternoon was expensive. And the bank—they said they'll get back to me on Monday because the loan officer wasn't in. I guess I should have expected that on a Saturday."

The pizza settles into a hard lump in my stomach. I pause

on my way into the bathroom and lean against the doorframe. "Rhonda?"

"Yeah?"

"Are we gonna be okay?"

She closes her eyes. "I don't know."

I swallow against the tightness in my throat and head into the bathroom to get ready for bed. Rhonda saying she doesn't know is never a good sign. Rhonda always knows. Or at least, she thinks she does.

By the time I come out, she's already sleeping, a crease between her brows and traces of salt on her lashes. That's another thing about Rhonda. She always waits to cry alone. Her book still rests open on her chest, so I tiptoe over and carefully slide it out from under her hand, then slip her bookmark between the pages before placing it on our shared nightstand. The click as I turn off the lamp wakes her. She shifts onto her side and reaches out an arm.

Without a word, I leave the edge of my bed and climb into hers instead. She'll justify this as being there to comfort me, but I know Rhonda's the one who needs comforting right now. This day has taken its toll, and soon we've fallen asleep huddled together like the nights I'd had nightmares when I was little. Like the night Mom left. Like the night Dad died.

First, I dream of darkness. Rustling leaves and labored breathing, coolness against my skin. It brushes past me in light gusts, enveloping me as I fall. I fall, and fall, and fall, as a string—a shining, silvery thread like spider silk—stretches out and away from me, far into the distance, disappearing into the never-ending dark. A scream builds in my lungs, but I can't let it out, its pressure increasing as I continue to fall . . . until there's a tug at my middle, and—

My body jerks awake, the whisper of a just-missed word lingering among the edges of consciousness. Rhonda's arm tightens a little, holding me in place.

"Y'okay?" she mumbles.

"Yeah."

She relaxes her hug, and I realize the pressure was probably from that. I'm feeling cramped. "I'm going back to my own bed now, okay?"

"'Kay," she answers, but I think she's still mostly asleep. She rolls the other way as I transfer from her bed to my own. By the time I've pulled up my covers, she's succumbed to light snoring.

Remember . . .

The just-missed word peeks from the edges where it was hiding as I drift off again, then fades away as Rhonda's snores mingle with a distant rumbling. What could that be? Before I realize what I'm doing, I've drifted over to the doorway, drawn by the sound and something else. A feeling. Something familiar, though I can't define it. I step outside, barefoot, and land, not onto the wood porch but onto asphalt.

I'm standing in the middle of a street.

The rumbling grows louder, closer. Pops are followed by echoes of the pops, and my first instinct is to duck. My pulse quickens as I'm reminded of another time. Another place with pops and sparks and shadows and . . . Rob. Is he here? What's happening? The pops are coming from behind me. I turn, dreading what I might find.

The Roadhouse is gone, replaced by more asphalt. Another pop ricochets off blurred, indistinct structures lining the street as a boy jumps his skateboard onto the curb. He balances there for a second, then hops it back down onto the street and kicks off to get it moving again. Pop. Pop. Rumble. I relax . . . a little. There's no shadow here. No smoke. No smell of cordite, either. Just some guy on a skateboard.

He glides over and stops, flipping his board up with his foot and catching the end with his hand. He grins at me. "Heya."

"Hey," I return. He looks familiar, but my sleep-addled brain is having trouble placing him. His features flicker in and out of focus, like he's trying to hold them to a certain self-image but they're rebelling.

"Which one's yours?" he asks.

"What do you mean?"

He rolls his eyes. "Your tag, duh."

I turn in place—or rather, the place turns around me—and the structures reveal themselves: worn brick factory walls, concrete smokestacks, curved tunnels stretching far overhead. Every surface is covered with bright, sweeping designs and stylistic lettering in all the colors on the spectrum, overlapping in infinite layers.

They're . . . *beautiful.* Rainbows of personality, brightening what would normally feel so stark. So utilitarian. I've never thought of graffiti that way before.

"None of these are mine," I answer.

Once I speak it, everything changes.

The atmosphere grows heavy and gray. The colors darken. The designs shift and morph, restructuring themselves into harsh, angular letters. Stomach fluttering, I look to the skater to see if he's seeing what I'm seeing. But he's lost interest in the graffiti. He's staring at me now, eyes bulging, his features finally coming into stark relief. I do know him. Skateboard, graffiti . . . my jaw tightens. Which one is he? What were their names again?

"Holy shit," he says, backing away from me. Or is it from something else? His gaze shifts past my shoulder, making my skin prickle. I can feel it. Something creeping in the air. Something I recognize, tugging at my emotions. Strengthening them, drawing them out.

But when I look behind me, nothing's there.

His gaze flicks toward the buildings again, then returns to me. He drops his skateboard onto its wheels.

"I'm sorry, okay?" he says. "I couldn't back out. I'm not a coward anymore."

He kicks off to make his skateboard go, but it doesn't move. The wheels have sunk into the road.

"Back out of what?" I ask him.

At the same time, another voice seeps in from somewhere beyond. "Yes, you are," it says. "Coward."

The voice is low and high at the same time, raspy and smooth. Coming from everywhere at once yet nowhere definable. Like the fear I'm feeling right now. The fear, the anger, the shame, the guilt . . . it's all swirling around me and inside me at once.

In a panic, the skater crouches down to pull his wheels out of the asphalt, but they won't budge, and the walls are closing in around us. We're surrounded by the word *WITCH*, sprayed over and over again, at all angles, on every surface, even the road. Even the concrete sky.

The boy gives up and sits on his board. Pulling his knees in tight, he rocks back and forth.

"Stop," he begs. "I told you I'm sorry. Stop. *Please.*"

"Me?" *I'm* not doing this.

Am I?

The *I* in the most prominent *WITCH* grows. It grows and grows, morphing into a lanky, shadowy figure. And it's creeping toward us.

"I'm not doing this," I repeat to myself, backing away until I come up against the wall. "This isn't me."

But I'm not sure I believe myself. The shame I'm feeling, the guilt—it's so strong, I can't tell anymore if it's coming from the skater, the shadow, or from me. Maybe—maybe it's *all* me. I know this feeling so well. Ever since Dad died, it's been my constant companion, one I'm forever working to bury away. Maybe . . . this shadow is mine.

Witch, witch, witch.

Dark wisps bleed off the figure into the air, reminding me again of another time with flickering lights, sparks, shadowy smoke rolling through rows of shelves . . . and Rob. I remember the shadow enveloping him just before I awoke . . . and he didn't. *They found him in a coma.* But that has to be a coincidence. Because this is only a dream. That's all this is. A dream. A nightmare.

One of the wisps hits me, knocking me back to the present. *That didn't feel like a dream.* Another tendril lashes out, snagging my wrist as I bring my arm up to block my face. I tug against it, a dull ache building behind my eyes. Dad's face flashes across my vision—angry, frustrated, so disappointed. And the pain worsens—a throbbing, stabbing—until I manage to shake myself loose. The tendril retreats, and the pain and imagery retreat with it, leaving behind a horrible feeling in the pit of my stomach.

The dark figure pauses its attack and cocks its head, examining me. I have to hide. I have to get out of here. If only I could sink into the wall the same way this shadow emerged from it.

And then, in an instant, I do.

I'm falling as before, falling through darkness. There's a tug from my middle again, like a string pulled taut, and I snap awake, gasping in air.

My sheets are soaked. Throwing them off, I sit up and swipe my hair away from my damp forehead. Soft snores still emanate from the lump in the covers on Rhonda's side of the room, oblivious as the weak light of dawn creeps in around the edges of the curtains. Staring past it, I try to hold on to the fading remnants of the dream. But they're slipping away like sand slips between fingers until all that remains is an uneasy feeling in the pit of my stomach, like I've done something wrong. Something very, very wrong.

CHAPTER 11

This morning, Rhonda and I found our loaner car sitting on its rims in the Roadhouse parking lot, each tire sporting a gash several inches long. So now instead of heading over to the house to start cleaning, we're sitting in Madrona's tiny police station, waiting to talk to Chief Burke while the officer sitting at the front desk clacks away on her keyboard.

My face is hot; I can feel my pulse in it, and my chair scrunches whenever I change positions. Part of me wants to scream. First the graffiti, now this. The rest of me is . . . tired. It doesn't help that I'm still uneasy over last night's dream. And even more uneasy that I can't quite remember what happened in it to make me feel so uneasy. It's similar to how I felt after the dream about Rob, which I also couldn't remember at first. And that makes me *even more* uneasy. Because Rob's in a coma now. I'm sure it's a coincidence. I mean, it must be, because they're just dreams. Except these felt different somehow.

"So, this guy was Dad's friend?" Rhonda whispers, interrupting my internal spiral of doom.

"That's what he said." I examine the framed pictures lining the walls—photos of everyone who's ever served on Madrona's tiny police force. Chief Burke's portrait is right in the center. The label on his frame tells me he's only been the chief of police for about five years.

"When?"

"When they were kids, I think. He said they went to school together." I wonder how close they really were. Were they best friends or just classmates? It sucks that I don't know. This is something I should know.

"No, I mean, when did he tell you this?"

The door opens, and a lanky, dark-haired officer pops his head in. He looks inquiringly at the woman at the desk, who nods at him then tilts her head toward us.

"Come on back," he says.

The chief's office doesn't look like it's been updated since at least the seventies. Cheap wood paneling lines the walls, negating the window's effort to cheer the place up.

"Thank you," he says to the officer who led us in. The officer backs out and closes the door while Chief Burke half stands, leaning over his desk to shake our hands. "Hello again, Eva. And you must be Rhonda. Please, take a seat."

"So." He folds his hands on the table as Rhonda and I settle into our chairs. "What can I do for you?"

Rhonda fiddles with the hem of her shirt. "My sister said you, um, told her that if we ever need anything . . ." She trails off, unable to complete the sentence, because heaven forbid she ask anyone for help. Even if they've offered.

"Your sister's correct." Chief Burke looks to me and attempts

94

what I think is meant to be a smile, but it comes out more like a wince. "Anything for Alex's kids. What's the trouble?"

"Okay, so first, our car wouldn't start yesterday," Rhonda says. "The mechanic said it looked 'fishy.'"

"Fishy?" He leans farther forward. "How?"

"I don't know. Like, tampered with, I guess. But he wouldn't go into any details without a more thorough look. He seemed a little . . . intense?"

"Ah, yes, that would be Charlie," Chief Burke says.

"Yeah. Charlie. So, anyway, I didn't really take it seriously. But now someone's slashed the tires on the loaner he gave us."

Chief Burke leans back and lets out a heavy sigh. "Is there anyone specific who you've had an altercation with within the last two days? Besides Rob Petersen, that is."

A lump forms in my stomach. I never did get around to telling Rhonda what happened in the gas station. I was hoping I wouldn't have to. Especially with everything else going on.

"An altercation? No, of course not. Who's Rob Petersen?" Rhonda asks.

Petersen. Where have I seen that name recently, and why does my chest feel tight? Was it also embroidered on Rob's shirt? I think it just said *Rob*.

I clear my throat. "So, you know how Cal showed us how to get to the house? That was . . . well, that was because the gas station attendant—that's Rob—he kind of freaked out when he saw our last name on your credit card and refused to help."

Confused, she opens her mouth as if to respond, but nothing comes out.

"And now I guess he's in a coma or something?" I add, cautiously looking to Chief Burke for confirmation.

"Where did you hear that?" he asks.

"Cal told me. Because you wouldn't."

"Ah. Of course he did. Must have heard it from my son, who likely overheard something he shouldn't have." He sighs again. "My point is, as gruff as Rob can get, I can't imagine him doing that, but obviously, I can't rule anyone out. Being in a coma's a pretty good alibi, though, wouldn't you say?"

"Is he going to be okay?" Rhonda asks.

"I, uh, can't discuss that. It's a HIPAA thing." He gives me a pointed look. "Which is why I wasn't going into details with you yesterday, Eva. Anyway, has anyone else bothered you, threatened you at all, done or said anything to warrant suspicion?"

Rhonda and I look to each other.

"Well . . ." I think for a moment. "There was this old couple giving me dirty looks yesterday." I picture them gleefully slashing someone's tires in the middle of the night and realize how stupid that sounds.

"Eva, seriously?" Rhonda shoots Chief Burke an apologetic look.

"You weren't there. They were being creepy." I go silent as I remember what their stares led to: me ducking into the gift shop, and then Chief Burke walking in and . . . I look down at my lap.

"I guess I've had a few strange looks, too," Rhonda says. "But we're strangers in a very close-knit community, right?

96

The only other incident *I* can think of happened our first night here. When we got to Miriam's house—that's Eva's great-aunt—and . . ."

Chief Burke holds up a hand here. "I'm sorry, *Eva's* great-aunt? That's an interesting way to put it. I was given to under-stand the two of you are sisters."

"We are," I mumble. Guilt seeps through me as I'm reminded yet again that Miriam never mentioned Rhonda in the will. Just me. Rhonda hasn't said much about it, but I know it hurts.

"We're half sisters." Rhonda's face tinges red, and I can tell she's annoyed from the edge in her voice. "Same mom."

Rhonda took the Sylvan name along with our mom when Mom and Dad got married. He's the only dad she's ever known, and he always treated her as if she was his own. Or so I thought. More guilt as I think of how the pictures on Miriam's mantel are only ones of me. Either Dad never sent any of Rhonda or Miriam chose only to display mine. Either way, it's wrong. I need to take them down before she sees them. I wish I'd thought to do it when I was there yesterday. I reach over and squeeze Rhonda's hand. She squeezes back.

"I'm sorry," Chief Burke says. "I just wanted to make sure I have everything straight. Please. Continue. What happened when you got to the house?"

"We chased some teens away who were vandalizing it. Drink-ing and spraying graffiti all over the place," she tells him. "It was creepy, too—the graffiti, I mean. Part of that song, you know, the one from *The Wizard of Oz*? Ding-dong—"

"The witch is dead," Chief Burke finishes for her. He slouches

97

a little more in his chair. "I'm disappointed, but I can't say I'm surprised. All right, so we've got graffiti, slashed tires, and whatever it was that was allegedly done to your car. I'd say this qualifies as harassment and could certainly be the same person."

"Troy," I say automatically as a flash of last night's dream finally comes to me. There's graffiti all around me. And a boy—a terrified boy. And a shadow. I shiver involuntarily.

Chief Burke sits up straighter. "Excuse me?"

"I mean, maybe." I double back. "Someone told me they thought the graffiti was by someone named Troy and . . . Chris? I think? They recognized Troy's tag."

"Who recognized it? I'd like to talk to them."

I hesitate, then say, "I . . . don't know everyone's names yet. Sorry." I add a little sheepish shrug at the end, but I'm not sure I've sold it. It's technically not a lie—I don't know everyone's names yet. It's also not an answer. But I'm not sure how happy Chief Burke would be to know his kid had been traipsing around the "dangerous old Sylvan place" yesterday. Or to know he could recognize a graffiti tag when he saw one. My dad wouldn't have been too thrilled about it, and he wasn't even a cop.

Chief Burke thinks for a moment, and I find myself tensing. But instead of questioning me further, he scoots back his chair and stands. "Interesting. All right, well, now that I have some information to go on, I'll start looking into it and see if there are any connections." He reaches across the desk to shake our hands again.

There's an abruptness to it that makes me wonder if I've said something else he didn't like. Maybe I should have told him it was his son who recognized the tag after all.

"Well, that was awkward," Rhonda says once we're back out on the sidewalk.

"Yeah, a little."

"Why didn't you tell me about what happened at the gas station?"

"I don't know. I guess I didn't want to stress you out over it."

She stops and pulls me aside. Placing her hands on my shoulders, she looks me earnestly in the eyes. "Don't you dare worry about stressing me out, got it? We're in this together. We need to be able to talk to each other. You need to be able to talk to me about things."

Tears well up, forcing me to blink to hold them back. "I'll try. But the same goes for you. I know I've—I've been kind of a jerk lately."

"I know. I have, too." She smiles, but her eyes are sad as she pulls me in for a hug.

A boy on a skateboard whizzes by, bumping our shoulders and jolting us apart.

"Hey!" I call after him, but he doesn't slow down or even acknowledge having heard me.

"Is it just me, or did that feel like it was on purpose?" Rhonda asks.

My jaw tightens as I watch him and his white baseball cap speed away. "That's one of them. I think."

"One of who?"

"One of the graffiti guys. I saw them out skateboarding yesterday."

Rhonda squints after him. "Are you sure? Lots of people skateboard."

The rumble of the board and the pop as he hops it from curb to street brings me another flash of last night's dream. *Is* it the same guy? I rummage around in my memory, trying to unearth a clearer image, but everything's so fuzzy. I don't think it's him, though. This guy—which one is it? Chris or Troy? This guy is shorter and bulkier than the one in my dream. More compact.

I blink, then hurry to catch up with Rhonda, who's already walking again. Of course he's not the guy in my dream. This is real life, and that was just some horrible nightmare. That person probably doesn't even exist. But I've had plenty of nightmares before and this didn't feel like those. This felt real. Even more real than the ones right after Dad died.

"I guess we now know why Dad wouldn't talk about his life here," I say. "This town obviously has something against our family." Now the wheels are turning. "And when Miriam died, they thought she was the last Sylvan, right? Like, they were finally rid of us. But then you and I showed up."

"I don't know. That seems a little . . . paranoid? What could be so horrible about us?"

"Okay, but would you believe there isn't a single Sylvan in the cemetery here? Not that I could find, anyway, and I looked all over that place. They aren't even buried with the rest of the town. I think, whatever this place's issue is, it's been going on for a long time."

"Evangeline," Rhonda sighs.

I bristle, but I don't correct her. "What?"

"Why on earth were you hanging out in a cemetery? Is that where you were 'walking' yesterday?"

Before I can answer, there's a jangle of bells behind us and a woman shouts, "Hey. You. You're those Sylvan girls, aren't you?"

My spine stiffens. That was an accusation, not a question. Slowly, I pivot. The woman steps out from the doorway of the shop we've just passed—Petersen's Gifts—the store I darted into yesterday to escape that creepy old couple who kept staring at me. As the door jingles closed behind her, I notice something carved deep into the doorframe, past the layers of paint, down to the bare wood. Another one of those strange symbols I've been seeing all over town, except this one is fresh. I'm positive it wasn't there yesterday.

The woman lurches toward us, shoulders squared, arms swinging stiffly at her sides. I recognize her as the woman from behind the counter who received the bad news yesterday and take a steadying breath.

Rhonda raises her chin. "Can we help you with something?"

The woman's nostrils flare. She stops inches from us, forcing us to take a step back. "Yeah. You can. You can pack up your bags and go home to whatever hellscape you came here from, that's what you can do for me."

Rhonda's jaw drops.

I'm hit with a wave of dizziness as the woman then turns her focus on me. She sticks out a finger, nearly poking me in the face with it. "You. What were you doing in my shop yesterday? Were you there to gloat? To see if it worked?"

I take another step back, struggling to find my words. "I don't know—I don't . . ."

The walls of the shops close in around me. Crowding me. People stare out of windows, stop on the sidewalk, watch from across the street.

"Okay," Rhonda coaxes. "Clearly there's been a misunderstanding. Let's all just calm d—"

"Calm down?" the woman gasps. I zero in on the fine spray of spit exiting her mouth with each hard consonant. Her finger is up in my face again. "My dad called and warned me about you last night. Right after you left, he called and told me the Sylvans were back. Sounded terrified. Wasn't making much sense. Said there was gonna be trouble, and he was right. There *is* gonna be trouble if you don't undo whatever it was you did to him. *Right. Now.*"

There's gonna be trouble. And then it clicks. I look past this woman to the sign above her shop again. Petersen's Gifts. Petersen. *Rob Petersen*, Chief Burke had said. *That's where I knew the name from.* "Rob? That's your dad?"

As soon as the words leave my mouth, I wish I could swallow them back up. The woman goes from red to ashen, and now I know the bad news Chief Burke delivered to her yesterday was about him. *Didn't show up for work*, Cal had told me. *Found him in a coma.*

And she thinks *I* did that somehow? It's so completely ridiculous, I'd laugh in her face if I didn't think one of those balled-up fists would end up in my own. But it doesn't matter how bizarre the whole thing sounds. In her mind, I've confirmed it.

The gift shop's door rattles again, and that white-baseball-capped skateboarder pokes his head out. He hesitates, then comes over and gently tugs at the woman's arm. "Mom, come on."

"Christopher! Go back inside. Stay away from these two."

Christopher. *Chris.* Heat creeps up the nape of my neck. I was right. He *is* one of them. "You—you were at the house. With Troy." The red dripping letters of the word *WITCH* plastered across Miriam's house are now plastered across my mind's eye.

The two go absolutely still.

"Eva," Rhonda warns. "Let's go."

My heart thumps in my chest. She's right. We should go. But my body's not cooperating. Nerves are tugging me one way and anger is tugging me another, creating a standstill. They're bullies. I saw the way they treated Cal yesterday. I wouldn't put it past them to have slashed our tires, too. I can feel myself shaking. I should listen to Rhonda and go, but I can't.

Ms. Petersen is shaking now, too, but I don't care anymore. She should know what her son and his friend have been up to. She turns to Chris and hisses, "House? What house? What did you do?"

He shakes his head, eyes wide.

"Tell her, Chris. Tell her what you and Troy spray-painted all over Miriam's house." *Stop, Eva. Just shut up.* My stomach is churning, and I feel like I might vomit. I hate conflict. I hate it. But this has been building and I can't get myself to shut up. I knew I was upset about what they did, but I didn't realize *how* upset until now.

There's a light touch on my arm, opposite the side Rhonda's standing on.

"Eva, come on." A guy's voice. I think it's Daniel, but I don't turn to look.

"Come *on*." And that's Bethany.

When I don't move, she hands Daniel her coffee to-go cup and steps in front of me. "Bethany . . . ," he warns, but she waves him off. And instead of coaxing me to leave, she faces Chris and his mom, staring them down as if challenging them to say anything else.

Chris's mother puts her arm in front of him, and they retreat . . . a little. Only a few steps, but it's enough to satisfy Bethany. She turns her back to them. "Come on, Eva." Taking hold of my shoulders, she spins me around as well, adding through her teeth, "They're not worth it."

Faces draw away from windows and pedestrians give us a wide berth as we book it to the Roadhouse. Our rapid pace helps to work some of the fight out of my system, but I'm still feeling shaky by the time we reach the steps leading up to the room.

"When I told you not to worry about stressing me out, that's not what I meant." Rhonda massages her temples. "I think I'm getting a migraine."

"I'm sorry." A heaviness washes over me as the implications of my behavior back there sink in. Whatever people thought about the Sylvans before, I've hardly helped.

The whole town saw that. Okay, so maybe not the *whole* town, but it might as well have been with how quickly news travels around here.

Rhonda trudges up to our room to lie down while Bethany shoos Daniel away, telling him she's got this, and leads me through the door beneath it, into the Roadhouse kitchen. The pungent smell of bacon and eggs and grease turns my already nerve-addled stomach.

"Hey, Dad. Coming through."

Bethany's dad flips four sizzling eggs in rapid succession and turns around just as we're darting behind him. He's wearing one of those slick-looking black double-breasted chef's shirts, but better, because on the back is a silk-screened design of a cartoon spatula playing an electric guitar. I think I like him already.

"Oh, hey! This must be the Eva I've been hearing so much about. Great to finally meet you!"

I open my mouth to say hi back, but Bethany continues to push me forward.

"Not a good time, Dad. Sorry," she says with a warning shake of her head.

"Uh-oh, I know that look. What happened?"

"Diane Petersen happened," she calls back, which must be explanation enough because I can hear him grumbling as we pass through the flapping doors. It seems he's also not a fan. I would have liked to have at least had a moment to say hi, but he looked busy, and I'm still shaky, so Bethany's probably right.

"Sorry for the mess," Bethany warns me as we approach her family's apartment. She ushers me inside, then slips off her shoes and places them neatly beside the door. "We're in the process of replacing some of the Roadhouse's tableware."

She waits as I crouch down to loosen the laces of my boots. The apartment doesn't seem that messy to me. Some boxes are stacked by the dining table, which is covered with an array of dishes, glasses, and silverware, but other than that, there's not a lot of clutter here. Or maybe it feels that way to me, because it's much more spacious than our apartment back in New York. It feels like a small house, with the kitchen in a different room and an actual hallway separating the bedrooms and bathroom from the rest of the living space. Our apartment would have felt cramped with their overstuffed sofa and wide-screen TV, next to which is a large bookshelf with knickknacks strewn here and there among so many novels and cookbooks. Here, it feels comfortable. Inviting.

No way we'd ever afford a place this big back home, even with Dad's income, I muse as I follow Bethany down the hall to her bedroom. And yet, I get the feeling this isn't considered large for around here.

The first thing I notice when we enter Bethany's room is the large poster over her bed featuring a grainy photograph of a UFO and the words *I Want to Believe*. A shelf above her desk displays figures with oversized heads of characters from sci-fi and horror movies.

Bethany shuts the door, then groans and plops down on her bed. Her purple comforter poofs up around her. "Why the hell'd you have to go and bring up Troy?"

She stares at me, waiting for an answer, but I don't have one. Why'd I have to go and say any of the things I did? I'm not sure why mentioning Troy would be any worse than the rest of it.

"Of course," she says quietly, more a reminder to herself. "You wouldn't know." She exhales, then explains, "Troy's in the hospital. His mom couldn't get him to wake up this morning. People were talking about it when Daniel and I were getting coffee."

I wrinkle my brow, not quite understanding.

"He's in a coma," she clarifies. "Like Diane's dad?"

Oh. "W-well—how was I supposed to know that?"

"You weren't," she sighs. "Of *course* you weren't." Again, like she's reminding herself. Or . . . convincing herself? "But you've basically made her case stronger, ridiculous as it may sound to you."

"I'm still not clear on what her case is, exactly."

She flips over onto her stomach and props herself up on her elbows. "You really didn't know anything about your family before you got here? Nothing about Miriam? Your dad didn't even give you a hint?"

I lower myself into a cross-legged position on the floor. "No. He never talked about his childhood here. Ever."

"Well, shit. That was probably your hint."

I can feel my face flushing again. As if we'd *planned* to move here. As if Dad could have *known* he was going to get shot while trying to save someone's life in a car accident, and somehow warned us not to move here as a result. As if we'd wanted *any* of this. "Could you enlighten me, then? Why was everyone so scared of Miriam? Why would that lady—"

"Diane," she reminds me.

"Why would *Diane* automatically assume I had something to do with what happened to her dad?" And Troy, probably, too. Because apparently everyone knew about him except for me. I recall how still Diane went when I said Troy's name. She absolutely thinks I did something to him, too. And I've announced to the entire town that I'm pissed at him. My stomach is churning, made worse by the smell of food wafting up from the restaurant below. Images of graffiti—*WITCH*—sprayed over and over, peek out from the corner of my mind. A boy huddled over his skateboard, begging me to stop as a shadow peels out from the wall . . .

"I don't know the history, really," Bethany says. "My parents didn't buy the Roadhouse until I was seven. We lived up in Vancouver before that. I just know everyone was always afraid of Miriam. Called her the town witch. Said the Sylvans had a history of being witches. And you've gotta admit it's not hard to see why, with Miriam being all reclusive and stuff, living way out in the woods in that creepy old house. No one saw her around town much in person, but somehow, it was like . . . it was like she was always nearby anyway, watching. Like . . . in the backs of our minds." She looks up from weaving her fingers together. "I— Well, this is going to sound weird, but I used to dream about her sometimes when my grandma was dying of cancer. I was scared of Miriam, too, at first, because of what everyone had said, but then I realized that in my dreams, she was . . . I don't know. Trying to comfort me or something?" She looks down at her hands again. "I mean, they were just dreams, obviously, but well . . . I've never told anyone that before."

Just dreams. "I promise I'll keep it to myself. I'm so sorry about your grandma."

"Thanks," she says. "She lived with us. We were very close." She pauses for a second, as if lost in thought, then sighs. "Anyway, my point is, everyone here is weirdly superstitious. You've noticed the carvings on several of the old buildings around town, right?"

"I've been meaning to ask about that."

"They're supposed to be protection against witches."

As in, protection from the Sylvans. "Diane has a fresh one carved on her store," I say.

"Yeah, I saw that," Bethany says. "There's a fresh one on the coffee shop, too, which surprised me. But I'll bet you haven't noticed that there aren't any streets or addresses with the number thirteen around here. Also, be prepared for half the shops to be closed on full-moon days. It's so ridiculous. And you know me, I love all things paranormal and creepy, but even I don't believe in any of that basic superstitious shit. And neither do my parents."

Still . . . I remember the way Mrs. Lieu's expression changed when she looked at Rhonda's driver's license. I suppose whether you're superstitious or not, it might be risky for business to have Sylvans staying in your establishment.

"But," Bethany continues, "you've got to admit, to those who do believe, it doesn't look good when two people fall into mysterious comas the minute another Sylvan arrives in town."

I take a steadying breath. "So basically, by bringing up Troy, I've reinforced all of this"—I gesture vaguely at the air—"whatever it is."

"But you know what?" She slaps her hands down onto the bedspread and pushes herself up. "Fuck 'em. They're all ass-holes anyway, and Diane's literally the worst. I think you're cool.

Granted, I love everything spooky. But Daniel thinks you're cool, too. He said so. And, *obviously*, Cal thinks so."

My stomach flutters. "He does?"

"Uh, yeah," she says, eyebrows raised. "You couldn't tell?"

I hope my cheeks aren't giving me away. "I think you guys are pretty cool, too."

CHAPTER 12

Monday's a better day. I accompany Rhonda to the bank, where we relay our pathetic tale of woe to the loan officer in person. I think it helps that she doesn't live in Madrona—she just works here—so our last name doesn't affect her in any way. But our story does. She agrees that under the current circumstances we qualify for a month extension. Now we get to hold our breath and hope Dad's life insurance benefits finally make it to us before then. In the meantime, we'll have to hunt for other ways to scrape together the cash we'll need—not only for the mortgage but for an electrician so we can finally move into the house and stop accumulating debt at the Roadhouse because the credit card's nearly maxed out. And then there's the situation with the car.

Charlie, the mechanic, mercifully doesn't charge us for the tires on the loaner. "I'll charge the asshole who did it, though, once I find out who it was," he grumbles as he cranks on the car jack.

I like Charlie. He's friendly, easygoing, and a bit of an oddball for a town like this. Like a puzzle piece that got sorted into the wrong box but still kind of fits if you ignore the big splotch of orange where green leaves should be.

He hovers around longer than necessary after changing the

tires, chatting with my sister. She doesn't seem to mind, I notice. Her cheeks are rosier than usual, and she's forgotten what to do with her hands.

Soon, we're armed with not only new tires but two battery-powered lanterns, a cooler, some extra tools Charlie just *happened* to have lying around, and even a headlamp from that one time he went spelunking with his buddies down in Mexico. He also suggests that if things go sour with the bank, we could always squat for a while. I can't tell if he's serious or not.

"We're *not* squatters," Rhonda tells me as we head to the house. "The house is still technically yours."

"Ours," I correct her.

She doesn't correct me back, but I get the sense it's hovering behind her lips.

The first thing we do is remove the plywood from several downstairs windows so we can use the daylight to work. Next, we clean a year's worth of science experiments out of the fridge and freezer, with frequent breaks to breathe. After that, we weed out any expired canned and dry foods from the pantry. I discover a large stash of homemade jams and pickles in the back with no dates on them. Running my fingers over Miriam's handwriting on the labels—raspberry, blackberry, strawberry-rhubarb—I marvel at the perfectly formed loops and swooshes. I wish I could write half as well. It looks almost like art, and I hate to throw them out, but there's no way to know how old they are. I pick one up, then hesitate, and place it back on the shelf. I'll deal with them later.

We're about halfway through scrubbing the cabinet doors when Rhonda stops and turns to me. "I've been thinking. I'll bet there are lots of interesting antiques in this house. Maybe we could, you know . . ." She fiddles with her gloves instead of finishing her sentence.

"Yeah," I say, picking up on her train of thought. I considered this, too, while eyeing the chandelier the other day. "We should sell some stuff. That would be a good idea. I mean, as long as it doesn't look important or like an heirloom or something."

"Great."

Her tone is just shy of curt, and it hits me how weird it must be for Rhonda, unpleasant even, to feel she has to ask me permission. It drives home the point that, technically, none of this is hers to sell. She was right when I tried to correct her back in the car. Per Miriam's will, all of this—the house, the kitchen cabinets, the furniture, even the curtains on the windows—belongs to me. If I wasn't a minor, I would have been the one dealing with the bank, not her. I would have been the one talking to the lawyer, arranging the move. Not her. But as my legal guardian and trustee, she gets all the burden and none of the perks.

"Hey, Rhonda?" I call after her as she heads into the dining room.

She leans back around the corner. "Mm?"

"I—" I'm not sure how to put what I want to say. "Do you need a hand?"

"Nope, I've got it. You can take a break if you want."

"I'll take one soon. I'm almost done."

I spritz some cleaner on my rag and make it through one more cabinet door before the creep factor of being by myself in a dead person's house finally hits. Probably because I don't

113

actually *feel* like I'm alone. Every time I turn my back toward the door leading to the dining room, I get that skin prickle on the nape of my neck like someone's lurking in the shadows, staring at me. Then again, I've been inhaling lots of cleaning chemicals today. Maybe Rhonda was right about that break.

"Actually," I shout into the other room, "I'm gonna get some fresh air. Back in a bit."

"'Kay," I hear from somewhere in the house.

Despite the humidity, stepping outside is a huge relief. A breeze has blown in, whisking away the stillness. I settle onto the concrete steps and listen to it rustling through the leafy chaos that used to be a garden. Now it's hard to tell which plants are weeds and which are flowers or herbs left unattended too long.

It's getting late; the sun kisses the treetops as their branches sway gently along the edge of the woods. I catch myself swaying along with them. Physically, I'm exhausted, but my mind becomes restless as the sun sinks lower behind the trees and the shadows grow longer. I shiver despite the heat. We should return to the Roadhouse soon, unless we want to keep cleaning by lantern light.

"Rhonda?" I call out once I'm inside. She doesn't answer. Must be upstairs. I hesitate in the doorway to the darkened dining room, then make a mad dash through to the living room. With the sun at the other side of the house, it's not as bright as I'd like in here, either. But it's also not dark enough yet for me to justify going back for one of Charlie's emergency lanterns.

The wood floor lets out a long, slow creak beneath my feet. A vague shuffling comes from somewhere overhead, sending another shiver down my spine. I stand still and listen. That's . . .

probably Rhonda walking around on the floor above me. It's totally normal for old houses to make weird noises. It's not a ghost, just old wood settling and shifting. Right? Right.

"Rhonda?" Still no answer. It must be her, though. *Relax.* I shake away the shivers and head across the room to check out a box by the curio cabinet. There are shapes in the dust between items left behind on the cabinet's shelves—footprints of antiquey-looking things that are now in the box. A fancy teapot. Some china figurines. A clock. I wonder how much those might go for on eBay. Probably not a lot, but anything is better than nothing.

While scanning the room for anything Rhonda may have missed, my heart skips a beat when I come to the pictures arranged across the mantel. *Crap.* I forgot to do something about those. Rhonda must have noticed them by now, but maybe she hasn't looked too closely. I'd better get rid of them before she comes back downstairs. I grab an empty box and pack them away, one by one.

Each picture conjures a memory, and each memory, an ache. I work quickly, not allowing myself to pause for too long. I'm not in the mood to deal with these feelings right now. *Push 'em down, Eva. Stow them away.*

I'm mostly successful until I come to a small, facedown frame. My hand hovers. I should slide it as is, straight into the box. I don't need to see that again right now. To see eleven-year-old me, sitting on Daddy's ambulance, grinning and cocooned inside Daddy's work fleece, surrounded by everything *Dad*.

But . . . Dad.

I steel myself and flip it faceup. But the frame . . . it's empty.

Am I remembering wrong? Was this not that picture after all? There aren't any other facedown frames. And none of the ones in the box hold *that* photo. It must have slipped out. I set the frame down and check the floor. Nothing. I lift the edge of the rug to see if it slid underneath. Still nothing. I get down on my stomach and peer under the sofa, but it's too dark and narrow underneath to see, so I put my back against it and shove, straining against its hefty, solid frame.

"What are you doing?"

As though on a spring, I straighten and spin to find Rhonda standing in the foyer archway. One arm cradles a vase; a creepy antique doll dangles from the other. Rhonda's eyes dart from the couch, to me, to the box. Then to the fireplace.

Her shoulders sag. "Eva."

"I'm sorry." I sit down heavily on the couch.

Rhonda places her found items in the box filled with knick-knacks, then comes to sit beside me. "You're packing the pictures away."

"I meant to do it before you saw them. But I forgot."

"Why?"

"Because—" It comes out nearly a whisper. "Because there aren't any of you."

"Hey." She hooks her arm around my shoulders, and we lean together. "That's not your fault."

"I know, but I don't understand. There should be pictures of you, too. Why would he do that?"

"Maybe it wasn't him."

True. Maybe it was Miriam's choice to display only mine. I'd wondered this before. "It still isn't right."

116

She gives me a squeeze and points at the empty frame. "What happened to that one? Maybe that one was me." She's joking, which means she's hurting.

"That's why I was moving the couch. It slipped out somewhere."

"Maybe it was always empty." She shrugs, then hops to her feet. "Let's call it a day. How about we go back to our room, order a large pepperoni, and watch junk TV while we pig out. Oh! And look what I found!" She digs into her pocket and grins as she pulls out a wad of twenties.

"You found those here?"

She grins. "Seems Miriam didn't *always* trust the banking system. These were hidden inside that vase." She points to the box where she's stashed it. The antique doll peers over the edge at me with its dead eyes. Gotta admit, I'm not looking forward to sharing a hotel room with it tonight.

"It's not a lot," Rhonda continues. "But it'll do for a few meals. Might even cover one of our nights at the Roadhouse. I won't be surprised if there's more squirreled away around here, too. Somewhere."

Wouldn't that be something? A twenty here, a fifty there—if we're lucky, the house will end up paying for itself. Okay, so not likely, but we can dream.

I take one last look between the couch cushions as Rhonda hefts up the box of antiques. Still no photo. I'll have to look again the next time we're here. It can't have gone far. Can it?

Chapter 13

That night, I dream of the dark again. But this time, I'm not falling. I'm running. My feet thud against packed earth as a light breeze caresses my face. A child's voice calls to me to come on, hurry up, so I pump my legs harder and harder until I spy a pinprick of light ahead.

"Come on! I'll help you, come on!"

The voice is coming from the light, but it feels so far away. As I run closer, it takes shape. It's a person. A young girl. She leans forward and reaches out, beckoning me with both arms.

I'm trying. But the darkness surrounding us is so thick, it's like running through syrup. I'm exhausted.

"Don't give up! Come on!"

I work harder. The dark loosens some of its hold on me. And the girl in the light—her dress, her braids, her wide eyes become clearer. I know her! She's . . . she's me! A wave of relief washes over me, and I know I'm going to be okay. If I can just get to her, everything will be fine.

As our hands are about to touch, I feel a tug at my middle and another voice overtakes the girl's. "Come on, wake up."

I groan in disappointment as my eyes flutter open.

"Finally," Rhonda says. "You were *out*."

"You interrupted my dream," I tell her, yawning.

"Yeah? Was it a goooood one?" She winks at me, prompting me to pull my pillow out from under my head and chuck it at her.

"Watch it! You could break something."

Everything from Miriam's has been removed from the box and laid out across her bed.

"I need you to double-check there isn't anything here you don't want to sell. Then get dressed, because we're taking these down to that antique place by the coffee shop right after breakfast. I figure we should check with them first, before going the eBay route. Faster cash, and no shipping. Unless it's consignment. Hmm."

My stomach flips over the idea of going back down to Main Street so soon after the Diane incident. Resisting the impulse to cocoon under the covers, I give the items a cursory scan. There's the teapot and some of the figurines from the curio cabinet, the vase, and a few other trinkets she must have found somewhere else. I notice she's flipped the dead-eyed doll facedown.

"Looks good," I say, then haul myself out of bed to get dressed.

Jolee's Attic is aptly named. For one thing, it smells like one— like fading mothballs and musty cardboard, with a hint of Christmas potpourri. For another, it's filled to the brim. I don't know if she'll have room on the shelves for what we want to sell her. It doesn't look like she has a fast turnaround.

"Hmm, I'll have to fetch the Big Book for these," Jolee says. She's a tiny flower of a woman in her sixties, maybe even her seventies, with a soft, breathy voice. But any perceived timidity is made up for with her head full of thick, unnaturally orange curls and her bright emerald eye shadow reaching all the way up to her eyebrows. Bold, bulky jewelry weighs down her slight frame, bangles rattling and clacking whenever she moves. I don't know how to respond to the strange, knowing looks she keeps giving me. It's like we're having a conversation in her head that only she can hear. I wonder what I'm saying in there.

As I think it, she gives me another look, raising an eyebrow before disappearing below her counter, which doubles as a display case for more bulky jewelry. A moment later, she reappears with a groan as she heaves a massive volume up with her, then thumps it down onto the glass top. I cringe, expecting the counter to shatter, but fortunately, it doesn't.

Rhonda leans over the book as Jolee flops open the cover, licks her thumb, and flips through the tabs. I try to act interested, but soon, my eyes are glazing over. It's pages and pages of plates, figurines, and furniture, and it doesn't take long before everything starts to look the same.

"It's all right if you want to go explore," Jolee tells me without glancing up. "Your sister and I can take care of this."

I look to Rhonda, who nods, then goes back to discussing makes, models, and years with Jolee. I step away from the counter and wander off to peruse the clutter.

As I poke at a jingle bell hanging from the frayed hat of an old clown doll, movement catches my eye. Cal waves at me from the sidewalk through the front window display. Then Daniel jumps into view behind him and makes gruesome faces at me over his shoulder. I stifle a laugh as Cal points next door, then shoves

Daniel in that direction, who responds by making an exaggerated show of tripping over his own feet, then righting himself; he smooths out his shirt, sticks his hands in his pockets, and strolls out of view. Cal rolls his eyes before following after him.

I tap Rhonda on the shoulder. "Okay if I head next door?"

"Hmm? Yeah, sure."

Amusement flickers across Jolee's face as she and Rhonda return to haggling over the value of Miriam's things, though I'm not sure what's so funny. Gratefully, I make my escape to the coffee shop via Jolee's shared interior door.

Just inside, I nearly collide with Charlie.

"Oh, hey . . . Eva, right?" He peers over my head into the antique shop. "I thought I spied your sister in there, and—"

"Is it about the car?" I cross my fingers it's not, unless the stuff from Miriam's house is worth more than I'm guessing it is, because we can't pay him yet.

"No, not about the car. Sorry. Still waiting on a part. I just, uh, thought I'd say hi." He looks down and scratches absent-mindedly behind his ear. "See how the, um, the tires are working out. She looks busy, though . . ."

The tires. *Sure.* "The tires are great." I catch Cal's eye and wave as he and Daniel get in line at the register.

Charlie frowns. "Speaking of tires, you might want to tread carefully with those two."

Speaking of . . . I resist rolling my eyes. "Why?"

"There's some 'off' history there."

"What do you mean?"

"It's hard to explain. But maybe consider keeping your distance."

I glance back over and catch Daniel watching our conversation with a curious look on his face. Something about his expression stirs up another one of those flutters of guilt. There's no way he can hear Charlie over the espresso machine, can he? He holds his arms out to the side as if to ask, "What's keeping you?" as Cal examines the baked goods on display, oblivious.

What could Charlie mean by an "'off' history"? They seem like best friends. And while most of the people in this town have treated me like a disease, Cal and Daniel haven't, even if I do get that weird vibe from Daniel sometimes. He's never done anything to justify it, so it's probably just me.

I must not be good at keeping my thoughts off my face, because Charlie nods and says, "I know, I get it. They're your friends. But be careful, okay?" He leans in and lowers his voice even more. "There was this kid one of them used to hang around with a few years back. Graham Yeats. Heard of him?"

The name sounds familiar, but I can't put my finger on why. I shake my head.

"Hmm," he says, then louder, "I'll let you know as soon as that part gets in. Any day now." He takes one last look into the antique shop, sighs, and adds, "Tell your sister I said hi."

I steady my nerves as I watch him head back across the coffee shop and out the front door.

"You know quad means 'four,' right?" the barista is asking Daniel as I finally join my friends.

Daniel gives her a Look.

"Okay, it's your vascular system," she says, dubious. She rings Daniel up, then asks Cal, "What can I get for you?"

"Hold on." Cal turns to me. "Want anything?"

I feel my ears heating up. Is it that obvious we're broke? "No, I'm good. Thanks, though."

He shakes his head at the barista, and she heads over to the espresso machine to make Daniel's quad whatever.

"You're not getting anything, either?" I ask.

We all move off to make room for the next customer.

"Not really my thing," Cal says.

We cringe as the espresso machine assaults our ears. Daniel perks up and bounds over to the pickup area, soon returning with an enormous to-go cup. He immediately takes a sip, then yanks it away, wincing. "Holy shit, that's hot."

"She just made it," I laugh. "Give it a sec."

He bounces on his heels, literally unable to stand still.

"How much caffeine have you already had today?" I ask him.

He gives me his signature shrug.

"Maybe you should consider cutting back?"

"That's what I keep saying," Cal joins in. "Pretty sure he's gonna give himself a heart attack."

I cock my head. "Is everything okay? Did you not sleep last night or something?"

Daniel's brows twitch almost imperceptibly—and I get that guilty flutter in my chest again. Like maybe I should keep my questions to myself.

He lets out a dark chuckle. "I'll sleep when I'm dead," he says, then shrinks back when he catches the look on Cal's face. "I mean, not like . . . it's only an expression."

Cal's jaw twinges. I think I'm missing something here. Is it because my dad's dead? Is he worried the very word is going to trigger me or something?

But before I have a chance to ruminate on it, Daniel's shoving his coffee into Cal's hands and marching for the door, fists balled. That's when I notice Chris outside on the sidewalk shooting death glares at us through the window. Cal and I exchange looks and rush after Daniel. A few steps ahead, Cal makes it to the door first, swings it open, then freezes as Chris says something to Daniel that I can't make out over the espresso machine shrieking behind me. It must have been bad, though, because Daniel replies, not with words but with a swift right hook.

Whump! Chris reels backward, hand flying to his face. His eyes register shock before narrowing into murderous slits as he works his jaw. Daniel shakes out his fist, then clenches it again, muscles tensing for another go. I need to stop this, but Cal's blocking the doorway, still frozen. Squeezing past him, I hurry out to the sidewalk to get in front of Daniel. Probably not the best decision, because now I'm also in swinging range, but it works. Sort of.

"Out of the way." Daniel tries to dart around me, but I thrust my hands out to stop him. I can feel people's eyes on us from behind the coffee shop's picture window. And I can feel Daniel's heart thumping in his chest through my palms as he pushes against them. My heart is thumping, too, to the point where I can't tell which is his and which is mine, their staccato beats mingling unpleasantly. I don't know what I was thinking; he's stronger than me and could easily knock me over if he wanted to.

He looks down at my hands, at his own balled fist, then at

my face. Now it's his eyes that register shock—no, shame—as he realizes what he's doing. Shame so intense I can practically feel it myself. All this within a span of what I'm sure is only seconds, but it feels like forever.

He stops pushing against me and backs away as Cal, finally coming to life, leaves his spot in the doorway and hurries over to join us. I can see that he's shaking.

"Fuck you," Chris spits out, then throws down his skateboard and skates the opposite way, speeding past Charlie, who's stopped down at the corner, a witness. Charlie catches my eye, and I turn away.

For a minute, it looks like Daniel might chase after Chris, but when Cal and I both move to block him again, he stumbles backward instead.

"What the hell was that?" Cal snaps at him.

Daniel doesn't answer. Wincing, he inspects his knuckles.

"Are—are you okay?" I ask. My heart is still racing. I reach forward to check his hand—gingerly, as if there's a chance it'll spring out at me like a jack-in-the-box.

"Back off," Daniel barks before turning and storming away.

"Let him go," Cal says. As if I have any intention of following.

"What did Chris say to him? Did you catch it?"

Cal stares after Daniel's retreating figure. "Yeah. Some of it. He, um. He asked what Daniel's doing hanging out with the witch." Then, bitterly, "As if the 'head case' isn't bad enough."

The witch. That's me, obviously. But . . . "Excuse me, the *what*?"

Cal turns and faces me. "You know. Because of my—" He

stops and looks down at his feet. "I wish Dan wouldn't do that. I don't give a shit what anybody calls me."

But from the way Cal's avoiding my gaze, I don't believe him.

I recount the entire event to Bethany while she's on her lunch break. We're hanging out in my room this time, munching on a basket of fries someone ordered and decided they didn't want.

"Dan gets *really* defensive about Cal," she says. "Which is pretty ironic seeing how much they used to hate each other."

"For real?" I can't picture that. "They act like best friends."

"They are—now." She pauses, mulling something over. "This is between you and me, okay? But when we were younger? Cal was kind of a bully."

I snort, nearly choking on my french fry. "No way. I know I just got here, but Cal's the last person I could ever picture bullying anyone."

"It's true. He and—" She stops herself. "Um, I mean, I don't think things were very good in Cal's house when he was younger. His dad's a serious asshole, in my opinion. And Cal seemed to be easily influenced by—" She stops again, like she's editing herself or something. "Anyway, he was always teasing everyone. Shoving kids in the hall. Pulling mean pranks. And Daniel was his main victim—I'm not sure why. But then he had this ... accident. We don't really talk about it, but you're basically part of the group now, and I think you should know. He was hurt. Badly. He ... almost died."

"Almost died?"

126

"Mm-hmm. We didn't see him at school again for a whole year. He used to be a grade ahead of us, you know. He skipped a grade in elementary school, and then, because he missed so much, he was put back with us again."

"That must have been hard." I can't imagine what it must feel like to be so smart, you get to skip ahead, but then have to go back again and face everyone you left behind.

"You would think so, but he didn't act like it. When he came back to school, he was a completely different person. Nice, friendly, quiet most of the time. And really awkward, honestly, but don't tell him I said that. Then *he* was the one getting bullied. So, Daniel stepped in and started looking out for him."

"Wow, really?"

"Yup. Most people don't understand why he would do that after the way Cal treated him for so long, but that's the way Daniel is," she says. "He's just super empathetic, you know? He didn't like people bullying the new Cal the way the old Cal had bullied him."

I think back to some of my own run-ins with bullies over the years. As much as I hate to admit it, I don't think I'd have it in me to do the same, personality change or not.

"I can see why you like Daniel so much."

She smiles a little, then sobers. "Please don't let them know I told you all that, okay? It's kind of a sore subject."

How badly must Cal have been injured that it would take him an entire year to recover? There's a twist in my gut, and I want to ask for specifics. What happened to him? How was he hurt? But something tells me that is all she's willing to say.

"Okay," I assure her. "Promise."

This must be that "off" history Charlie was talking about. But I can't imagine why he would feel the need to warn me away. If anything, it makes me want to get to know them even more. But there was something else, too—that name he mentioned. I *know* I've heard it somewhere before, and it's been bugging me ever since.

"Bethany? Do you know anyone named Graham Yeats?"

Her body goes rigid. "H-how do you know about Graham?"

"I don't. Someone mentioned him to me, and I—"

"Graham's dead," she says quietly. "He . . . died a long time ago." She stands and heads for the door, grabbing her work apron off the back of the dinette chair on her way. "I'm sorry, I need to get back to work. My next shift's about to start."

Conversation's over. I'm being shut down.

As I listen to Bethany's footsteps clomping down the wood stairs outside, I run her about-face over and over in my head. Obviously, I hit a nerve. I wonder if she and Graham were close. *Graham Yeats.* I know I've come across that name before. I know I have. But where? *Graham . . . Graham's dead.*

The graveyard. I can picture the headstone now, the crows scattering as I approached, clear as day. I can even smell the popcorn Cal sprinkled over his grave. Cal had some kind of accident . . . and Graham Yeats is dead. I remember now. Cal even told me how it happened—he said his friend fell. Did they both fall? Is that why I'm not supposed to talk about it? With the way Bethany kept stopping herself midsentence, it was like she was purposefully leaving something—or some*one*—out. There's more to this story, and I can't let it go.

That night, as Rhonda snores softly under her blankets, I

try googling Graham's name. It takes forever over the Road-house's crappy Wi-Fi, but once my search goes through, I don't find much. Exhausted and bleary-eyed, I wade through a list of shady background-search sites and business profiles for people who are much too old to have been hanging out with a bunch of kids several years ago. Some social profiles for people in other states. Someone's pet-grooming service.

I try searching his name again, this time including the words *Madrona* and *accident* to narrow it down. And then, there it is! Two results down is a link to a five-year-old article in the *Madrona Gazette* archives. My thumb hovers over the headline: SERVICES TO BE HELD FOR LOCAL BOY, GRAH—The search engine cuts the rest off, but it has to be him. I tap the link and wait while the article struggles to load. The full headline comes into view:

SERVICES TO BE HELD FOR LOCAL BOY, GRAHAM YEATS, AT MADRONA EPISCOPAL CHURCH

Yeats died tragically last week when he fell from—

And that's as far as I get before a pop-up window fills the screen. *To read this article, please subscribe.* It lists a few subscription plans, none of which are free.

Damnit. A stupid paywall. It takes everything I have not to throw my phone. I was so close to answers. I already knew Graham died from a fall. But *how* did he fall? Was it the same accident that injured Cal?

A further search only brings up other paywalled articles that

I can't afford, and honestly, I'm not sure I even *want* to know anymore. And I can't, for the life of me, figure out why Charlie thought it was necessary to bring it up. Frustrated, I switch to a random phone game and knock off a few levels before my eyelids droop and I finally fall asleep.

CHAPTER 14

Something is making a low, rumbling sound. I follow it, gliding through the hotel room door onto a lonely forest road. Lonely, except for the tow truck idling on the shoulder, its headlights cutting a path through the night. Scanning the trees, I search for the source of the feeling that drew me here. Something I've been feeling a lot lately—darkness, fear . . . guilt. As I approach the truck, my gut twinges with nerves. Maybe I shouldn't be here. I feel like I'm doing something wrong.

The letters on the truck's door won't hold still, but I'm able to catch them a little at a time. *Ma . . . dr . . . Moto . . . Madrona Motors*. Is that Charlie's truck? But where is he?

"Where'd you go?" His voice echoes out from somewhere in the woods. "Come back here."

I hear footsteps. A twig snapping. And soon, Charlie emerges from the trees, bathed in the glow of his truck's lights. "Damnit," he says.

"Charlie?"

He puts his hand up to shield his eyes as he peers into the dark. "There you are," he says. "What are you doing walking alone along this road at night? You're lucky I have sharp eyes."

The trees rustle behind him, conjuring up dread.

"Come on, I'll give you a ride home," he says. "Your dad must be worried."

"My . . . dad?" Doesn't he know my dad's dead? Everyone else seems to by now. Should I say something? Or not? But before I can make up my mind, the trees rustle again. My pulse quickens, a staccato thumping in my chest and head. There's something else emerging from the forest. Something dark. A shadow.

The shadow sweeps around the truck and passes in front of me so fast I'd wonder if I imagined it if not for the wave of guilt that follows. Guilt, and anger, and even more fear. They pull at me like an undertow, leaving me off-balance. Siphoning. Feeding.

No, no, no. Not this again. The inside of a gas station swallowed by smoke flashes through my head. *WITCH* painted over and over, dark tendrils whipping about. In my memory, smoke envelops Rob. TENDRILS curl around Troy. They're both in comas now. *Charlie,* I think. *Charlie's not safe. I need to get him out of here.*

"Let's go!" I yell, rushing toward him and the truck. Maybe we can out-drive it. Is that possible? We have to try. But when I step into the headlights, he freezes.

"Y-you?" He falls back, his mouth open in shock, and that's when the shadow returns. It's larger now, circling the lit road, closing in. Closer, closer. As it grows, so does that horrible feeling in the pit of my stomach where every bad thing I've ever done rests. We need to run, to get out of here, but I can't move. My feet are planted in place as the shadow passes in front of the lights, making them flicker. The truck's idling engine goes dead. Silent.

"Here I am, Charlie," the shadow taunts in a deep yet somehow also high, childlike tone. Two versions of the same voice overlapping, reaching us from every direction at once. "You found me."

The shadow swirls in and out, around and between us, a hurricane of inky wisps threatening to pull us into its core. My head pounds. My chest tightens, seizing up on itself. Everything hurts. I need to get out of here, let me out, let me—

I'm covered in sweat. I claw at the blanket and yank it off my face, gulping in the cool air of the room's crappy air conditioner. Rhonda snores in the other bed, curled up with Dad's old copy of *Dune*, oblivious.

I was dreaming again. That's all.

Just dreaming.

Again.

"Eva, I need to t—" Rhonda begins at the same time I say, "Don't you think—"

I stop. "Sorry. You go ahead."

Rhonda looks down at her bowl of the Roadhouse's special blend of granola. "No, that's fine. You go first."

"We should call Charlie and check up on the car."

"Uh . . ." Rhonda pauses mid-bite. "I assume he'll call us when it's ready. You talked to him yesterday, right?" She focuses on her bowl again and mutters, "I wonder why he didn't come over and say hi."

I pick at my scrambled eggs. They seemed like a good idea when I ordered them, but now my stomach's telling me otherwise.

I can't shake that horrible dream.

"Are you okay?" Rhonda asks. "You don't look so good."

"I'm fine." I attempt a smile, but I'm not sure if I've succeeded.

"You sure?" She reaches across the table to feel my forehead, but I bat her hand away.

"I'm *fine*. I just slept badly, that's all."

But I'm not fine. Bits of the other strange dreams I've been having are weaving their way into my thoughts, too—snippets and extra details I hadn't remembered until this morning. Now they're all so clear, like my subconscious has been working in the background, piecing things together, and it's ready to give me its final presentation.

In my mind's eye, the forest road from last night flickers into a graffitied streetscape, flickers into a dimly lit mini mart, flickers into darkness. There's Rob. There's Troy. There's Charlie. And running circles around them all, a shadow. A shadow I can *feel*. Still feel, even now, while I'm awake.

Rob's in a coma. So is Troy. I need to check on Charlie. If he's okay, I can get Diane's nasty voice out of my head: *There is gonna be trouble if you don't undo whatever it was you did to him.* Did I do something? Did I?

"Eva." Rhonda's staring at me. "Evangeline."

I blink. "Sorry."

"I'm getting worried about you. You've been sleeping badly since we got here. Is this like"—she stirs her granola around—"before? Or is there something else going on? Because you can talk to me, remember?"

Like before? She must mean the nightmares I was having

right after Dad died. But those were completely different. Those were normal nightmares—awful but nothing like these. And, as far as I'm aware, no one ever ended up in a coma afterward. These, though—these feel like I'm somewhere else, outside my own head.

"No, seriously, I'm fine." I'm not fine. But I don't know how to talk to her about this. I don't even know what "this" is.

Her mouth screws up like she's chewing on a thought, but she keeps it to herself and instead asks, "Do you want to go take a nap before we head over to the house?"

"No," I answer a little too quickly. No naps. No way. I cram a few bites of egg in my mouth and force them down, then put my napkin on the table and scoot out of our booth. "I'm gonna go for a walk and check on our car."

"Eva—"

"Back in a bit."

Madrona Motors is about a half mile down the road on the opposite edge of town from the gas station. It's a plain brick building, painted white, with two large garage doors and a tiny front office. A myriad of junkers in various stages of being fixed fill the lot around it. The cars are in such a jumble, I almost miss the police cruiser parked out front.

Two gloved officers emerge from the building. I recognize one as the officer who led Rhonda and me back to Chief Burke's office when our tires were slashed. I haven't met his partner before. She raises a hand for me to stop and stay where I am.

I try to remain calm, my palms breaking out into a sweat. I know I haven't done anything. I haven't. But . . .

"We need everyone to stay clear of the area," the officer tells me as she approaches. The other officer taps her and leans in, quietly relaying information that I suspect has to do with me. And, from the way her expression changes, I don't think it's good. She sets her mouth firm and nods, then continues forward. "I'd like to ask you a few questions."

"Okay." I try to keep my voice from shaking. "I was just coming to check on our car."

"How long has your car been in the shop?"

"Um." I do some quick counting in my head. "Almost a week?"

She asks me some more questions— questions about the car, questions about Charlie and when I spoke to him last. If he'd shown any indication of being ill yesterday at the coffee shop.

"No." I swallow. "He seemed fine." Sort of.

"What did you talk about?"

"Just the car," I lie. I don't want to go into the whole thing about Graham Yeats. My gut tells me it wouldn't be a good idea. "He—he said he was still waiting on a part."

"Did he give any indication it would be here today?"

I shake my head.

"But you came to check on it, anyway."

Mercifully, Chief Burke chooses that moment to pull up. He calls over the officer who's questioning me, holding up his finger for me to wait as my legs twitch for me to spin on my heel and go.

What has happened to Charlie? Is he in a coma now, too? With two police officers combing over his garage, this feels worse.

Could he be . . . ? Is he . . . ? I won't allow myself to complete that thought. But it's obvious that whatever happened, Charlie's very much not okay.

And if it *is* a coma, that's number three. Three dreams. Three people out of commission. This can't be a coincidence anymore.

Chief Burke sends the officers back to their investigation, then makes his way over to me.

"You okay, kiddo?"

I'm not sure how to answer.

"This must have been uncomfortable to stumble upon. Officer Sontag, she didn't know. She's just doing her job, trying to get more information."

It takes me a minute to figure out what he's getting at. Then I remember: the gift shop. He saw my reaction to Diane's bad news—how I fled. Which means I'm doing a terrible job hiding my emotions right now. I try not to show my relief over his assumption. And at the same time, my relief is a gut punch. I shouldn't be glad not to be thinking of Dad for once. That shouldn't be allowed.

"Did something happen to Charlie?" I ask.

He nods, poker-faced.

"He's not . . . *dead*. Right?" The word "dead" catches in my throat, coming out half-formed.

"No." Chief Burke relaxes his stance. "No, no, no. Charlie's not dead." It's like a switch has flipped, transforming him from his officer persona to his parental one. To him, I'm a scared little kid. Which, honestly, isn't far from how I'm feeling right now.

"He's in a coma, isn't he? Like those other two." I can't hide the shake in my voice any longer.

He doesn't answer, which is answer enough for me. Instead, he bends down so we're eye to eye. "This is not your fault, got it? No matter what Diane Petersen said to you, you understand? Yes, I heard about that."

My eyes are stinging. When did that start? I know I must be overreacting. I didn't even know Charlie that well. But Rhonda— I'm going to have to tell her what's happened to him, and I can tell she was starting to like him, and she doesn't need another blow like this right now.

"Do you understand?" he asks me again. "This isn't your fault."

He waits for my nod, then straightens back up. "I can't believe how long these old town superstitions have stuck around. This isn't seventeenth-century Salem, for Christ's sake." Then, catching himself, he smiles apologetically. "Sorry. Just don't let them get to ya, got it?"

"Got it." I take a deep breath. He's right. Dreams aren't real, for one thing. And it's not like I can control what my jerk of a brain decides to do while I'm asleep. Yet with each dream, I've felt, above everything else, that overwhelming sense of guilt. It feels *so much* like it's my fault.

He gives my shoulder a pat and turns to head back to the garage.

"Wait." I stop him before I even know what it is I want to say.

"Hmm?" He pivots.

"I . . . Why was everyone so scared of Miriam? What did she do?"

He looks uncomfortable as he considers the question. "Well,

she—" He stops and tries again. "She, uh . . ." His face scrunches as he tries to come up with an answer, but I don't think he has one. It's like when I asked Bethany. The best she could come up with was that it felt like Miriam was always around, even though she wasn't.

"You know," he says, giving up, "I think the best person to help you with that would be Jolee. Jolee Harmon. She owns the antique store. Used to be good friends with Miriam."

The woman who kept giving me those strange, knowing looks while flipping through the "Big Book" of antiques with Rhonda? If Jolee was such good friends with Miriam—possibly Miriam's only friend, from the way this town acts—why didn't she mention it when we were in her shop?

"Jolee. Got it. Thanks."

"Good luck," he says.

I thank him again and head for Jolee's Attic.

CHAPTER 15

Jolee's Attic is closed today. There's a number to call for appraisal appointments outside of store hours, but as I reach for my phone, I find it's missing. *Crap.* I remember setting it on the table at the Roadhouse. I must have left it behind—*again*—when I ran off to check on Charlie. I hope Rhonda grabbed it. She'll probably threaten to staple it to my forehead the next time she sees me.

"Is that her?" I hear a high voice say. "Is that Eva?"

I turn to see Cal standing on the other side of the street with a very excited little girl, waiting for the light to turn. She's blond, like him, with two curly pigtails that bounce whenever she does, which is constantly. I wave, and the girl returns it, then steps out into the crosswalk. Cal lurches forward to grab her arm and pull her back, shooting me an exasperated look. When the light changes, they hold hands and cross safely.

"Are you Eva?" the little girl blurts out as soon as her foot hits the curb.

"That's me."

"I'm Ginny. I'm five. Cal's my big brother, and he talks about you all the time."

I stifle a giggle as Cal turns crimson.

"I . . . I don't . . ."

"Yes, you do," Ginny says. "Mom's making Cal take me to the park to get me out of her hair," she explains.

I cover another laugh with a cough. "Wow, sounds fun."

Poor Cal looks like he's already been having lots of "fun" chasing his sister around all morning.

"Come with us!" Ginny grabs my hand with her free one, pulling me along.

"Oh. Uh—" I hesitate. I should be getting back, but . . . "Okay."

"You don't have to," Cal laughs, but there's an edge to it.

Crap, he thinks I don't want to. "Sorry. I've had kind of a rough morning," I explain. "I'd love to come."

"Stop yanking our arms," Cal tells Ginny, so she drops our hands. Then Cal and I fall into a leisurely pace while she bounds ahead of us, circles back, and bounds ahead again.

"Wait at the corners," he yells after her.

"I *know*," she says, and off she goes again.

He's acting like a mother hen. It's kind of adorable.

"Sorry you had a bad morning," he says to me. "Want to talk about it?"

For a brief moment, I consider it. For a brief moment, I feel a tug in my heart urging me to open up. *I'm having nightmares, Cal, like you wouldn't believe. And the people I dream about aren't waking up.* But I can't. He'll think I've gone completely bananas.

"It's nothing major. Just, you know, stuff."

He side-eyes me. "What kind of stuff?"

He's not buying what I'm selling. But it's not exactly any of his business, is it? Still, something about the look and his tone dissolves the shield I'm trying to put up. Not all the way—not

141

enough to tell him what's really going on. But . . . "I wanted to talk to Jolee about some things, but she's not around right now."

"Jolee? From the—the, um." He snaps his fingers while he looks for one of those words on the tip of his tongue. "The place with the, you know, the old stuff."

"The antique shop? Yeah. Someone said she might be a good person to ask about—" I hesitate. "The history of the town. And about my family."

"Ah. Family." I can see him chewing over a thought, but I can't read whether it's a good one or a bad one.

"Is something wrong?"

He sighs. "My dad just got back from a 'business trip'"—he does the international symbol for air quotes with his fingers— "and he's already saying he's going on another one next week. Mom's not happy."

"Oh." I look down at the concrete passing beneath my feet. "I'm sorry."

"It's fine," he says.

It's not fine. But he could have dodged the question like I'd tried to do, and he didn't. That means something. Something like . . . well, trust, I guess. He doesn't know me well. He has no reason to trust me with something so personal, and yet, he did. I used to be like that, too. I want to be like that again—but I don't know how anymore. I force myself to make eye contact. He shrugs and flashes a sad smile back. And my armor dissolves a little more.

Cal and I choose a park bench while Ginny goes off to play with the other kids. At first, we watch her run around for a while in silence, neither of us knowing what else to talk about. I can feel Cal's leg bouncing ever so slightly through the bench. Fingers laced together, he fidgets absentmindedly with his thumbs as his eyes follow his sister's trajectory around the play structure, up the ladder, down the slide, and around again.

My mind slides to yesterday's scene at the coffee shop—the fight outside, the way Cal froze up when Chris called him a head case. The way he couldn't look at me when I asked him about it. I wonder if Bethany warned him that she told me about his accident. Or that I asked about the boy in the grave again. Maybe when he said I didn't have to come with him and Ginny to the park, he was really saying *he'd* rather I didn't.

"What were you hoping to find out?" he suddenly asks.

My muscles tense. "About?"

"Your family."

"Oh." I relax. "I mostly want to find out more about Miriam. The only thing I know is that everyone around here was scared of her for some reason. But whenever I ask anyone why, they either don't know or they don't want to talk about it."

"I hate that," he says, angling his body to give me his full attention. "Why do people always tiptoe around about stuff?"

"Yeah," I say, feeling emboldened now, though I notice he isn't volunteering any answers, either. "I get it with my dad, too. Like, if they say the *d*-word, they're afraid I'll start bawling right in front of them or something."

His baby blues widen with recognition as he nods emphatically.

"I mean, okay, I might," I continue. "It depends on the situation. But why is that so scary? Why am *I* so scary?"

143

"You're not scary." His voice softens. He shifts again; our knees touch, and my chest thumps in response. Panicking a little, I spring to my feet.

"I am, though. Look. Even she's scared of me." I tilt my head in the direction of a mom standing on the far end of the park, nursing an iced coffee while her two young kids play. Except to check on her children, her eyes haven't left us the entire time we've been here.

Cal stands now, too, and we wander over to the edge of the play structure where Ginny is playing Lava Monster with the other kids. In response, the woman moves to a nearby bench where she can keep a closer eye on us.

Cal watches her warily, then turns back to me with a sigh. "She doesn't know you."

"Neither do you, really."

"Yeah, I do," he says quietly, then hurries to add, "I mean, enough to know you're not scary. Even if you do enjoy . . ." He hesitates.

He's standing close. Very close. I swallow. "Enjoy what?"

One corner of his mouth quirks up in a half smile. "Wandering around graveyards just for the heck of it. Pretty creepy if you ask me."

"Bethany talked to you."

"Tip-toe-ing," he says in a singsong voice. He jumps up and grabs on to one of the monkey bars, dangles with bent knees, then hops back down. Ginny runs past him, up the wood steps onto the play structure above. He watches protectively as she swings from bar to bar, a good distance between her feet and the ground.

He's right. I *am* tiptoeing. I still can't bring myself to ask him what I really want to know.

"All right." I deflect with the truth. "I was in the graveyard looking for Miriam, but she's not there. None of them are. No Sylvans anywhere. If they've been living in this town for so long, where are they?"

He stares off into the distance for a second, then leans up against one of the play structure's poles. "I know where they are. At least, where everyone says they are."

"You do?"

"Oh yeah. It's a 'thing.' You ready for this?" He pauses for dramatic effect. I take the bait and lean in closer.

"They're buried *on their own property*. Well, your property now, I guess."

"Like, in the backyard or something?" He's messing with me. He has to be.

He laughs. "Not in the backyard. Out in the, uh . . . um, you know, with all the trees."

"Are you telling me my whole family's buried in the woods?" I picture mounds of dirt sprinkled among the trees—something a serial killer would do. But I doubt that's what he means. I *hope* it's not what he means. "Is that even legal?"

"I guess." Cal shrugs. "But even if it's not, no one's gonna argue with a Sylvan." He leans in conspiratorially and whispers, "They might hex you."

I snort. If it was coming from anyone else, it wouldn't be so amusing, but I'm finding it's hard to be annoyed with Cal for longer than a second or two. How he could ever have bullied anyone is mind-boggling.

He glances at his watch, then looks up at the sky. "I should probably get Ginny back."

With a sinking feeling, I follow his gaze toward the dark clouds forming in the distance. There wasn't even a hint of bad weather twenty minutes ago. It must be moving in fast. I haven't thought much about the rain my new home is known for. It's been so sunny and warm since we got here, I guess I figured it was all hype. But as I watch the dark clouds inching toward us, I can already imagine the damp chill creeping along my bare arms and legs.

"Yeah," I say. "I should be getting back, too."

I'm not a fan of rain. And besides, I've been gone too long without my phone again. My sister's going to be pissed.

Rhonda isn't in our room. She's left me my phone and, below it, a note scrawled beneath the Roadhouse's retro letterhead: *At the house. Cleaning. Without you. Hope you're having fun.*

In other words, she hopes I choke on my "fun."

I try calling her, but it goes straight to voice mail, reminding me once again that Miriam's house is a complete and utter dead zone. I guess I'm stuck here.

I mess around on my phone for a bit to pass the time, and before I know it, I'm searching for the Sylvans and turning up nothing. Then Graham Yeats. Again, nothing more than what I've already found. Frustrated, I toss my phone over onto the other bed and switch on the TV, but it's all news and reruns of reality shows, so after a short while, I switch it off again. I'm not paying attention, anyway.

The clouds must have finally found their way to town, because the light from the window is turning gray. So are my thoughts. Gray like stone, and graves, and unasked questions. My eyelids grow heavy, then my head does, too. It falls forward, then jerks, jolting me awake for a second before doing it again.

Stark fear courses through me. I hop off the bed and walk around the room to stay awake. If I sleep, I might dream. Who will it be about this time?

Maybe some caffeine will help. I open the mini fridge and grab the Coke I've been holding on to since the night we got here. As the bubbles settle in my throat, I remember how Cal rushed outside to give it to me when I'd left it behind at the gas station. How he'd felt so familiar, though, up until then, I'd never seen him before in my life. How even now, despite our limited interactions, he'll say things that feel like he's known me forever. Obviously, a coincidence. I don't really know him. And he doesn't really know me. But . . .

Yeah, I do, he'd whispered when I'd pointed out as much at the park. And maybe he does a little. I've lost someone close to me, and so has he. And now I'm wishing I wasn't alone. I'm wishing we could have stayed longer at the park. I'm wishing it didn't have to rain. I hate rain. I especially hate being alone when it rains.

A plan forms in my head. Maybe I don't have to be alone right now. Maybe Cal could give me a ride to the house. If he can get away from watching his sister for long enough. Or if not, he could bring her with him. He'd only be dropping me off. He wouldn't have to stay . . . if he didn't want to.

I retrieve my phone from Rhonda's bed and pull up his

number from my contacts. I smile, remembering how after our adventure at the house, Bethany suggested they pass my phone around so they could all add their numbers to my contacts list. Daniel sent me a funny meme later that day—something about a ghost bear. And Bethany and I have texted back and forth quite a bit. But this will be the first time I've texted with Cal. Will he be weirded out?

It's just a text, I tell myself. Why would that make me so nervous? Maybe it's because I'm asking him for a favor. *But he can say no. It won't hurt to ask. He can say no if he'd rather n—*

The phone vibrates in my hand. Startled, I choke while swallowing another sip of soda. The phone vibrates a couple more times while I cough it out, and when I look again, eyes watering, I'm greeted by a short series of texts.

Hey, it's Cal.

Are you busy?

This is Eva, right?

> *Yeah it's me. So weird, I was just about to text you*

Oh weird. Why?

> *Rhonda left for the house without me*

I was going to ask if you
could give me a ride

If that's ok

I wait as my phone tells me he's typing. Then he stops. Then he's typing again. Then nothing. I take another sip to distract myself from my nerves as I wait. What was he texting me about? Did I ruin it by asking him for a ride? Maybe he's sick of always being asked to drive his friends places. Maybe he thinks that's all I see: a guy with a truck who can—

Sure, I can do that

Phew! Took him a while to decide, though. Then I remember he texted me first. Something must be on his mind.

Thanks

What were you texting me
about?

Another long pause as I wait for him to respond. When he does, I almost choke on my soda again.

I need to get out of here.
Maybe we could go grave
hunting.

I'm giving you a ride over there
anyway. You want to?

Grave hunting? Well, that's about the last thing I expected.

. . . Isn't it about to rain?

Wear boots

Yup

I always wear boots

CHAPTER 16

Cal pulls up in his truck, and I dash down the stairs and out to the street to meet it. The mid-song guitar riff of Soundgarden's "Fell on Black Days" greets me as I open the passenger side door; the first raindrops of the storm speckle the windshield as I pull the door shut. I'm still buckling my seat belt when Cal eases his foot onto the gas.

"You said you needed to get out of there," I remind him. "Is everything okay?"

He shrugs.

"Wanna talk about it, or do you want some space?"

He takes a breath. "Space," he decides.

"Okay."

His rain jacket rustles as he changes gears, and I realize I'm not wearing one. Oops. At least I remembered my umbrella.

He starts the windshield wipers as Chris Cornell finishes his song, asking, "How would I know that this could be my fate?" Then Fleetwood Mac comes on and Stevie Nicks's distinctive voice takes over with "Landslide," sending chills up my spine and taking me right back to lazy Sunday afternoons listening to Dad's vintage vinyls and CDs. And I'm surprised to find I'm not sad about it. Just happy to have found another musical kindred spirit.

None of my friends back home understood my alternative and classic rock obsession. I make a note of the radio station, right near the end of the dial. I wonder if it always plays this stuff, or if it's having an "Oldies Lunch Hour" or something.

"You know, it's funny," Cal says, as though thinking out loud. "You chose to move here, of all places, and all I've ever wanted to do is leave."

I bristle. "I didn't exactly *choose* to move here."

Cal's eyes dart to the side. "Right, your dad. I . . . I'm sorry."

"Why do you want to leave?" I throw the subject back to him, hoping it will break the awkwardness now hanging in the air between us.

He thinks. "I was going to say because of *my* dad, but that's not it. He's not around much, anyway."

"Why, then?"

"Hmm. Anonymity, I think."

I can understand that. Everyone knows everyone here. I can't imagine growing up with that. I just got here, and it's weird how many people already know who I am, or act like they do. And yet . . .

"Anonymity isn't all it's cracked up to be," I say, surprising myself. "It can be kind of lonely."

How different this experience would have been had we moved the other direction. I've barely been here a week, and I already have friends. I already have enemies, too, which I could do without, but I also have support. Real support, from Cal, from Bethany, and maybe even from Daniel. From Officer Burke and Charlie, too, in their own ways. This would never have happened this quickly being a newbie in a big city like New

York. Even having grown up there, we didn't have much of a support structure in place. We did have some friends, of course, but it wasn't the same. And Dad was always a bit of a loner. Maybe he moved to New York seeking anonymity, too.

"You're probably right," Cal says. "I guess something in between would be nice. But it can be . . . What's the word when you can't breathe?"

I think for a second. "Suffocating."

"Yeah. It can be like that living in a place where everyone seems to know more about me than I do."

Cal turns into the wilds of Fay Road, and our conversation gives way to the scraping of foliage and rattling of the truck's chassis as we rumble over the potholed ruts leading to Miriam's house. I take a moment to prepare myself for Rhonda's wrath over disappearing yet again without my phone, leaving her to do all the work. But when we pull into the gravelly area in front of the hedge, the loaner car is nowhere in sight.

Cal sets the parking brake. "I thought you said your sister was here."

"I thought she was. Her note said she was." I glance at the clock on the dashboard. It's almost one. "She must have gone to get lunch. Or maybe she found some more stuff to sell." And with no cell signal out here, I can't call her to find out. "She'll probably be back later."

His brow furrows. "Stuff to sell?"

"It's . . . it's nothing. Don't worry about it." I unbuckle and grab my umbrella. Cal hops out and comes around to join me. It's still only drizzling, but the air is thick, threatening a downpour. We should make this quick.

153

"Okay." I pop open my umbrella and breathe in the fresh, piney air. "I'm ready. Let's find some graves."

A suppressed smirk glints at the corners of Cal's lips.

"What?"

He leans under my personal shelter, so close I can feel his warmth. "You know how you can tell around here if someone's from out of town?"

"How?" My face is tingling. I hope it doesn't show.

"This." He flicks the edge of my umbrella with his finger, then ducks back out again. Lifting his face to the sky, eyes closed, he allows the rain to wash over him.

In that brief moment, he's the picture of bliss. I can't help but stare. And at the same time, it conjures an ache. An emptiness. I wish I could feel the same. I wish I could revel in this cool, fresh reprieve from the summer heat. But I'm no longer able to enjoy the rain.

He laughs, then ruffles the moisture from his dripping hair before pulling up the hood on his jacket, whatever good it will do him now. "All right. Feeling better. Let's go."

I mention the trail I saw at the edge of the woods the other day, and we decide to explore there first. There's not much left to it anymore; ferns and nettles and underbrush weave across it, covering some sections completely. Cal kicks through with his thick jeans while I follow along his newly created path with my bare shins. I regret my choice of shorts today. Too late now.

"Which way?" I ask when the trail forks.

Cal shrugs. "Pick one." He's grown somber again, but it could be the exertion from the hike. Or the remoteness, so quiet except for the patter of rain through the trees.

154

I examine both pathways. Neither looks more frequented than the other, so I close my eyes and grip my umbrella tight with one hand while sticking my other arm out like an arrow. "Spin me," I say.

"What?"

"Spin me around a few times, and we'll take whichever one I land at."

"Um. Okay." Cal's jacket rustles behind me. His fingers are cold against my bare arms, but his palms are warm, his touch light and hesitant as he guides me around in a circle, once, twice, a third time. I trip over my feet and bump him with the edge of the umbrella, eliciting apologetic giggles on my part. By the time he stops, I'm wobbling and laughing over my blind dizziness.

I'm cold, my legs and boots are splattered with mud, I have no idea where we're going, and I think . . . I think I'm actually enjoying this. I came out here fully expecting the weather would dredge up bad memories, but instead, a sense of adventure has taken over. It helps to have Cal here with me.

"Left," he says.

Satisfied, I open my eyes and wait for him to take the lead again. But he stays where he is, uncertainty all over his face.

"What's wrong?" I ask him, deflating.

He considers his answer. "Maybe this wasn't the best idea."

"It was *your* idea."

"I know." He stares off down the trail, hands wandering to his coat pockets. "I, um . . . I didn't think it would rain this hard."

It *is* starting to pick up a little. And it's getting chillier. I'm even starting to shiver a bit. But I can tell that's not really the problem. It's like when he got cold feet after driving all of us out here to find the fuse box. And he was right. I hadn't been ready to stumble across those photographs. Especially *that* photograph. Especially in front of someone I hardly knew. This is different, though. These are the graves of strangers—they share my DNA, yes, but they're strangers just the same. I may not know Cal well, but I know him better than the people in those graves. I'm fine. Totally.

"It's only rain," I tell him, even though I hate the rain. It comes out harsher than I intended, my stupid armor clinking around me again. He frowns and I feel bad, but I'm determined to find my family. We've come all this way. I forge on ahead; he can follow if he wants to.

I'm simultaneously rewarded and punished for this decision. I've barely gone ten feet when the clouds burst open, pelting my umbrella with thick drops. If Cal's still behind me, I can't hear his footsteps over the percussion above. My muscles tense. I almost do an about-face, but up ahead is a bend in the path, and at the edge of it, a rusty, wrought-iron fence post pokes out of the bracken. My pulse quickens. I pick up my pace. That has to be it.

It feels appropriate, somehow, that a low roll of thunder sounds overhead the moment I lay eyes on my family's final resting place. I stop at the edge, frozen, taking it in. They're simple graves, unassuming. In the back, the rough-hewn, chiseled headstones are green with moss and lichen, the forest welcoming them in, reclaiming them. The newer ones toward the front are less so, but they'll be welcomed, too, eventually.

I feel light and heavy at once. I've found, for the first time, who I came from, and who came before them. My family. And yet, I'm just an observer. An outsider looking in. I don't know these people. I don't know their stories, their personalities—I don't even know what they looked like. I'm a part of them, but they are not a part of me.

And that's when it hits me. The one link between us isn't here. This place, this gorgeous, peaceful place, is missing a member.

Even Miriam's grave is here—someone knew where she belonged and made sure she could join her family. But there's still plenty of room between her headstone and the side of the fence. A Dad-sized gap I can *feel*. I can *feel* it in my chest. Like I've walked around the corner straight into a sledgehammer. I should have known about this. I should have thought harder about where he'd want his final resting place to be. Maybe he did want to be here. His will didn't say. But maybe—

A hand rests on my shoulder. I'd forgotten Cal was here.

"You okay?" He asks me that a lot, I've noticed.

"Yeah, I'm fine." I wipe the moisture from my face. "You were right. It's a lot of rain."

His gaze flicks up to my umbrella, my shelter, calling me out.

And that's all it takes. My face and voice contort against my will. "*He's* not here."

Fresh water mingles with salt water as my umbrella drops to the ground. I don't have control over my body anymore. It heaves with gasps and sobs as Cal squeezes his arms tight around me, holding me in, holding me up. Holding me together.

I don't know how long we stay huddled like this, getting soaked while I struggle to bring myself back under control. His chest moves in slow, deep breaths, and eventually, I figure out

157

how to match them. My pulse calms; the tears take longer, but finally, I find my footing again.

"Come on." Cal's warm breath tickles my ear. "We know where this is now. We can come back another time when the weather's better. Okay?" When I'm more ready, he means.

He loosens his hold, and I pull back, nodding, wiping my face. I can feel his eyes on me, but I can't meet them. Maybe if I stare at the ground long enough, it will open up and claim me, too.

I focus on dumping the water out of my upturned umbrella instead. It's useless to me now, anyway. I'm fully drenched, inside and out. But not drenched enough, apparently, because as I'm closing my umbrella, there's a flash and another roll of thunder overhead. The sky opens even more—something I didn't think possible—but instead of rain, white pebbles of hail pelt our heads and the ground around us.

Cal grabs my hand. "Come on!"

We book it back the way we came, leaping over the sticks and stones in our path until we're out of the tree line, around the side of the house, and on the front porch. I still don't have my own copy of the keys, so I reach for Dad's pocketknife, prepared to break us in again, but Cal tries the handle and the door swings open with a loud creak. It's not like Rhonda to forget to lock up after herself. Maybe I should be concerned by that. But for now, I'm just happy to be inside.

Cal tries the light switch without thinking, then shrugs off his jacket and hangs it from the dusty iron coatrack. Miriam's coat is no longer there. Rhonda must have packed it up to be donated or sold. Unable to shed my outer layer, I stand dripping in the middle of the parquet. Note to self: Keep a spare outfit here until we've completely moved in.

"So," Cal says.

"So," I say back. The storm chimes in with more thunder. "I guess we're hanging out for a while, huh?"

Cal's eyes wander from dark corner to dark corner, over to the stairs, then back to me. "I guess so."

The basement door's ajar, a crack letting the darkness through. I push it closed. "We literally just hunted down a graveyard in the woods. If anything was gonna get you, it would have been there."

He shoots me a look filled with reproach. "I'm not afraid of your house."

"I know. Sorry." I was trying—badly—to lighten the mood. I'm feeling exposed in more ways than one—exposed in my clinging, soaked-through T-shirt, exposed for freaking out about my dad. If Cal didn't realize what a disaster I am before, he most certainly does now.

The number of boxes in the living room has grown exponentially, evidence that Rhonda really was here at some point this morning. They're even labeled: *Consignment . . . Jolee's . . . Ask Eva.* Where *is* she? If she'd gone to lunch, she should be back by now. And if she'd gone to sell more stuff, she would have taken these boxes with her. I wonder if something came up with the bank. I hope she wasn't caught out on the road in all of this.

The storm has darkened the daylight, deepening the shadows in the corners of the room. The house creaks and moans in the wind as if it's breathing, while rain and hail rap against the windowpanes demanding to be let in. I shiver in my damp clothes. If only we had wood for the fireplace. If only I knew how to build a fire.

Cal grabs the moth-eaten throw off the back of the sofa, shakes out the dust, and wraps it around my shoulders. We hover close, face-to-face, neither of us making a move to sit or even step apart. Neither of us quite sure what to do now.

The noise of the storm is soon overshadowed by my pulse thrumming in my ears. My gaze trails from the freckle on the tip of Cal's nose to the tiny flecks of gray among the blue of his eyes. I linger there and he lingers back, until I grow uncomfortable and shift my gaze to his forehead. Neutral territory. Or so I thought. A faint scar peeks out from the hairline above his left brow. I've never noticed it before. Usually, it's covered, but he's slicked his dripping hair off his forehead, exposing it. I inhale sharply as it registers: *Is that from the accident?*

Cal takes a quick step back. His eyes dart toward the fireplace. "You, um, you took down the pictures."

"Yeah." I retreat to the farthest end of the sofa. "Wouldn't you?"

Without answering, he takes a seat on the opposite end and leans forward, arms on his knees. One of his legs bounces, shaking the cushions.

"I wonder how long this is supposed to last." He pulls out his phone to check, then remembers it's useless here and tucks it back into his pocket.

I was right. He does think I'm a disaster now. He'd rather not be stuck here with me when I could go off again at any minute.

"I'm sorry."

He cocks his head. "About what?"

"About, you know." I make a vague gesture in the direction of the forest. "Back there."

"Don't be sorry about that."

I nod, looking down at the floor.

"It's just that I left to pick you up without telling anyone. I was angry, and I didn't care. I just wanted to get out of there, you know? I should probably get back soon before I get into too much trouble, but the roads right now . . . The truck's tires aren't great. And I only got my . . . my . . . you know, my card . . . thing. For driving. I only got that a few months ago."

"Dad won't let me get my license." My heart skips a beat, picking up on my mistake. "Wouldn't." I hate it when I do that. "The, um . . . insurance. And you know, we had the subway."

"Dan's dad won't let him drive yet, either," Cal says, turning a little pink.

I've made him uncomfortable, bringing up my dad again. *Find another subject already, Eva. Or maybe let him talk about his own problems for once.* But my jerk of a brain has other ideas. "It was raining. That . . . day."

Cal's knee stops bouncing. He sits up more—turns his body toward me, giving me his full attention. His eyes grow soft and wide with interest. Even in the dim light, their calm blue bolsters me, which in turn unnerves me, and now I'm the one looking down at my twisting hands. Can't take it back now.

"It was raining hard, like this."

And it was late. Dark. But I was still up. I'd just gotten home from being out when I shouldn't have been, and I was alone. Rhonda was home from college for the weekend, but she was out with friends, as usual.

A lot of that night is a blur to me now, a swirl of feelings and senses and images all mixed up as one. Sharp and distant at the same time. Except for the rain. And me just . . . standing there. After the police officer told me my dad had been shot. That he was in the hospital in critical condition. I just stood there, staring at the puddle forming in the hallway around his shoes. Not hearing anything else he said. Only the rain pounding rapid-fire on the windows behind me. Then the splash of tires in puddles as our neighbor drove me to the hospital, stopping to pick Rhonda up along the way. The windshield wipers squeaking as they swished back and forth, back and forth as taillights blurred and came into focus, then blurred again through the ever-persistent damp.

"I get that sometimes, too," Cal says, bringing me back to the present.

I straighten and scoot farther into my corner of the couch, tucking my legs up under me, giving him some space. Cal stares ahead at the fireplace.

"I do understand, you know," he says. "I mean, I *sort* of understand. I lost someone, too. About five years ago. But I don't have the memories like you do. There's just this gap where someone used to be, and now they're not."

I shift in my seat.

"I know you've been asking around about him. You want to know more about who Graham Yeats was, right?"

I nod, silent.

"Yeah," he says. "Me too."

CHAPTER 17

The howling storm fades to the background as Cal speaks, words tumbling out of him in halting bursts. He's been waiting for this. Waiting for a blank slate—someone who knows less than he does so *he* can be the one to tell, not be told about his best friend. The best friend he can't remember.

"All I have are bits and pieces. A smell here, a feeling there—sometimes they'll trigger not so much a memory but like . . . like the shadow of a memory. Like I'll know something without knowing why I know it. Does that make sense? Like—popcorn." His voice takes on a far-off quality. "I don't have the first clue what my best friend looked like, but I sure do know he liked popcorn."

I don't know what to say. I can't imagine not being able to remember what Dad looked like. Though I do have to concentrate sometimes to bring up the details. His laugh lines, his freckles—they're already fading. Like the sound of his voice.

"You don't have pictures?"

"I've seen some, but they don't—" He takes a breath and starts over. "The thing is, I can't picture what *anyone* looks like if they're not in front of me. Not the way you do."

I shift a little in my seat. "You—you don't—Like, if I were to—" *If I were to walk away right now, you'd forget me?* is what I want to say, but that can't be right. I must not be understanding, because clearly, he knows who I am when I'm not in front of him. He texted me. And his sister said he's talked about me.

"No, no, no," he's quick to say, clearly guessing where my thoughts are going with this. "I remember you. I do. I know what you look like. I just can't *picture* you." He closes his eyes and takes a Zen-like breath. "I can tell you that your hair is long, and light brown, and . . . smells like berries. Your eyes are brown, too. And friendly. And you have a really great smile, but you only show it when you're caught off guard." He opens his eyes now and raises his eyebrows. "Like now."

My gaze drops down to my hands again, a flush forming on my cheeks.

"But these are memorized details," he adds. "I can't actually form a picture of you in my head. Or anything. When I close my eyes, it's all blank. It's this condition called aphantasia."

My smile fades.

"I think I used to be able to picture things. But some people are born with it, so maybe I've always been this way. Like I said, I don't remember. Not since my head injury." He taps the scar on his hairline. "I'm told I was lucky, though. Graham wasn't. We fell out of a tree, and I hit my head, but Graham, he—he broke his neck."

"The accident," I murmur, remembering what Bethany told me.

Cal nods. "They said I was unconscious for something like two weeks. They weren't sure I was going to wake up at all. But then, one day, I just . . . did. Everyone said it was a miracle. But then I was in rehab for a year. I couldn't talk for a while. And other things. I also have trouble finding the right words sometimes," he continues. "When I'm, um . . . when I'm . . . well, like now."

When he's nervous. I think back to how often he's done this around me. How he had so much trouble remembering the word for "cemetery," and "cookies," and "antique shop." *Maybe*, I think, biting down on another smile, *I make him nervous.*

Lightning fills the room again, followed immediately by a burst of thunder that rattles the house. I startle, pressing my hand into the couch cushion between us. Cal's hand brushes against it. Our fingers interlace. Our eyes meet.

"I'm sorry for tiptoeing," I tell him. "I should have just asked you."

"That's not—It's not—" He gingerly retrieves his hand. A lump rises in my throat. Why don't I ever know the right thing to say?

Gathering himself, he tries again. "I had to tell you all that—I *wanted* to tell you all that—to explain. Because . . . well, please promise me you won't be mad."

Heat inches up my spine. Promise you won't be mad usually means I'm about to have a good reason to be mad.

"Why?"

"Because I wasn't completely truthful just now. There's one picture I *can* bring up when I close my eyes, but *only* one. She's been there ever since the accident."

She? She who?

My pulse quickens as he leans forward to pull his wallet out of his back pocket. What's he doing?

"You're going to think I'm a creep," he mutters, almost under his breath.

165

Why? What's he getting? It briefly crosses my mind that I'm alone with him in a spooky, abandoned house in the woods with no cell service, and nobody else knows I'm here.

Now his words come out in one long string with barely a pause or a fumble. It's like he's gone past nerves and entered into panic. "I swear I didn't mean to, okay? I just—you seemed upset by this, but once the lights were on, I had to double-check. And I didn't want you to get upset again, so I had to be quick, but then it fell out and I couldn't get it back in, and I—There wasn't time."

"There wasn't time for what? What are you talking about?"

"You remember back at the gas station? I *knew* you from somewhere. You know, like the popcorn. I didn't know *how* I knew you. I just did, and it was bothering me because I couldn't figure it out. But then we came here, and I saw this."

I stiffen as he slides a small, wrinkled photograph out of his wallet and hands it to me. Jaw tight, I stare down at my miniature self, grinning while sitting on the back of Dad's ambulance.

"You *took* it?" My voice sounds strangled, foreign to my own ears. I didn't promise. I didn't promise I wouldn't be mad.

"I didn't mean to, but I had to double-check. You have to understand, when I say I can't see you in my head, what I mean is, I can't see you as you are *now*. But the you in that picture, when you were little . . . that's what I see. It's the only image I'm ever able to come up with when I close my eyes, and it's *your* face. So, I was right. I do know you. But I don't know how."

I've heard him, but I'm not processing it. This picture hurts to look at. It hurts so much. But it's also *very* important to me. It isn't just about my dad. It's so much more. And he *took* it. The blanket drops from my shoulders as I rise to my feet.

"You don't, okay?" I hurry over to the box where I stashed the other pictures and snatch up the empty frame. "You *don't* know me."

And he doesn't understand. He will never understand. Because while this picture was being taken—the very minute it was snapped, for all I know—my mother was climbing into a cab, never to be heard from again. This picture was the last moment my family was complete. Shaking, I fumble with the photo, trying to slide it back into the frame, but my fingers aren't cooperating.

"I'm sorry," he tries. "I know it sounds weird. But there's more. You need to look at the back."

He's next to me now. I don't know how he got there. And this stupid frame won't cooperate.

"The back." With a light touch, he steadies my hand. "Look."

I see it. The empty frame drops into the box, forgotten. There's a message scrawled on the back of the photograph in a strange, hurried script: half-printed, half-cursive. *It's time to Dream Again, but be Wary, Evangeline, and Remember.*

This isn't Dad's handwriting. Miriam wrote this. I'm sure of it. The cursive bits remind me of the jam labels on the jars I found in the pantry.

"It's weird, right?" he says, as if the rest of what he's told me isn't bizarre enough. "I think maybe it's a code."

I huff in disbelief. A code? Seriously? I reread the words as, still shaking, I return to the sofa. Cal scoots closer to me so he can read it again, our shoulders pressing together. I'm still angry, but I don't push him away. If he hadn't taken this picture from me, I would never have known this was here. I would have packed it safely away with the rest, oblivious. Still, that didn't give him any right to take it.

"See?" He points from word to word. "These are capitalized for no reason."

"D-A-W-R," I spell out. *Dream, Again, Wary, Remember.* "I think she was just writing quickly."

"Your name, though, that's capitalized, too."

"Okay, but even then, it still doesn't mean anything. Unless they're initials for something."

"Or someone's last name."

"I guess?" I doubt it. "Do you know anyone named Dawer?"

He shakes his head.

I don't think it's a code. The writing does look rushed. And the message itself is ominous enough. It may not mean anything to Cal, but it does to me. At least, some of it does.

Dream—I've been doing a lot of dreaming lately. *But be wary*—and the people I've dreamed about aren't doing so well. But that last word—*Remember*—I can hear it in my head in another voice. A familiar voice I can't quite place, that for the briefest moment made me feel like I'd glimpsed something missing within me. And now what Cal told me doesn't sound so strange after all. Knowing without knowing. Remembering without remembering.

"Cal? Can I ask you a question?"

"Of course."

I flip the picture to the front and trace my finger along the caduceus on Dad's jacket. "If you can't see things when you close your eyes, how do you dream?"

"I don't—" He sounds momentarily confused, as if he's never thought of it before. "I don't think I do."

A faint ringing reaches our ears from somewhere in the house, barely audible over the storm. It may have been ringing for a while. Is that a phone? We exchange glances, then it clicks—that old rotary in the kitchen—and we're both up and headed that way.

"How is it working without electricity?" I wonder aloud as we hurry through the dining room.

"I don't think landlines need electricity," Cal says.

Well, that's handy. But I don't know anyone who would have this number besides Rhonda, or maybe the police. It better be Rhonda, because if it's the police . . .

She's still not back. The rain still hasn't stopped. *Where are you, Rhonda?*

CHAPTER 18

I never thought I'd be so relieved to be yelled at over the phone.

"*There* you are!"

"It's Rhonda," I mouth to Cal. Though he can probably hear that for himself.

"Jesus Christ, Eva, people are dropping like flies around here, and you couldn't be bothered to text?"

"Dropping like—"

"Charlie," she tells me. "But you probably already knew about that, didn't you? Since you were in such a hurry to go check on him this morning you couldn't even be bothered to take your phone. Again. I'm not even going to ask why you thought you needed to check on him. What I want to know is why you didn't think I'd want to know he wasn't okay." The hurt in her voice is palpable.

My grip tightens around the earpiece. I *told* her she should call Charlie, and she blew me off. And now she expects me to have somehow found a way to communicate . . . what, with her, exactly? That I wanted to check on Charlie because I had a scary dream? She would have blown that off, too. *I* would have blown that off if it hadn't been the third time this week.

"You'd already left by the time I got back. Thanks for stranding me, by the way."

"You obviously made it there somehow," she counters. "Did you forget we have a working landline at the house? You know, the one we're talking on right now? You could have reached me on that, and I would have come back to pick you up."

Yes, actually, I did forget about the landline. It's not like I don't have a million other things on my mind right now. And besides, without electricity, I didn't expect it to work. I take a steadying breath. "Well, it doesn't matter anyway, because I found another ride."

There's a pause. "From that boy you keep talking about? Cal?"

I look over at him leaning in the doorway. I hope he didn't hear that. He looks nervously back at me.

"Yes. So I could join *you*, but *you'd* already left."

"So . . . you're alone? With a boy you barely know?"

I wish she'd lower her voice. I groan inwardly and reiterate. "I wouldn't be *if you hadn't left*." I decide to leave the grave hunting out of it. She's being unreasonable, and maybe it's because of Charlie. Maybe it's because of Dad. Maybe it's because of something else, but I wish she'd get to the point. "What's going on?"

She pauses again. Her breath hits the mouthpiece as she exhales. "I need to talk to you about something."

"Okay, I'm listening."

"In person."

Cal catches my expression and questions me with his eyes. I shake my head at him, mouthing, "Nothing."

"Why?"

Another sigh. "I found these journals, okay? And I—I need

171

you to see them. I brought them all the way back here to show them to you, thinking you would be here."

"Journals?"

Cal shoots me another questioning look, and I shrug at him. Why would something she'd read in some old journals be so urgent? Could they be Miriam's? But why would that be urgent? Unless . . . my heart flips. What if they have stuff in them about Dad? Rhonda gets angry when she's upset. Maybe she saw something about Dad and she just needs me to be there right now. "Okay," I say. "As soon as the rain slows down, I'll—I'll have Cal—"

"Cal's parents have been trying to get a hold of him, too. You think *I'm* pissed? Uh-uh. They're about to send Chief Burke out looking for him, so he'd better give them a call ASAP, then get both your butts back here."

"But the storm . . ."

"It's just rain, Eva." She hangs up before I can explain the whole new-driver thing, which probably wouldn't help, anyway.

Cal gets an earful from his mom as well. The word "grounded" travels clearly enough through the earpiece, even I can hear it. What I can't hear anymore is the pounding rain. I guess even the storm knows it's time for us to go.

Tucked back into the truck, a ballad on the radio, windshield wipers swishing lazily back and forth, I lean my head against the cool window. I'm exhausted. *But I won't close my eyes.* I yawn. *I can't.*

Bad dreams . . . running through the storm in the woods . . . emotional outbursts . . . one thing upon another, upon another . . .

172

The rain is dripping, dripping on my face and down the back of my neck from my saturated hair. My feet stick in the mud as I slog through the forest. Squish, suck, slurp. Each step heavy, laborious, holding me back.

"Eva! Evangeline!"

My name echoes, bouncing off the trees like chaos.

"Evangeline!"

"I'm here! Where are you?" My own words fall short in front of me, washed away by the rain.

"Evangeline! Eva! I'm sorry, please come back. Come back. I'll do better. I'm sorry."

It comes at me from all directions, sweeping through the openings in the trees, brushing past and around me like swallows chasing mosquitoes.

"Rhonda?" I'm sure it's her, but she sounds younger. Much younger. Where is she? What is she doing out here?

The mud loosens on my shoes, and the ground hardens, becoming slippery. I pick up my pace as the trees widen. They stick together, then turn gray. Concrete. Sidewalk. Cars and taxis swish through the puddled street.

"Evangeline!"

There she is, standing in the middle of Times Square, screaming out my name. Rain and tears mix, sending streaks of mascara down her cheeks and stringy bangs in her face. She runs up to a man and a woman huddled under an umbrella taking pictures of the lit signs and billboards.

I'm not close enough to hear her when she's not yelling, but I can see her gesticulating wildly. She holds her hand out, palm down, waist-high. She grabs her hair in two fists, tugging to indicate pigtails, maybe braids. She's describing a little girl, not me. Not current me, anyway.

The couple shakes their heads, so she moves on to a man in a business suit and a trench coat. Then to an older woman, hunched and gnarled, with a plastic-weave shopping bag and a plastic kerchief protecting her fluffy white perm from the rain.

I remember this. Well, not *this*, but from my own perspective. She was supposed to be watching me while Mom went to go "talk to someone." She'd told us not to tell Dad. It was no big deal, but he was "already so stressed, you know? Stay with your sister. You understand?"

And I meant to. I really did. But one second, I was standing next to Rhonda in the crowd, marveling at the lights, and then somehow I wasn't. I don't remember much else, just that Rhonda found me again and screamed at me for wandering off, neither of us told Mom, and that was the end of that.

Guilt washes over me. But Rhonda's not sixteen anymore, and I'm not the ten-year-old she's describing.

She stops again in the middle of the square and turns in circles, searching the crowd desperately. They're all kind of fuzzy now—one amorphous mass of blurry, generic faces.

"Evangeline!"

"Rhonda! It's okay! I'm right here!"

She looks up, confused at first as I run toward her, then she backs away, eyes widening in fear.

"Rhonda? Hey. It's just me."

She shakes her head and continues to retreat, one frightened step at a time.

The square darkens. Is night falling? It doesn't feel like night.

It feels . . . different. Oppressive. I shiver. The crowd disappears. The images on the billboards lose their color, their definition, then fade away completely. Walls of nothing close in around us as the sound of the absent crowd morphs into an eerie scratching noise. Skittering . . . squeaking.

Rats.

"Where are you?" Rhonda's voice is low, husky, drenched in fear. "Why are you doing this?" She hugs her arms around herself, rising to her toes, trying to get as far from the ground as possible. Her entire body jerks as a rat scrambles past us. Then another and another.

"Rhonda, I'm right here. Don't you see me?" But my words are drowned out, spoken over by someone else.

Some*thing* else.

"No one else can know." It's that voice: low and menacing yet high and childlike at the same time. The shadow's voice. It's here.

A throbbing in my head follows, forcing my eyes into a squint. I duck, too late, as something dark passes through me, overwhelming me, filling me with shame and self-loathing. It mixes with my own emotions, drawing them out. Almost . . . like it's feeding on them. Or the other way around. Or both. I turn to see a murky figure rise up, poised to come at me again, dark tendrils billowing around it like branches whipped up by a storm. I reel with dizziness as I try to focus past the pain in my head and my chest now, too, readying myself for another attack.

"No!" Rhonda screams. And then, to my horror, it shifts away from me, staring her down instead.

"Eva!" she yells. "Listen! It's—"

"Rhonda!" I cry as a tendril whips out, covering her mouth. She braces herself, hands thrust forward, face twisted in fear, as the rest of the shadow rushes toward her. And I'm frozen in place. Paralyzed. I can't do *anything* as it swirls around her and . . .

. . . there's a nudge to my arm. I jerk awake.

"Hey. We're here."

Here? Where's here? I take a second to reorient myself. *Here* is Cal's truck, not moving. Idling. Parked.

Yawning, I blink the sleep out of my eyes, adjusting their focus on the front facade of the Roadhouse and its great big sign. *Jumbotron. Rats. Shadow.*

My hand shoots up to my mouth.

Cal's brow furrows. "What's wrong?"

"Can you come up with me, please?" My voice is shaking. I'm shaking. *Rhonda. Not Rhonda.*

"My parents . . ."

"Please." I grip the door handle, but I won't—can't exit the car until I know he's coming with me.

"Okay." He switches off the ignition and unbuckles his seat belt. "Okay."

I'm out of the truck so fast, I'm halfway around the hood before I hear my passenger door slam shut behind me. Cal's on my heels as I run down the sidewalk, heart thumping, then up the stairs leading to our room, taking them two at a time, gripping the side rail tight with each leap to keep from slipping on the slick, wet wood.

I fumble with my key. It slips from my fingers. I retrieve it, then try to jab it into the keyhole, continually missing until Cal's warm hand closes around mine.

"Hey," he says. "Deep breaths." But I notice his own fingers are trembling, too, as he takes the key and unlocks the door for me.

It swings open to silence. There's a heap of leather-bound books on my bed. *Those must be the journals Rhonda wanted me to see.* And beyond them, propped up on her own bed, is Rhonda. One of the journals is open, facedown on her chest, mid-read. But she doesn't say anything as we enter the room. No "hello." No "well, it's about time." She doesn't say anything because she's asleep. As fast asleep as someone can be. And it doesn't matter how much I call her name, how hard I shake her, she won't wake up.

I dreamed about Rhonda, and now she won't wake up.

CHAPTER 19

Different hospital, same smell. If anxiety, fear, and waiting could be distilled, then chased with a healthy dose of antiseptic—that would be the odor entering my lungs with every breath, stealing my oxygen away.

It's not the fluorescent lights, a sickly yellow that turns even the rosiest complexion jaundiced. Not the monitors beeping from behind curtains, ticking off the endless seconds. It's not even the flurry of nurses and doctors flitting about, their stark white sneakers squeaking on the linoleum with every hurried step. It's the smell that takes me back.

If I close my eyes, I can hear the doctor again—one of Dad's colleagues—his voice calm, methodical, carefully controlled to omit all emotion. Except he doesn't quite make it. He falters, his voice catching on the last word. But he doesn't have to say it. We know. Rhonda, who never cries in front of anyone, crumples into a sobbing heap. But me, I do nothing. I don't cry. I don't yell. I don't even try to comfort my sister. I'm numb. I'm in a dream.

I hate this smell.

"Come on, let's stretch our legs." Chief Burke unfolds from his chair and stands, waiting for me to join him. I don't want to stretch my legs. But I don't want to sit here having flashbacks, either, the knot in my stomach working its way farther up my esophagus with each sensory assault on my memory. Cal squeezes my hand for reassurance, and I reluctantly follow Chief Burke out of the waiting area, leaving Cal behind.

All I can focus on is placing one foot in front of the other as we aimlessly wander down the hallway. The speckled linoleum reflects a shadowy blob of myself back at me.

"Rough day all around, huh?"

I don't answer.

"Okay," he says, unruffled. We stroll a few more feet before he clears his throat and says, "I have to ask you these, you understand. It's strictly procedure. Was your sister acting differently in any way before this happened?"

Wow. Right to the point. "I . . . I don't know," I mumble. "I hadn't seen her since breakfast. But she seemed fine then." I don't include how I'd ditched her to go check on the *last* person who wound up in a coma. Besides, he can probably figure that out since he found me there. He'd even made it a point to tell me it wasn't my fault. I wonder why he felt the need to tell me that if he didn't think it was a possibility. I wonder if he's changed his mind. If he knew about the dreams, he would. Maybe I should tell him.

"But you spoke to her on the phone—not long before you found her." He must have interviewed Cal while I was talking to the doctor earlier.

"She was worried about where I was," I say. "Because of the storm."

I tell him about the note she'd left at the Roadhouse, how Cal had given me a ride to Miriam's to meet up with her. I leave out the bit about going off to look for the family graveyard. It feels too personal. Maybe Cal already told him all of that, anyway. I hope he hasn't mentioned my embarrassing breakdown.

I do tell Chief Burke that Rhonda had already left by the time we got there, and how we were then stranded when the storm hit because Cal wasn't comfortable driving in it. "Oh, and she left the door unlocked," I remember. "She's always really diligent about that. So, I guess you could say that was unusual behavior."

"Hmm." He bobs his head, thinking everything over.

I wonder how pissed Cal's parents are right now, since he drove me here instead of going home. I'm not sure how long it's been. Time moves differently in the ICU, and I haven't been paying attention. His parents probably wanted him home hours ago.

Chief Burke assured us he took care of things with Cal's parents, and Cal's been updating them via text, but—

"Did she mention anything on the phone about, oh, I don't know, headaches, or drowsiness, or anything of that nature? Did she mention where she'd been or who she'd spoken to during the day?"

I shake my head, then remember: "She said Cal's parents were looking for him. So, she must have talked to them. And she knew about Charlie somehow, too. She was . . ." I stop before betraying the feelings I suspect she's developing for him. "She also said she needed to talk to me about something."

"Oh?" He perks up. "Did she give any hint as to what that might be?"

180

"No, she said it would be better in person." I feel like I'm forgetting something. My thoughts are so sluggish, so disordered right now, it's hard to think.

He nods, his face blank again, but I can tell he's frustrated. A nurse bustles down the hall and stops us. Chief Burke tells me to hang tight for a second while he moves off a short distance with the nurse. They speak in low voices; he nods a few times, then signals to me that I can go back to the waiting area.

The journals, I remember as I trudge back down the hall. *I forgot to mention the journals she wanted me to see.* But maybe it's better if I don't say anything until I'm able to take a look at them myself. I need to know what Rhonda saw that made her so upset. It could be something personal. My stomach twists into a knot. If they belonged to Miriam, there could be something about Dad in them, or even me. Judging from the plethora of photographs above her fireplace, Miriam obviously knew about me. But they also might finally give me some context for why so many people in Madrona were afraid of her. Even if the journals belonged to someone else in the family, they'll surely give me at least *some* insight into why so many people have issues with the Sylvans.

It's still a little chilly, but I keep the window cracked on the drive back from the hospital to help keep me awake. The doctor told me that, as a family member, I was welcome to stay overnight with my sister. That they'd pull up a cot for me. But she said it would be better if I went home and got some good sleep.

Ironic, since me sleeping is what sent my sister to the hospital in the first place. I dreamed about her, and now she's in a coma. Just like Charlie, and Troy, and Rob. No one should want me to get a good night's sleep right now. Who knows who I might dream of next?

But I can't avoid it forever. I'm exhausted now that the adrenaline is wearing off, and the more I think about not sleeping, the more my eyes want to close. Eventually, sleep will come for me. It's inevitable.

"Are you sure you're gonna be okay tonight?" Cal asks. "By yourself?"

By myself. Those last two words knock the wind out of me. I'm . . . I'm by myself. By. Myself.

"Yeah," I lie. "I'll be fine."

I don't think Cal believes me, so I deflect. "Were you really able to smooth things over with your parents?"

"About the hospital? Sure."

"But not about taking off with me in the middle of a storm, I'll bet."

He makes a face I can't quite read—something between a cringe and a grin. "Yeah, I'm definitely still grounded for that."

"I'm sorry."

He pulls up to the curb in front of the Roadhouse and sets the brake. "I'm not."

"You're not?"

He shifts in the driver's seat so he's facing me and shakes his head. The truck is idling. I should get out, but I know that once I unbuckle, once I open that door, I truly am on my own. Just like he said. I don't want to be by myself tonight. I don't want to sleep. I don't want to dream.

"Are you *sure* you're going to be okay?"

My pulse quickens as his eyes lock onto mine, drawing me out. Once again, he's calling my bluff. I'm not at all sure I'm going to be okay. In fact, I'm pretty sure I'm not. And he knows it.

"It's my fault," I blurt out, my pulse quickening as I fully realize what I'm admitting to. "I dreamed about her." *Why am I telling him this?*

He blinks. "Dreamed about—"

"Rhonda." My mouth keeps going despite the rest of my mind screaming at it to shut up. *Don't say it, Eva. Saying it makes it real.* "I dreamed about Rhonda in the car on the way home. From the house, I mean. Before we found her."

"Okay . . ."

"And I dreamed about Charlie last night."

"Charlie? He works at the—at the—"

"Madrona Motors." He probably doesn't know about Charlie. "He's in a coma, too." Cal's chin jerk confirms this is new information.

"They found him this morning." My words spill out of me a mile a minute, and I can't stop them. I can't take them back now. "And I dreamed about Troy the night before they found him, and I dreamed about Rob the night before they found *him*—"

"You've had a long day, okay? I mean, I guess I wouldn't know, but it's normal to dream about the people you run into during the day, isn't it? It doesn't mean anything."

"What *exactly* did Miriam do?" I ask him. "Everyone was so afraid of her. Why won't anyone tell me?"

There goes his knee again, bouncing like back at the house and the park. With a pained expression, he looks from my face to the passenger door handle behind me.

"I need to get back. My parents . . ."

I bite down hard, fumbling to remove my seat belt. "Right. Yeah. Sorry." I push open the door and hop out onto the pavement.

"Eva, wait. I'll call and check on—"

The door slams shut behind me, cutting off the last word. Head down, I dash around the front of the truck toward the alley. The sound of the engine revving and pulling away is both a gut punch and a relief. We were having a moment, but I ruined it. And now he hates me.

"What the shit, Eva?"

It's exactly what I want to say to myself, but Bethany's gone and done it for me. I stop and peer around the stairs to find Bethany standing underneath, wadded apron dangling from her fist. How much did she see?

"You're seriously not staying up there by yourself tonight, are you?"

"It's here or the Witch House," I tell her. It comes out pricklier than I intend.

"Or my room, silly. Grab your pj's and stuff. Mom already said it's fine."

I open my mouth to express my gratitude, but it threatens to turn into a sob that I immediately choke back.

"Aw, come 'ere," Bethany says, pulling me in for a hug. "Do you need help gathering everything up?"

I shake my head.

"Okay, then, take your time. I've got the rest of the night off."

What with the paramedics and those two police officers from Charlie's tromping around in here earlier, I'd expect the place to look more disheveled. But it appears untouched since Cal and I stepped in and found Rhonda unconscious. Except . . . something's missing. Where are the journals?

I think back. Rhonda was holding one to her chest, open, facedown, like she always does. But I'd been more concerned with trying to get her to wake up to pay much attention to what happened to it. I think I remember Cal sliding it out from under her hands and setting it down somewhere—probably with the rest of the journals. Or is my mind just filling in the blanks?

And where are those? I should be gathering up my things to stay with Bethany tonight, but my brain is now zoomed in on figuring out where so many books could have disappeared to. They were on my bed, and I remember moving them so I could sit down when the paramedics were here. I stacked them . . . on the table in the kitchenette, didn't I? Yes, I'm positive that's where they were when Cal and I left for the hospital, but now they're gone.

Did the police take them? What reason would they have?

Or . . . did Cal? When he took the one out of Rhonda's hands, did he not actually set it back down? It's not like he hasn't taken things that don't belong to him before. I bite down on the thought the minute I have it. No, he wouldn't do that again. And besides, it doesn't explain where the rest went. It's not like he could hide all of them under his shirt.

I slip the photograph out of my pocket and rub my thumb over the emblem on Dad's jacket. Cal doesn't understand. He acts like he's trying to, but he doesn't. He doesn't remember the person he lost. And if you don't remember the person you've lost, have you really lost them at all?

Yes, I scold myself. *Yes, of course it still counts, Eva. What's wrong with you?*

But as for me, I'm out three for three now. My mom, my dad, and now . . .

Something hardens inside me. Nope. Not Rhonda. She's still here; she's just sleeping. And if she's sleeping, she can wake up. I just need to figure out how to make that happen.

I flip the picture over and reread Miriam's message to me: *It's time to dream again* . . . If I did dream Rhonda and the others into a coma, there must be a way to dream them back out. I can fix this. I *will* fix this.

CHAPTER 20

Last night's dreams were about aliens, so unless there's been an invasion, I think everyone's fine today. Bethany, Daniel, and I had an *X-Files* marathon. I said I hadn't watched the show before, and apparently that was not okay, because Bethany has every single season on DVD—even the newer ones where everyone's old—plus the movies, and she's watched them so much, she has them memorized. Cal would have been invited to come watch, too, if he wasn't grounded. After his reaction when I opened my big mouth about my dreams, though, I'm glad he wasn't there.

I'll admit, the show *would* have been a great distraction if my current situation didn't feel like something belonging on Mulder's desk. I could use his and Scully's help right now. I guess in their absence, I'll have to do my own investigating.

I hop on the bicycle Bethany has been kind enough to loan me and pedal my way down to Jolee's Attic. Unfortunately, I've failed to consider how early it is. The lights are off, and the closed sign is prominently displayed in the window. And yet I swear I hear some movement coming from inside. I hold my breath and listen, but whatever it was has stopped. Still, I give the door a light tap, just in case. Silence.

I must have been imagining things. At least I have my phone

this time. I take a picture of the sign with the number for appointments and am halfway down the block when bells chime on the shop's door behind me. I twist around to find Jolee's curly head poking out from the doorway, bedraggled red locks bouncing around a pair of purple reading glasses pushed down to the tip of her nose. A chain hangs from the frames, looping back around her neck.

"Did you knock? Was that you?" Her voice is high and sing-songy.

"Sorry. I know you're closed."

She beckons me over. "No apologies allowed for curiosity. Get on back here. Come in."

I walk the bike over to the shop and lean it against the wall.

"Come in," she beckons again, her voice coaxing like I'm a scared puppy or something.

Maybe I do look a bit like that. My heart is thumping as if I'm about to discover all of life's secrets. And before I know it, I'm in Jolee's apartment above the shop, sitting in her vintage kitchen at a chrome-and-Formica table, complete with a pair of red vinyl diner chairs.

"How do you like your tea? That is . . . if you like tea?" Jolee asks, but before I can say I'm not much of a tea drinker, she adds, "Well, you'll like this tea, anyway. I make a good cuppa." She stretches up on the tips of her toes to retrieve a box from an upper cabinet. "I'll start you off with milk and a couple of sugar cubes. Yes, I think that would be the best introduction."

"Um, okay." I feel disoriented, like my time machine got confused and I've stepped into some strange mash-up of the fifties and eighties. It's a lot. The pink enamel stove—one of those old-fashioned ones with drawers and cupboards and levers—is surrounded by baby-blue cupboards topped with a gold-flecked Formica countertop. Novelty canisters and kitcheny knickknacks take up most of the counter space. There are so many shapes and colors, my eyes can't decide where to look.

"I was wondering when you'd be coming around," Jolee says, placing teabags in two china teacups decorated with a spray of pink rosebuds. "I was expecting you yesterday."

"You were?" She must have me mistaken for someone else. I haven't made an appointment yet. Unless—my stomach knots—she was expecting Rhonda to come by with more things and figured I'd be with her again.

She plops a sugar cube in one cup and adds a little milk, then gives it a quick stir before setting it in front of me. She then sets her own down across from me and places her hands on her hips. "Evangeline Sylvan," she says with awe. "Well. Just look at you."

Her smile makes her jaw sharper and her cheeks rosier, and I catch myself checking if the tops of her ears come to a point.

"You look exactly like her. Do you know that?" she says. "Well, except for the torn clothes. Why do you young people purposely ruin your clothes like that? My goodness, what a bizarre fad."

I could say a few things about her own style choices, but I keep it to myself. "Who do I look like?"

"Why, Miriam, obviously." She cocks her head. "Though I suppose you wouldn't know that, would you, hon? Poor dear. Never met her, did you? Or . . . perhaps you have and you don't remember it." One eyebrow rises, just for a second, before she's distracted by another thought. "Oh! I almost forgot! Can't have tea without something sweet!" She turns and retrieves a half-empty package of Oreos from another cupboard and places it unceremoniously in the center of the table before finally settling into the seat across from me.

Leaning back in her chair, she appraises me again.

"You know, actually, I think you might resemble May even more."

I don't know who May is—another relative, I presume—but I can't find my voice to ask. My senses are overwhelmed, and I'm feeling unprepared. It's setting me a bit on edge.

"So? You'd like to know more about her, yes?" she asks. "Miriam, that is. Isn't that why you're here?"

"Y-yes. I mean, no. Well, I do, but I want to know about all of them. The, um, the Sylvans."

She nods patiently. "Well, I can certainly help you with that. But are you absolutely sure?"

I resist the urge to squirm in my seat. I *thought* I was sure. "Yes, of course."

She sighs. "See, what you have to understand is the Sylvans were—*are* . . . How should I put it? Different. But I think you already know that, don't you?"

"*How* are they different?" A little voice in the back of my head nags at me that I already know that, too. That I know exactly how they aren't like everyone else—how *I'm* not like everyone else, as much as I wish I could be. But that little voice won't give me a satisfactory answer. At least not one that makes any sense.

"I'm sure you've noticed the symbols carved on many of the buildings throughout the town," she says.

"Yes. My friend Bethany told me they're meant to ward off

witches. I got the impression she meant my family." She isn't about to tell me the Sylvans really were witches, is she?

Jolee nods, thinking. She takes a moment to sip her tea and nibble on an Oreo while I try to rein in my growing frustration. *Just tell me. Someone just tell me* something. *Please.*

"I don't know how much I should say," she utters, more to herself, it seems, than to me. Her eyes narrow in concentration. "There's something, like a block . . . like some sort of shadowy—" She sets her teacup down with a clatter. Some of its contents slosh into the saucer, but she's too busy staring intently at me to notice. My skin is crawling. It feels strange, like she's looking through me to the inside. I have the urge to slap her hands away from my head, except her hands aren't anywhere near me. They're flat on the table.

She closes her eyes, then opens them again with an embarrassed smile. "Sorry." She takes up her teacup again. A few drips fall from the base, joining the puddle in her saucer. "What I mean is, you've had a lot of things kept from you, haven't you? To not even know who May is! My goodness."

My skin prickles. I think back. "I . . . I never said I didn't know who May is." I didn't, did I? I'm positive I only thought it.

"Didn't you? Oh. Well, of course you *wouldn't* know her, though." She nods at my untouched tea. "Basic English breakfast. Nothing strange, I promise."

I can feel my ears getting hot. I pick up my cup and take a test sip to keep calm. It's not bad. Sweet and warm and earthy. But it doesn't help. The heat spreads from my ears to my face and neck. It doesn't matter *who* I talk to, it's always the same.

This is my family I'm asking about. I have a right to know about them. What was wrong with them? What's wrong with *me*?

My hand shakes. I set my tea down so I won't spill it. "I don't know who May is because no one tells me anything. I was told *you* probably would, though, and now you're not sure you should? I just want to know why everyone was so frightened of Miriam. And the rest of my family. And of *me*. I need to know. I need to know what's wrong with us so I can figure out how to stop it." I suck in my breath. I didn't mean to say that last bit.

"Stop what, hon?"

"Nothing," I say quickly.

"Doesn't sound like nothing." She pushes the package of Oreos toward me. I don't take one.

"Eva, hon, I can tell you're feeling a lot of, well, *feelings* right now," Jolee says. "I'm willing to listen. I promise I won't tell a soul. That's what we did for each other, you know. Miriam and me. We had some . . . things in common. So, whatever it is, let it out. It'll do you some good. And then I promise I'll tell you what I can. Think of this as your safe space."

I consider doubling back on what I said. Or knocking my teacup over to create a diversion so I can run away. But there's something about the warmth in her eyes right now—something that says she of all people won't judge me for what I have to say. And that maybe, just maybe, she *can* help me after all. *You have to let people help you, Eva.* And if opening up is what it will take to finally get some answers, fine.

"I keep putting people into comas, and I need to know how to stop."

"Oh!" Whatever it was Jolee expected me to say, that was

obviously not it. She reaches across the table and places her hand on my arm. "Oh, honey. Who says you're the one doing *that*?"

"I—I do. Well, and the lady who owns the gift shop. Diane Petersen?"

Jolee looks to the ceiling with a heavy sigh. I get the feeling she's not at all surprised by Diane.

"She blames me for her dad being in a coma," I continue. "And I think she might be right, because I dreamed about him that night." It feels so strange to be saying this out loud again, when the only person I've told is Cal in a moment of panic. Which he didn't react well to. But I force myself to keep going. "Then I dreamed about a boy named Troy. Then Charlie from the garage, then my *sister*. And now they're all in comas."

"Oh. Well," she says, retracting her arm and grabbing another cookie along the way. "You dreamed about them because you're a Sylvan."

"I don't . . . I don't know what that means."

She sighs. "Do you know what telepathy is?"

Telepathy? "Doing stuff with your mind, right? Like, communicating and moving things around?" Like in that old horror movie *Carrie*—locking gym doors and starting fires, oh God, am I like Carrie?

Jolee nods. "Right. It's like that, but with dreams. What the Sylvans can do, that is."

"Telepathy . . . but with dreams."

"Exactly. Dream telepathy. Or you could call it astral dream travel if you want to get all New Agey about it. Ooh, or oneironautics. That's a fun one. Like a dream astronaut. Sounds exciting, right?"

I don't feel excited. I feel ill.

"Basically," she continues, "you can go inside other people's dreams and, you know, rummage around a bit. Explore. That kind of thing. Lots of Sylvans could do it. Not all, mind you. Your father couldn't, as far as I'm aware. But Miriam could. And so could your grandmother, Rose. And May." Her eyes take on a faraway look.

"Who is May, anyway?" There are so many more pressing questions I could ask, but this is the third time she's brought her up and she still hasn't told me who she is.

"Didn't I say? Or did I just think it? May was Miriam's youngest sister. There was Miriam, then Rose, then May. She passed away very suddenly back in the seventies. Very young. About your age, I think. No, that can't be right. She must have been a bit older. Was she still in school? No, she'd definitely graduated by then. Must have been her early twenties, then. Hmm. Anyway, all three sisters were *quite* skilled at dream telepathy, like many other Sylvans through the generations. Sounds like you've inherited the skill as well."

All the time she's speaking, my stomach knots tighter and tighter. "So, it *is* my fault."

"What's your fault? The comas?" Her brows knit. "I . . . don't know about that. As far as I'm aware, no Sylvan has ever put anyone into a coma. Even the less-than-savory ones."

Doesn't mean I haven't, I think. *There's a first time for everything, isn't there?*

"But why else would this be happening now?" I ask. "I move here, I dream about people, they don't wake up. And now you're telling me my family can *actually* enter people's dreams." Which sounds so much more bizarre even than what I've admitted to,

I'm shocked I'm not having any problem accepting it. My gut was right: Somewhere deep down, I already knew. And besides, it's the only thing that fits. "It has to be me."

Jolee's brows furrow as she watches my response. "Oh, honey, you're holding on to so much *guilt*." She shakes her head sadly. "So much."

Something about the way she says it hits a nerve. It feels intrusive—like she's prying into my private thoughts, poking and prodding at personal wounds. My pulse quickens. I need to get away.

Head swimming, I spring to my feet "I . . . I have to go." And without further thought, I'm speeding for the door with Jolee on my heels.

"You have to get it under control, or it'll eat away at you," she says. "Eva. Eva, listen to me, honey. His death was not your fault."

Stunned, I whirl around to face her, heart thumping so hard I can hear it in my eardrums. My mouth opens, but nothing comes out. Her intentions may be kind, but her words are daggers in my chest.

"I know you blame yourself," she says. "But it's important for you to understand. Critical, even. You *must* let the guilt go. Before it—" She stops herself and repeats instead, "It's not your fault."

"I *know* that." It comes out hoarse, quieter than I intended.

"No," she calls after me as I hurry out the door. "You don't."

195

I circle my thumb over the back of Rhonda's hand—the hand without an IV needle taped to it—and wonder if she can hear me. The nurse told me I should talk to her. That, depending on the coma, it's believed people can still be aware of what's going on around them. Which sounds horrifying to me. But she said it might be comforting for my sister to hear a familiar voice, so I'm trying to think of something to talk about. Something boring. Because what's really going through my head wouldn't be comforting at all.

I'm still reeling over what Jolee said to me as I was rushing out the door. I *know* Dad's death isn't my fault. How could it be? *I* didn't pull a gun on him while he was trying to save someone's life. *I* didn't cause the car pileup that sent him to the scene. I wasn't even there. I was at Riley's when it happened. I wasn't supposed to be, but I was.

My stomach lurches with the memory, like it always does when I allow myself to think of that night. Riley's parents were out of town, but they didn't want to pull her out of school. Which was why she was having a party on a weeknight. Dad said I couldn't go, not just because it was a school night, but because he was well aware her parents weren't going to be there. And he never did trust her after the incident with the liquor cabinet. But when he got called away, I took the opportunity to go, anyway. And I didn't even have any fun because all I could think about was how much trouble I'd be in if I lost track of time and didn't make it home before Dad did.

I'd felt so relieved when I walked in the door to find he wasn't there. Giddy, even, for being so rebellious and getting away with it—so unlike me—like I'd gone through some important rite of passage. My gut does another twist. How could I have known Dad wouldn't be coming back at all?

I try to think of another subject. Something I *can* talk to Rhonda about. "I finally got some information on our family," I start, then change my mind. That's not comforting, either. What would I say, exactly? That the Sylvans can intrude on other people's dreams, which is probably why the town hated them so much? That apparently I can do it, too, so it's definitely my fault she's lying in this hospital bed right now? No, I need to talk about something else.

"I, um, I stayed with Bethany last night. She introduced me to *The X-Files*. You used to watch the reruns with Dad sometimes, right?"

The curtain draws back, and a nurse sticks his head in. "Don't mind me. Just here to check vitals. Routine stuff."

I scoot over to give him room as he sets a garbage bag on the other chair. "These are your sister's clothes. Thought you might want to take them home with you, give them a good wash. Don't want them to get misplaced or anything like that." My chest tightens. They're expecting she'll be here a while.

He switches out the saline bag and examines Rhonda's monitor, jotting things down onto her chart.

"Was there a book with them?" I ask. "Brown, with a leather cover. A journal."

"With the clothes? Um, I wouldn't know, sorry. Wasn't my shift yesterday. But if it came here with her, it'll be in there."

"'Kay. Thanks."

I wait until he leaves, then take a peek through the sack. No book. But as I'm shoving Rhonda's jeans back down inside, something crinkles, and I yank them out again. A folded piece of paper has slipped halfway out of her pocket. It looks like another letter from the bank. Heart in my throat, I snatch it out and unfold it, then exhale in relief. It's from *our* bank. Dad's insurance has finally landed in our account. Thank God, something has gone right today.

Then the ache settles in. This isn't something that has "gone right." This is compensation for a lost life. Dad's monetary value as a person. *Your dad got killed while doing his job, and since we can't bring him back, here's some cash instead.* I know I should feel grateful. This is meant to take care of us, I get it. And I *am* grateful. But nothing feels "right" about it.

I fold it and slip it in my pocket. It doesn't matter. I doubt much will be left anyway after paying off Miriam's debt. If there's enough here to even do that. And besides, this isn't the only thing Rhonda had in her pocket. There's another crinkle as I lift Rhonda's jeans off my lap to stand up. Another bank statement?

I glance around instinctively, as if someone's going to reprimand me for going through my sister's jeans, then pull out a smaller slip of paper—yellow and lined, torn from a spiral notepad of some kind. Unfolding it reveals a string of numbers in a nearly illegible script. Definitely not Rhonda's handwriting. Hers is tidy and round. This is sharp chicken scratch.

Maybe she already went to the bank. Could this be an account number? But if she'd already gone to the bank, I would think she'd have deposited that check.

What were you up to yesterday, Rhonda?

Her chest moves slowly up and down, her monitor beeping at a steady rhythm. I refold the note and slip it in my pocket with the bank statement. Then I go through the rest of Rhonda's pockets to make sure I haven't missed anything else. Nothing there but lint.

"Gotta go." I give Rhonda a kiss on the cheek. "But I'll come back when I can. Love you."

I sweep through the curtain, mumbling, "'Scuse me," as a woman stops short to let me through. Fingers close tightly around my arm.

"Hey!" I jerk automatically and tug back in an unsuccessful attempt to free myself before recognition hits. The woman who's grabbed me, face stark, eyes hard, is Diane Petersen.

"What," Diane snarls at me, "are *you* doing here?"

My voice catches in my throat. I glance back at the curtain.

Diane's bony fingers dig deeper into my biceps as she reaches across me to take a peek inside. With a gasp, she releases my arm, whipping around to face me, eyes round with shock and disgust.

"Your own *sister*?"

"I'm a Sylvan, aren't I?" I answer quietly, rubbing my arm. "What else would you expect?" Swinging Rhonda's bag of clothes over my shoulder, I revel in Diane's stunned silence as I turn my back to her and shakily walk away. My lips twitch into something resembling an attempt at a satisfied smirk for the briefest of seconds before it's overshadowed by the stinging in my eyes.

CHAPTER 21

Bethany pauses while wiping down a table. The Roadhouse is empty, that dead couple of hours between lunch and dinner. I'm helping her clean up so she can take off a little earlier and we can go hang out.

"Maybe it's a safety deposit box number."

I already thought of that. I even dropped by the bank and asked if it looked like anything from their system, since I'd found it with a bank statement. They said it didn't. Googling didn't come up with anything that made sense, either. Just like everything else I've searched for in this town. Sometimes I feel like by moving here, I've entered some kind of void or traveled back in time.

"If it is, it's not for this bank. It's too long for a safety deposit box, anyway. I think." To be fair, I've never seen a safety deposit box, but I doubt that's what this is for.

"Hmm." Bethany pushes in a chair and moves on to the next table.

"What are you guys talking about?" Daniel strolls in from the kitchen, munching on a croissant.

"Don't lean on that table with your buttery fingers!" Bethany barks at him, but I detect a laugh behind it. "I just fuckin' cleaned it, gawd."

His eyes go wide, and he backs away. "Yes, ma'am. Sorry, ma'am."

Grinning, she throws a rag at him. "And help out."

"You gonna pay me to do your work for you?" He shoves the last half of the croissant in his mouth and bends to retrieve the rag he hadn't been prepared to catch.

Bethany ignores this question, answering his first one instead. "We're trying to figure out what this mysterious number Eva found is all about."

Great. I'd rather have kept this conversation between the two of us. She misses the dirty glance I shoot her way, but Daniel doesn't and now he's intrigued. Still chewing, he saunters over to where I'm cleaning, then audibly swallows his lump of masticated croissant.

"Lemme see." He holds out his hand, waggling his fingers. "I'm good with numbers."

"It's not a math problem or anything, just a random string of digits."

"Lemme see," he repeats. Casual, but insistent.

I retrieve the crumpled scrap of paper from my pocket. I regret telling Bethany about it now. What if it turns out to be something private? It's like our conversation about Cal's accident. She said not to tell anyone she'd told me about it. And then she went ahead and told Cal, anyway.

Word travels fast around here, I remind myself.

Daniel plops his rag down on the table and smooths the note out next to it.

"Huh. I think this is a case number or something." His

201

expression darkens as he looks it over, then his easygoing demeanor returns. It happens so quickly, I wonder if I imagined it.

"A case number? Like, a police case number?"

"Yeah."

"How do you know?"

"It's my dad's handwriting." He points out a double seven. A single line cuts across the middle, tying them together like two *t*'s. "It's terrible. Where'd you find this? Someone's probably looking for it."

"Her sister had it in her pocket," Bethany volunteers for me. This time she does catch my look and mouths, "What?" at me.

"I'm not even gonna ask why you were fishing around in your sister's pockets," Daniel says. "Gross."

I snatch it back from him. He gives me a mock-affronted look, which I ignore, along with that weird urge to apologize that I always get with him, and shove the paper deep into my own pocket for safekeeping. Then I get back to wiping down the last of the tables in my corner.

Daniel thinks for a minute, and again, I catch a flicker of darkness behind his eyes. Then it's gone. "I'll bet it's from when your tires got slashed. I wouldn't worry about it. If it was a big deal, Dad would've brought it up with you by now." He turns to Bethany. "Can I steal a Coke from your fountain machine?"

"Sure, consider it a free refill of your last fifty free refills. Tell my dad while you're back there that I'm almost done. We'll meet you outside in a sec." Then, once he's out of earshot, "As if he needs any more caffeine. I don't know how the fuck he even sleeps. And he could really use some, too. He's starting to act weird."

"Weird? Like, how do you mean?"

"Like . . . I don't know. Moody and kind of, like, not caring about anything at the same time, if that makes sense."

I have noticed that, but I don't know him nearly as well as she does. "He's probably scared," I tell her. It makes sense. "Scared to sleep, you know? I don't blame him. For all he knows, he could be next. You could be next. Cal could be next."

Bethany stops cleaning to stare at me. I bite my lip and focus on a stubborn sticky spot on the table.

"I hadn't thought about it like that," she says quietly. "Shit."

I scrub harder. I wish I could tell her. I could tell Riley. Could *have* told Riley. Riley could keep a secret. But Bethany . . . then again, when I opened up to Cal about my dreams yesterday, it didn't end so well. Even after everything else, after what he'd confessed to me.

I wonder if Cal was being serious when he said he doesn't dream. I hope so. Then, maybe he'll be safe. Is that how it works? Is the victim the dreamer, or is it the other way around? Or maybe he does dream, but he doesn't remember because it's all . . . dark. *Like a shadow.* An unwelcome suspicion pops into my head, making me sway on my feet. What if Jolee's right and it's *not* me doing this? What if I'm just a witness to someone else's darkness?

I take my feelings out on what looks like a lump of hard-ened barbecue sauce. Cal never did call to check on me last night, after I'd told him about my dreams. Even though he said he would. But that's fine, because I was busy hanging out with *his* best friends, pretending to watch *The X-Files* while trying to ignore the irony of it all. My dreams may very well be trapping other people into sleep. I'm Madrona's monster of the week.

It's strange sitting in the hotel room at night by myself. I keep glancing over at Rhonda's bed, expecting to see her there, reading. Bethany tried to convince me to stay in her room again, but her mom didn't seem to be on board with the idea. She said she was fine with it, but her face told me otherwise. She kept giving me strange looks this morning, too, when I came down with Bethany to breakfast. I'm getting the feeling Bethany's friendship is the only thing keeping her from kicking me out completely.

So I told Bethany thank you but I needed some time alone. Maybe I should have taken her up on it, though, because now that I *am* alone, my thoughts are taking me to some dark places.

I pull the cap off my pen with my teeth and write: *Dear Dad.* At least there's someone I can talk to.

My handwriting is frantic, scrawling. I'm sure my sentences aren't making any sense, but I don't care. That's not the point. I write and write, dumping every thought I have onto the page. *Why didn't you tell me, Dad? Didn't you know? Did you think by not telling me, you were protecting me somehow? Protecting me from my own dreams? Or from someone else's? Protecting me from this place? From this town? From the shadows?*

Shadows.

These dreams—they always end with a shadow. Not *just* a

204

shadow—it's something more than that. Not an absence of light, but a stealer of it. A thief. A thief of light, of day, of wakefulness, and I don't know how to stop it.

To stop . . . me.

It *must* be me, because everything about that shadow, everything I fear about it—the pain, the guilt, the anger roiling off of it—I've felt it all before. Feel it constantly. It's everything I've felt since . . . since that night. Everything I've kept locked inside me, hidden away in the shadows.

I stop and close my eyes, chewing the pen cap to a smashed, pockmarked mess. I'll never get it back on the pen now, and I don't care. What I care about is figuring out who might be next. If I know, maybe I can do something about it. What is it that brings each of my victims together?

I write down the first name. Rob. Was it because of the way he treated me when he realized who I was? But his daughter's been much worse, and she's still walking around, free to be as awful as she pleases. I have a fleeting hope that she'll be the one who's next. And then my stomach lurches. *What's wrong with me?* I spit out the pen cap, then take my head between my hands, pressing my palms into my temples, forcing the thought out before it can take shape. Before it can become another one of my avenging shadows.

Focus, Eva. Who was next? Troy. I write his name under Rob's, circling my pen around and around the *o* as I think. I'd barely met Rob, and the same goes for Troy. But I was angry with him from the start, even though I didn't know who he was at first. He was there when we arrived at the house, vandalizing it. And I'd witnessed him being an asshole to Cal. Twice.

But Chris was always there, too, and he's still awake. Maybe it was *supposed* to be Chris, and I mixed them up somehow. Troy is Chris's friend, and Chris is Rob's grandson. Maybe this has more to do with them than me. All three of them are connected. And then Charlie came next, and for all I know, he could also be connected to them in some way.

"But what about Rhonda?" I mutter, interrupting my own train of thought. Rhonda isn't connected to Rob at all. She never even saw him that day. And though she's the one who chased Chris and Troy off that night, she didn't know who they were at the time. She wasn't there when Daniel pointed out that Troy was the one who'd graffitied our house. My temper flares as I picture the phrase once again. *Ding-dong, the WITCH is DEAD.*

Long live the witch, I add in white-hot letters in my head.

The pen drops.

That's it. That's got to be the connection. Anger.

I was angry with Rob for treating me unfairly, solely based on my last name. I was angry with Troy for teasing Cal and for defacing my aunt's house with no respect for the dead. I was angry with Charlie—yes, I was—for trying to warn me away from my newfound friends. And for being so damn cagey and cryptic about the whole thing. And maybe Diane *will* be next, because I sure as hell am angry with her.

And Rhonda.

I was angry with Rhonda.

All day, I'd been angry with Rhonda. All week. All *month*. For acting on that deed when she found it in Dad's things. For dragging me out here, away from the only life I've ever known. For trying to be a replacement parent instead of the sister I need.

And I'm angry with her now, for leaving me all alone like this, stranded, in a town that doesn't want me, that's afraid of me because of who I am and what I can do.

I'm angry with Rhonda.

I'm angry with Dad.

I'm angry with Miriam.

I'm angry with *me*.

I'm angry.

ANGRY.

I write it over and over again on the page, pressing my pen into the paper until the letters rip through to the sheets below. The pulse of karaoke night vibrates up through the floor, reminding me of the night this all started, only a week ago. The bass beat emphasizes each stabbed period until that's all I'm doing— stabbing my pen into the pages because I'm so angry.

So! Angry!

I get in a few more stabs, then pick up my journal and fling it across the room. It sails over Rhonda's bed and hits the wall with a satisfying smack, falling to the floor on the other side of where Rhonda would certainly be sleeping right now *if she were here.*

Time stops. I sit and stare at the spot on the wall where it connected. Slowly, I heave in a lungful of air as a tear forms in the corner of my eye and stays there, refusing to fall.

"I'm sorry," I whisper. "Daddy, I'm sorry."

I rush around Rhonda's bed and crouch down. My mangled journal—my letters to Dad—lies splayed open on the floor, its pages bent and wrinkled. I curl them back the other way to straighten them, pressing my fingers against the creases and tears. It's not working, but I keep trying anyway, bending and pressing, bending and pressing, over and over again. As if fixing the pages will fix what I did. Fix *me*. But I don't know how to fix this. I don't know how to make it stop.

Finally, I give up. Rocking back and forth, hugging the journal to my chest, I allow myself to cry. No one will hear me over the karaoke below. No one will know. I cry until all my tears have run out, and when I open my eyes again, swollen and stinging, my gaze lands on my own impish face, grinning up at me, swaddled in Dad's jacket.

"You again." I retrieve the photograph from the carpet where it's escaped from the pages of my journal. "If only you knew then what you know now."

But what do I know now? Nothing. Not really. I flip the photo over and reread the note Miriam wrote on the back. *It's time to Dream Again, but be Wary, Evangeline, and Remember.* Remember what?

"Dawer, dawer," I mutter, recalling Cal's theory that the random capitals might not be so random after all.

"Dawer," I try again. "D*r*awer."

My hand shakes. How had I not caught that before? Both the *d* and the *r* in "dream" are capitalized. I probably didn't notice because, despite being capitalized, the *r* is the same height as the lowercase letters that follow. It would be easy to overlook as a quirk of Miriam's handwriting, except it's the only *r* besides the first *r* in "remember" that's written that way. All the rest are proper lowercase *r*'s. That can't be an accident.

Before I know it, I'm on my feet, my boots are on, and I'm out the door.

I need to go back to the house. I don't care how late it is. No one's around to stop me. I can do what I want.

My arms and legs break out in goose bumps as I speed through the dark, empty streets on Bethany's bike. It's the middle of July, but chillier at night than I'm used to. I'm still only in my tank top and boxer short pj's. I should have grabbed a jacket. Too late now.

Reaching the outskirts of town means leaving the streetlamps behind. I navigate through the pitch-dark by the dim, narrow beam of one of Charlie's flashlights, which I've made into a headlight by fastening it to the handlebars with a hair tie. No time to worry about what monsters roam the woods beyond that beam, what critters lurk in the grasses and weeds brushing against my ankles as I leave the smooth pavement of the highway and turn up the overgrown wilds of Fay Road.

It's time to Dream Again, but be Wary, Evangeline, and Remember. DRAWER.

There's something in a drawer that's going to help me remember something. Something about dreams. *Again.* It's time to dream *again.* Could it be that I've done this before? But when? In the back of my head, I worry I'm grasping at nothing. But nothing is all I've got. I need to find this drawer.

CHAPTER 22

There are a lot of drawers in this house.

I start in the kitchen because it has the most. And also, because I'm tired, and emotional, and not thinking very clearly. Why would she hide all the answers I need in the kitchen? Besides, I've been through all of these drawers before. I'm the one who cleaned them, so I'm pretty sure I would have found whatever it is already. But it's possible I overlooked something, especially if I didn't know there might be something to over-look. That's the main problem, isn't it? How do you find something when you have no idea what it is you're looking for?

By the light of one of Charlie's lanterns—better than the flashlight—I rummage through utensils and Tupperware lids, boxes of zip-top bags and aluminum foil, and random lost junk like screws and paper clips and ballpoint pens. All normal things you might find in kitchen drawers. Nothing that makes me think, *Ah, yes,* now *I remember. Now I know how to fix everything.*

I slide the last drawer shut with the creeping fear that this behavior isn't normal. I've been up all day, I haven't slept well in twice that long, and I've been left to my own devices so soon after losing my dad and moving across the country and . . . *This would be a very bad time to come unglued, Eva*, I tell myself.

I could have waited until the morning for this, I think as I poke around in the laundry room. It still smells sour, despite throwing out the mildewed clothes and bleaching the washer three times. *I could have—should have—slept first.* But sleeping equals dreaming equals people in the hospital. So, no. I'm doing exactly what I should be doing. Finding a drawer. With a thing in it. I hope.

The laundry room comes up empty, as does the attached bathroom. I wander through the rest of the downstairs, checking the drawers of a china cabinet, a desk, a bureau. Like a cat burglar, except a cat burglar usually has at least some idea of what they're after, and I still haven't the foggiest clue. I try to ignore the creaks and pops and shuffles of the old house—try to pretend I'm not unnerved by what might be lingering in the corners, just beyond the reach of the lantern light. In an abandoned house. In the middle of the woods. In the middle of the night. Where no one knows I've gone . . .

I pause at the bottom of the stairs, gazing up into the darkness above, having second thoughts. I haven't been up there yet. Not just tonight, but ever. Rhonda's been up there, but I've stayed anchored to the ground floor. That's weird, right? That's not like me, not to be curious. Not to explore.

But still, I remain fixed in place. It's colder in this spot. I shiver and rub my arms, trying to steel my nerves. The bedrooms are up there. Including Miriam's bedroom. Where she died. But . . . bedrooms have dressers, and dressers have drawers.

Okay. I can do this.

I take one shaky step up, then another. And the farther I go, the more I have to fight against this strange mental resistance, like pulling against a rubber band and dreading the inevitable snap. When I reach the top, I hold up my lantern, illuminating the hallway.

It feels older up here. Darker and danker. Cobwebbier. Floral wallpaper bubbles and peels around doorframes and hanging pictures. Black-and-white and sienna portraits of people I don't know.

My family.

Is this what I've been avoiding? I thought I wanted this. Hell, I'd hiked through the woods in a rainstorm just to see their graves. But cold, carved stone is one thing. Faces are another. Faces look back.

I feel dizzy, brushing my fingers along the yellowing flowers of the peeling wallpaper as I walk down the hall, taking in each photograph in turn. The clothing changes, the picture quality increases, but the family resemblances remain throughout them all. I see my dad's eyes in some, my angular face in others, and the sharp nose belonging to both of us in nearly all of them.

It feels . . . strange. I've never seen any pictures of any of my relatives before, on my dad's side *or* my mom's. Not even old pictures of my dad from before my parents' marriage—which wasn't long before I was born. I used to wonder if they would have married at all if it hadn't been for my impending arrival. I wondered what he saw in her in the first place, but I know better now. He saw someone he thought he could save. That's who he was. And though it didn't work out with her, he still did save someone. He saved her daughter Rhonda.

Now *I* need to save Rhonda. I need to stop looking at old pictures and find that drawer.

I've come to the end of the hall. Somehow, I've managed

212

to bypass all the doors along the way, distracted by the photos, and here I am, standing in front of the very last room. And—there it is again—that pushback. I can feel the resistance, like I did on the stairs. A prickling in my scalp, conjuring up dread. *Be wary, Evangeline.* Behind this door, I'll find what I'm looking for, whether I want to or not. I can feel it.

Slowly, I turn the knob and let the door swing open. The weak light from my lantern creeps into the room. I can make out the shape of a fluffy comforter on a four-poster bed, a nightstand with a lamp, and that's about it. But this is definitely Miriam's room. I don't know how I know it, but I do. This is her room, and that four-poster bed is where she spent her last moments. I know it in my gut, as if I were there.

I take a deep breath and try to shrug off my creepy thoughts. What if she *did* die in that bed? She isn't *still* in it. *Get in there, Eva. Go look.*

I take a tentative step inside. A hush falls over me as if I'm in a museum. Or a mausoleum. To my right is a vanity: old, oak, beautifully carved. It's adorned with what I think might be old bottles of perfume and cosmetics, and I doubt they've been used in years. Decades even, maybe. Gross. There's nothing in its drawer except more of the same. Double gross.

It occurs to me that Miriam's mind might have been going. Dementia maybe, or Alzheimer's. From the state of her house, the things she kept . . . her handwriting on the back of that picture. What if it isn't a clue at all? What if there is no drawer—just the disordered thoughts of an old woman grasping at memories as they fade away?

I'm so exhausted. The rush of emotions earlier, and the bike ride in the night air, and the search, this obsessive search—why am I searching at this hour? The bed that had me spooked a moment ago looks so inviting now. I'm tempted to curl up on it and rest, dust and all, until I remember again that its last occupant would have been Miriam's dead body.

My stomach jumps into my throat, and my legs twitch with the urge to run back out into the safety of the hall and call this a night. To go back to the Roadhouse, or even the couch downstairs, and collapse into much-needed sleep.

But I can't sleep. I'll dream if I sleep.

And I haven't checked the nightstand yet. But as I reach for the handle, the light from the lantern shifts, glinting off metal. Neatly arranged beneath the shade of the bedside lamp is a collection of small brass containers—about the size of lip-balm jars. I set the lantern down beside them and pick one up. They could actually *be* lip balm—just more old cosmetics from the vanity. Or maybe medication or something. *I'll probably regret this but* . . . I twist open the top, then quickly clap it back on when I catch a glimpse of something dark inside, twisted and crumbling. Not lip balm. Definitely not pills. I tighten the cap, then turn it in my hand looking for a label—something I probably should have done first. A sticker on the bottom has handwritten instructions. I recognize Miriam's tight cursive, matching the note on the photograph and the labels on the jam jars in the pantry.

1 pinch snuff
or
2 pinch tea

The other containers have similar labels. *2 pinch under tongue, 1 tsp gargle, 1 tsp smoke*. Smoke? What exactly was Miriam into? It's no wonder she had a heart attack. This looks like some seriously sketchy stuff.

But these aren't what I'm here for.

I replace the brass containers and slide open the nightstand drawer. "Please let this be it," I mutter to myself, hoping this strange midnight excursion will soon be over. That I haven't been sent on some wild-goose chase fueled by dementia or whatever the hell is in those containers.

Inside the drawer, I find an empty hot water bottle, a crossword puzzle book, tissue packets, and other odds and ends anyone would expect to find in an elderly woman's nightstand. No cryptic notes, no mysterious skeleton keys, no Pandora's box to provide the answers I'm looking for. Nothing.

"Damnit!" I shove the drawer closed, rattling the lamp shade and, without thinking, plop down onto the bed. A cloud of dust rises, sending me into a fit of sneezing and regret.

But once it settles, I notice something. The drawer face—it's too big. It isn't nearly that deep inside. And, now that I think of it, it felt clunkier and heavier than it should have as I slid it open.

I crouch down to examine it, opening it just enough to run my finger along the bottom and see if there's a lip, like the drawer's face was made larger for aesthetics or something. But there isn't one, and the inside is definitely shallower than the outside. With a flutter in my chest, I pull out the entire drawer and dump its contents on the bed, disturbing even more dust.

215

Flipped upside down, the bottom of the drawer remains intact, which means either it's nothing or the false bottom requires some trick to remove. I'm positive it's that last option, because the drawer still feels heavier than it should, even when emptied. I press, and pry, and tilt without any luck.

Then, moistening my lips, I flip the drawer upside down again and press along the edges of the bottom until, at the very back, it depresses with a click, then snaps up again—farther up. Heart beating with anticipation, I hook my finger into the gap and pry it open.

There, taped to the underside of the false drawer, is an envelope—a large yellow mailer stuffed full to nearly bursting. Written where the address should go, in Miriam's tidy, looped handwriting, is my name. And underneath that, a single word: *Remember.*

CHAPTER 23

"It's cold."

"I know, honey."

"I don't want to go in there. It's dark."

"You must."

"Why?"

"Because I can't. He won't let me. But he'll let you."

"Why?"

"Because I'm a scary old witch. And you're a harmless little girl."

"You're not scary."

"Thank you, honey. But to him, I am."

"And I'm not harmless."

"That's not your fault."

"Okay. I'll go in. And then what?"

"And then . . . find him. Figure out what's holding him there and bring him back out."

"That's it?"

"That's it."

There's a falling sensation and my body jerks, jolting me awake. I clutch at the papers as they threaten to slide from my chest and sit up, dazed. Where am I? What time is it?

The rest of the contents of the manila envelope are spread haphazardly across the coffee table. I add the letter I fell asleep with to the pile, my eyes scanning across the pages. Random sentences jump out at me, telling half a story.

It's a story about me, and I don't remember any of it. I've spent all night reading and rereading, trying to piece it all together, and I can't. I just can't. I have a sinking feeling that was by design. Dad wanted me to forget.

> *Here's a picture of Eva at the beach. She mentioned you while we were there. "I want to build a sandcastle as big as Mimi's," she said. It took me some questioning before I realized "Mimi" was you. I didn't know you were visiting her. Are you sure that's a good idea? So far, I haven't seen any evidence that she's inherited anything, but I'd rather not tempt it. I hope you understand.*

In a later letter, he's written:

> *The only way to break the cycle is to stop feeding it. Stop visiting her. Stop teaching her. This has gone too far. I don't want to lose her, too. You of all people should understand.*

Mouth dry, I check the date again. That one was written about five years ago—not long after Mom left.

Another letter, dated a month later, is short and to the point. It simply says:

218

Because another child is in danger, I'll allow it this once.
But only on one condition: As soon as she's finished helping
you, you help her. Help her forget again. Please. She's come
so far.

"Why?" I whisper. Has all of this happened before? Did I go on some kind of coma-inducing rampage when I was a little girl? And if so, how did I fix it? *Did* I fix it?

I feel ill.

And why letters? Did Miriam not have email? *Of course she didn't have email,* I remind myself. *Have you seen any computers around here? She didn't even have a TV.* She must not have had our phone number, either. Just a return address from the pictures Dad sent. I don't know why, but that makes me feel even more off-kilter. It's so strange. This entire situation is *so strange.*

I gather the letters, folding them exactly as they were. Tucking them back into their individual envelopes, exactly as they were. As if somehow, this will reverse everything. Return things to exactly how they were. Before the search, before the note, before the comas and the dreams. Before moving here. Before Dad died, before Mom left. I rubber-band them securely together again and pick up the yellow mailer to stow them away when something shifts inside it. It's still heavy. I missed something.

I return the letters to the coffee table and pry the mailer open. With the way my headlamp is positioned, it's hard to see inside and shine the light in at the same time, but it looks like . . . some sort of stick? In goes my arm, up to my elbow.

It feels like a stick. I fish it out and hold it up into the light. It *is* a stick—a thick section of branch, bent, notched, and broken.

And stained.

I let it drop. It hits my knee and clatters to the Persian rug, rolling under the coffee table.

It's sap. Just sap. It has to be.

Or maybe paint.

I take a breath and retrieve it, then dangle it between thumb and forefinger in the light. It's an awfully dark red for sap. And it doesn't look like paint, either. But it wouldn't be blood. It looks like blood, but of course it isn't *actually* blood, because why would Miriam put a bloodstained stick in an envelope filled with cryptic letters from my dad with a note on the outside telling me to remember, with *no explanation*? Nope, it couldn't be blood.

It really does look a lot like blood.

I can't think straight. I've barely slept in forty-eight hours.

And dawn is already creeping over the hedge outside Miriam's living room window.

I drop the disgusting stick into the mailer, then shove it and the letters into my backpack. Time to go.

I let Bethany's bike fall without bothering with the kickstand. Legs like rubber, I barely make it up the steps and into my room before I'm shrugging my backpack onto the floor and flopping down onto the bed. I can't sleep. I might put someone else into a coma. I can't sleep. I can't. But my head's *so heavy*. And my eyes . . . won't . . . stay . . . open. And the next thing I know . . .

. . . It's cold.

I can't see anything.

My head is throbbing.

Why is my head throbbing?

"Where am I?" I call out.

"Graham?" I hear. And then, when there's no answer, "Graham?!"

I take a step forward, lurching, and stumble into something. Someone hunched low. I can't see them, but I don't need to. I know who it is.

"Graham?"

"No." I crouch down, too.

Hands clasp mine, and slowly, as if my eyes are adjusting to the dark, a young boy comes into focus. Except my eyes can't really be adjusting, because he's all I can see.

"Who are you? I know you," he says.

I shake my head. "You don't. But you will."

He nods resolutely, as if he knows what I mean. I don't even know what I mean. Not on the surface. And yet, somehow, some part of me knows what I'm doing. Remembers.

"We have to go," I tell him.

"But . . . Graham," he says.

"Graham's not coming. I'm sorry. He had somewhere else to go."

The boy stares at me. I drop one of his hands and tug a little on the other, but he tugs back.

"No, he's here. He's here somewhere." Still holding

my hand, he turns. "I have to—" And then he's cut off
as the ground beneath us gives way and we sink, then
fall.

    We fall,

            and fall,

                    and fall.

    Clasping each other's hands, tumbling in the
pitch-darkness until it no longer feels like falling,
but floating, weightless in the void. And still, all I
can see is myself and the boy. And two glimmering,
shimmering threads stretching out from us, twisting
together as we tumble. Those are our lifelines, those
threads, and they will show us the way home. I don't
know how I know it, but I do. I remember.

    "Pull," I say, indicating the threads.

    "But Graham . . ."

    "Pull!"

    He won't do it. Not as long as he continues to look
for Graham. So, I do it for both of us, pushing down
the doubt. I grab hold of both threads, feel the energy
surging through them—so strong for how thin they are.
Nearly microscopic yet still visible to my dreaming eye.
I grab hold and I pull and—

I gasp in air, as if I've been holding my breath in my sleep.
Maybe I have. I can still feel the remnants of the tug to my
insides and look down at my stomach expecting to see the thin
silvery line stretching off into nothingness. Instead, I see the

short knot of my drawstring pajama shorts and, upon scanning farther down, my boots, still on my feet.

Panic hits me—I was sleeping. I was dreaming! Who was it? Who did I dream about this time? There was a boy there . . . but where was the shadow?

I don't think there was one. No attack, either. I relax. This dream felt different than those. More like a memory. Or a memory of a memory. And then it hits me—there was no shadow because *everything* was shadow. The boy was my only source of light. And the boy was looking for Graham.

Remember.

The tugging sensation twists into a gurgle. Turning to check the clock, I find I've slept through both breakfast and lunch. It's nearly three in the afternoon. I was going to visit Rhonda this morning. Crap.

I stumble over to the kitchenette and grab a banana. It's green toward the top, but I wolf it down, anyway, then change into a fresh tank top and my denim shorts from yesterday. Paper crinkles in the pocket as I pull them on. The note! Almost forgot about that.

I glance over at the spot where I'm positive I'd stacked those missing journals before Cal and I left to follow the ambulance to the hospital. *Not missing. Stolen.* Then, I think back to Rhonda's urgency on the phone. Her insistence on waiting until she could speak with me in person. And now I have this weird note from her pocket of what is, according to Daniel, a case number of some kind? I think he's wrong about the tires. Sure, his dad said he'd look into it, but I don't think he ever opened an official case. He was in too much of a hurry to get us out of there. Weirdly in a hurry. Could he be hiding something?

I run my fingers through my hair, pull my boots back on, and head out the door. The only way to find out what this number's for is to ask. Visiting Rhonda will have to wait.

CHAPTER 24

W hoa! What's the hurry?"

I come to a screeching halt outside the police station, narrowly missing Daniel as he steps onto the curb. He leaps backward out of the way, coffee splashing from his to-go cup.

"Shit, I'm so sorry! You okay?"

Fumbling, he switches hands so he can suck the scalding liquid off his wrist. "What's the hurry?" he tries again, muffled.

I hesitate. If I tell him, he might ask the reason. But his green eyes are fixed on mine with genuine concern, and I can't come up with any other excuse as to why I'd be rushing to the police station on a borrowed bicycle. And then I feel guilty about wanting to come up with an excuse in the first place. "I need to see your dad."

He wrinkles his brow. "Something happen?"

"I . . . Maybe? I'm not sure."

"All right." He pauses, then says, "I'm heading in to see him, too. I'll get you past the front desk."

"Thanks," I tell him, though I'd rather be doing this alone. I follow him up the steps, waiting while he takes a sip of his coffee before opening the doors.

"Hey, Sonya. She's with me," he tells the policewoman at the front desk. She nods, then goes back to typing on her computer.

I continue following Daniel into the main office and stand behind him while he knocks on his dad's door, then opens it without waiting for an answer. I get a strong whiff of musty papers and stale cigarettes and have to take a step back. I had no idea Chief Burke was a smoker. He looks up from hunching over a bulky file.

"Hey." He sounds tired. Looks it, too. "Danny. I was about to send Sonya after you." His gaze shifts to me hovering in the background. "Oh. Hi there, Eva. To what do I owe the pleasure?"

"Hi," I say, still hanging back. I'd prefer to talk to him alone.

"Well? What can I do for you?" He beckons both of us in, then sweeps his hand toward the chairs opposite his desk. "Hanging in there? Been to see your sister today?"

Daniel opts to take a seat in another chair tucked off in the corner. I catch his eye and shrug, trying to convey to him that I'd like to speak with his dad privately. But either he's not understanding me or he's choosing to ignore me. I suspect the latter. His face shows boredom, but he's leaning far forward in his chair, clearly curious.

"So, um." I swallow and glance at Daniel again, who's still not taking the hint. "Um, I found this note. And I think it might be a case number?"

Daniel's chair creaks as he shifts in his seat. I hand the tightly folded paper across the desk to his dad. A line forms between Chief Burke's brows as he unfolds it and gives it a once-over.

He clears his throat. "Dan, could you give us a minute, please?"

"Yessir," Daniel mutters, his face reddening as he gets up

and shuffles out of the room. The door closes mercifully behind him with a click. *Finally.*

Chief Burke eyes the door suspiciously, then pokes at the note with his finger. "Where'd you find this?"

"My sister had it."

"It's not a case number."

"It's n—"

"It's the file number for an autopsy report."

I take a moment to process this. Why would Rhonda be carrying around the number for an autopsy report? I think back to her phone call, replaying it in my head. She was upset that she didn't know where I was. She was upset about Charlie. But then she got *really* upset when I told her I was with Cal. Weirdly upset. She hadn't had any issues with him before. And she needed to speak to me, but not where Cal could hear my end of the conversation. She needed to speak to me about those journals *alone.*

"Wh—who is it for?"

Graham. The answer flashes into my head before Chief Burke can say it. My dream. The boy was searching for Graham. Because Graham died. And . . . Charlie—it was Charlie who mentioned his name while warning me about my new friends. He must have said something to Rhonda at some point, too. *You're alone? With a boy you barely know?* Did she suspect Cal had something to do with it? Like, on purpose? Bile threatens to rise from the base of my throat. He couldn't possibly. He's not like that. But then again, according to Bethany, Cal was a *very* different person before the accident. Maybe he . . . maybe he . . . I can't complete this thought, because if I do, I will absolutely vomit, right here, all over Chief Burke's paperwork.

"It's for Miriam," Chief Burke answers.

I jerk involuntarily. "Miriam?"

Not Graham. Not Graham at all. And not Cal. Thank God. But my sigh of relief gets caught in my chest, because *Miriam?* Why? We already know how Miriam died. The estate lawyer told us.

Chief Burke must be able to read my expression because he bobs his head in agreement. "I know. Doesn't make sense, does it? Miriam's death was cut-and-dried. But your sister was pretty worked up about it, so I looked up the number, wrote it down." He cocks his head. "But then I remembered, your sister isn't a blood relation of Miriam's. Legally, she doesn't have any rights to the report."

My jaw tightens. I can imagine how well that must have gone over. Also, I don't think that's a thing. Is it? I'm fairly sure it's not. She's still *legally* family. Dad adopted her. Blood shouldn't have anything to do with it. It sounds more like an excuse. But why wouldn't he want Rhonda to see the report?

"And then, somehow, this note"—he thumps it with his finger and gives me a pointed look—"disappeared off my desk."

So, Rhonda wasn't buying it, either. She knew something. And I think Chief Burke does, too. It feels very much like he's hiding something. And I want to know why.

I press the soles of my boots hard against the wood floor as I sit up straighter in my chair. "Well," I tell him, "*I'm* a blood relation. And I'd like to see the report."

He pauses, then offers me a wan smile. "Of course." With a groan, he pushes himself to standing and takes the note over to a filing cabinet. "I figured you'd also be around asking for it at some point, so I went ahead and printed it out. It's not that interesting, though. Pretty straightforward."

My breath hitches as I catch sight of a stack of unmarked leather-bound books peeking out among the clutter behind where he was sitting. Are those the journals? Buried under paperwork and other books, I can't tell for sure. He's turned away from me, sifting through files. If I can just lean forward far enough, I might be able to—

"Your sister got this idea in her head somehow that Miriam's death was, well . . . not entirely natural."

My eyes dart up to meet his back. "Not natural?"

"That was how she put it. But . . ." He pauses to yank out a thick file, closes the cabinet drawer, and places the file on the desk, smack on top of the one he'd already had open. "As you've no doubt already been informed, your great-aunt Miriam passed away in her sleep of natural causes."

He flips it open and sifts through the pages. "Let's see. Here it is. Standard autopsy. Says here, she died of . . . yup, a ruptured brain aneurysm. As I'm sure you already knew."

Hairs rise on the back of my neck. "An aneurysm?"

"Yes," he says, tilting his head. "Was that not what you were expecting?"

"We—" I hesitate. Why would we have been lied to? Or is he the one lying? "We were told she'd had a heart attack."

He frowns and scans down the page. "Ah." His eyebrows go up. "Yes, it appears she had a heart attack *and* a ruptured brain aneurysm." He shudders, but his tone doesn't match this senti- ment. His voice is tight. Like he's growing impatient with me.

"One must have triggered the other." He flips the folder closed. "Still, not murder."

My entire body goes cold. *Not murder.* According to him, Rhonda didn't ask about murder. The way he's jumped from "not natural" to specifically "not murder" isn't sitting right.

"My grandma—" I pause, not sure where I'm going with this, but I know I'm going somewhere. "Dad's mom—she also died of a brain aneurysm. Aren't they supposed to be kind of rare?"

"Hmm." He tosses the file on the stack of paperwork behind him. Right on top of the pile covering what I'm positive now are the journals. "Might run in the family, then," he says. "Perhaps you should get your head checked."

"That's . . . that's not—" I take a shaky breath and try again. "That's not funny."

"Neither are you and your sister's misuse of my time."

Heat returns to my face and neck. Who is this? What happened to Mr. Sensitive Officer I'm-Here-For-You? Something isn't right. The stack of journals, half-hidden behind him, taunts me. I want to grab them—dash behind him, grab them, and run. Maybe I should. *Assertive. Be assertive.* But assertive doesn't mean stupid. None of this is right.

I try to keep my voice steady, but internally, I'm a quivering mess. "Rhonda wouldn't have come to you with a suspicion like that without a *very* good reason."

He goes quiet. And very still. I tense, preparing to get kicked out.

"I'm sorry," he says instead. He takes another moment to regroup, closing his eyes and pinching the bridge of his nose.

Then with an exhale, "I didn't mean to snap at you. You've got to understand, I'm dealing with a very stressful situation right now. Word's spreading about what's happening here, you know, with the comas. I've got panicked people calling at all hours, wanting to know what's going on, what I'm gonna do about it. As if there's anything I *can* do. Hell, I'd just finished a conference call with the CDC and the DOH before you and Dan came in here. You know they're considering putting this entire town under quarantine?"

I shake my head. Maybe . . . maybe I should tell him. Maybe I should tell him, and they can put *me* under some kind of quarantine instead. It's me. I'm the problem. Not some virus.

"But then, of course you've got your own stuff going on," he continues. "You have your sister to worry about. And so soon after . . . jeez, after—" He cuts himself off with another exhale, his hand fluttering up to his chest.

My dad, I finish in my head. My fingers curl into the underside of my seat. *So soon after my dad.*

"And here I am complaining about phone calls. Look, if you . . ." He pauses, choosing his words. Here it comes. "If you need to, you know, talk to someone about all of this, just to, uhhh . . . sorta sort things out, I can recommend a wonderful—"

"I don't need a therapist," I say a little too sharply. He thinks I'm cracking under the stress. That I'm being paranoid. Just like Cal thinks. But I'm not being paranoid. I'm not. And besides, I've seen a therapist before. This is not something a therapist could help me with.

He holds his hands up. "Okay. But who's taking care of you? Who are you staying with? Do you need—"

"I'm fine. I don't need anything." I take a breath, forcing temporary calm, then stand.

"You sure about that?"

"I'm good. Really."

I can see the protest forming. The parental-like concern kicking in. I back toward the door, feeling behind me for the knob. "I gotta go. I'm—I'm sorry for wasting your time."

His face falls, and I know my words have hit their mark. I almost feel guilty about it. But I just want to get out of here before he starts trying to set me up with foster care or something. I finally find the handle and open the door. Daniel steps aside to let me by. Crap. I forgot about him. Has he been standing there the entire time? How well does sound travel through oak?

"Everything okay?" he asks. He moves as if he's going to accompany me out.

"Wait just a second, Danny," his dad calls out from behind his desk. "Don't think you're getting out of that talk you owe me."

Daniel sighs. "I hate it when he calls me that. Catch up with you later." He smiles and winks—or was that an eye twitch?—then slips past me through the doorway, clicking it shut behind him.

I took so long talking to Chief Burke that it's too late to go to the hospital now. Visiting hours will be over soon, so I call to check in with the nurse's station instead. No change for Rhonda. Still fast asleep. No degradation of her condition, but no signs of waking up, either. About what I expected. Still, I feel guilty for not being there in person.

I wish I could tap into Rhonda's subconscious via the phone and ask her what it was she'd read in those journals. What did she see that would cause her to go to Chief Burke and ask for Miriam's autopsy report? If I knew how to dream about her on purpose, I'd ask her that way. Then again, if I could dream about her on purpose, I'd wake her up. Maybe. I don't know how I caused her to fall into a coma in the first place. What makes me think I would know how to pull her back out once there?

Pull . . . The thought pricks at my subconscious. I feel a residual tightness in my abdomen, a tug. As if pulled on by a rope—no, a string. *Or a thread so thin it's barely there, shining like silver in the dark. Two of them, twisted together.*

I shake my head. There's too much. Too many puzzle pieces, and I can't make sense of them all. I wish I had *someone* I could talk to about this. Someone who could help me order my thoughts. Someone who wouldn't hate me, or be afraid of me, or think I've lost all sense of reality. I'm reminded ruefully of how even Cal, when I opened up, when I let down my guard for that brief moment of panic in the truck—even he thought I was losing it. Maybe I am losing it.

I miss having someone I can tell anything to without being judged. *You're not bananas,* I can hear Riley saying to me right now, as if she were here. *I'm the bananas one, remember? No way I'm handing over that title so easily.* My fingers itch for my phone. God, it would be great to hear her voice again. A little bit of home.

Riley was the one person I could tell anything to. It was only when I stopped—

My throat constricts as I remember *why* I stopped. There are some things that cannot be expressed. Not adequately. Not right away. Not even now. That was the one thing Riley could never understand. She thought I was pushing her away, when all I needed was time, and space, and my family.

But maybe there *is* one other person I can talk to. I'm just not sure I want to, after the last time ended with me running away in an angry panic. But she's the only one who knows— *really* knows. And the only one who might have some idea what Miriam was trying to tell me.

I rest my hand on my phone, hesitate, then, with a steadying breath, pick it up and call.

Jolee answers on the first ring. "I'll see you in about fifteen minutes, all right? I just need to finish closing up."

My breath catches, and I wonder if maybe she's been expecting a call from someone else. "I—I haven't told you who this is," I manage to stammer out.

"Oh. Right. Sorry, I get that backward sometimes. Let's start again. Hello? Who's calling?"

Is she serious, or is she making fun of me? Maybe this isn't such a good idea after all. "It's . . . Eva. Eva Sylvan."

"Eva! I was wondering when you'd be calling. I'll see you in fifteen minutes. Oh! And bring those letters. All right, see you soon." *Click.*

CHAPTER 25

B efore I give you these," I say, hugging the bundle of letters to my chest, "I want to know how you knew about them."

I'm sitting at Jolee's kitchen table again with another cup of tea and the same package of Oreos, but emptier.

"Didn't you tell me?" Jolee sets her teacup down. "Ah, yes, all right. As I said, sometimes I get these things backward. Or did I not say that, either? That's the problem. Sometimes I'm not sure what I've said and heard out loud, and what I've picked up on intuitively."

I hug the letters tighter. "So, you're psychic?"

Up until a few weeks ago, I never believed in any of that stuff. But after the last time—*you're holding on to so much guilt*— I've had a suspicion.

"I'm a little psychic, yes. Some days more than others. Didn't I say? Must not have. But that's why Miriam and I got along so well. We understood each other more than anyone else could."

"So, you can, like . . . read minds? Can you do the whole dreaming thing, too?" I have a flicker of hope that she can, and that she can teach me how to control mine. But wouldn't she have said so the last time? Unless she thought she had but had really only told me in her head.

"Oh, no. I'm sure the Sylvans aren't the only telepathic

dreamers out there—that would be bizarre, wouldn't it? But I'm not able to do that. And I wouldn't say I can *read* minds exactly, either. It's more that I can pick up on emotions, and if the emotion is strong enough, sometimes—not often, mind you—I'm able to put an image to it. Those letters must have been very strong on your mind for me to pick up on them over the phone like that. There are a lot of things strong on your mind right now, so it's all a bit confusing. But for the splittiest of split seconds, the letters must have been the strongest. So." She holds out her hand and makes a *gimme* motion with her fingers. "May I?"

"Please be careful with them." I hand them over, and she peels off the rubber band. "They're very important to me."

"Mm-hmm." She nods, taking an initial glance through the pages. "Of course they are. They're from your father." Then she goes silent except for the occasional "hmm" and "huh" as she reads through each page.

I curl and uncurl my toes in my boots, clench and unclench my jaw, fiddle with my knuckles—until I accidentally pop one, eliciting an irritated glance from across the table. I'm uncomfortable letting someone I barely know read Dad's words. These words weren't even meant for me, much less public consumption. Worse, they're *about* me.

She puts the last letter down and pats the papers gently with her hands as if to smooth them out. Or maybe to calm them down. With her, it's hard to tell. Then she slides them back across to me and folds her hands in her lap.

"And do you remember any of it? What he's talking about?"

"Nope. None of it."

Her brow furrows. "Are you sure? Perhaps you do, but you don't know you do."

"Well, it would help to know the context." If only I had the other half of these letters—the ones Miriam must have written back to him.

"Hmm," she says again.

She munches on an Oreo while she thinks, then washes it down with a sip of tea. "Sounds to me like Miriam was helping you hone your dream telepathy skills. Your father probably didn't like that because that's how he lost his mother, poor soul."

The aneurysm in her sleep. And Miriam's, too. "Rhonda figured it out," I mutter to myself.

Now it's Jolee's turn to be confused. "Come again? I'm sorry, you have so many things in your head right now, I'm having trouble parsing them."

I close my eyes to regroup, then, after a moment, I tell her. I tell her everything up through my disconcerting visit with Chief Burke. I tell her about the autopsy report, and the missing journals, and how Rhonda had been reading them.

"I spoke with her on the phone just before the, um, the dream. She said she needed to talk to me in person about something she'd read in those journals—but she wouldn't tell me what it was. She was really upset." *Because she was scared.* It's obvious now. Rhonda gets angry when she's scared. I should have picked up on that. She'd already lost Dad, and now she was scared she was going to lose me, too. That's what she was dreaming about, except in the dream, I was already lost.

"I think," I say, blinking back the sting in my eyes, "I think she was looking for the autopsy report because of whatever it was she read in those journals."

At my mention of the journals again, Jolee claps her hands together, a wistful gleam in her eyes. "You know, they must have been the dream journals! I haven't thought about those in years! Miriam and I used to sneak down to the basement when we were kids and read through them, looking for juicy gossip and embarrassing little tidbits about everyone in the town. Of course, we kept everything we learned to ourselves," she assures me. "They go way back, you know. All the way to when the town was founded. Before that, even. There was practically a whole wall of them."

She finally notices my expression—or maybe she starts picking up on my thoughts or emotions or something again because that nostalgic glow drains from her face. "They've gone missing?"

"Well, some of them. Not an entire wall's worth. Just Miriam's, I think. I never got a chance to look inside them. But I don't think you're understanding me. These letters"—I stab at them with my finger—"were cherry-picked and left, *hidden in a false-bottomed drawer*. For me. Like . . . like Miriam knew something was going to happen to her. And—and—" I fish around in my backpack and pull out the photo with Miriam's note on the back. "And she wrote me this note to lead me to that drawer, and Jolee . . ."

I'm starting to piece things together now as I'm saying them out loud. I reach into my backpack again, pull out the mailer that originally housed the letters, and turn it upside down over the table. Jolee jumps as the stick slides out and rocks back and forth, settling into place on the letter pile, barely missing her teacup.

"The letters were with this bloody stick."

"Well, there's no need to swear," she says.

"No, look at it."

She looks at it, then looks at me over the top of her glasses. Slowly, she pushes her chair out from the table, grabs a pair of dish gloves from the sink, and puts them on. Then, the same as I did, she picks up the stick by its very end between forefinger and thumb and holds it up in front of her face, turning it this way and that.

"Well, that's rather gruesome. Miriam, Miriam, Miriam, why-ever would you keep such a thing?" She takes it over to the kitchen window to examine it in natural light. "That does look like blood, doesn't it? Old blood. Hmm."

"I'm starting to agree with Rhonda," I tell Jolee as she scowls at the stick. "I think Miriam knew something she wasn't sup-posed to know. And I think it has something to do with me. In this last letter"—I pick it up—"Dad's giving her permission to have me help her with something. What if I know whatever it is Miriam knew, too, but forgot? Or what if—what if I *did* some-thing? What if I did *that*?" I point at the stick as Jolee gently returns it to the table and removes her gloves.

Without a word, she reaches across the table and snatches Dad's last letter from my hands, then takes it out into the living room.

I shove my chair back, scraping it along the floor, and hurry after her. "Didn't you hear what I said?"

"Of course I heard you. It was hard not to." It's not in anger but in a stoic, nonchalant kind of way that only serves to irritate me. "It got me thinking, that's all."

She doesn't stop in the living room but bids me to take a seat on the sofa while she disappears down the hall, Dad's letter tucked under her arm. I hear some rummaging around, and some grunts, and soon she reappears hefting a large paper file box. *Mad Gaz* is scribbled on the side in permanent marker. With an *oof*, she thumps it down between the couch and the coffee table, barely missing my foot. Then she takes a seat and pulls off the lid. The box is crammed full of newspapers, divided into tabbed folders by month.

"You save newspapers?" I didn't think anyone got physical copies of newspapers anymore.

"Just the *Madrona Gazette*," she says, checking the date at the top of the letter. "When you sell antiques, old newspapers can help put items in context." She walks her fingers along the tabs in the box until she comes to one labeled for May through June of five years ago. The same time Dad's last two letters were written.

"But how will five-year-old newspapers help you with antiques?" I ask.

"Well, they won't *now*. But someday, they might. Glad I saved them, too," she continues as she works to tug the file loose. "The *Gazette*'s building burned down a few years ago, taking their entire physical archives with it. They have the more recent years online, fortunately, but—call me old-fashioned—if I'm going to pay for something, I'd prefer to be able to hold it in my own two hands."

"Yeah. I got blocked by their paywall," I commiserate. I wish I'd known Jolee had these earlier when I was searching for information about Graham. Is that article in this box, too?

240

It must be. Is it the one she's looking for? I lean forward with apprehension.

Finally, the file comes loose. She sets it on the couch cushion between us, then shifts to face me.

"I never thought Miriam's death was a fluke." Her eyes pierce mine. "But you. Did. Not. Do. It. Do you understand?"

I can feel the burn in my nose and eyes as my tear ducts threaten to do their stuff. I can't deny that very fear has popped up. More than once. And she saw it. Chest tight, I maintain eye contact. "Do you know who did?"

"I do not. Do you?"

I shake my head.

"Are you *sure*? Somewhere in there"—she swirls her finger in the air around my forehead—"lies all the info."

"What's in those newspapers?"

"Hopefully, a clue."

Chapter 26

It's late. The sun has dipped below the hills on the other side of the valley, and the long, slow summer twilight is creeping in. It's dark enough that half the streetlights have turned on, and light enough that the other half have not.

I hardly notice any of it. My mind is on overdrive, and my body needs to move. I don't even know where I'm going. I just go.

But I'm also exhausted. My adrenaline can only take me so far. Silent tears stream down my face. Wiping them away, I stumble over a crack in the sidewalk and slow my pace.

I wish Miriam's will had never been found. I wish Dad had taken our mom's name when he married her so no one would know who I am. I wish we were still in New York and I didn't know what I know now. Had never known what I know now.

And yet, I still know *nothing*.

I stop on the sidewalk in front of a house with white siding, black shutters, a freshly mowed front lawn, and an old blue Chevy parked in the driveway. There's a light on in the front room, pierced with the unmistakable blue flickering of a television set.

Is Cal the one watching it? Or has he been banished to his room? That seems extra harsh, so probably not. What if

I feigned ignorance and knocked on the door? Then maybe I could explain things to his parents and . . . and to him, and . . .

But then I remember the last time Cal and I spoke. His big blue eyes, drawing me out, inviting me to open up, and then me responding with what must have sounded like complete nonsense. This is going to sound even worse. *Hi, Cal,* I practice in my head, *you know how I told you I dreamed about each coma victim? Well, guess what?*

The sound of rumbling, then the slam of a gate stops me mid-thought. I scurry out from under the streetlamp as a dark, shadowy figure comes around the corner of Cal's house, pushing a garbage can out to the curb. I'd better get out of here before I'm caught creeping. What else would this look like? As I turn to leave, the rumbling stops.

"Eva?"

I take a steadying breath and pivot back.

"Oh, hey," I say, trying to sound casual, as if this was some random coincidence and I wasn't, in fact, staring at his house. *He's not stupid, Eva.*

Cal finishes pushing the can to the curb, then, after a glance toward the front window, jogs the short distance over to me. "What are you doing here?"

"I was, um, I was just out for a walk."

"All the way to my house?" He flashes me a confused smile.

I shift from one foot to the other. "Not on purpose."

His smile fades, and I want to kick myself.

"Well, it might have been on purpose. I just didn't . . . know? . . . It was on purpose?" No, that's worse. *Damnit, Eva.*

"I—" And there are those stupid tears, collecting in the corners. Shit, shit, shit. I sniff to keep them in check.

He looks back at his front window again. The flickering from the TV has stopped, and there are shadows of movement behind the curtains. "It's okay. Stay. Please? And I'll— Actually, wait over *here*." I let him lead me into the shadows around the corner of his house. "I'll be right back. Okay?" His eyes lock onto mine, urging me not to take off.

I nod; then he disappears through the gate, slamming it shut behind him, harder and louder than necessary. Angrily?

I thought for a minute there we were okay, but I guess not. He's still pissed. He's grounded because of me after all. And here I am, showing up after dark all teary-eyed. More proof I'm a disaster. He probably only wants me to stay so he can come back out and tell me so.

I'm considering breaking my promise and leaving, when there's a metallic squeak. Cal carefully undoes the latch and opens the gate again, just a sliver. The toe of a tennis shoe peeks through, nudging a small rock into the crack to prevent the gate from closing again. "I'll be right back," he whispers.

I let out a breath.

Cal's footsteps rustle through the grass of his backyard. I hear the sound of a back door rumbling open, then shut. And I wait, leaning against the side of the house, tucked safely in the shadows out of view from the street, praying he won't get caught sneaking out again to talk to me.

What, exactly, am I going to tell him? I hadn't intended to come here. It just happened. I haven't prepared. I haven't even fully processed everything I've learned tonight. I still don't know what to think. *Or what it might mean.*

"Hey," Cal whispers, startling me. A shiver runs down my arm as he brushes up against it while squeezing through the crack in the gate. "Let's go."

"Where?"

"Just down a few blocks. To the cemetery."

"You serious?"

"Yeah, it's quiet there. You scared?" he asks, picking up on my hesitation.

Kind of. But not for the reason he thinks. "Did you forget I'm moving into the 'Witch House'?"

He snorts as he suppresses a laugh. "Good point. Come on," he says, heading for the sidewalk. I sprint a few steps to catch up, then settle into pace beside him.

Okay, so maybe he's not mad at me. He actually sounds kind of giddy. Or relieved. And then it hits me. All this time I've been thinking he's pissed at me, he must have thought I was pissed at him. And I was, a little. Maybe he was a little with me at first, too.

I still think it's weird to build a neighborhood around a cemetery, but at least we don't go far inside—just past the barrier of trees to a stone bench. It's a nice spot, actually. Surprisingly un-creepy, and still plenty dark. Most importantly, we're completely alone and likely to stay that way. Cal must have sensed that was important. Now I understand why he chose this spot. No one to overhear or eavesdrop through an open window. And dark-ness to hide my face.

But if he can't see my face well, maybe he can't picture it well, either. Like when he closes his eyes, like he told me. He can't see me in his mind. Not the current me, anyway. I resist the urge to grab his hand, as if otherwise he might forget me completely, though I know that's not true. Besides, our eyes will adjust to the dark soon enough. But then he takes hold of my hand instead, and its warmth melts away all my apprehension.

"I've been worried about you," he says. "I'm sorry I haven't been able to call. I wanted to, but they took my phone, and—"

"It's okay," I stop him. I don't want apologies. I want to believe him. I choose to believe him. To trust him. "How much longer are you grounded for?"

"Just through the weekend. But I might not get the keys to my truck back for a while. And, um." His hand squeezes mine. "My parents don't—" He swallows. "They don't want me hanging around you anymore. Not that they can stop me," he's quick to add.

The only thing surprising about this is that I'm not surprised. I guess in the back of my mind, I'd suspected as much. Still, it stings. And . . . "Honestly? Maybe they're right."

His fingers twitch against the back of my hand. "Don't do that."

"I found out some things today."

He inhales deeply. "This isn't about those dreams again, is it? Because that's just a—just a—" He stops and regroups. "You're letting people get to you."

So, he may not be mad at me, but he still thinks I'm being irrational. Awesome. This is going to suck. "Listen, okay? It's like this—you know how you told me you thought I looked familiar? From that picture?"

"It wasn't just that you looked familiar. I actually remembered your face."

"Right. And I blew you off. That must have felt pretty crappy. Being so sure about something, finally getting up the courage to tell me about it, then having me dismiss it like that."

He shifts next to me on the bench. "I'm listening."

Good. Still, I have to restrain myself from gripping his hand with both of mine to keep him from taking off. Here we go.

"You know how you thought that message on the back of that picture of me was a code?" His hand twitches again, ever so slightly. "You were right. And it led me to some old letters Miriam had kept for me, hidden away in a drawer. They were from my dad. And yes, okay, they were about dreams—my dreams."

I pause to give him a chance to respond. He remains silent, waiting for me to finish. At least he's still listening.

"In the last letter? My dad gave Miriam permission to have me help her with something. He didn't say what, except that it involved another kid. The letter was from June. Five years ago."

I can hear Cal's breath beside me, in and out, in short, shallow bursts. But still, no words.

"Cal," I coax. "What day did you wake up from your coma?"

His hand jerks free from mine. He stands up. *He's taking off,* I think. *I went too far.* But no—he's pacing.

"According to the local paper, it was June 13. Five years ago," I answer since he won't. "Cal, listen to me. I found out what it is the Sylvans do." I'm speaking louder now, stronger. I need him to really hear this. To really understand. "I know why I've been having those dreams, and I know why you remembered me—the younger me—from that picture."

Still no response. Just more pacing.

"Say something. Please?"

I stand up, too, and the pacing stops. His back is toward me. I can't read him, here in the dark, with his face turned away. I can't read him like he can't picture me. Right now, in this moment, is he angry? Sad? Is he . . . processing? Thinking?

"It's not you," he finally says. His voice doesn't sound right. Lower, a little husky. Almost . . . ominous.

Goose bumps form on my arms and legs. "What do you mean?" My voice doesn't sound right, either. Like something's caught in my throat. What does he mean, it's not me? He couldn't be about to tell me . . . No, he can't be about to say it's him. I can't pretend my mind hasn't gone here before, but every time the suspicion pops up, I'm quick to push it down. I don't want to think it. Yet he sounds so sure it's not me, I can't help but wonder why. *He was in a coma, Eva*, the suspicious voice in the back of my head chastises me. *And he doesn't dream. He closes his eyes, and everything is pitch-dark. Like a shadow.*

"You—you helped me. After my accident, when I was in a coma. I've had a lot of time to think about this, and I'm positive that's why I recognized you. I can almost . . . *almost* remember it. It's like it's *right there*, somewhere in my head, just out of reach. You were there, somehow, and you helped me wake up, didn't you? That has to be what your dad's letter was talking about. And that's why I know it can't be you. You don't put people into comas. You pull them out."

I touch his shoulder, urging him to turn around. He does, and we lean into each other.

"I thought if I told you I'd met you before in, well, in a dream, you'd think I was creepy," he says. "Or weird. Or . . . not even, maybe . . . sane. But then you were starting to blame yourself for all of these comas, and—I just know it can't be you. I don't know who else it could be, but it's definitely not you."

"I don't think you're weird, Cal. Not even a little. I thought— well, I thought you thought I was."

"Maybe we're both weird," he says.

"A couple of weirdos," I agree.

"I mean, I guess it's better to be weirdos together, right?"

I let out a laugh, then stop short, my pulse racing as what he said sets in. "Together?"

"I—I mean, if—um—if you don't—"

I clasp my hands gently behind his neck, slow-dance-style. He responds by slipping his hands around my waist. Our fore-heads touch, and after some hesitation, I tilt my chin forward. So does he. Heart pounding, we draw closer, closer, until, at the very last minute, I panic and take a hard left. Cal's lips brush against my cheek as I move in for a hug instead.

Damnit, Eva. I rest my head on his shoulder, unsure what else to do. I started it. I *wanted* it. And I ruined it. What's wrong with me?

He tenses a little, then relaxes and eases into the hug, his breath tickling my skin as it disturbs the wisps of baby hairs that have come loose from my ponytail. My eyes close. I feel warm and tingly all over. And dizzy. Like I'm falling . . .

. . . We're falling together . . . falling together through the dark . . .

With a jerk, I pull away, startled by this sudden flash of imagery. The light summer breeze rustles the leaves in the trees around us as I struggle to regain my footing.

Cal steps back. "I—I'm sorry. I—"

"No." I step close again and, after some hesitation, give him a light peck on the cheek. "Don't be sorry," I tell him. "I'm not."

CHAPTER 27

I've developed a bit of a spring in my step as I head back to the Roadhouse through the neighborhood streets. A goofy smile keeps sneaking onto my face, my cheek tingling from Cal's missed kiss.

But then that flash of imagery returns again—the two of us, falling in the dark—and my smile fades a little, betrayed. Should I be this happy? The only reason we met the first time—in a dream, that is—was because of his injury and his friend's death. And now we've found each other again, in person this time, which is great, but if Miriam hadn't died, and then my dad, I wouldn't be here. Again, we're together because of death. How can I be happy with the result of *that*?

It's okay to be happy, I tell myself. *It's okay to be happy and still wish that happiness had come about a different way.* I haven't felt happy— not truly happy—since Dad died, and I refuse to let my stupid jerk of a brain chase that happiness away. My therapist would be proud.

But my happiness only lasts two more blocks.

When I reach the intersection at Main, flashing red lights catch my attention from down the street. My gut automatically reacts by twisting itself into a knot. *Brains are jerks*, I remind myself. *Brains are jerks, brains are jerks, brains are . . .*

My feet obey the knot in my gut rather than the voice of reason in my head. Instead of crossing, I turn toward the lights. Within a block, it's clear which building the ambulance is parked in front of.

But it can't be another coma. Something else must have happened. Because I haven't been asleep for hours. *Something else must have happened.* My heart thumps against my rib cage as the ambulance pulls out from in front of the police station. Flashing lights only, no siren. Because there's no rush. Which can only mean one of two things. It isn't an actual emergency, or . . . I break out into a run.

I don't stop to think. I'm on autopilot as I yank open the front doors to the station and find myself face-to-face with Officer Sontag.

"Miss, you shouldn't—" Recognition crosses her face as I cut her off.

"Who was it?"

"Miss Sylvan, I'm going to have to ask you to leave."

"Eva?" Bethany stands up on the other side of the room. She looks . . . confused. A little angry, even. My heart sinks. What's she doing here? Was it one of her parents?

The door opens—the one leading to the main office—and a disheveled-looking Daniel steps through. He's carrying a bundle of things in his arms, and draped over the top is a black uniform jacket. And then it registers: That's his dad's. Daniel's expression is dark. It darkens even more when he sees me.

I feel far away, detached, as if I'm watching the scene unfold through a layer of film. Officer Sontag abandons me to go speak with Daniel while I hover inside the doorway. Bethany rubs his back, nodding along with Officer Sontag's words but occasionally looking past her to glare at me. I feel a rush of guilt. I'm intruding. I shouldn't have come in here. My feet are itching to leave, but it's too late now. I can't. Not until I know what's going on.

Daniel doesn't appear to be listening to Officer Sontag at all. As she speaks, his eyes remain fixed on me. But I can't read them. Is he also angry with me for barging in? Or is he looking for my support?

"What's she doing here?" he interrupts Officer Sontag. His voice is flat. Expressionless. I understand that voice. That was how my voice sounded, too.

"Your . . . dad?" The last word catches in my throat as I try to confirm what I already know.

Daniel's head snaps back, as if I've slapped him. He wobbles a little on his feet; the bundle of his dad's things shift in his arms. With another glare in my direction, Bethany hurries to take it from him. As she transfers the pile to the nearest waiting room chair, something slips, threatening to tumble out of the heap. She jerks to catch it and tucks it back into the safety of Chief Burke's jacket, but not fast enough. I've already seen it. It's a leather-bound book. One of *the* leather-bound books.

I take an involuntary step toward it, but Daniel leaps up and pushes past Officer Sontag, darting over to me before I can go any farther. Right up to my face. So close, I can see the vessels in his bloodshot eyes and the dark sleepless circles underneath.

The smell of stale coffee hits me when he hisses between his teeth, "This. Is. Your. Fault."

All of the oxygen is sucked out of the room. I stand

breathless, stunned, no words with which to defend myself. Bethany's glares turn to daggers as Officer Sontag comes over and retrieves him, gently guiding him back over to the chairs. I don't understand. I take a step toward her, and she stiffens as if she thinks I'm going to attack her or something, so I retreat, realization hitting me like a fist to my gut. Bethany's not just angry with me. She's *afraid* of me. Does she also think this is my fault?

Daniel slumps forward in his chair, burying his face in his hands as Officer Sontag comes back to deal with me.

"You really need to go now," she tells me, firm but not unkind. "This isn't a good time."

"Please," I whisper. I beg her with my eyes to be straight with me. I'll leave in a second—I just need to know. "Did he . . . ?" I can't bring myself to say my fear out loud.

Her mouth a straight line, she shakes her head.

I let out a breath, only slightly relieved, because I know what the other option is, but I don't know how it's possible. I've been awake this whole time. "Coma?" I mouth.

She tilts her chin down, then up. Yes.

I steal a final look past her at Daniel, palms in his eyes, and at Bethany sitting next to him. She's rubbing his back again, up and down, up and down, but keeping me within sight out of the corner of her eye.

The edge of Miriam's book—the book Rhonda was reading, I'm sure of it now—still pokes out from beneath Chief Burke's personal effects. My fingers itch for it. I need it. But how can I explain that right now? I can't. I never should have come here in the first place.

"Go," Bethany mouths at me, scowling.

I nod, turn, and hurry out the door.

My thoughts are all over the place as I throw my things into my backpack and suitcase, and all of Rhonda's things into hers. How am I going to get all of this stuff to Miriam's without a car?

Daniel's wrong. It isn't my fault. Not this time. *It really isn't my fault.* I didn't dream about Chief Burke. I wasn't there. I wasn't even asleep! I haven't so much as catnapped since I saw him last. But now my friends have turned on me. To them, I'm Miriam's grandniece, so of course it must be me. I thought they didn't believe any of that stuff. I thought they were different. But they're not. And I should have known better.

"Assholes," I mutter as I shove my own journal into my backpack, then recoil. Daniel's actions tonight aren't his fault. He's hurting. People act like that when they're hurting. *I* acted like that. *But still.*

I go into the bathroom and collect our toothbrushes and toothpaste. I toss our hair and makeup junk into a floral toiletries bag, then go into the shower stall to retrieve our shampoo and body wash. The sweet lingering scent of strawberries and botanicals sends me spiraling back to missing Rhonda. Damnit, I really need her right now. More than ever.

Why did Daniel have that journal? Had his dad fallen asleep while reading it, too? Like Rhonda? Could the journal actually be the problem? No, no, no. That doesn't make sense. That

255

doesn't explain everyone else. So why did Daniel think to grab it, then?

After a quick, final check under the beds and behind the nightstand—should I leave the food in the mini fridge and count my losses?—I lug our suitcases down the stairs and out to the loaner car. I can't carry all of this to the house on foot. But I also don't have a license.

I pause with the key in the trunk. Who would know? It's not *that* far away. And it's a straight road. And it's late enough that not many people would be on it. *And it's also late enough that it's pitch-dark once you leave the main road, Eva, and you've never driven before in your life. What's wrong with you?*

I twist the key and pop open the trunk. I'll keep what I can't carry in here for now, and then figure out how to get the rest to the house later. I've got my basics in my backpack. I left the room key on the nightstand with a scribbled thank-you and apology on the Roadhouse stationery. They should already have Rhonda's card on file. I just hope there's still enough money on there to cover it.

My fists tighten around the straps of my pack as I take one last look up toward the room. I'm making the right decision. I'm positive by morning I won't be welcome here anymore.

My eyes trail down the steps, then over to the Roadhouse's kitchen door below. I stare at it, willing it to open. Willing Bethany to pop her head out and ask me where I'm going. To tell me no, I've misunderstood. But she won't. Of course she won't. And besides, even if she is back by now, Daniel's probably with her. Probably staying with her family like I did that first night when I, too, was left all alone.

I play the scene from the police station over and over in my head. Each replay is amplified a little more than the last. Daniel's face, inches from mine. Spitting blame. Bethany behind him, *agreeing* with him. I know she believed him. It was all over her face. So much fear. So much disgust. And the irony of it all. Because this is the one time I know for sure I didn't do it.

"It wasn't me," I whisper into the night air.

I'm going to figure it out, though. This can't keep happening. I need to make it stop.

But I'm going to have to do it from somewhere else. I can't stay here anymore.

Loosening my fists, I adjust the weight of my backpack's straps on my shoulders and let my arms drop to my sides. Then, without looking back, I head out on the moonlit trek to Miriam's house. This time, to stay.

CHAPTER 28

Tonight, I sleep without the fear that someone else won't wake up in the morning because of me. I almost hope I find myself staring down another shadow. Maybe, no longer paralyzed by self-blame, I'll be able to find a way to stop it. Or at least get some clues as to who's behind it. And why.

But tonight only holds regular dreams for me—fuzzy unpackings of the day's events. I dream of a police station made entirely of books. It turns into a maze through which I chase after long strings of numbers. I dream of streetlamps, gravestones, and kisses that never were, stolen under the cover of night. I dream of running, running, running—chased by guilt and false accusations. And I dream of trying to dream and being unable to do so.

I wake up between each one, and each time, I suffer a moment of panic, forgetting where I am. My eyes dart from shadow to shadow, the edges made starker, more sinister by the moonlight seeping in through the dirty window. Then realization sets in, and pushing my panic and hurt deep down, I shift my position; the old sofa creaks and groans beneath me, and I fall back to sleep to deal with my feelings in yet another discomfiting dream.

Clouds move in overnight, and in the early morning hours of a drizzly gray dawn, I dream of Dad. But this feels different than the others, more memory than dream, except certain things are off. I'm not in my bed at home in my old room, which I most definitely would be if this was a true memory. Instead, I'm still here at Miriam's, prone on the sofa, dressed in the clothes I walked here and fell asleep in. But it feels like my childhood bed. And Dad's crouched beside me. He has on his sweats and an old T-shirt—the same things he'd always slept and loafed around in back home.

"I'll be right here the whole time, you understand?" he tells me. "Even if you don't know it."

"Okay," I say. It's my voice as it is now, but I feel much smaller. Still a child. "But, Daddy?"

"Yes, Bug?"

"I thought I wasn't supposed to go with her anymore."

He squeezes my hand. "I know. But it's okay this once. There's a little boy who needs your help."

I don't like how his voice sounds. He's afraid. And Daddy saves lives for a living. He's never afraid. He's brave. Not like me.

I close my eyes and a woman's voice echoes in my head: "He *is* brave. And so are you. Bravery isn't the absence of fear."

I hear a buzzing in my ears. Her voice continues over it. "Bravery is doing the thing that makes you afraid, despite that fear."

The buzzing grows louder. So loud, it's deafening. It fills my eardrums, my head, my entire body. I try to sit up, to push away from it, but as I sit, my body stays behind. I have two bodies now. I can feel two bodies at once. I lift an arm out of my arm. It shimmers.

"What do you wish to see, Evangeline?" The woman's voice sounds like music. "Do you know yet? You need to see to remember. I can help you."

Now I'm truly afraid. I'm terrified. But unlike my dad, I'm

259

not brave. My heart skips a beat, and it snaps my second body back down into the first. And I'm awake.

My eyes—my real, physical eyes—fly open. I turn my head—my real, physical head—to ask Dad what the hell just happened. Never mind that he wouldn't like me cursing. But he's no longer there. He's been replaced by a dusty coffee table and an empty mantel, all of its pictures—its memories—removed and packed away.

My limbs are lead; my heart is clay, sluggish and dull. I stare at the space where Dad used to be and breathe until my body feels almost normal again. Until I feel I can sit without leaving it behind. Rain patters against the window. I tense and listen, waiting for thunder, but the only rumbles I hear are the protests of my empty stomach.

Of course, I didn't really *leave my body*, I convince myself as I rummage through the pantry for something remotely breakfast-like. *You don't* actually *leave your body when you dream. Do you?* Green beans, no. Crushed tomatoes, no. Baked beans, hmm . . . no. Not cold, anyway.

I pick up a jar of Miriam's homemade jam. Strawberry. *It had to have been a dream because I'm already having trouble remembering parts of it.* If only I had some toast. And any idea of how long ago she made this. For all I know, it could have been decades.

Cold baked beans it is.

I eat them straight out of the can while standing over the sink. Out the window, the overgrown garden revels in the rain. As if the storm a few days ago wasn't enough, it's turning even more lush and green, right before my eyes.

That's how rain used to make me feel, too. Refreshed. Back

before it became the backdrop of the worst night of my life. But the memory—the association—has now been overlaid with another feeling. Over the deep, gut-wrenching chill of loss, I've layered on the warmth of Cal's chest, the squeeze of his arms around my back, supporting me against the storm trying to pummel me down. My thoughts slide to last night. I absent-mindedly touch my fingers to my cheek.

Turning from the window, leaning my back against the sink, I stare at the phone on the wall. One more day. He's only grounded for one more day, and then . . .

The fluttering in my chest picks up. What if Daniel talks to him before I do? They're best friends. What if he shows him that journal? I don't even know what's in it, but what if whatever's in there is what made Dan and Bethany turn on me last night? Will Cal change his mind about me, too?

He was so quick to say it wasn't me. So certain. And he was right. But if it's not me, who is it? That little voice of suspicion in the back of my head chimes up again. *Maybe he was lying when he said he didn't know who was doing this. Maybe he was so certain it wasn't me, because he knows exactly who it really is.* As soon as I think it, I push it back. I refuse to go there. Cal couldn't possibly be doing this. He's too . . . nice.

But he didn't used to be, says that annoying inner voice. *Remember what Bethany said? He used to be a bully.*

Cold beans threaten to make their way up my esophagus until I remember, it *can't* be him. He was with me last night when Chief Burke was attacked, and he was driving when I dreamed about Rhonda. It can't be him. He was awake both times. *Unless he doesn't need to be asleep like I do.*

261

No. I grip the edge of the sink and swallow my suspicions down. I'm not doing this right now. I have to focus.

I have to find out what's in those journals.

I'm positive now Daniel flipped through them while gathering his dad's things. But getting them away from him is going to be tricky. Maybe if he knew that if I could only see what's in them, I might finally know how to help everyone, including his dad. If I can even get him to listen to me in the first place.

I steel myself, push off from the sink, and unhook the antique rotary from its cradle. The dial tone hums in one hand as I scroll through the contacts in my cell phone with the other, looking for Daniel's number. There it is. But . . . I hesitate, picturing the flash in his red-rimmed eyes, the fire in his breath as he hissed at me: *This. Is. Your. Fault.*

My stomach churns. He's not going to talk to me. Not when he thinks I'm to blame.

What I need is to talk to someone who can give me some advice. I scroll to the *J*s instead and dial. It takes forever on a rotary, my anxiety growing with each long, slow spin and release. Three, *click-click-click,* eight, *click-click-click-click-click-click-click-click . . .*

The first thing I'm going to set up in this house, as soon as the electricity gets fixed, is internet for Wi-Fi calling, because this is ridiculous.

There's a pause as the phone system catches up, then the beginning of a ring, immediately cut off by Jolee's groggy voice.

"The journals," she yawns deeply, "were in the basement, hon. Remember, I told you that."

I decide not to ask how she knew what I was calling about. She'll probably say they were strong on my mind. "The—the journals were stolen. Remember?"

A sigh. "Not Miriam's journals. The rest of them. Stop avoiding the basement and go down there already."

"I haven't been avoid—"

"Yes, you have. I suspect—" She's cut off by another yawn.

How early is it, actually? I hadn't thought to check.

"I suspect," she tries again, "you were meant to avoid what's down there. The journals, and . . . other things. But circumstances have changed now, so hop to it."

I don't have a clue what she's talking about, and she doesn't enlighten me.

"The basement," I say. "Right. Th—"

"You're welcome. And good luck. I'm going back to sleep now." And with a click and a dial tone, our conversation is over.

I stick an arm out to brace myself against the wall. You'd think each time I spoke with Jolee, I'd feel a little less disoriented, but I doubt I'll ever get used to it.

The door under the stairs creaks open. I stand in the gap, bracing myself against the dark passageway. Beyond the light from my lantern, the end disappears into shadow below. I feel tipsy on my feet; that falling sensation is back. I *have* been avoiding going down here. Just as I'd been avoiding going upstairs until the need to find that drawer pushed me past my discomfort.

And now I need to find some journals. I should focus on that.

It's like stepping through a cobweb. You don't want to do it. Every part of you is against it, until the need to get to the other side is greater than the fear, so you close your eyes, scrunch up your face, and then, barely feeling a thing, you step through.

My avoidance is like that—a webbed barrier in my mind convincing me not to pass it. I switch the lantern to my other hand and grip the railing tight, descending carefully onto the first step, then another. But the closer I get to the door at the bottom, the more I realize the stairs aren't the problem. It's what's at the end of them. It's whatever I might find beyond that second door. I reach the landing and give my head a shake as if to recalibrate.

Maybe it has something to do with why I can't remember helping Miriam before. Was that something else she was able to do? Block memories? In that last letter, Dad asked her to help me forget. And the journals . . . the journals might remind me.

With one enormous steadying breath, I push past my resistance and snatch at the doorknob, quick, as if it will suddenly sprout wings and fly away. *I have it now. Here we go.*

I try to turn it, but it sticks.

I give it a rattle and try again. Still nothing. Now I'm blocked in an entirely different way. The door is locked, and I don't have the key. *Why, Rhonda, why? Why would you feel the need to lock this door behind you when you didn't even bother to lock the front of the house? Who's going to break in here?*

It's not like I can't go get the key. It's upstairs in my pack on the ring with all the other old keys Rhonda carried with her, but I know if I turn around, if I go back up those stairs, there's a real chance I won't come down again. The resistance was that strong. It's *still* that strong. Maybe this is a sign Jolee's wrong and I'm still not supposed to read these. Maybe something bad will happen in my brain if I do. I don't know how erasing someone's memory works. Maybe it's like a trip wire, and if I try to get my memories back, I'll—

No, Eva. Stop it. I can't turn around now, and I won't.

I pull Dad's Swiss Army knife out of my pocket and get to work. Unlike the kitchen door, this one gives me some trouble, but the challenge—and concentration required—helps distract me from the urge to run away. Finally, after several failed attempts, I manage to catch all the tumblers. As I turn the tweezers in the lock, it still catches some resistance, but I know it should work, so I crank a little harder, and then . . . there's a snap as my hand jerks down and away. The tweezers are now tweez*er*—singular and single-tined.

Tears well up before my brain can even process what just happened. I can't believe I broke it. This is part of Dad's knife! He'd carried it with him since he was a kid. It's the only thing I know of from his childhood here that he kept. He entrusted it to me, and now part of it's jammed in the lock and I'll never be able to get it out, and I can forget about getting this door open now, and all of this will have been for nothing. In my frustration, I reach out to rattle the knob again, just to prove to myself how much I've really screwed up.

But it doesn't rattle. It turns easily and with a long, low creak, the door swings open.

I inhale a shaky lungful of stale, musty air. Maybe it wasn't for nothing after all. I kiss my fingertips and touch them to the jammed keyhole as I step over the threshold into the shadows beyond.

CHAPTER 29

The room is small with a worn stone floor and worn brick walls lined with worn wood shelves holding the strangest assortment of things. There are clocks (no longer ticking) and hourglasses, scales and other brass gadgets, jars and casks filled with who-can-tell-what at this point. And covering them all, a thick layer of dust. Some look valuable. Others, more sentimental, like the slumped teddy bear missing a button eye. And a few have no reasonable explanation at all as to why they've been displayed so prominently. I pause and hold the lantern up to a plain gray stone resting on a wooden pedestal. Next to it sits a chipped and barnacled mussel shell.

I find empty spots here and there, where missing items have left behind shapes in the dust. I have a feeling they're in the antique store now. My chest tightens a little. I don't know why, but it's bothering me.

These things may not have had any meaning to us days ago, but from the way everything has been so carefully displayed down here, they must have meant something to someone. It's not like guests would see them tucked away in the basement like this. They feel important. And strangely familiar.

But they're not why I'm here. I'm here for the journals. And damn, are there a lot of them.

Lantern held aloft, I stand in front of the massive bookcase, scanning the rows and rows of leather bindings. They differ in size and color; the ones at the top are clearly much older than the ones at the bottom. But they all have one thing in common: They're unlabeled and soft-spined so they'll lie flat for writing in when opened—as all the best journals are. I know this, because they're like mine. Dad gave it to me years ago. And I kept it, unwritten in, until he died. Now I know where it came from.

I skim down the rows until I come to the gap at the end that was formerly occupied by what I assume were Miriam's journals. There are fresh streaks in the dust in front of the gap where Rhonda must have slid them out. Should I start with the ones that came before those, or should I start at the very beginning?

I decide to test the waters with a random book in the middle. I carefully slide one out, blow off the dust, and settle down cross-legged on the cold concrete floor. Lantern by my side, I begin to read.

When I finish flipping through that book, I grab another. Flip through it, grab another. It turns out all I needed was to start. Now I can't get enough. It's as if I've been starving my entire life without knowing it, and now a feast has been placed before me. I'm finally—*finally*—beginning to understand.

These are dream journals. But they aren't about the writers' dreams. They're other people's dreams. Each new entry, no matter who the journal belongs to, is marked with the date and the name of the person whose dream they were visiting.

It doesn't take long before I'm able to see why everyone's so suspicious of the Sylvans. It's not that they were collectively evil. But they weren't all saints, either. Many of them had no problem using what they found in people's dreams—their private fears and shames—as fodder for leverage and gain.

They didn't seem to care that people avoided them as much as possible—as one of my ancestors wrote in 1910, "You can run from us during the day, but you can't run from sleep. It will always come for you eventually." Another talks about the protective symbols people in the town put on their doors, calling it an "ineffective, silly superstition." They're baffled it still persists. This was in 1923. I wonder what they'd say if they knew it's still going on, even now.

This same relative also talks about "taking up the silver cord" to find out someone's deepest, darkest secrets in order to manipulate their dreams and use those secrets against them. I have to put the journals down for a minute after that because I feel ill. *I'm not like that*, I want to scream at the town. *I refuse to be like that.*

I see cords mentioned in several journals. Sometimes they're called threads instead. Sometimes tethers or lifelines. From the way they're talked about, I think they must be a metaphor for something taboo.

Fortunately, the next few journals I skim through aren't quite as awful. I'm relieved to find not every Sylvan entered dreams with malicious intent. At least, not always. Sometimes they were just curious, and sometimes they were actually trying to help people, dispelling nightmares or working through grief. Though from what I'm reading, the people they were helping rarely understood this. In their confused, dreaming state, the dreamers often associated them with the very thing they were trying to help with. It reminds me of something my history teacher said last year when we were studying the Salem witch trials. He said people accused of witchcraft were usually misunderstood healers. Obviously, that doesn't apply to everyone in my family. But now I'm starting to wonder . . . was Miriam actually a healer?

I think back to what Bethany told me after my first encounter with Diane. How, despite being a recluse, it was like Miriam was always around in the backs of people's heads. *Like a specter*, I think. *A phantom.* But Bethany said she thought Miriam was trying to comfort her, even though she was scared of her at first. It all makes sense now. Miriam was trying to help, but with what I'm reading about the Sylvan family's history of behavior, it's completely understandable why people would assume she meant harm. A misunderstood healer, Miriam was labeled: witch.

But something's still nagging at me, a feeling of déjà vu—a conversation at the tip of my consciousness. Obviously, Miriam didn't let her reputation stop her from trying to help people, but why, then, didn't she help Cal herself? Why did she recruit me to do it?

I stare again at the gap where her journals should be. Reading my family's history through other people's dreams is insightful and all, but it's still not telling me what I need to know. So far, I haven't read about anything quite like what's happening now.

The shadowy figure, the comas, the letters, the stick. Cal's accident. Graham. I know they're connected. I can feel it in my gut. But how?

There was an accident. Cal was in a coma, and Graham . . . had somewhere else to go. I remember saying that to the boy in my dream. To

Cal. Graham had somewhere else to go, because he was dead. And I remember a sense of urgency. Like if I didn't get Cal to wake up, he, too, would have somewhere else to go.

What happens if you die in a dream?

In a flash of memory, I picture two thin, glittering threads. One extending from my middle, the other extending from his. Twisting and tangling together as we fall, tethering us to something beyond sight. Tethering us to ourselves. *Those are our lifelines, those threads, and they will show us the way home.* I feel a faint tug in my abdomen as my body remembers as well.

Silver cords. What if it isn't a metaphor? What if it's a *literal* cord, sort of like an umbilical cord, tethering our dream selves to our physical selves? And if that's the case, could it also literally break?

That inside-out pulling sensation before waking—I feel it again, stronger now, as my gaze shifts a little to the left, from Miriam's gap to the books before it. I swallow against the dryness in my mouth. Then I reach forward, stretching across the cold floor, and grab the very last one.

There's that prickly, tickly, cobwebby feeling again. All over my skin. At first, I think maybe I've caught a real one this time. Spiders love cold, dark basements after all. I swipe my hands up and down my arms, across my face, trying to brush it away. But there's nothing there. The feeling remains as I stare hard at the worn leather cover resting in my lap.

Whose words will I find in here? Could this be Dad's? *No,* I remember with some relief. Jolee said he couldn't do that whole dream telepathy thing. And besides, it doesn't match the blank one he gave me. It's darker and it looks too old. *My grandmother,*

I think with a mixture of excitement and dread. *It's going to be my grandmother's.*

My pulse speeds up. I've always wondered what she was like. But now, after some of the things I've read today, I'm not sure I want to know anymore. The binding crackles as I open the journal to the first page. Leaning into the lantern light, I squint down at the placard on the inside cover.

PROPERTY OF:

May Evelyn Sylvan
October 1973 –

But my grandmother's name was Rose. Who is May? In my surprise, it takes me a second to remember. Jolee—I think back—yes, Jolee talked about May the first time I met with her. How could I forget, after she'd made such a big deal about me not knowing who she was? Three sisters—Miriam, my grandmother Rose, and May. All three gone now. That's what Jolee said, that May had passed away a long time ago. In the seventies. I remember now. And there's no ending date to this journal. Which means she probably never got to it. This must be the last journal she wrote in before she died. I feel a surge of, not quite excitement, but expectation. This is what I need to read. I don't know why, but I'm certain of it.

I flip to the next page. Then the next. Soon, a pattern emerges. May was one of the helpers. But, unlike anyone else I've read about so far, she actually *would* ask permission first. Not in the waking world, because again, that's a conversation that likely wouldn't go well. But if she came across someone who was experiencing nightmares, she would help work through them if, in the dream, they were willing.

The more I read, the more I like May. She reminds me of Dad, constantly finding people to help. Constantly putting others before herself, and not even appearing to realize it. I can sense the lantern dimming beside me as its batteries wear down, and still, I read on. *Maybe I should take this upstairs. After this page. Okay, maybe after the next one.* I lean closer into the light as I speed through entry after entry.

As I'm skimming an entry about a man named Bobby, the word "shadow" jumps out at me, and my heart does a somersault. This is it! This is what I need. With a mixture of excitement and fear, I hunch over the pages, racing against the dimming light, soaking up the information within.

Bobby was a soldier in Vietnam. His nightmares took him back there. May doesn't go into detail about the gruesome scenes themselves, which I'm grateful for. Instead, she focuses on a menacing shadow figure that chases after her whenever she tries to help. Like it's protecting Bobby, in a way, but holding him captive at the same time. Each night, Bobby accepts May's offers of help, but then the shadow rushes in and pushes her away. And each night, it grows stronger, more threatening. More dangerous for both of them. The more I read, the more my muscles tense. My pulse races in recognition. I turn the page . . .

I know what I have to do. But I don't know what will happen if I do it. I panicked last night. It was coming. I tried to stand my ground this time. But when it lashed out at me, I felt it. It grabbed hold of me, and

I felt its fear. It filled all of my senses. I could even smell it. And its anger. And guilt. So much guilt. And so much pain. Not just emotional pain, but physical pain coursing through my entire dreaming self. It felt so real. All I could think about was waking us both up to get away.

I know I should have asked permission before grabbing on to his lifeline like that, even if it was just for a second. He's angry with me now, I know it. But I'm not sorry. Because just before waking, it gave me the glimpse into his soul I needed and now I know everything. I know everything he's kept hidden from me, and even from himself. I saw what he did. And now I understand what's fueling his shadow, down to its very core.

It's not his fault. If I can only get him to see that, to face it and accept it. If he could only forgive himself, I think he could get these nightmares under control.

If I could just get him to face it. To face his guilt. I think he could control it and stop it from taking him over completely. But I'm fooling myself to think it will be that easy. His guilt is too strong, and it will take a lot for him to let it go. If this doesn't work, there's only one other thing I can think to do. And if he can't forgive himself, I hope, at least, he'll be able to forgive me.

I turn the page again and find it blank. And the one after that, and after that. With a sinking feeling, I flip through the rest of the pages to make sure. Whatever it was May tried to do, I don't think she made it back. And I don't like to think of what might have happened to Bobby, if his shadow took him over.

I close May's journal and drum my fingers on the cover, a swirling mixture of dread and relief. On the one hand, I feel a little lighter now, like I can finally breathe. This is the confirmation I needed—I'm absolutely, positively not the one causing these comas. But on the other hand . . . I know the shadow May's describing. I know how it feels, and I know its scent, that odor of guilt that clings to me after each dream. Could it be the same one? It was fueled by whoever this Bobby person was, but could it be possible he didn't create it, and now, somehow, it's moved on to someone else? Or is this new? Either way, I know for sure now Jolee was right. I'm not the one who's doing this. But I still don't know who is.

As much as I don't want to, I still need to see what Miriam's last journal says. If it ended similarly to May's, that would explain why Rhonda wanted Miriam's autopsy report. And why she wanted so desperately to talk to me without anyone else around to hear.

Can someone be killed by a nightmare?

I stare again at the darkened space where Miriam's journals should be, jaw set. A small part of me wants to binge on coffee and energy drinks like Daniel's been doing and never sleep again. But my sister's been taken, and so have others, and it will keep on taking people unless I do something about it.

And Miriam knew it. She knew something like this might happen. She had to have, or she wouldn't have left me all of those clues. And Dad knew, too, or he wouldn't have asked Miriam to make me forget how to dream like she could. He must have thought that would protect me somehow. That if I couldn't remember, this kind of danger couldn't reach me.

"But you were wrong, Dad," I say aloud. "It found me anyway. And now, because you didn't want me to remember, I have no idea what to do."

My memories are *trying* to wake up. Things are coming back to me in tiny bits and pieces—like that dream that felt like a memory where Cal and I fell and fell. Where Graham had somewhere else to go. But it's not enough.

I tuck May's journal under one arm and stand, shaking the pins and needles out of my legs. The lantern swings as I retrieve it; the shadows shift. I freeze, tensing, then slowly exhale. I'm awake, not dreaming, and those are normal, everyday shadows. I need to get out of this basement, back into daylight. I'm psyching myself out.

Just to make myself feel better, I take one last look around the room. All is as it should be. Every odd knickknack is in its place. The stone and shell sit on their pedestal, the teddy bear winks at me with its missing eye, and the glass and stoneware jars remain clustered in the far corner with . . . is that another book?

I leave my post by the bookshelf to take a closer look. Not a book. A binder. Like what I use for school. Except older— black and vinyl with cracks in the seams. I hook the lantern on my arm and slide the binder carefully out from where it's been nestled among the jars. Some of them remind me of Miriam's jam jars up in the pantry. Maybe that's what they are, but it's too dark in the waning lantern light to tell, and the writing on the labels is faded. But if they're just jams and pickles, why stash them all the way back here to be forgotten about, instead of keeping them in the pantry with the rest?

I blow the dust off the binder and take a quick peek inside. It's filled with what appear to be old clippings and drawings. Like a scrapbook. I'll need better light to know for sure, though, and if I don't head upstairs soon, I'll have to navigate the treacherous steps by feel. I've waited longer than I should have already.

CHAPTER 30

After spending all morning in the dark basement, the kitchen feels like a solarium. Sitting at the tiny table, I flip through the binder's delicate pages. It *is* kind of like a scrapbook, but for recipes. From the looks of it, they've been carefully collected and curated over generations until someone finally decided to put them all together in one place.

These, however, aren't like any recipes I've ever seen before. There are soups and stews meant to "nourish after a lengthy slumber" and drops "for fever sleep." There are oils, and potpourris, and bundles of herbs for "purifying." I skim through recipes for "clarity teas," and "quick sleep tonic," and a tincture simply titled: "float." I assume it's not the root beer kind.

Some use common herbs, like oregano and rosemary. Some involve less common ones, like mugwort and calea leaf. I've heard of mugwort. I haven't heard of calea. I wonder if it's dangerous. In fact, quite a few of these recipes look a little sketchy. There's a deep sleep tea that calls for a *lot* of poppies. Aren't poppies used to make opium? I'm pretty sure I heard that somewhere. But it's not like there's anything *really* dangerous in here, like "how to make meth." And I doubt any of these work the way they claim to anyway, if they do anything at all.

A breeze from the kitchen window tickles my shoulder and

rustles the paper as I turn another page. I hop up to close it, and as I return to my seat, a slight movement by the dining room archway catches my eye.

It's so quick, I'm not sure I saw anything at all. It was probably a trick of the light or a speck of dust in my eye. But it isn't sitting right with me, so just in case, I go over to the doorway and poke my head out to investigate. Of course there's nothing there. Not a sound besides my own shallow breathing and the first trickles of a new wave of rain pattering on the window behind me.

It was nothing. Of course it was nothing. Just the spookiness of this old house getting to me again. I yawn and shake my head. I've also been staring at words too long. My eyes are swimming from deciphering so much old handwriting. Time to give them a break.

I head back to the table and move to flip the book shut when a familiar set of instructions catches my eye:

1 pinch snuff or 2 pinch tea,

hold that which you wish to see.

1 pinch snuff or 2 pinch tea. I've seen that before. Where? Not in this book—or at least, not both together. There are recipes for snuffs, and recipes for tea, but this is the first I've come across that could be used either way. No, I saw this somewhere else, and not too long ago.

I scan the ingredients as I search my memory. Unfortunately, this is one of the much older scraps that's been pasted into the book, and a popular one, too. Stains from spills obscure some of the already faded writing. I can't make everything out. But what I can read doesn't seem bad. Not that I'm paying very close attention, anyway. I'm too busy racking my brain while running the poem through my head. *What you wish to see . . .*

What do you wish to see, Evangeline? I hear the woman's voice in my head again, clear as it was in this morning's dream. Guiding me to be brave like Dad because a little boy needed me. But I wasn't brave. I was terrified. That buzzing sound, the lightness I felt as I began to break away from my heavy, stubborn limbs, it's all flooding back to me. *You need to see to remember,* she'd said, just before I'd snapped back into my body. Could that have been Miriam? My chest thumps with the memory. *I thought I wasn't supposed to go with her anymore,* I'd said to Dad in the dream. Yes. That was her! That was Miriam! And I think—yes, I think I remember where I've seen those instructions. She was giving me another clue! I spring from my chair and dash upstairs to Miriam's room.

I return with the small brass canister from her bedside table. The one with the label on the bottom: *1 pinch snuff, 2 pinch tea.*

Shoving dried herbs up my nose doesn't sound pleasant, so I choose the tea. That way, I can test it out one sip at a time. But without electricity, I don't have any way to heat the water. I'll have to brew it at room temp and hope that's good enough. Wrinkling my nose, I sprinkle two small pinches of the crumbly herbs and who knows what else into the bottom of a mug, which I then fill under the faucet. It immediately turns a sickly shade of pond scum.

I let it steep for a while and turn the canister over and over in my hand. What if it's expired? Miriam didn't write a date any-where on it. The freshest it could possibly be is a little over a year, assuming she hadn't had this for very long before she passed. And that's assuming a lot.

Fear pricks at the back of my mind. What if she was using this *when* she died? What if it wasn't the shadows that killed her, but this? *This is really stupid, Eva. You don't even know what this stuff is.*

But I need to see to remember, she'd said. See what? Her journals maybe? I don't have them, and the instructions say I need to *hold* that which I wish to see. And since, if I'm holding something, I can probably see it, too, it must mean a different kind of seeing than the kind you do with your eyes.

I think for a minute, then grab the envelope full of letters from my dad. These were what she'd saved for me after all. Not the journals themselves. Maybe all this time, I've been chasing after the wrong thing. Because it's strange, actually, that she didn't set aside the journals for me as well. Then again, pretty much everything Miriam did was strange and cryptic.

I eye the "tea" suspiciously. Most of the mixture has floated to the top, creating a grainy layer that stays there even as I try to stir it down. The swirls of unincorporated herb spin in my spoon-powered whirlpool, pulling my thoughts toward its center.

What do you wish to see?

Dad.

I might as well be honest with myself. I grabbed the enve-lope, not because Miriam set it aside for me but because the letters inside were written by Dad. But the letters mostly explain themselves—their half of the puzzle, anyway. I've been assum-ing the journals are the other half, but what if the other half has been right here with the letters all along? I *want* to see Dad. I want to see his smiling eyes. I want to hear his voice that's fading from my mind. I want to hug him with all my strength, squeeze him until he laughs and says, "Oof! Bug! Give me some air!" I want to tell him I'm sorry.

It's tempting. It's *very* tempting. But what do I need to see right *now*?

I remove Dad's letters and, with a heaviness in my chest, set them off to the side. Cringing a little, I reach my arm all the way into the envelope and pull out the broken, bloodstained stick. The letters never mention this stick, but Miriam clearly saved it with them for a reason. It must be important. Maybe it's what I need to "see." *Maybe*—I shiver—*it will tell me how it became covered with blood.* Before I can change my mind, I hold my breath and take a slug of the tea.

The *spicy* tea. I slam the mug down onto the counter and rush over to the sink to cup fresh water into my mouth with my free hand. It only helps a little. I turn off the faucet and watch as the last remnants trickle down the drain. And, grasping the stick tightly in my fist, I wait.

Besides my tingling tongue, I don't feel any different. Then again, the effects probably won't be immediate. I'll need to digest the tea first, and it will need to work its way into my bloodstream, and *whoa*.

The room has completely shifted around me. What just happened? I'm still in a kitchen, but it's not Miriam's. I hold the stick up under the light of the window,

*examining it with a dish-gloved hand. It has a bit of
a halo around it—blurred, and yet clear to me at the
same time.*

"That does look like blood, doesn't it?"

*I haven't felt my mouth move—I'm not in control
of any of my movements—but the words seemed like
they were coming from me in a voice that's not my own.
And . . . were they backward? I think so, but I could
still understand them as if they weren't.*

*The room swivels around me. I catch a glimpse of a
girl beyond the stick, sitting at a square kitchen table
with a cup of untouched tea. She's wild-eyed, like she
hasn't been sleeping well. And she's—hold on. She's
me! And this is Jolee's kitchen. But does that mean I'm
Jolee right now?*

*Before I can fully process this revelation, the lighting
changes, bright and focused, like a spotlight. My dish
glove has disappeared, and I'm in a completely different
room. This time, I'm holding the stick barehanded
between thumb and forefinger, twisting it this way and
that under a harsh light, with darkness all around. I'm
pretty sure that's my own hand this time, but I'm still
not controlling it. I remember this, though. This is when
I first found the stick along with all the letters from my
dad. And a moment ago—that was when I showed it
to Jolee. Which happened afterward. I think . . . I'm
traveling backward through time. The timeline of the
stick.*

The lighting shifts again, and so does my hand.
It's wrinkled and speckled with age spots. It's also
a little shaky as it carries the stick backward down
some curved, creaky stairs. Then down another set of
stairs—narrow, worn stone, to the basement. I pass
the bookshelf filled with journals and stop, holding the
stick up to a light bulb to get a better look. A feeling
of sadness washes over me, overwhelmed by the pang
of old hurts and remembrances I don't understand,
because I don't think they belong to me. Then I turn
and place the stick next to the one-eyed teddy bear on
one of the basement's dusty wood shelves. Although, if
this is backward, I think I might actually be picking it
up. Is this Miriam's hand? Is this where she'd kept the
stick before hiding it in her false-bottomed drawer?

The next thing I know, I'm outside. It's night, but
bright with the light of the full moon. And I'm having a
panic attack. The stick is flying through space, flung, a
backward ricochet that ends with a crack as it becomes
whole again—longer now, heftier—as my smaller,
younger, dirt-splotched hand yanks it back from—oh
God—from . . . is that a head? And hair. And blood.

I hear in reverse, but again understand as if forward,
the slurred speech from the owner of the head: a young
boy, wobbling on his feet, hands held up protectively
as I dash backward in a panicked rush, branch held
aloft. His hands go down, and I get a clearer look at
him as he tracks the stick, then me, horror dissipating
into confusion as I continue to run in reverse. His hair

*is blond, his face bloodied, and his blue eyes dull and
unfocused. Oh—oh no. I know those eyes.*

"*Get help. What are you doing?*" *the blond boy
yells. I stop moving, frozen with terror as he looks down
sharply, then rewinds into kneeling.* "*Graham?*" *he
says to another boy lying at the base of a massive tree.
The branch blurs as my focus shifts to the broken body.
His limbs are splayed in odd positions, and his head—
his head is turned much farther than it should be. Eyes
wide open. Unseeing. Lifeless. I feel sick.*

*The kneeling boy falls forward and lies next to
him, unmoving, as I creep backward. Heart pounding,
unsure of what to do, I crouch down and set the branch
onto the ground—or really, pick it up in reverse—as
there's a bang, a flash, and everything goes dark.*

*I hear yelling. I'm yelling? No, someone else is
yelling. I shake. And shake some more. I can't stop
shaking.*

"Damnit, wake up. Come on, wake up. Come on, come on.
Eva! Shit, come on."

I'm shaken again, and my eyes flutter open in front of a pair
of blue circles. Denim circles. Knees.

"Can you hear me? Look at me."

There's the sound of rapid snapping. A flutter of movement
accompanies it. My eyes focus, then blur, then focus again. I
turn my head and follow the knees up to a navy T-shirt, then a
wide-eyed pair of baby blues. I know those eyes.

285

Chapter 31

"Cal? You're 'kay." My words come out hoarse and slurred. I prop myself up on my elbow. It's a mistake. The world spins, and I flop back down. Where am I again? I instinctively reach out and brush my fingers against the denim circles in front of my face, exploring the feel of the soft cotton. Hands clasp my cheeks, and I'm gently turned to face Cal again.

"What did you take? This? Did you take this?" He thrusts his hand forward. In it is the tin filled with powdery herbs.

I nod, which makes me dizzy again. My head's splitting open.

"Why would you do that? What is this? Do you even know?"

I answer with a groan, and he finally lets me lay my head back down on the cool wood floor. I think for a second about his question, then wind my arm out from under me to show him what I'm holding.

"I was this shtick." That doesn't sound right.

His mouth opens slightly, his brow knits in confusion.

I try again. "I had to see. To 'member." I pause, trying to untangle the jumble of images in my brain. "I was this stick. I hit you." No, that's not right. Try again. Enunciate. "I mean, someone hit you. With this stick." My eyes wander toward his forehead, then up to his scar, peeking out from beneath his disheveled hair. I did that. No, the stick did that. No . . . whoever was *holding* the stick did that. Who was it?

He carefully takes it from me and scoots back while I ease myself up to sitting.

Which is another mistake. A big, big mistake. My stomach lurches, pushing its contents up my esophagus. Very quickly. Spurred into action by this new development, I manage to pull myself up to the counter and lean over the sink just in time to heave into it, clearing the god-awful tea from my system.

"Oh, God," I moan, and crank on the faucet to wash it all down the drain. But I'm not done. I succumb to another bout of heaving. And another. My body has decided everything must go.

I feel a lot better once I'm done. Except for my pounding head. And the burgeoning realization that Cal has been subjected to my most epic stomach-content expulsion since I ate that bad Fourth of July potato salad two years ago.

Also, I think I may have told him I was a stick?

Also also, I have just now remembered this sink doesn't have a garbage disposal. Or the electricity to run one even if it did.

I rest my elbows on the counter, gripping my head, wishing I could disappear. But I can't stay leaning here forever. Eventually, I'll have to turn around and face Cal.

I take another moment to collect myself, rinse out my mouth, splash more water on my face, then turn. Cal's still kneeling on the floor, but now his back is to me. Understandable.

I approach slowly, carefully. I'm still a little wobbly and have to shoot my hand out at the last second to brace myself as I crouch down next to him. He doesn't move. He doesn't even acknowledge I'm there. He's too busy staring at the stick, though I wonder if he's really seeing it at all. His mouth is set in a hard line.

"Cal?" I place a hand on his shoulder, trying to find the words to apologize. He jerks and shrugs it off, and I have to catch myself from falling over again as he rises to his feet.

"I thought you'd be at the . . ." His jaw twinges. "At the . . ." He takes a deep breath. "At the place—the Lieus' place. I thought you'd be there."

The Roadhouse. I sit all the way down and pull my knees to my chest. "I thought you were grounded until tomorrow."

My voice sounds small to me, not at all how I'd meant it to sound. How long has it been? Maybe it *is* tomorrow. True shock over the risk I've taken is finally hitting me. *Hitting.* The image of younger Cal's bloodied face, his dazed expression, flashes across my vision. Yes, that was Cal. *That was Cal. And Graham. That was dead Graham.* I blink and shake my head to clear the image as my stomach threatens me again.

"It got Bethany," Cal says.

"What g—"

"She's in a coma, damnit."

I can't think. I—Bethany? Now Bethany? And so soon after Chief Burke—that's two comas in one night. *It's accelerating.* I get back to my feet, wobbling.

"And then I come here and . . ." He sweeps his hand toward me, then the floor, then the stuff on the table. He's still holding the stick in it. My eyes follow it as it swings around.

"I'm going to the hospital," he finishes, letting his arm flop in defeat. And without so much as looking at me again, he turns and heads for the dining room while I remain rooted in place, unable to even speak. He's going out the front way. Doesn't even want to pass by me to go out the kitchen door. And he still has the stick.

As he disappears around the corner, I don't move to stop him. A few long seconds pass, ticked off by the pounding of my pulse, and then he reappears, annoyed. "Are you coming?"

I release my breath. "Yeah." I blink. "Yeah, give me a sec. I'll be right there."

He leaves again, and I slump back against the counter, listening to his footsteps as they disappear toward the foyer. Aspirin. I should take some. I turn and reach for the cupboard above the sink, and that's when I discover why Cal was really going out the front way. The kitchen door doesn't work anymore. It's askew in its frame, splintered around the latch.

Did he . . . kick it open? To get to me? I thought that was just a movie thing. I blink and blink again. I don't feel fully awake, yet I know I am. I must be. The slam of the front door carries in from the foyer, spurring me back into action. I pop an aspirin in my mouth and wash it down with a full glass of water, then dizzily hurry out the front to join him.

We're past the gas station before either of us speaks. The silence, the tension in the truck cab is squeezing the breath out of me. He doesn't even have the radio on. He always has the radio on.

Finally, I can't stand it anymore and break the ice by blurting out the most observant statement ever. "They let you have your truck back."

"So I could give Daniel a ride to the hospital."

"Oh." Yeah. So, there's also that. "You heard about his dad."

He shoots me a sharp look out of the corner of his eye, then returns his focus to the road. "He wasn't home, and he wasn't answering his phone. Thought maybe he already took the—the bus. Or got another ride."

I nod. That makes sense.

"So I thought instead I'd see if you were around. But you weren't answering your phone, either. Or the room phone. So . . . and then . . ."

He's pissed, so pissed, and I deserve it. I know what I did was dangerous and stupid. But I was desperate. I had to *see*. I dig my nails into my palms, waiting for him to gather the rest of his words. Waiting for the worst.

"I went inside. To ask if anyone knew where you were. I thought maybe Beth . . ." Her name cuts off like someone has stolen his breath. I touch his arm to calm him. He shakes me off again, then wrenches the steering wheel to the right, bringing the truck to a squealing stop in the shoulder, my heart leaping into my throat as another car blows past us, blaring its horn.

He turns off the ignition, then twists in his seat to face me. His eyes bore into mine, his words flowing easily now, fast and furious, taking me by surprise. "Beth's dad told me you checked out last night. No explanation. You just took off and left the key. Why'd you do that?"

There it is. I knew it was coming, but it still stings. He didn't even need to talk to Bethany or Daniel to come to the same conclusion they did. My own actions have done that. But last night, *he told me* it wasn't me. He knew it wasn't me before I did.

I take a slow, deep breath, forcing myself to hold eye contact. "I didn't know about Bethany," I tell him, keeping my voice as steady as possible. "And I didn't dream about her, either. The last time I saw her, she was at the police station comforting Daniel."

"You were there? Last night?"

Crap. That doesn't look good, either. Especially since . . .

"Before?" he asks quietly. "Or after . . . ?"

"After we . . . talked." "Talked" isn't the right word. It was more than that. We were more than that. My chest feels tight. I'm forgetting how to breathe.

"On my way back to the Roadhouse," I try to explain. "I saw the ambulance leaving the police station, so I went over to see what happened." I think I see the red lights again, glowing behind Cal, but I blink, and they disappear. Almost like I fell asleep for a second, but Cal would have reacted to that. Unless I'm still—no, I'm definitely awake. But I think that tea's still messing with my head.

I reach out for Cal's arm again, not for his sake, but for mine. This time he lets my hand stay, but his muscles are tense under my fingertips.

"I didn't dream about Dan's dad, Cal." I can't hide the shake from my voice now. He needs to believe me. *I* need him to believe me. "You know I didn't, because I was with you. And before that, I was with Jolee, looking through old newspapers. Remember? I told you that. And I didn't dream about Bethany, either. You were right. It's not me. I'm not the one doing this."

It doesn't matter to me anymore what anyone else thinks, as long as Cal believes me. He has to believe me. After a long moment, he nods and relaxes, but only a little. Then, with a deep breath, he turns the key in the ignition, the truck rumbles to life, and he pulls back onto the road.

I hug my arms to my chest and stare at the blur of trees speeding past my window. The shadows between their branches morph into menacing figures, taunting me until I force myself to look away. I know this discussion isn't over. Even if he does believe me now—does he? I think he does. But after all he's already been through this morning, what must he have thought when he found me lying unconscious on my kitchen floor? The way he was kneeling over me, trying to wake me up . . . *He was kneeling over him. Over Graham. Graham is lying there on the ground. He's kneeling over him. Graham's just lying there. His neck is twisted. It's twisted.*

I blink, and blink, and blink, trying to wipe the images from my vision, pushing them down. Away and down. *Brains are jerks,* I remind myself, bringing my feet up and curling into the corner of the truck cab where bench seat meets door. I wring the shoulder strap of my seat belt with both hands, gripping it tight. *Brains are jerks.*

CHAPTER 32

They've moved Rhonda to her own room. It's nice and quiet here if I shut the door, which I've done, and dark if I draw the blinds, which I should do for the sake of my head, but haven't. I'm grateful for the more comfortable chair in here, and the small table to rest my elbows on.

My brain still feels fuzzy, but a 7 Up from the vending machine, courtesy of Cal, has helped keep my stomach calm and leveled off the shakes. He's gone in search of Daniel alone. I told him Daniel won't like me being here, and he didn't ask why. He hasn't asked or said much of anything since confronting me back in the truck. When he's done looking for Daniel, though, I think we're going to see if they'll let us visit Bethany together.

I check the clock above the door. It's a little after six. Later than I thought.

Rhonda looks peaceful at least—or as peaceful as someone can with a feeding tube up their nose. The heart monitor beeps at a slow, steady pace. I match my breaths to it—two beeps in, two beeps out.

With her long lashes fanned out on her pale cheeks and her dark waves cascading around her head, she reminds me of a sleep-spelled Snow White. But something as simple as a prince's kiss isn't going to wake her up. It isn't going to wake any of them up. To do that, I'm going to have to figure out how to get back inside their heads—on purpose this time. My thoughts wander toward the "recipe" book again, and to the tea. I reach for my 7 Up and take another sip as my stomach also remembers the tea.

I'm never using anything from that book again. I'm going to have to rely on myself this time. I "saw." I did what I was told, or at least what I think I was told. I saw to remember. But remember what? To "just say no"? That wasn't the kind of remembering I was going for.

Just say no. A humorless chuckle escapes me as I conjure up the memory of Dad repeating the oft-mocked slogan in front of a classroom full of twelve-year-olds while I sat in the back, slumped in my chair, pretending I didn't know who that guy was up there. As a paramedic, he'd seen a lot of overdoses, and when he found out my seventh-grade health class was doing a unit on drugs, he volunteered to come in and talk about it. I got called a narc in the hallways for a week after that.

My chest feels like it's being squeezed, gripped by a vise, as it often does when I dare think negatively of my dad. I get up and go to the window to find something to distract me. But the ocean of cars in the parking lot below is just as depressing. How many of those cars will leave today, minus one of their passengers?

Jesus, Eva.

I need to knock it off.

As I'm turning away from the window, I catch a glimpse of dark movement out of the corner of my eye. It startles me and, thinking someone's standing by Rhonda's bed, I finish turning around more quickly than I'd planned, bringing about another rush of dizziness. But there's nothing. Still, the hairs rise on the back of my neck. I could have sworn someone was there. I glance over toward the door. Still closed. I would have heard the latch, I think.

It was no one. Nothing. I'm being paranoid now. And I am never ever trying anything from that recipe book again.

A voice out in the hallway snaps me back to reality. "Be right back," I tell Rhonda before cracking open the door. I spy Bethany's mom through the gap and freeze. She's pacing while talking frantically on the phone in Vietnamese. Her usual composure is gone, mismatched clothes thrown on haphazardly, hair down and loose, unbrushed.

I forget myself and allow the door to swing open, a lump in my throat. Mrs. Lieu sees me and quickly ends her call before rushing over.

"You," she says. "You know something."

I shake my head.

"But . . . my husband says you checked out last night. You left a note. It said 'sorry' on it. What were you apologizing for?"

I can feel the shadows closing in around me, tunneling my vision. *No, Eva, you're awake. Snap out of this.* I swallow hard. My words catch in my throat, and I'm unable to respond.

"You can tell me," she tries again, coaxing. She sounds sincere, but after Bethany's hostility toward me last night, I don't know if I can trust her.

"Please, if you know anything—" She stops short, her frown deepening as her gaze shifts. I turn to see what she's looking at and find Ms. Petersen standing by the open door of another room. Of all the people I'd rather not run into right now, Diane's at the top of the list. Chris comes out of the room behind her, catches my eye, reddens, and heads back inside. *Must be Rob's room*, I think.

"I told you she was trouble," Diane says to Bethany's mom. She saunters over with a smug look on her face. "And I warned you that letting her stay at the Roadhouse would be dangerous. But you wouldn't believe me. You even defended her, remember? Tried to make me sound like some kind of conspiracy theorist."

Mrs. Lieu blinks, stunned. Her mouth opens a little as she looks from me to Diane. "What?"

"She's the one causing these comas." Diane points an accusing finger at me. "Haven't you figured that out yet? She's doing this."

"I'm not," I whisper.

"It's okay," Bethany's mom says quietly, and places a hand reassuringly on my arm.

Diane steps closer. "I know you haven't lived in Madrona long—"

"Eleven years," Bethany's mom retorts.

"—but if you had," Diane continues, "you'd understand that *all* the Sylvans are dangerous. Always have been. For generations. Every last one of them. This one's the same as the rest."

"You're right," I say, catching both of them off guard. I've even surprised myself. But I'm so tired. Tired of the accusations. Tired of being judged for the actions of family members I've never even met. But most especially, I'm so sick and tired of Diane Petersen.

She cocks her head to the side, confused. "Come again? I don't think I heard that right."

My fists clench and unclench at my sides. Something has shifted in me. Things are clicking into place. "I said you're right. I *am* the same as the rest of my family. But not in the way you think." I'm trying to sound calm, but my voice is shaking. My whole body is shaking. "I'm. Not. Doing. This." And for the first time, I truly, *truly* believe it. This isn't my fault. It really isn't.

I turn my back on Ms. Petersen and face Mrs. Lieu. "But I promise you," I assure her, "I'm going to find out who is. And I'm going to stop them." This I believe a little less. But saying it out loud cements my determination.

She nods and mouths, "Thank you."

"Mrs. Lieu?"

I look past Bethany's mom to find Cal standing down the hall. I don't know how long he's been there, but his face is flushed and his expression dark, so probably long enough. He makes eye contact with me for a split second before turning his attention back to Bethany's mom. She lets her shoulders droop. Tears return.

"I've got her," Cal tells the nurse, and shoots me another look I can't quite read, as Bethany's mom allows him to walk her back down the hall.

"Come on, Mrs. Lieu," I hear him say as they turn the corner. "I saw them bringing her back from her MRI."

"My husband should be here soon. I should text him and let him know . . ."

I retreat into Rhonda's room. The door clicks shut, and I lean my head against it, closing my eyes tight. I breathe in, then out. In. Out. A few more times. Then I push off from the door and go perch on the edge of Rhonda's bed.

"Hey, sis." I take her hand. It lays warm and heavy in mine. "I have to go now. I'm sorry. I might not be able to come back for a while. But I swear, I'm going to figure out how to get you out of here, okay? You first. Then the rest. Whatever it takes." I kiss her cheek and brush a stray hair away from her forehead, then give her one last look before I leave.

But the second I'm out of Rhonda's room, I'm in trouble again. I thought I'd given Diane enough time to move on, but unfortunately, she's still here. I think she's even been waiting for me. Her son, Chris, has come back out of his grandfather's room and is standing off to the side, looking like he'd rather be anywhere but here. And he's been joined by a woman I recognize from the gift shop—the one who was talking with Diane in hushed whispers when I ducked in that very first day. What could she be doing here?

"Nice little promise you gave to Bethany's poor mother just now," Diane says, while her tone says the opposite. "I think she even believed you."

My mouth goes dry. I look from her, to Chris, to the woman standing with him.

"She said she's not the one who put my dad and your son and everyone else into comas," Diane says to the woman, her voice dripping with sarcasm. "But she's going to find out who is and stop them."

The other woman—Troy's mom, I now know—doesn't say anything. She stares, stony-faced. And just past her, a movement catches my eye, farther down the hall. I notice just in time to see a dark figure pop back through a doorway. It was quick, but it looked a lot like Daniel. A wave of cold washes over me.

I'm sure it was him, but something looked off. I can't put my finger on what, exactly.

"Well? Are you?"

My attention snaps back to Diane. "Of course," I tell her.

She pokes her chin toward the door behind me. "Your sister in there?"

The hairs rise on the nape of my neck. She knows she is. Why else would I have been in there? She just wants to remind me she knows. I swallow hard. And nod.

"You'd better keep that promise," she says with another pointed look at Rhonda's door, "and you'd better do it soon, before the whole damn town winds up in here because of you."

She starts to walk away but stops in her tracks when I call after her, "Wait."

Surprised, she turns and stares at me. I know I should have let her go, but I've had enough. I'm much too angry now to stop myself.

She raises her eyebrows. "Excuse me? Do you have more empty promises to make?"

I'm shaking on the inside, but not with nerves this time. She threatened my sister. "Do you still seriously think I'm the one doing this?"

"Of course you are," she says.

I hold her gaze. "Then explain to me what you're still doing awake."

Eyes widening, she takes a step back. I can almost see the fear roiling off her, like billowing smoke. That dream—the first one, with Rob and the boys and the smoky shadow—creeps into the periphery of my vision, as the dream world tries to edge into this one. I can't let that happen. Not here. Not now.

It dissipates as I turn my back on the three and walk away. I need to get out of here. Get myself together. Nervous energy courses through my veins as I hurry to the elevator and punch the down button. It opens right away. I step inside.

"Wait up." A hand blocks the door as it starts to close. It slides back open, and Cal joins me, still flushed and out of breath. "I'm your ride, remember?"

I attempt a smile, but I don't think it works. He reaches across me to push the button for the lobby, and for a split second, I think I see blood—blood on his forehead, and then it's gone. My stomach lurches, and I sway on my feet as the elevator jolts into its descent. I really, *really* need that tea to wear off. Now. I can't take much more of this. Would it have hurt for whoever wrote that recipe to have listed the side effects?

"How's Bethany?" I manage.

"Well, uh . . . she's asleep."

Asleep. I bite down a retort to his retort. "What about Daniel?"

"Don't know. He isn't here."

"But I thought I saw him."

He shakes his head. "The woman at the nurse's station said he hasn't come by. They've been trying to get a hold of him all morning."

"He wasn't in his dad's room?"

"I checked his dad's room as I was coming back from helping Bethany's mom. And then I saw you taking off and had to catch up."

Another hallucination. Of course. That would explain why Daniel didn't look right.

The elevator stops on the next floor, the doors open, and a woman and two young children step on.

"Is Daddy gonna have a scar?" the youngest asks. The mom hushes her and shoots us an apologetic look. I flash a polite smile at her, then concentrate on my feet.

"Is he going to have amsena?" asks the youngest one again.

"Am*ne*sia," the older one corrects. With a blink, she's Rhonda at that age. With another blink, the similarity's gone.

"I don't know," the mom says, clipped. "We'll see."

Cal's fingers brush against mine. I accept, and we clasp hands as my gaze shifts from the floor to a smudge on the wall. When the elevator stops, the mom and kids get off.

Alone again, Cal leans close. "I'm sorry for being so angry with you earlier. I think I understand now why you took the risk."

"No," I say. "*I'm* sorry. What I did, especially alone, was dangerous. You have nothing to apologize for."

He gives my hand a squeeze, then lets go as the elevator stops again and an elderly couple hobbles on.

"Oh, how precious. Don't you mind us," the woman says, patting her husband on the shoulder to turn around. He grins and winks at us before shuffling around to face the door.

Cal and I exchange amused looks. Then, as the elevator lurches again, he puts an arm around my waist, drawing me to his side. I lean into him, and for a brief moment, I feel safe. *Together*, he'd said. We're in this together. And we have been for a long time, whether we knew it or not.

CHAPTER 33

On our way back to the house, we stop by the Roadhouse parking lot to get the rest of my stuff out of the rental car. Then, suitcases sliding around the truck bed, we head back to Miriam's. Cal pulls up in front of the hedge and cuts the engine. But as I reach around to unbuckle, he lightly puts his hand on my arm to stop me.

"Please don't take this the wrong way, but I don't—I don't like the idea of you staying here again tonight. Um . . . alone."

A slight thrill travels up my spine as I think about him staying, too, then turns to butterflies of anxiety over what that could mean. Then more butterflies at the thought of staying alone again in this creepy old house still plagued with the effects of that tea. Dreams can be freaky enough on their own. But this dreaming-while-awake thing is much worse. Every time I think it's starting to wear off, I'll see something else that makes me question whether I'm even awake at all. It does have to wear off eventually, though, right? It's been a few hours, so soon, I hope. But as much as I want Cal to stay, he's in enough trouble already.

"I promise, I'm not going to try any more of that tea if that's what you're worried about. Learned my lesson."

"I know. I trust you." His knee is bouncing. "But the attacks seem like they're sort of . . . ramping up. Daniel's dad and Bethany in the same night? And if it's definitely not you . . ."

"It's definitely not me."

"I know. But that also means you could be next. Haven't you noticed how all the attacks seem to be, well, circled around you?"

Yes, I've noticed. It would be hard not to. "I'm more worried about you being next," I admit.

"I don't think you have to worry about that." He looks uncomfortable. "It's happening through dreams, right?"

He doesn't dream. For his sake, I hope he's right. I finish unbuckling and scoot closer to him. "Well, I'm not going to be next, either. Because I'm going to make sure there isn't any next."

"How?" His gaze holds mine. "How will you do that?"

"I don't—I don't know. I'll have to dream on purpose somehow. I did it before, right? When I helped you. I'll figure it out." I don't feel nearly as confident as I sound. Now that I've had time to get over my initial relief, it's bothering me that I didn't dream about Chief Burke or Bethany last night. I dreamed about the rest. Why not them? What's changed? Is it a coincidence, or am I being purposely shut out?

"That was a different situation." He breaks eye contact and stares out the windshield, focusing in on something. I try to follow his line of sight, but I don't see anything out of the ordinary. Just the unruly hedge and the rusty iron gate. And I'll admit, I feel a bit relieved by this, because not seeing anything out of the ordinary must mean that tea is *finally* starting to wear off.

He points. "It happened right there. I didn't tell you before."

I look in the direction he's pointing, but the only thing there

303

is that large, rotted-out tree stump just outside the hedge near the gate. It must have been a massive tree once. *Perfect for climbing*.

"That's where you fell?" He's had to pass that thing every time he's come out here. Had to pass the spot where his friend *died*.

I couldn't even walk within a city block of where my dad was killed. I'd go out of my way to avoid it. It doesn't matter that I never saw him get shot, my brain has come up with a good idea of what it would have looked like. And it can be relentless. Cal might not remember any of it consciously, but I'll bet his brain does the same thing, except without the imagery. I saw his face when I almost fell down the stairs. His mind went somewhere else.

Like mine's doing right now, because by thinking about that city block, I've given it an in. I was wrong. The tea is still affecting me and making my jerk of a brain worse. Made-up images of Dad getting shot overlay my vision, but now they're swirling together with the very real images of Cal being hit and Graham sprawled on the ground with his twisted neck, running in an endless loop. I need to tamp down on this before it gets out of hand—shove the loop back into the darkened corners of my mind to deal with later. Focus on Cal's voice. He's still talking. Pay attention to that.

"I guess I wasn't the nicest kid," he's saying. "People won't talk about it, but it didn't take me long to figure that out. When I came back to school, everyone avoided me. And then they were surprised by everything. By how I acted, by what I said. And then they avoided me again, but in a different way. If that makes sense."

I know this part. Bethany told me. That's about all she told me, though, when I tried to ask why Daniel was so protective of Cal. *They used to hate each other*, I remember her saying. *But then he came back a different person.*

"I don't remember climbing that tree," he continues. "But I know it would have given me a great view over the hedge— into the witch's house." He says "witch's house" as if he's tasted something bitter.

"You were kids," I tell him, though I know it won't help. "Kids do stuff like that."

Without warning, Cal doubles over. At first, I think he's about to be sick, but then I see he's fishing around for something under the seats. When he straightens up, he's holding the stick.

I forgot he took that from me earlier. Or had I given it to him? I feel a little sick again myself as I realize I can't quite remember. The aftermath of the visions is fuzzier than the visions themselves. It's harder to tell what's a dream and what's real.

He stares at it for a moment, then turns his gaze back out the window. "You said you were this stick. Before."

The sudden intensity in his voice sets me on edge. "Did I? That tea—"

"Where did you get it?"

"The . . . tea?"

"No," he says, turning his full body to face me again. "The stick."

I hesitate. *See to remember.* Maybe Miriam didn't mean *I* was the one who needed to remember. But memories aren't always a good thing to have. I've been feeling sorry for Cal, not being

305

able to remember his best friend. But after what I saw—keep seeing . . .

I recoil as the images from that horrible stick flash before me yet again. I don't want to tell him what it showed me. I wouldn't wish that memory on anyone. But bad memories or not, he has a right to know. He *needs* to know what was done to him. He needs to know all of it. I take a steadying breath. The images fade.

"It was from Miriam."

And then everything tumbles out. I tell him how the stick was in the envelope with the letters from my dad, with no other explanation. About my early morning dream, where I saw my dad, then Miriam—or who I assume was Miriam—and that she told me I needed to "see." I tell him about the journals, and what I read in them—about what my relatives could do, about how they used it, some for bad, some for good. I hesitate again, then I tell him about May's journal. And the shadows she saw. And that she died. I tell him everything I've learned since I saw him last night.

He listens quietly, without interruption, and I can't read him. I don't like not being able to read him, so I avoid his face most of the time, looking down at my hands, off toward the tree stump with shadows swirling all around it that I have to blink away, down at the stick grasped tightly in his hand, so tightly, his knuckles are white. I don't give myself the chance to wonder what he's thinking, or I might stop talking. Or I might run away. Or I might throw up again. Because now I'm coming to what I saw when I drank that god-awful tea while holding that god-awful stick, and I know I'll need to tread carefully.

"What people have told you," I say, "that's not the entire story. But I don't think they *know* the entire story." Finally, I look up at him. He's facing the front again, his jaw clenched so hard, I can see the muscle pop where it meets below his ear.

"Someone else was there that night," I continue with caution. "You did fall. Your head was injured. But that's not what put you in a coma. That stick was."

He blinks and looks down at the stick. "It's too small for that." His voice is quiet. Flat. It's the first thing he's said since I started.

"Well, I mean, it broke. That's only a piece of it. It hit you so hard, it broke when it—when they . . ." I trail off as the image assaults me yet again. "And besides, you were already in bad shape. I don't think it would have taken much."

He nods as he takes in everything I've said. "I was trespassing."

He says it in such a matter-of-fact way, it's disconcerting.

"Do you think this was your fault? That because you were trespassing, you somehow deserved what you got?" And then it hits me—he thinks it was Miriam defending her property.

"This isn't your fault," I stress. "Look at me. It's connected, but it isn't your fault. And it wasn't Miriam, if that's where you were going with that. The hand I saw swinging that stick was too young to be hers." It was, wasn't it? I search my memory. But, of course, now that I actually *want* to see the images again, I'm having trouble bringing them up. The hand was dirty. I remember dirt. And it was small. But no . . . no, it definitely wasn't an elderly hand. I'm sure of that.

"Someone else was there that night," I continue, "and you

307

saw them, and I don't think they wanted you to." Graham's neck, bent much too far. That feeling of panic as Cal got up and looked toward the wielder of the stick. He recognized them. I'm sure of it. "Someone's hiding something," I continue. "From you, from me, from everyone in this town. Someone we know is guilty, and—"

I suck in my breath as what I've said hits me full-on. That's it. That's the connection I was looking for. Guilt. Shadows that feel like guilt. So much overwhelming guilt. Guilt mixing with my own. Growing stronger . . .

Who was there that night? Whose hand held that stick? I'll bet anything that's who I need to stop. Miriam knew who it was. She must have. And she would have tried to help them, like May tried to help that soldier. But their shadow was too much, their guilt too strong, and now—now that I, someone else who might interfere, am here, their shadow is back. I can even feel it now, swirling just beyond the edges of my vision. Or is that another waking dream?

I shake my head. Why, then, does it seem to be going after everyone *but* me? There's still something I don't understand. In May's experience, the shadow always acted as if it was coming for her. She never mentioned it attacking anyone else.

Because when I moved here, I brought something with me. My own baggage—my own guilt. And the guiltier I've felt, the stronger the shadows have become. And the stronger they've become, the guiltier I've felt. As if we've been fueling each other. Jolee tried to warn me, too. She told me I had to get my own guilt under control. But I didn't understand, and now it's gotten to the point where the shadow doesn't even need me anymore. For

Chief Burke, for Bethany—it was strong enough on its own. Damnit, I need to know who was holding that stick.

"Eva, I think you need to go home." Cal's words rip through my train of thought, knocking me off track.

I blink. I think I missed something. "I *am* home."

"I mean New York."

My eyes sting. "I don't understand. You want me to leave?"

"I don't *want* you to leave—" His voice catches. "I want you to be safe. And New York's as far from all this as you can reasonably get."

"But the stick . . ."

"I don't care about the stupid stick!"

I flinch as, without thinking, he tries to chuck it out of the truck. It catches on the edge of the half-open window, ricochets off, and lands in his lap. Then, in a further spurt of frustration, he violently sweeps it onto the floor between my feet. When he looks up at me, I flinch again. I've never seen him act out like that.

His eyes widen. "I'm sorry." He holds his hands in the air around me like he's afraid to touch me. Like he thinks he'll break me.

My whole body has gone rigid.

"I'm so sorry," he says again.

I let out a slow breath. "You don't need to apo—"

"I don't—I don't care about the stick," he tries again. "I care about you. And that shadow you read about in . . . in . . ."

"May's journal." So, he's finally connecting the dots.

"Do you think that's what happened to Miriam, too?"

I can't bring myself to answer that, but he takes my silence as a yes.

309

"Do you think that's what's happening to everyone else?" he asks. "Have you—Eva, have *you* seen shadows, in those dreams?"

I probably shouldn't tell him I'm seeing shadows even now, flitting about the hedge. But they're not real. *They can't be, because I'm awake. It's that tea. It's just the tea.* The shadows disappear, and I take a breath.

"I'm not going to run away and abandon everyone just because there's a chance I might fail. If I don't try? If I run off to be 'safe'? That's failing. It's failing everyone back at the hospital. They need me. And besides," I remind him, "I don't think distance matters when it comes to dreams. It didn't with you."

"Eva, please listen. You could die," he says. "If you fail, you could die."

Yes. Yes, I could. But I can't think about that right now. "It's gonna be okay," I tell him. I don't know that. Of course, I don't know that. But what else can I say? "I promise."

"That's not a promise you can make."

"I'm making it, anyway. So now I have to keep it, okay?"

He nods. The bench seat creaks as I scoot closer. We lean together, foreheads touching, like last night . . . in the cemetery . . . when we almost . . .

My pulse quickens as his hands slip around my waist. I pause, then tilt my chin toward his. And this time, I don't dodge at the last minute. I'm surprised by how soft his lips are. How warm. How perfectly they fit with mine. He draws back slowly and searches my face. I nod, my heart pounding, and this time, our lips part as they connect. My nerves light up, and the rest of the world falls away. I want to stay like this forever, his palms pressing into my hips, my fingers tangled in the waves of his hair. Lungs in sync, falling, falling . . .

Because we know. We both know my promise is a lie.

We both know I'm going to have to fall.

CHAPTER 34

My lips are still tingling as we drag my suitcases into the house. Cal thumps Rhonda's down next to the couch. "I still don't think you should be on your own tonight."

I raise an eyebrow, and he rolls his eyes, but he's grinning. "You know what I mean."

Shadowy movement flits past me, and I blink it away. He's probably right. But . . . "You're not supposed to be hanging around me, remember?" I can't stand the thought of him getting grounded again right now. I can barely stand the thought of him having to leave at all. I can barely stand.

"They think I'm staying with Daniel."

My stomach flutters at this, and not in a good way.

"As you should be," I tell him. "He needs his best friend right now. I don't like not knowing where he's disappeared to."

I think I hear a creak, then a quiet shuffle from somewhere deeper in the house, but I shake it off. It's the house making strange noises as usual. Nothing to worry about.

"I don't like it, either," Cal says. "I'll try calling him again." He pulls out his cell, then remembers—no service—and puts it back in his pocket. We head for the ancient phone in the kitchen. "If he doesn't answer, maybe I can try calling the hospital to see if he ever—"

Cal and I skid to a halt just inside the kitchen doorway.

"Oh, hey," Daniel says without bothering to look up. "You found me."

My chest thumps. "*You found me.*" Where have I heard that recently? And why don't I feel relieved now that I know where he is?

He's sitting at the kitchen table, casually flipping through the Sylvan family recipe book like a waiting room fashion magazine. May's journal pokes out from underneath. And the letters—*Dad's letters*—are spread out all around it. That's not how I left them. My hands ball into fists.

"You two seemed a little, uh ... busy." He licks his finger and flips another page. "So, I went ahead and let myself in. I hope that was cool with you." He twists in an exaggerated way to look at the back door. He's managed to prop it open, but it's still askew. When he turns to face us again, he finally makes eye contact. "It was unlocked."

Under normal circumstances, I'd be mortified. Daniel saw us. Walked right on past us while we were having our make-out session in the truck. But my cheeks don't even have the decency to flush. It's hard to blush when you suddenly feel so cold.

Now that Daniel's lifted his eyes to us, I can see how red-rimmed they've become. Even more so than last night. Huge dark circles have formed underneath. His cheeks sag, and his head has become too heavy for his neck. He can hardly keep it straight between his shoulders.

"Daniel?" I ask, careful to keep my voice steady. "When was the last time you slept?"

He lifts his hand and jabs at the air in my general direction, a

313

bemused expression on his face. "You've asked me that before. It's a weird question to just ask someone, you know? It's like you're obsessed with it or something." Scooting his chair back, he plants both hands on the table to push himself up but stumbles and sits down hard on the very edge of his seat. If I didn't know better, I'd think he was drunk. But I know sleep deprivation and mismanaged grief when I see it. Has something else happened with his dad? Has his condition worsened?

Cal rushes over as Daniel makes another attempt to stand. He hooks an arm around him, catching him to keep him upright. I hurry over, too, and help to prop Daniel from the other side.

"Come on," Cal groans as we half lead, half drag Daniel through the house and out to the truck. "I'm taking you home."

Daniel's body is behaving like a cat that doesn't want to be picked up—suddenly longer and heavier than it should be. It takes all our strength and ingenuity to help him climb into the truck cab and get him buckled in. It doesn't help that I'm still feeling twitchy from the aftereffects of that tea.

"No!" Daniel's attention perks up with the click of the seat belt. "No, no, I'll fall asleep. Cars make me drowsy."

"Dude, you fell asleep at least five times on the way out here from the kitchen," Cal tells him. I shoot Cal a Look.

"Well, he did."

"No, no, you don't underst—"

The passenger door swings shut on him mid-protest, and Cal and I move off a ways so we can discuss what to do next.

"He must have heard about Bethany," Cal says.

"That, and he's scared he's going to be next," I add. "He's been pumping caffeine into his veins all week."

314

Cal exhales heavily and hooks his thumbs in his pockets. He looks from the truck to the house and back to me, weighing his options. Daniel's gone quiet again, but I can tell he's still fighting sleep. He keeps blinking and staring down at the floor of the truck. What could be so fascinating about his shoes?

"Should we take him back inside?" Cal suggests. "We could take turns keeping an eye on him that way. Make sure he's *just* sleeping, like normal sleeping, and not, you know . . ."

"Not sure how you'd be able to tell until it's too late."

I take another peek at Daniel. His chin is now resting on his chest. I can't see his eyes, but I think they've finally closed. He doesn't look peaceful, though. I don't like this. Everything about this is off. Where's he been all day? Why would he come here, after being so pissed at me last night? He was going through my stuff. Reading through my very personal, very private things. My stomach knots. I don't want him here.

"No, take him home," I tell Cal. "He'll sleep better in his own bed. And then call me when you get there, okay?"

"But what about you?"

"I'll be fine. He needs you."

Cal gives me a hug, then presses his lips softly to my forehead before climbing into the driver's seat. "Promise me you won't do anything about . . . you know . . . while you're alone, please, okay? Wait for me to come back."

"Promise," I tell him.

Daniel lifts his head with a jerk when the door slams shut. As the truck pulls out, he turns to watch me and continues to turn, looking out the back to maintain eye contact as they drive away. But just as they're about to pass out of view, his gaze shifts and his eyes darken. I barely catch it, but it's enough to make my stomach twist. I look behind me, then around me. There's nothing there.

He's so sleep-deprived, he's probably hallucinating. *Like I've been doing,* I realize. *Half dreaming, half awake.*

Even the constant flow of caffeine running through his veins can barely keep him awake. He'll fall asleep soon, he has to, and everything will be fine. Cal will get him home just fine. Then he'll call me, and we'll figure out what to do next. It'll be *fine.*

But no matter how hard I think the word "fine," I can't push away the feeling in my gut that this is *not* fine. Something's really off about Daniel. Something more than sleep deprivation. I think back to the hospital. How I was so sure I saw him, but he didn't look right. If that wasn't him, who was it?

Was there anyone there at all? I think as I head back into the house. There can't have been, because I was hallucinating, obviously. Right? The tea was—*is*—still affecting me. But . . . now I'm not sure. Because what I saw, that Daniel-shaped figure down the hallway—the figure I was so positive was him—it looked an awful lot like a shadow.

All the blood drains from my face. Daniel didn't look like *a* shadow. He looked like *the* shadow. All the caffeine, the fear of sleep, his disappearance after his dad's coma—how hadn't I seen it before? *Oh my God, it's him. It's Daniel.*

In a flash, I'm back out the door. They can't have gotten far yet. The dirt-rutted road doesn't lend itself to fast driving. The most he could be going is, what—five miles per hour? Ten?

Parking lot speed. I haven't run track since middle school, but I might be able to catch up to that.

My legs are pumping faster than they've ever pumped before. Shadows flick in and out of view around me, just on the edge of my vision. I don't turn to confirm that they're there. They both are and they aren't. I know that now. My eyes have *not* been playing tricks on me. Ever since I drank that tea, I've had one foot in the waking world and one foot in the dream world.

And so does Daniel. It's him. It's *his* shadow. He's so tired, so exhausted, I think he must be dreaming even while awake. We're both dreaming while awake, and that has to be why I can see it. Daniel's protests on being put in the truck have taken on a whole new meaning. It's just a guess, but as long as he's semi-conscious, maybe he can control it, but the minute he falls asleep all the way . . .

I need to stop them before they get too far.

I reach the hill; my thighs burn as I push them harder so as not to lose momentum, only to come to an abrupt stop at the crest.

"No," I murmur. "No, no, no . . ."

Cal's truck. It's veered off the dirt road and is idling against a large boulder in the middle of the field. I take off running again, down the other side of the hill and into the brush. I curse the tall grass for slowing me down as I wade through it, my shins and ankles collecting a million scratches and stings.

I yank open the driver's side door and move to catch Cal as he slumps toward me, but his seat belt locks, holding him at a gruesome angle. A purpling goose egg is already forming on his browbone. And Daniel's gone. The passenger side door is hanging open, and Daniel is nowhere to be seen.

"Daniel?" I call out. Nothing. "Daniel!"

Still no answer. And despite me yelling right beside him, Cal remains unconscious.

"Wake up, Cal, come on, wake up." I know it's useless, but I keep trying, anyway. I push him upright in his seat. I clasp his face, I shake his shoulders, I scream at him, "Wake up!"

His face remains slack, but his chest moves in and out in a steady rhythm. *He's okay, he's okay,* I tell myself. *He's not dead. But he's been knocked out. And now he's asleep and he won't wake up.* Then, *Damnit, you told me it wouldn't happen to you. You don't dream, Cal, so it can't happen to you. It can't.* But I guess that doesn't matter anymore. If Daniel's dreaming while awake, all it must have taken was a single moment of unconsciousness for his shadow to find its way in.

I suck in my breath as it hits me full force—if Cal doesn't dream, how will I reach him to wake him up? Could it be that he's wrong? He must dream, because that's how I reached him before, when we were kids. That was *after* his fall. He could still dream then, which means his head injury didn't cause that. He must not remember them when he wakes up. Right? That has to be it.

Right. It'll be okay, it'll be okay. I try to steady my own breaths to match his, to calm myself so I can think more clearly. But I can't. The rhythm of my lungs remains ragged and erratic. My hands shake as I reach over him and turn off the ignition. I go to set the parking brake as well but find that someone's already done it. Daniel. Anger boils up inside me. Where is he? He did this, I know he did, and then he just left! He left Cal like *this* and ran off. *He fucking ran off.* With a roar of frustration, I kick the front tire as hard as I can.

This was not supposed to happen. I was supposed to fix everything before anything else *could* happen. I need to find Daniel and stop him before he can strike again, but . . . I can't leave Cal injured and unconscious in the middle of nowhere.

I bite my lip, then make a decision. I'm not strong enough to carry him. I'll have to drive him back to the house and call an ambulance. Then I'll go after Daniel.

Yes. This should work. I undo Cal's buckle, ease him down to lie along the bench, and scoot him over to make room for me to climb up and take his spot. He's taller than me, and I can't get the seat to adjust. I have to perch on the edge to reach the pedals.

What the hell am I doing? I don't know how to drive. *Right is go and left is stop, right?* My palms are sweating, making the steering wheel slick and hard to grip. Then it occurs to me that for someone who doesn't know what they're doing, this is actually the perfect spot to figure it out. We're in the middle of a freaking field. There's nothing here to hit except this boulder, and that's already happened. I crank the key, and the engine revs to life. It takes me a second to figure out how a steering column works, but I finally manage to slot it into reverse, then with a jerk, I get the truck to back up, away from the boulder.

Okay. This isn't so bad. I continue to back the truck around in a wide arc until I'm turned around and lined up with the wheel-rutted road that leads back to the house. From here, it'll just be a matter of applying enough pressure to the gas to get the truck up the hill, then applying the brake enough to ease it back down the other side without soaring like a roller coaster straight into the hedge.

I shift into drive and ease up the slope and over the crest of the hill, and am just starting down the other side when I stomp on the brake, shooting my arm out to the side to brace Cal from rolling off the seat.

There's Daniel. I can see him up ahead, sitting on the edge of the stump by the gate. The remains of the tree where this all began. *Where he did what he did.*

I ease off the brake pedal and creep the truck down the hill, parking crookedly in front of the hedge.

Like back in the kitchen, Daniel doesn't bother to look up when I get out of the truck. He's focusing hard on something cradled in his hands. I can't see it from here, but I can make a pretty good guess as to what it is. It wasn't his shoes that he was blinking at back in the truck. It was the stick.

Red-hot rage tints my vision. Before I can think, I've shot out of the truck and closed the distance between us. I grab Daniel by the shirt collar with one fist and pull back my other, poised to swing. I've never punched anyone before. Never even come close, until now. The stick tumbles out of his hands and lands at his feet with a thud in the dirt.

He finally looks up at me, his face twisted into a tearstained grimace. Like he's *relieved* that my fist is about to make contact with his face. He *wants* me to beat the shit out of him. He believes—he *knows* he deserves this and so much more. The guilt is so thick in the air, I could choke on it.

All the fight in me evaporates. I let my arm flop. With a shove, I release his shirt and take a step back.

Daniel blinks at me once . . . twice, then slowly reaches up and adjusts his stretched-out collar. "It was in the road. I thought . . . I mean, I saw it."

"Saw what?"

"That shadow. I thought I saw it. In the road. Cal didn't. So I grabbed the wheel. And—" He swallows hard.

"And then you just *left* him there." My fist clenches again involuntarily.

He shakes his head, but he's not disagreeing. "Why'd you have to come here? I thought it was finally over."

He thought it was over. I'm hit with a wave of nausea as it dawns on me what he means. "Did you kill her?" I ask him through gritted teeth. "Did you kill Miriam?"

He stares down at the stick now resting in the dirt between us, a glaring beacon of shame and guilt. "I didn't want any of this to happen," he says, exhaustion seeping out of every pore. "But I can't control it, Eva. I can't make it stop."

The hairs rise up on my arms. I can feel it. His shadow—I can't see it, but it's somewhere near.

"Miriam was trying to help you, wasn't she? Because you were having nightmares." I nudge the stick toward him with my foot. "Because of what you did."

He looks up at me. Anger briefly flashes in his eyes, then dissipates just as quickly. I can feel the shadow growing but resist the urge to look for it. I'm pretty sure it's coming for me no matter what I do. Unless . . . I can get him to face it. I think back to May's last journal entry. *If I could just get him to face it. To face his guilt. I think he could control it.*

"I didn't mean for it to happen like that," he says. "I only wanted to scare them. Get back at them for all the mean shit they did." The anger in his eyes returns and stays a little longer this time. And the shadow—the shadow grows. I can see it now in my periphery, lurking at the edge of the woods.

"I only wanted to scare them," he repeats, almost as if he's trying to convince himself more than me. "I didn't mean to hurt them."

"But you did hurt them." I don't know what he did to cause Graham and Cal to fall out of that tree. Maybe that was a mistake. But what he did afterward—you don't swing a stick at someone's head like that by accident. "And now people are getting hurt again. Daniel, you need to stop this."

"I knew they were coming out here," he continues as if he hasn't heard me. "They were bragging about it all fucking day. But it was just a prank! A mean trick! I wanted them to think Miriam was casting some kind of spell, like a hex or something, so I . . . I threw a firecracker into this tree. It wasn't even a big one. All I wanted was to scare them. I thought maybe then they'd leave her alone. I didn't know it would make them fall. I didn't." He's rocking back and forth now, staring through me as if I'm no longer here. In his mind, he's twelve years old again, watching the events of that night play out, over and over as the shadow at the edge of the woods moves closer.

I glance over at the truck where Cal is sleeping, fighting the growing urge to run away. *He's okay*, I remind myself. *He got knocked out, or stunned, or something—like falling asleep—and the only*

322

reason he won't wake up is because it got him. What if I let it get me, too? What if I stop running and just let it? Then maybe I can find him and wake him up along with everyone else.

"So you saw them fall, and came out of your hiding place." *Come out of your hiding place, shadow.* I don't need Daniel to tell me the rest of this story. I've seen it. It plays out backward in my mind, and I turn it around. "You saw the piece of a branch that broke off when they fell. You picked it up." I reach down and pick it up from where he dropped it when I almost punched him. He flinches, but I keep going, relentless. "And then you saw Graham. And he didn't look right." *He needs to understand what he did. Like May's Bobby, he needs to face it.* "And then Cal—he got back up. And *he* saw *you.* You realized Graham was dead, and Cal knew it was your fault. So, you panicked, didn't you? You panicked, and you were already holding a big stick, and you didn't think. You just swung and hit him over the head with it. You hit him so hard he was in a coma for two weeks."

"Stop it!" His face contorts. He can't hold back the flood of tears anymore. He doesn't even try.

"You're guilty, Daniel." I drive it home, piercing him with each syllable. *I saw what he did.* May's words run through my head. Her revelation about Bobby's shadow hits me as if it was my own. *I know what fuels Daniel's shadow.* And it's growing. Reaching beyond the edge of the woods. Stretching toward us.

"You've been holding on to that guilt for years and years." *Don't panic,* I tell myself. *Don't panic this time.* "And you've been trying to make up for it all this time, haven't you? By being there for Cal when he needed it most, defending him when people bullied him the way he and Graham used to bully you. But that isn't good enough. The guilt is still there, festering, turning into nightmares that have taken on a life of their own."

"Stop it," Daniel warns me again through gritted teeth.

"And then when Miriam tried to help you, she *died*, and you felt even more guilty. Which made it worse. And then I showed up with my own guilty baggage, which fueled yours. Which made it even w—"

"Stop!" Daniel screams at me. He's closing his eyes, clutching his head. "You have to stop! It's coming!"

The shadow bursts out from the woods, growing, flowing, roiling toward us, darkening everything in its path.

"You have to run!" Daniel cries. "It's going to take you, too!"

I have to fight every muscle in my body against following his advice. He's not going to face it on his own. He's too scared and his guilt is too strong. *There's only one other thing I can do.* Was this how it played out with May? And Miriam? Is this how they died?

"It's coming, Eva, it's coming," he says again as I dart forward and grab his hands away from his temples. I hold them tight, forcing him to look at me.

"I know. And you're coming with me."

This better work. Please don't let me die.

I close my eyes, willing my waking half to join my dreaming half. Giving myself over to sleep. The shadow washes over us, and everything goes dark.

CHAPTER 35

Surrounded by darkness, we fall.

Fine threads of silver stretch out from each of us, perceptible only if I don't look directly at them. I'm holding Daniel's hands in a death grip as he struggles to break free, wriggling and panicking as if I'm pushing him underwater. What I'm really trying to do is keep him from drifting off, sinking away into the oblivion of his shadow, drowning in his own guilt.

"Daniel, stop fighting this," I tell him, and yet my mouth hasn't moved. I guess it doesn't need to here. I get the feeling he can hear me in his head. Because that's where we are, I think. "You need to stop running away from your guilt and face it."

But he won't. *What was it that you knew you had to do, May? What am I going to have to do?*

"Face my guilt?" Daniel scoffs in my head. "You mean like *you* have?"

A surge of energy shoots down his arms and up my own, breaking him free as the ground catches our feet. He's off and running while trees, massive trees, erupt from the dirt all around us.

I try to run after him, but I can't. My legs are heavy and slow, as if slogging through waist-high mud. All I can do is watch helplessly as he disappears into the distance; his silver thread stretches so far behind him, so thin, until it, too, fades from my perception and the forest envelops him, leaving me surrounded by nothing but trees. So many trees. The same tree, stamped over and over again so every direction is identical.

What the hell do I do now?

Focus. I wonder if I can shift the dreamscape around me somehow, close the distance to bring him back to me, or appear in front of him. I'll bet my ancestors knew how to do this. I feel like I should know, too, that maybe I even used to be able to once. But I can't remember for sure. I don't know how far Miriam got in teaching me these things before Dad told her to stop.

I need to try. I need to remember. I close my eyes to help me concentrate, but it doesn't matter because my eyelids won't block out the dreamscape. Trees still fill my vision. *That's because my eyes are already closed*, I remind myself—*have been this entire time.* I keep trying, though, as my heart rate speeds up—*has it sped up for real, or is that an illusion, too?* I feel a growing sense of urgency, like when images of my dad intrude on my mind and I can't make them stop. It's the same. It feels the same. *Go away, trees. You're not really here. None of this is really*—

Sirens scream in the distance.

Lots of them.

"No," I whisper.

The trees close in, fusing together into walls. The dirt softens beneath my bare feet. Where are my shoes? I squish my toes into carpet. Brown shag. My nose fills with the aroma of garlic and spaghetti sauce. Rain pitter-patters against the window.

"No."

There's an alarm sound. A phone. Dad's phone.

"No. This isn't what I meant."

"Then what did you mean, Eva?" Dad snaps. He checks his phone, sighs, then slips it back in his pocket. "Great."

He turns away from the stove after clicking off the burner and raises a finger at me. "We will discuss this when I get back. And I do expect you to be here when I get back to discuss it."

You're putting me on house arrest now? Like some kind of criminal? Riley's dad's the cop, not you. That's what I'd said. Among other things. Worse things. Just before he left.

"No." Panic wells up inside me. I step in front of him, blocking him from leaving the kitchen. "You can't go."

"Eva, I have to."

"You *can't.*"

He gives me a frustrated look. "Come on, Eva. I don't have time for this. Out of the way."

I plant my feet. "No."

"Evangeline!"

"No!"

His face softens, and he stops trying to dart around me. "You can't stop this from happening, Bug. You know that." He reaches out and puts a hand on my cheek. It's calloused and warm and feels so real.

"Yes, I can," I plead, tears streaming. "Just don't go. Just this once, stay home. It's your night off. You don't have to go."

"I do. They need me for this one."

"*I* need you," I tell him. "I'm sorry, okay? I'm really sorry. Please don't go." This is real again, it feels *so real.* I'll say anything, do anything to make him stay. "I won't go to Riley's party, like

327

you told me. I'll stop complaining about it. I'll—I'll fix my attitude. You were right. A house party while her parents are out of town is a terrible idea."

I can still remember how drunk everyone got. Especially Riley. And how nervous I felt, knowing I was already in hot water for helping her break into her dad's liquor cabinet weeks before, just to show her I could. Knowing that if Dad found out I'd gone to the party when he'd expressly forbidden me to do so, and that, worse, alcohol had been present, it wouldn't matter that I was one of the few people there who'd opted for soda instead. It would be the end of me being allowed to hang out with Riley.

"Damn right it's a terrible idea." His impatient tone is back. He looks at the clock. "Where is your sister? Never mind. I gotta go. You stay here. No party."

It's not working. What do I need to do to stop him from leaving?

I try another tactic. I tell the truth. "Okay, then, I . . . I *won't* stay. *You'll* have to stay to keep me here. If you leave, so will I. I'll go. So . . . so you have to stay. *Please.*"

"It's too late, Eva." Shadows form in the corners of the room. "Nothing you can do will stop this from happening." From the corners of his eyes, shadows drip down. "Because it already has."

They're streaming down his cheeks, obscuring his face. I have to stop them. I have to get them off. I raise my hands to wipe them away, but my hands are covered in blood. Blood and shadow, blood and shadow. I hear screaming, relentless screaming. It's coming from me. I stumble backward and scream some more.

This is a dream, I remind myself. *This feels real, but it isn't. It's a dream. It's—it's Daniel's dream.*

The shadows take over Dad's entire head, then his chest,

his arms, and his body all become a billowing cloud of thick, smoky tendrils. He inches toward me as I inch away. And the rain pounds rapid-fire on the windowpanes.

"Daniel?" I call out. This has to be him. "Stop! Why are you doing this?"

"This is *your* fault," the shadow that used to be my father bellows at me. "If only you'd been a better daughter, if only you'd fixed your attitude, I wouldn't have left that night."

Those aren't his words. They're mine. He's echoing the things I'd let slip to my therapist in a moment of weakness. Once I'd said them, I'd immediately wanted to take them back. Because logically, I knew it wasn't true. I still know it isn't true, but in my darkest moments, I believe it, anyway. Logic doesn't exist when you're suffering.

This isn't my dad. And it isn't Daniel. This is me. This is *my* shadow. *I'm* doing this. I need to get it under control. How can I help Daniel if I can't even help myself?

The shadows close in around me, closer and closer, shrinking the room.

"I would have stayed if you had shown any appreciation for how much I was trying to protect you. But no," the shadow bellows again, sounding more and more like me than him. "All you could think about was Riley's party, how it wasn't fair, how I was mean, and you hated me, and why couldn't I trust you and let you go like the other parents. You're selfish and ungrateful." Each word feels like a bullet to the chest.

"Dad would n-never have said that to me." It's true. He never would have. But did he think it? Was that the last thing he thought?

329

"I would have stayed," the shadow continues. "I didn't have to go. I was off that night and—"

"You would have gone no matter what," I whisper. "It—it wasn't just your job. It was who you were. You had people to save."

I have people to save. And in order to save them, I have to save Daniel. Which I won't be able to do unless I can figure out how to get this under control. *What is wrong with me? Why can't I just . . . get this . . . to stop?* If I can't, I'll end up stuck in a coma like the others, and I'll never get them free, and it will all be my fault.

My. Fault.

I gasp as the shadows around me home in to my thoughts and become more solid. I'm doing it again. I'm blaming myself. I'm feeling guilty for feeling guilty, and my shadow is growing stronger because of it.

Jolee tried to warn me about this. *You're holding on to so much guilt,* she'd said before I stormed out of her kitchen. I wasn't ready to hear it then. But I know now that she was right. *You must let the guilt go,* she'd said. *Before it*—And that's when she'd stopped herself. She must have sensed it would have been too much for me to hear right then, but I know now what she was trying to say. *Before it turns to shadow.* Just like it has with Daniel. That's what's going to happen to me if I keep going down this path. But . . . if I can get my own guilt under control, maybe I can help him do the same.

And where *is* he? This is his dream; he has to be seeing this.

The shadow retreats but only a little. "I would have gone without your nasty words following me out the door. The last words from you I would ever hear."

330

I can smell it—*my* guilt—as tendrils lash out at me from the surrounding shadows, threatening to snag me and carry me away. "I hate you," one mimics in my voice. "I wish it was you who left, not Mom," mimics another. "*She* would have let me go."

It would be so easy to give in right now. To let it overtake me. To let myself believe I deserve it. It's probably for the best. But . . . I can't. I can't let it take on a life of its own like Daniel has. I refuse.

"No," I say firmly, though I feel anything but. "I'm not going to do this." I remember now what the therapist told me when I'd let that awful admission slip. "I'm a teenager. Attitude is par for the course."

"That's no excuse," the shadow hisses at me. It's the same thing I'd said to her.

And again, I draw on my therapist's words. Words I've tried and failed to embrace, over and over again. "I know it's no excuse. I'm not—I'm not excusing myself. But I can't change what happened."

The shadow retreats a little more. I can't change it. I want to change it. I can't. Just like Daniel will never be able to change what he did. He will always feel regret.

My therapist told me I needed to forgive myself. I'd told her I never could. She said I could, and I would, when I was ready.

"Forgiving myself is not excusing myself." I repeat her words to the shadows around me, trying desperately to believe it. "And it's not forgetting. It's—it's accepting. And learning. And changing." I stand taller, firmer. I think I understand the difference now. And I think I almost *do* believe it. *I hope you're watching, Daniel.* Because I'm not just doing this for me, I'm doing this for him, too. Like putting my oxygen mask on before that of the person next to me, I need to forgive myself before I can even begin to help Daniel do the same. *This is what it's going to take, Daniel. This is what you're going to have to do.*

And holy crap, is it hard. But I can do this. I have to. I face my shadow. "I'm ready to start forgiving myself. Right now."

The shadows go still, waiting, like a held breath.

"I—" I swallow. I have to mean it. "I forgive you, Evangeline."

At first, nothing happens. Why is nothing happening? I don't know what else to do if this doesn't work. But then, like the release of a sigh, the shadows retreat.

Light returns, the pounding rain becomes a soft pitter-patter, and the sirens fade off into the distance. The walls peel away as the floor melts back into oblivion. All that's left is my dad. *No, not my dad.* "Don't go," I cry, reaching out for him. He simply smiles as his image shimmers away. I fall to my knees and breathe. And breathe.

"So that's it? That's the 'baggage' you brought with you?" comes a quiet voice beside me. Daniel's reappearance is so seamless, it feels as if he's been here this entire time.

"I *have* been here this entire time," he says, reminding me I also don't need to say things out loud for him to hear me. "It's my dream, remember?"

"Good," I say. "Then you understand what you have to do."

He offers me his hand, helping me up. "Do you feel better, though?"

I don't feel better.

I don't feel like any weight has been lifted from my shoulders. More like that weight has shifted a little. Like it's sitting in a way that makes it easier to carry. And maybe, for a start, that's enough. My shadow and my guilt aren't gone—not completely—but I think maybe I'm less afraid of them now.

"No," I tell him. "But I will. And so will you, eventually. If you let yourself."

He shakes his head. "It's too late now. Even if you did feel better, my shadow's grown too strong. It doesn't need to feed off yours anymore."

"Wh-what do you mean?"

The ground shakes as if in answer, and I find myself sinking again. No, wait . . . everything around me is rising. I struggle to stay on my feet as trees sprout from the ground right and left. The same tree over and over again.

"You'll see. This is *my* dream, remember? Or should I say my nightmare. My mental hell. And you actually chose to come here." He lets out a bitter laugh. "Welcome, I guess."

The shaking stops and all around us, the trees blink out. All . . . except one.

CHAPTER 36

We're back where we started. There's the hedge that surrounds Miriam's house—my house. There's the gate, in slightly better condition than when I last saw it. And next to us, where the stump should be, is a fully grown oak.

Darkness surrounds us, but I can see everything clearly by the moonlight. If I could see an actual moon, I might be fooled into thinking I was awake.

"Here's the thing," Daniel says in a soft voice. "There's no way I'm gonna be able to do what you just did. It's not possible."

"You have to try. I'll be right here with you," I assure him.

He shakes his head. "It's one thing to forgive yourself for back-talking your dad. But this? How can you possibly expect me to forgive myself for this?"

There's a flash of light and the deafening pop of a firecracker overhead, a yell, the snapping of branches. I choke on the smell of cordite wafting down through the air, then jump back with a gasp as two small bodies land at my feet with a sickening thud. One lies contorted to a grotesque degree, eyes staring at nothing, dead. Graham. Next to him lies a younger version of Cal, and if I didn't know better, I'd think he was dead, too. Bile rises in my throat. I gag, bending in half, bracing myself with hands on my knees, but nothing comes out since, in reality, there's nothing there. *We're not really here*, I remind myself. *None of this is real.* But it *feels* real.

"You see?" he says.

Oh, I can see. I can't stop seeing. I close my eyes, and I can still see because eyelids do nothing in this place.

"This is unforgivable," he continues as the battered image of a much younger Cal pushes up to his knees right in front of me. Red slicks his blond hair where his head came in contact with the ground. How he's at all conscious at this point is beyond me.

Focus. I need to focus.

Graham? Younger Cal says, then wobbles to his feet. He's off balance. He's going to fall. I rush forward to catch him, but my hands go straight through him, because he's not really here. He looks through me to another boy. Daniel—not the Daniel whose dream I'm in, but the young Daniel from that night. Younger Cal's expression changes as he recognizes him. At first, in relief.

Get help, he says. Then his gaze shifts to the branch the younger Daniel is holding. His brows furrow. *What are you doing?*

The younger Daniel looks down at Graham, his eyes widening with panic. He looks back to the younger Cal, pauses, then rushes at him, holding the branch high in the air with both hands. With all his strength, he brings it down onto Cal's head. There's a loud *crack*. My stomach lurches again as the branch snaps in two and the younger Cal crumples to the ground. I crumple, too, in another bout of dry heaves.

I need to catch my breath. I need to focus. This isn't really happening. I'm in Daniel's subconscious. His dream. Okay. And what am I doing here? I'm stopping Daniel from attacking anyone else. I'm waking everyone up that he's already attacked.

I force back the nausea and collect myself. "What about everyone else, Daniel? Where are they?"

Daniel blinks. "Everyone else?"

"There are people in *comas* because you can't get your own guilt under control. People who have nothing to do with this."

"They have everything to do with this," he says darkly.

"How?" This doesn't make sense. Why would his shadow lash out at people who weren't even here? What's the connection? *Like Rob*, I think. *A grouchy old man who works at a gas station. Why attack him?*

"Rob sold me that firecracker." Daniel points up to the top of the tree, where thin wisps of smoke are still mingling with the branches. Wisps of smoke were in the dream I had of Rob in his gas station. And sparks, the smell of cordite reminding me of the Fourth of July. I remember them now, as vividly as if I was in that dream instead of this one. Or . . . if Rob was *here*. The scene resets as if nothing's happened, the images of the boys fading away like ghosts, but when I turn back to Daniel, I find another person has materialized behind him: Rob.

He's frozen, feet wide, mouth open, as if someone has hit the pause button. A thin tendril of shadow has twisted up from the ground and wrapped itself lazily around him like a vine or errant root, holding him in place. Daniel doesn't seem to know he's there. But he must, even though he's not facing that way. Like he told me, this is his dream. And yet, he's not reacting, so I try to keep from reacting, too. Just in case. If Daniel *doesn't* know he's there, I don't know what will happen if he finds out.

336

Crack! The firecracker goes off again. I whip back around at the sound of it, then brace myself for what comes next: the fall.

"Troy was supposed to come with me," Daniel says. "He was supposed to be here, too. But he chickened out. He was scared the witch might hex him. Coward."

No. I can't watch this again. I flinch and turn away as Graham and Cal hit the ground with two sickening thuds. But at the same time, Troy materializes behind Daniel, next to Rob. He's frozen, too: a crouching statue with his arms up over his head. Cowering. Exactly as I saw him last—in *his* dream. Tendrils of shadow hold him hostage, too. They look like scribbles of graffiti.

Again, Daniel is oblivious. I don't know what this means. Are Rob and Troy really here? Or are they more manifestations of his guilt? I can't tell, but just in case, I need to keep Daniel talking—keep him focused on his own words so he doesn't pick up on the ones running through my head. Both Rob and Troy appeared when he mentioned their names, when he remembered their roles on this horrible night. I need to try to get him to think about the others as well. And I can't let him catch on to what I'm doing.

I force myself to turn back and watch as Cal struggles onto his knees—*Graham?*—then works to push himself up to his feet. So young, so confused, so scared. It's tearing my heart in two. *This isn't real. But it was, once.* Cal really experienced this. I want to run over and hug him and tell him he'll be okay. But I'd just go right through him like the last time. And besides, like the dream manifestation of my dad told me, I can't stop this from happening. What I *can* do is keep Daniel talking. See if I can get him to pull the others out of the shadows like he did Rob and Troy.

"And—" I fight to keep my emotions at bay, to keep my voice steady. "And Charlie?"

The younger Cal notices the younger Daniel. *Get help. What are you doing?*

My entire body shudders as the stick cracks over Cal's head. Again. As he crumples into the dirt. Again. And as the scene resets. Again. A sob rises in my throat. I choke it down.

"You saw Charlie warn me about the friends I was keeping, didn't you?" I continue. "Back in the coffee shop? I saw you watching. What did he have to do with all of this?"

"Charlie?" Daniel shakes his head as if the name threatens to bring him out of this sort of trance he's in.

I tense up. Not subtle enough. But I have to keep Daniel going. "Yes, Charlie," I say, trying not to sound too invested, merely curious. I've turned my head just enough to check for Charlie's appearance out of the corner of my eye. And there he is, right next to Rob and Troy, suspended in mid-stride, his legs ensnared. My pulse quickens. "How was he involved?"

"He—"

The firecracker goes off. I refuse to turn and look this time. I don't think I can handle it again. I keep my gaze steady on Daniel, watching his eyes as he follows the boys' descent.

"He—" Daniel sucks in his breath as I hear the boys hit the ground behind me. It's the first time I've seen him falter. His first real show of emotion over the horror playing on repeat before his eyes. But he recovers quickly. "He found me," he explains in monotone. "Wandering home after. I don't remember it very well. I—I think he gave me a ride back in his tow truck."

338

Charlie's dream comes back to me. His tow truck pulled over on the side of the road, standing trapped in his headlights as Daniel's shadow emerged from the trees, weaving its way in and out and around us.

I hear stirring behind me as twelve-year-old Cal gets up on his knees. *Graham?*

"I remember," Daniel continues. "Yes, I remember being in his truck, and all the sirens rushing past. Someone had called 911. Probably Miriam. Charlie would have pieced it together later. He's pretty sharp."

Get help. What are you doing?

Without thinking, I spin around at the sound of Cal's small, frightened voice. I wish I hadn't.

"He never said anything," Daniel continues as his younger self rushes toward Cal with the branch. "But he never trusted me after that night. I could tell. And then—"

I can feel Daniel staring at me as my own eyes track the piece of branch flying off toward the hedge after cracking apart on impact. I think I'm going to be sick again.

"—and then he started hanging around your sister a lot."

My heart skips a beat. It takes everything in me to stop myself from swiveling on the spot to see if she's appeared behind him.

"Rhonda?" I say her name, hoping he'll say it, too. Does that matter? Or does he just need to be thinking about her?

The scene starts over. *Crack!*

"I was there when Rhonda came into the station asking about Miriam," Daniel says.

339

I manage to sneak a glance, then quickly look away before the relief I'm feeling can manifest on my face. It worked! She's right there, held by shadow next to Charlie, arms thrust forward, face twisted in fear as I last saw her. I want to run over there and rip away the tendrils that are trapping her. To pull her out of her nightmare. I promised I'd wake her first. But I can't. Not yet. Not until *everyone's* here.

"I stayed to listen at the door because I was worried she was there to talk about the tires I slashed," Daniel says. "And the cut fuel line."

I hear the boys land, and I feel like I've landed with them, all the wind knocked out of me. "That was *you*? Why?"

"I was afraid . . . I . . ."

Graham?

". . . I needed you to leave. You were making it worse. I thought I'd finally gotten it all under control, and then you showed up, practically dripping with guilt. I could feel it every time I came anywhere near you."

So could I, I realize. How had I not put it together before? That uneasy feeling I had whenever he was around, like I'd done something wrong, or something he didn't like, and I didn't know what. Like during each dream. How didn't I see it?

"You were making everything worse," he says. "Even worse than it had been before. So, I thought—"

Get help. What are you doing?

"I thought maybe, if you believed the town was out to get you, you and your sister would give up and go home. Back to New York. As far from here as possible."

There's a whack and a crack behind me as younger Daniel bashes younger Cal with the stick. My stomach lurches yet again.

"You could have talked to me," I tell Daniel. "All this time, you could have just talked to me. We could have figured this out together, before things got so out of hand. I could have helped you. *Daniel.*"

"Things were already out of hand! Helping me is what killed your aunt! Don't you understand? That's two people dead. Miriam *and* Graham. Because of *me*. I didn't want to make it three. At least everyone else was just sleeping."

"How did she die? What was she doing to help you that would cause her to die?" And how can I avoid the same fate? Is there any way around it? I feel the slightest tug at my middle as my lifeline shimmers into visibility. No. I can't wake up now. Not without the others. I need to move this along. I need to get Daniel to talk about the last three. Next was his dad, then Bethany, then Cal. Then I can worry about what comes after. The tugging sensation evaporates.

"I don't know," Daniel says, panic creeping into his voice. "I don't . . . I don't remember. I just know she was—we were here."

I actively push back against my building dread. Who was next? His dad. "Her death made you even more guilty, though, didn't it? And things got *really* out of control when you realized I was starting to figure it out on my own. That we might end up right back here again. You were there when I went to see your dad. You listened to our conversation through the door, just like you did with Rhonda, didn't you?"

Crack!

And there's Chief Burke. Positioned as if asleep with his head down on his desk, except there is no desk, just air. The shadow wraps around him like a support. *How strange*, I think. *It's as if he'd been dreaming about being asleep.* Or—no. He must have *just fallen* asleep.

Now it clicks into place. I picture Daniel's bloodshot eyes inches from my own, the smell of coffee on his breath when he hissed at me that this was all my fault. His dad probably wasn't dreaming *at all* yet, but Daniel was. Half dreaming, half awake, his shadow was already poised to attack. It must have jumped in at the first moment of unconsciousness as Chief Burke was drifting off. Similar to what I think happened to Cal in the truck. But this gives me hope. If Chief Burke is here, maybe Cal isn't so far out of reach after all.

"You don't think my dad already knew what I did?" Daniel sits down hard and pulls his knees up to his chest as Cal and Graham hit the ground again. "He's been protecting me over this"—he nods his head toward the fallen boys—"for *years*. He never said, but I know he knew. He caught me sneaking back into my room that night, with mud on my shoes and acting guilty as hell. The timing, that leftover firecracker he found in my pocket when doing laundry, and—well, he's a police officer. He had to have figured it out.

"But he only knew I was the reason Miriam died from the journals Officer Sontag found in your room. I'll give Miriam credit—she never wrote down my name—she never wrote any names. But it wasn't hard for him to put everything together."

So Daniel did read through them.

342

Graham?

"And then"—Daniel gets back to his feet—"he was protecting *you* . . . when you came to ask about that number. I guess now that he'd figured out Miriam died because of me, then surely you . . ." He trails off. "You shouldn't have gone to him. You should have left him out of this! Dad was *your* fault. I never should have told you that was a case number. Why don't I ever think before I speak? Why—" He cocks his head at me, a curious expression crossing his face. "Why are you walking me through this? This isn't helping me forgive myself. This is making it worse!"

"And Bethany?" He can't stop yet. There's still Bethany and . . . and . . .

Get help. What are you doing?

—And Cal. I swallow. "Bethany knew all this time, too, didn't she?" That would be why she didn't want to talk about it. Why she shut me out when I brought up Graham.

"Bethany didn't know," he says quietly. Then, thank goodness, Bethany appears. She's very close to Daniel—mere inches away. Encased in shadow, she's curled up in the fetal position, bracing herself against what was coming for her.

"I told her that night. After you left, she walked me home, and I told her about Graham. And then . . . I told her about my shadow. And she—she got sick in the bushes. Then she called me a monster. Because it's true, I *am* a monster." He flinches and turns away this time as his younger self bashes Cal. He turns and sees everyone—all of his shadow's victims behind him—and his entire body goes rigid.

Oh no. Panic courses through me. I need to distract him again. I need to get him to talk about Cal. *I don't have Cal yet.*

343

The words tumble out of me a mile a minute. "And what about Cal? Daniel. You need to tell me about Cal. You found the stick in his truck, didn't you? The evidence. And you thought he would—"

"Bethany?" he says. He's not hearing me. "Dad?"

The scene resets, but he's not watching anymore.

"And *Cal*," I plead, tears running down my face. "We're still missing Cal. You need to tell me about Cal—"

He whirls on me. "Is this what you were doing? Did you know they were here?"

Not with a flash of light, but under the cover of darkness, the crack in the tree comes again, but drawn out, like a lot of cracks in succession. Like branches creaking and bending and knocking against each other.

"Did you?!" he screams at me.

"You're not a monster!" I shout back. "So stop acting like one. You can let them go. Right now, just let them go." *But Cal*, my heart pleads with me. Cal's not here. How am I going to find Cal?

"I can't." Daniel's chin quivers. Fear eats away the anger in his eyes. "I don't know how. You know I don't know how. I told you. I can't control it."

"Can't? Or you're too afraid to?"

The tree darkens. Not from smoke or char from the firecracker lobbed into its branches. From fear, from anger, from guilt—it turns to shadow.

Pulse pounding, I step between Daniel and the sleepers. "Daniel, look at me. Look. You were twelve. Just twelve years old."

"So were they," he sobs, gesturing wildly toward the boys

344

who are no longer there. "And Graham will always be twelve. Always. He never had the chance to grow up because of *me*."

The shadow's branches sway and touch down, sending out tendrils. Its shadowy fingers creep across the shadowy ground.

"And how can you change that?" I ask, firm yet desperate. Pleading with him to understand.

"I can't!"

"Exactly!"

I hear my dad's voice in my head, just before he turned to shadow. *You can't stop this from happening, Bug. Because it already has.*

I grab Daniel's shoulders and hold him steady. "You can't," I tell him. "You can't change what happened. You can't change what you did. You will never be able to fix it. You will never stop wishing you could." The shadows creep closer and closer. I can feel them, smell them, even taste them. My shadow may have been weakened, but it's not gone completely.

"And you will never *ever* forget it," I continue, trying to hold back the waver in my voice. "You have to accept that. Really accept it." *I have to accept that the last thing I said to Dad was that I hated him.* "Stop running from it, stop hiding, stop punishing yourself for something you can't change." *And beating myself up about it isn't going to fix it.* "Learn from it, take responsibility for it, and do better. That's what it means to forgive yourself, Daniel." *That's what it means. That's what my therapist was trying to make me understand. Will Daniel, though?*

I spin him around to face his shadow, like I faced mine. But I'm not nearly as confident as I sound. Below the surface, I'm a quivering mess. Daniel was right. His shadow is nothing like mine. Its roots are strong and deep, anchored into his very being, and it'll take more than a simple declaration of self-forgiveness to loosen them. He has to mean it. *Really* mean it. And ... I don't know if that's possible. Not after what I've just watched, over, and over, and over ...

And yet—

Daniel shakes off my grip and takes a tentative step toward the tree. And then another, his hands clenched at his sides. I hold my breath.

The tree goes still. As if listening. Or waiting.

Then, strangely calm, he says, "Let them go."

He takes another step toward the shadow tree.

"Let them go," he says, stronger. "It's me you're after. Only me."

"No!" I cry. "That's not what I meant!"

I move to go after him but am buffeted back by leaves and sticks and twigs. A new section of hedge shoots up from the ground, setting a barrier between us, and it goes on forever, as far as I can see. There's no way around it. He's trapped himself on the other side to face his shadow alone.

The last of the shadowy roots retreat, slithering between my feet until they disappear below the hedge. I can hear Daniel's voice, shouting, but I can't make out his words above the whistling howls of the shadow storm on the other side.

But I also hear movement behind me. And other voices. Confused, familiar voices.

CHAPTER 37

"Eva?"

Rhonda has me in a bear hug. I think she might be crying. As she holds me, the scene around us flickers in and out of a cityscape—skyscrapers and jumbotrons plastered with lights and advertisements, then forest. Buildings and forest, buildings and forest.

"I couldn't find you anywhere," she says, "and then the rats came, and they turned into this enormous shadow thing and—" She pulls away and looks around her. The flickering stops, and the city disappears. "Where are we?"

Echoes of "Where am I . . . ? Where are we?" come from the rest of the group as the last of the tendrils holding them in place retreat into the ground and their consciousnesses emerge into this warped yet familiar dreamscape. The storm continues to howl on the other side of the hedge, accompanied by cracks and thuds and Daniel's increasingly frantic voice. What will happen to him if his shadow wins? What will happen to *us*?

"Listen." I raise my voice over the din. "We are inside someone else's dream. You're okay now. It's just a dream."

I glance over at Rob and Troy, then scan the rest of the group. They're all staring at me. I should have known it wouldn't be as simple as telling everyone they've been dreaming to get them to wake up.

"Yeah," Troy says, his voice shaking. "We're in *your* dream. I knew it was you. I told Chris. I knew. You're a witch." He slowly backs away. "You're just like her. You're—"

"No, I'm—"

"She is," Rob cuts in, but there's no malice or fear in his voice this time. I remember the last words he said to me in his own dream, just before the shadow of the boy—of Daniel just before he grew and was about to envelop the store. *You're just like her, and that's why you need to go.*

"When I saw you were a Sylvan, I knew trouble would follow," Rob says. "It always does. You *are* just like her." His tone turns to regret. "She was so young when she passed. She was trying to help me. I shouldn't have let her. Now it's happening all over again, but you're even younger. I wish you'd taken my advice and gone. I knew you wouldn't, though. You really are so much like her. It's . . . remarkable."

She was so young? Miriam wasn't young when she died. And she was helping Daniel, not Rob. Unless . . . could he be talking about someone else? Could it be— And then it hits me. Rob . . . Robert . . . Bobby? Could he be talking about May?

Rhonda steps in front of me protectively. "No," she says to Rob, then turns to me, her words coming fast, desperate. "Don't listen to him. You could *die*. That's what I needed to tell you. I read Miriam's last journal. She wrote about a sleeping boy with a dangerous shadow, and I'm positive it killed her. Please don't go after it, or you could die like Miriam, and I can't—I can't lose you, too."

It's no wonder she sounded so desperate over the phone. *Oh, Rhonda, I'm so sorry. But I can't leave until I've found Cal.*

"Where's my boy?" Chief Burke asks quietly. It reminds me we don't have much time. I need to get them all to stop talking and just wake up. Catching my eye, Charlie sidles over to stand beside my sister.

"Is he in there?" Chief Burke takes a step toward the hedge.

"Daniel's back there?" Bethany doesn't move, but she looks torn—torn between fear for Daniel and fear *of* him. It makes my heart hurt.

"He's trying," I say. "He got his shadow to let you go, but he's blocked me out at the same time, and I don't know how much longer he can hold it back on his own. You need to wake up. Right now. All of you."

"And you," Rhonda says. "You too." Her eyes are pleading with me. She reaches out her hand, urging me to take it.

"I can't," I tell her, as much as it hurts. "I don't have everyone yet."

"H-how many more of us are there?"

"Besides Daniel? Just one." If I'm being honest with myself, I don't know if I can help Daniel anymore. But I refuse to leave without Cal. If I can't help Daniel, and his shadow takes over completely, if he traps himself inside his own dreamworld, I don't know if I'll ever be able to get Cal out. I'm the one who sent Daniel off in his truck. I'm the one who told him I didn't want Daniel to stay. He's here because of me.

And I'm getting a bad feeling about where in here he is.

"Then I'll stay and help," Rhonda says.

"You can't."

"The hell I can't. *Damnit*, Eva. You're all I've got now. I can't let you take this risk by yourself."

Charlie exchanges another look with me over her shoulder and nods.

I squeeze Rhonda's hand. "You're all I've got, too. And I made you a promise. You first."

Charlie puts his hands down on her shoulders. It startles her, bringing her lifeline shimmering into view. But she still isn't waking up. I'm going to have to do it. It doesn't feel right, but . . .

I reach out and give her lifeline a gentle pluck, like a harp string. It tightens, jolting her out of the dreamworld into wakefulness. With a gasp, she disappears before my eyes, as so many other things flash in front of them. Private things I should never have seen. Secrets she's kept locked away—the very fabric of her existence and her soul, and . . . *Mom*.

Reeling, I stumble backward. So much guilt. So much of it! The ache, the pain of it feels so familiar, but unlike mine, hers isn't about Dad. It's about *Mom*. The effects of Rhonda's darkest emotions linger, piercing my heart as if they were my own. It's *Rhonda's* fault Mom didn't get better. It's *Rhonda's* fault Mom left. I don't believe it for a second, but she does, and it hurts. It hurts so much.

I'm so sorry, Rhonda. I had no idea I'd see all that. I didn't think that would happen. I feel like I did the time I looked inside her diary when I was nine, but so much worse. So, *this* is why May was worried Bobby would be upset when she did the same to him. She saw into his soul. *I saw into Rhonda's soul.*

Queasy, I turn to the others. "Please don't make me do that again. You have to wake yourselves up."

Charlie nods. "I'll go check on her," he says. "But you'd better come back in one piece, or your sister's going to kill me." And then he's gone, too. A wave of relief washes over me. They *can* do this on their own, thank God.

"How'd he *do* that?" Troy asks, panicked. "Let me outta here. Wake me up, too."

"Wake yourself up," I snap at him. "Nothing's keeping you here anymore but you."

He blinks a few times as what I've said sinks in, then, mercifully, he disappears.

"Well?" I say to the remaining three. But Rob, Chief Burke, and Bethany don't move.

"You said someone's still missing," Bethany says. "Who?"

I shake my head. *Don't ask me that. Just get out.*

"It's Cal, isn't it?"

I can't trust myself to keep the panic out of my voice. All I can do is nod.

She swallows. "And what about Daniel? What'll happen to him?"

I tilt my head toward Rob. "I . . . I'm getting the feeling you should ask him."

Rob gives me a sad smile. "Eva, is it?" He turns to Bethany. "If Eva here truly is anything like the young woman I once knew, Daniel's going to be just fine. Eventually."

And there it is again. Young woman. Rob *must* be talking about May. It's the only thing that makes sense. He's Bobby. And if that's true, whatever it was that May did to help him must have worked. *But what did she do?* Is it the same thing Miriam tried to do? And will it kill me, too?

351

"And you?" Bethany's still not satisfied. "Your sister said . . ."

I'm not answering that. I'm not going there. And this has gone on for far too long. "Bethany, please. You need to wake up now. Your parents are worried sick about you."

"My *parents*? What about *you*? You're avoiding the question. What's going to happen to *you*?"

I take a deep breath. Fine. "I don't know. What I *do* know is that I can't leave until I find Cal and help Daniel stop this thing. But I might not be able to do any of that if I'm worried about the rest of you still being here. And also, in case I—" I stop. I take another breath, then say quietly, "I'll need someone to tell Rhonda I'm sorry."

Bethany nods, eyes glistening. Her lifeline shimmers into view. "Tell Daniel—" But before she can finish, her lifeline goes taut, and just like that, she's gone.

I take a moment to catch my breath. Whatever it was she wanted me to tell him, she can do it herself when he wakes up. Because he *will* wake up. I'll make sure of it.

I look to Chief Burke. "Your turn. Please."

He shifts from one foot to the other. "But that's my son," he says, staring at the hedge where Daniel's cries and yells can still be heard mixing with the storm of shadow and dirt and fear swirling on the other side. "He's all alone in there. He's still just a kid. He didn't—"

"I know. And he needs you right now, but he'll need you later, too. You can't help him in here. But you *can* help him—all of us—*out there*," I tell him. "Listen. Cal's in his truck in front of Miriam's—I mean my house. He's hit his head, it's pretty bad, and I don't know how long it's been or how long he'll be safe. Daniel and I are right here." I point to my feet. "Right here in front of the hedge, by the big stump. Come get us. Make sure we're safe." I lock eyes with him. "And send a . . . I might need a . . . well, you saw the report. You know what happened to Miriam. So please hurry."

His Adam's apple rises and drops as he swallows hard. He knows I'm right. He can do more for his son, for all of us, in the waking world than he can from here.

"Okay," he says. "Okay." With a nod, he disappears.

"Rob, wait," I call out to him before he can go, too.

Rob raises an eyebrow. I think he knows what I'm about to ask.

"When you said I'm just like 'her,' you weren't talking about Miriam, were you?"

He shakes his head. "Her name was May," he says. "Miriam's sister. I told her she needed to stop trying to help me, that it was too dangerous. But she wouldn't listen. She was stubborn. Just like you. You know, it's strange. You even look the same."

"You're Bobby. I read about you in May's journal."

With a sad smile, he raises his hand to his forehead in a salute. "Private Robert Petersen. Drafted the moment I turned eighteen. God, I was terrified."

"Please." My voice catches. "I don't know what to do. How did May help you? How did she finally make it stop?"

How did she die? Am I going to die, too?

He looks down at his feet, and for a second, I'm afraid he's going to wake himself before answering.

"She didn't," he says, and raises his head.

His eyes are inky. Even the whites. The ink seeps out like

353

ribbons of smoke, wafting around his face, then his body, building until he's fully enveloped in a dark storm cloud of shadow. My pulse speeds up, I feel a tugging at my gut, and it takes every ounce of concentration not to pull *myself* out of this nightmare, out and away.

But then his shadow gathers and consolidates. It collects around his arm, then makes its way down to concentrate in his hand.

"It took a long time, but I finally learned to control it." He whips his shadow out from his fingertips toward the hedge, clawing it open. "Reshape it." He draws the shadow back into himself. "And use it, rather than let it use me."

I finally allow myself to exhale when the darkness recedes into his pupils and disappears.

"But if it hadn't been for May," he says, "it would have consumed me. Like Daniel's shadow is consuming him, *right now*."

We both hurry to the opening he's made in the hedge to find Daniel rooted in place. Literally. He's struggling against hundreds of tendrils of shadow bursting up from the ground, bending down from the branches, curling out from the very air, and winding tightly around him.

Without a second thought, I run toward him, arms outstretched, ready to disentangle him. Gotta get him out of there. Gotta get it off of him.

"Don't touch it!" Rob yells at me. I stumble to a stop. "Never touch it."

He pushes me to the side and shoots his own shadow toward Daniel's bonds. Working with it as extensions of his fingers, he pulls off tendril after tendril. The shadow replaces them with new ones as quickly as he pries them away. And I can do nothing.

"Daniel, where's Cal?" I shout, but he doesn't hear me. Or if he does, he can't answer. But ahead of me, I hear another voice, blown along the shadow wind.

"Graham?"

My stomach drops. It's still playing out. Inside the storm, Cal and Graham are still falling, over and over again. But the voice. There was something different about the voice. It was lower.

"Graham?" I hear again. My heart skips a beat. He never said it twice before.

"Cal?" I whisper. That wasn't the voice of a little boy. That was *my* Cal.

I look at Rob and Daniel, occupied. I look at the storm of branches and dirt and darkness. I look at the heart of the shadow. Eyes closed, Cal lives in shadow. He *is* shadow here— the personal embodiment of Daniel's guilt. I know what I have to do now. But will Cal ever be able to forgive me?

"Graham?!" he cries out again.

I'm running. I hear protests behind me. I keep running. I hear Rob shouting, "No! It will kill you! Don't—"

It's cold.

I can't see anything.

My head is throbbing.

Why is my head throbbing?

"Where are you?" I call out.

"Graham?" I hear. And when there's no answer, "Graham?!"

I take a step forward, lurch, and stumble into something. Someone hunched low. I can't see him, but I don't need to. I know who it is.

"Graham?"

"No." I crouch down, too.

Hands clasp mine and slowly, as if my eyes are adjusting to the dark, Cal comes into focus. Except my eyes can't really be adjusting, because he's all I can see.

"It's you," he says, confused.

I nod, smiling. "It's me." But the nodding makes my head throb even more. The ache is building.

I wobble onto my feet. "We have to go."

"But . . . Graham," he says.

"I'm so, so sorry, Cal, but Graham's not coming. Remember? He had somewhere else to go."

Cal stares at me. His brows furrow. "I know. I said we need to find Daniel."

I drop his hands and clutch at my head. The pain. It's so bad.

"What's happening? What's wrong?"

"Nothing, I'm fine," I lie, taking his hands again. "I'm getting you out of—"

I'm cut off as the ground beneath us gives way and we sink, then fall.

We fall,

and fall,

and fall.

Clasping each other's hands, tumbling in the pitch darkness until it no longer feels like falling, but floating, weightless in the void. And still, all I can see is myself and Cal . . . and two glimmering, shimmering threads stretching out from us, twisting together as we tumble. Those are our lifelines, those threads, and they will show us the way home.

"Pull," I tell him. Another stab of pain shoots through my head, then radiates down my back and shoulder. I gasp.

"What's wrong?" he asks again, his voice filled with panic. "Eva, what's—"

"Pull!" I grab hold of both threads and feel the energy surging through them—so strong for how very thin they are. I grab hold and I feel everything. See everything. Our entire history together. I see all the way back to the beginning:

We're kids. Cal looks up at me for the first time, and I feel his understanding, his grief, his horror over his friend's death. He did see. He could see. He knew what happened. He understood his friend wasn't coming back, and he blamed himself, and I didn't know what to do. He was dying, too—I could feel his spirit weakening the longer he stayed, but I couldn't get him to leave. So I did the only thing I could think of. The thing Mimi told me I should never ever do. I took up his cord. His lifeline. I looked into his soul and reached into his memories, locking away everything—*everything*—I could find there of his friend.

I shrouded his memories in shadow. I made him forget.

I did that to him. It wasn't the concussion; it wasn't Daniel's stick. It was *me*. I have to fix it.

"Eva, no, wait—"

Too late. Memories and images of Graham come flooding back to him as I recover and pull. The pain shoots from my head down into my chest as we're ripped apart. Light surges through

357

his silver cord, it goes taut, and he disappears. He's awake! Pure relief washes over me. I did it. I saved him.

But something's wrong. Why haven't I gone with him? I was supposed to go with him. I land hard on my back.

My lifeline has snapped.

Chapter 38

*S*and.

The fine grains squish between my fingers as I push myself up to sitting. I'm on a pristine beach that goes on forever. Gentle waves slide onto the shore, then retreat again, slide, and retreat. I scoop up a handful of sand and marvel at how I can see each individual, microscopic speck. The grains consist of all colors on the spectrum, even those I've never been able to perceive before, all the way up into the ultraviolets and down into the infrareds. I let them seep from between my fingers in a rainbow.

Where am I? Is this another dream?

The pain in my head and my chest is gone. I feel . . . light. I get to my feet and turn in place, taking in the endless beauty and calm. By the time I've completed my circle, a castle has appeared. A giant, life-size sandcastle. The seven-year-old in me leaps for joy.

"Mimi?" I call out. I remember this! This is the castle Mimi and I built together in my dreams. We'd meet here sometimes when I went to sleep. How could I have forgotten?

But . . . Miriam is dead.

Miriam appears in the doorway of the castle, a gentle smile on her face. Her silver hair cascades in ripples down the back of her cotton house dress, which is speckled with tiny pink flowers. She holds out her arms to me, and I run into them for a hug.

Stroking my hair, she says, "My Evangeline, I'm so proud of you."

I burrow my head into her shoulder. "But I failed, Mimi. I didn't help him—I didn't know how."

She gives me a squeeze, then holds me out at arm's length. "If you think you've failed, you've missed the entire point. Just like I did. Just like my sisters did before me."

"The point? The point was to die?"

She shakes her head. "The point was to get to the heart of the shadow and release what feeds it."

"Cal?"

She nods. "Unfortunately, going that deep inside someone else's pain and removing its core is something like diving into a reactor and removing a fuel rod with your bare hands."

"Cal was a fuel rod?" I'm not sure I understand. Is he really safe? He was in there, too.

"All these years, Daniel has been trying to assuage his guilt by taking Callum under his protection. But all the while, Callum's inability to remember what truly happened that night continued to feed into Daniel's fear that someday he would. Maybe on his own. Maybe through someone else. And then none of what he'd done since would matter. In Daniel's mind, he's never deserved such friendship. Because this Callum, the post-accident version, was essentially created by him. The old Callum would never have accepted his friendship in the first place. Especially not after knowing what Daniel had done."

I shudder. I don't like to think of Cal like he was before.

Miriam continues. "To Daniel, it's all a sham, which adds to his guilt, which feeds his shadow."

"Cal wasn't the fuel." I think I understand now. "His lack of memory was the fuel."

"Exactly."

"Daniel's not the one who caused that. I am. Cal wouldn't follow me without his friend, but Graham had already moved on. So . . . so I put this sort of block on his memories. I made him forget about Graham so he'd let me wake him up." Daniel was right, and he didn't even know it. "This *was* my fault. All of it."

Miriam smiles sadly at me. "The fault was mine. I hadn't prepared you enough. The clock was ticking, and I sent you to complete a task you weren't ready for, because I couldn't do it myself."

"Why couldn't you?"

"Oh, believe me, I tried. But I never was very good at shifting my dream appearance. He recognized me as that scary old lady in the house beyond the hedge, and it was too frightening for him in the fragile state he was in. His mind was going, deteriorating from his injury as his lifeline grew weaker."

"He would have died if I hadn't done it," I say more for my benefit than for hers. If I hadn't interfered with his memories, he wouldn't have gone with me, either. He would have stayed there, lost, confused, searching for his friend forever.

"Yes, or spent his life in a comatose state. You did what you had to with the tools you had at the time—just like you've done now."

"I removed the block. I gave Cal his memories back."

And by doing so, I've rearranged his entire life, yet again. Maybe it's a good thing. As painful as it will be, he deserves to remember his friend. But this will change him again. He'll wake up grieving. He's going to have to deal now with the trauma that's been kept from him for five years, and it's not going to be easy. I should know. I would never wish that on anyone. It doesn't occur to me that with me gone, he now has two people to grieve.

"Is Dad here?"

"I've always been here, Bug." He appears next to Miriam in his paramedic uniform, jacket and all, looking shiny and new.

I throw myself into his arms. The tears stream heavy and fast. I can't count the number of times I've longed to hug him again, to see him again, to hear his voice. This can't be real. But it feels real. It feels more real than anything I've ever felt before.

"Dad," I sob into his shoulder. "I'm sorry. I'm so sorry."

A jolt stabs my chest. There's a flicker of darkness, so quick, it's nearly imperceptible.

"Hey. You have nothing to be sorry for, do you understand?" he tells me, pulling back so he can look me in the eyes. "Nothing."

"I needed to say it, though. Before—"

I'm hit in the chest by another jolt. Another flicker of darkness, slightly longer this time. Long enough not to ignore. "What's that? What's happening?"

Dad smiles at me. "Marcus," he says, and, picking up on my confusion, adds, "Daniel's dad. Remember? You told him to come get you, and he's come through. I knew he would. Everything's

362

going to be okay, Bug. Give Rhonda a big bear hug from me, and remember—"

Clear! It carries in from somewhere beyond here. There's another jolt. Electricity surges through me and everything goes dark.

"Dad!" I cry out. "Mimi!"

We're still here, Dad's voice echoes through my head. I feel like my skull is being stabbed repeatedly.

"And we always will be, even when you can't hear us," Miriam's voice chimes in; it's starting to fade away. "Now, go finish this."

I'm in so much pain I can hardly think. But my lifeline is back, shimmering as before. Except for one spot that's not quite as bright as the rest, tarnished. I wonder if it will always have that scar now. Pushing through the pain, I follow it, my crumb trail through the darkness, until I reach the edge of the shadow storm. It's already shifting from the hurricane it once was to something more like a strong breeze.

Rob is still pulling away at Daniel's personal cage, as if I'd never left. He falters when he sees me emerge; his eyes go wide, and his mouth stretches into a huge grin.

"Well, look at you," he says as I gently push him away and take hold of the tendrils myself. Then, concentrating through my pain, I manipulate them, reshape them. I pull the storm into them. I gather the branches, the roots, the entire tree into the darkness cupped within my hands, until I can get it as small as it will go: into the shape of a fragment of a branch.

I hold it out to Daniel. He recoils.

"Take it," I tell him.

"I don't want it."

"It's yours. You don't have a choice." I look to Rob. "Does he?"

Rob is staring at me with a mixture of awe and admiration.

"Daniel," Rob says, his eyes still on me. He blinks, then recovers. "Look. This is mine." He holds out his hand. Cradled in his palm is a round, egg-shaped shadow. A grenade . . . with a missing pin.

"Go on and take yours," he tells Daniel. "May has fixed it for you so you can manage it better."

May? I open my mouth to correct him, but then I think better of it. If he needs me to be May right now, that's fine. I nod at Daniel reassuringly, gritting my teeth against the pounding in my head.

Daniel hesitates, then reaches for his stick-shaped shadow.

"How did you do that?" He turns it over in his hands. But when he looks up for the answer, a crease forms between his brows. "What's wrong? Eva?"

I can't hide it anymore. It hurts too much. Sounds creep in from the corners of my consciousness. Beeps and low voices.

"I thought you were going to be okay. You made it out, and I thought—Rob, what's happening to her?"

"Hold on." Rob takes me aside. "I'll stay here and help him the rest of the way. I think it's time for you to go."

"But—"

"We'll be along."

It's okay, I tell myself. *They're going to be okay now.* I feel a tug at my middle. The darkness around me bursts into light.

CHAPTER 39

Waking after dying is nothing like waking from sleep. Of course it isn't. But I'm still not remotely prepared for how overwhelming everything feels. The light is too much. The beeps from my monitor are too much. The smell—that sickening smell of antiseptic hospital soap is too, too much. And the pain. My head, my chest, my entire body feels—well, like I died.

My brain is complete sludge, except for one thing. I saw Dad. That one thought is crystal clear. *I saw Dad.* I spoke to him; I hugged him. And I finally, *finally* got to tell him I was sorry.

"Eva?"

I turn my head to the side and the blob with Rhonda's voice slowly comes into focus.

"I saw Dad." My voice sounds strange to me. Thick and hoarse.

There's an intake of breath. Long, drawn out.

"I'll ... give you two some space." Another voice from another blob, haloed by the light from the window—too bright even with the blinds drawn. Charlie comes into focus as he unfolds himself from his chair. He gives Rhonda's shoulder a comforting squeeze before heading for the door. But halfway out, he pauses. "Eva?" he says. "Thank you."

Was that a waver in his voice, or is my hearing all jumbly?

Everything feels off-kilter and now my eyes are leaking, so everything's going blurry again, too.

The door clicks shut as Rhonda squeezes my hand. She puts it to her cheek, and I can feel her eyes are leaking, too. But . . . Rhonda never cries in front of other people.

"I thought I'd lost you for real this time," she says. Images of rats and billboards flash through my head, then disappear like puffs of smoke.

"Did it work?" I rasp. "Is everyone awake?"

Her brow knits with worry. "Everyone except Rob and Daniel."

"They'll wake up soon," I assure her. "Rob's staying behind to help Daniel figure out some things."

She nods, but I'm not sure she's convinced.

"I'll bet Diane's pissed I didn't bring her dad back with the rest of you, though," I add.

Rhonda snorts, then sniffles and clears her throat. "When is Diane *not* pissed?"

"What about Cal? His head . . ."

"Cal's fine. Concussed but fully conscious and constantly asking when it'll be okay to come see you."

Relief washes over me, but then I remember what I did right before my lifeline snapped—how I restored the memories I'd blocked so many years ago without permission either way, and my stomach lurches. He might not be very happy when he does come to see me. Which reminds me of another thing.

"I'm sorry I—I . . ." I can't seem to word it, so I continue past it. "But I had to. I promised I'd wake you up first."

A look of confusion crosses her face, then disappears. She

366

places her hand on her abdomen, remembering how I plucked her lifeline to force her to leave. Does she know what I saw when I did it? Is she angry?

"Mom wasn't your fault," I tell her. Does she understand? It's important she understands. It's dangerous to hold on to guilt like that. I should know.

She nods tearfully. Good. I think she does. My eyes grow heavy. I drift off again.

The next time I wake, Rhonda's gone and Cal is in her place. Mouth open, head lulled back against the chair, his chest rises and falls with his light snoring. My heart monitor's beeps accelerate as I'm hit with a jolt of panic.

Did it not work? Did I not wake him up after all? But then I remember where I am, and that Rhonda told me Cal was okay. Two steri-strips crisscross over a purpled goose egg on his forehead, but otherwise, he appears to be in good shape. I breathe a sigh of relief. This is normal sleep. No comas. No shadows.

He's okay.

As if sensing my stare, his eyes flutter open. He glances sleepily my way, then, with a jerk, sits fully upright.

"You're awake!" He rushes to scoot the chair closer to the bed, bumping the rolling bedside table on the way. Plastic dishware clatters. "Sorry," he says, catching the table to steady it. "I, uh, I ate your Jell-O. Rhonda said you hate it. She went to get some real food. Are you hungry? Do you— No?" he says as I shake my head.

Then the tears come again. Stupid eyes.

"What's wrong? What is it? I mean, besides . . ." He trails off.

These aren't sad tears, though. "I wasn't sure if you'd be happy to see me."

"What? Why?"

"Because I . . ." I'm struggling to find the right words to communicate properly. "I took your . . . your . . ." Damnit, what's the word?

I think he gets what I'm trying to say, though. *Memories. That's the word.* He lets out a long, slow breath. "I haven't had much time to process that yet," he says. "But I'm definitely happy to see you. So happy. Eva—" His voice catches. "They said you had a heart attack *and* a brain aneurysm. They said you were lucky to be alive, but they didn't know if or when you were ever going to wake up. They didn't even know how badly—if you have—you know, like me. If—" He takes a moment to collect himself. "All I've been able to think about is how if the paramedics hadn't arrived when they did, I—" And then he stops completely, misty-eyed.

"Hey," I say, reaching my hand out for him to take. "It's okay. I'm okay." And so is he. He scoots closer, interlacing his fingers with mine. His hand is so warm. I feel so safe.

Everything's going to be okay.

EPILOGUE

One Month Later

*E*verything's going to be okay.

  I wish I could say that was the case for everyone. That friendships were mended, old wounds healed, and people's pasts overlooked. That every*one* was going to be okay. But it wouldn't be true.

Daniel and Rob woke up the day after I did. Rob's awakening was met with celebration. But Daniel's . . . well . . . let's just say when you've trapped several people into comas with your guilt-fueled shadow, those people aren't exactly going to be thrilled to see you again. Daniel's dad being the exception, of course.

As for my own reception in Madrona, things have gotten better. While I was still in the hospital, Mr. and Mrs. Lieu held a bake sale for us at the Roadhouse that sold out within two hours. And Rob hosted a car wash at the gas station. The line caused so much traffic, Officer Sontag had to come help direct it. Now the house is no longer under the risk of foreclosure, we've already made some headway on the medical bills, and we're fully moved into Miriam's—I mean *our* house. Charlie didn't charge us once he finished fixing Rhonda's car, and his cousin Randy even came and fixed our electricity for free. Charlie says Randy owed him a favor, but he wouldn't go into any further detail.

I can tell Rhonda's uncomfortable with all the free help, but she feels a bit better about it now that she has a job at the used bookstore. Through a friend of Diane's, no less. Rob must have had a talk with her after he woke up, because, while she hasn't exactly turned friendly, she's at least been civil. I think she might even feel a little guilty. I hope she can forgive herself.

Rhonda's just left for work when I hear a knock on the door. My heart thumps with anticipation. Cal's supposed to be over soon to pick me up. That must be him.

"Coming!" I call as I carefully make my way down the stairs. But when I open the door, I find Daniel instead. He's holding a cardboard box, and from the strained look on his face, I can tell that whatever's inside is heavy.

"Hey," he says.

"Hey."

There's an awkward pause—I haven't seen him since the hospital, and then only briefly because Bethany was visiting at the time. Their reunion . . . didn't go well. I glance warily past Daniel toward the gate in the hedge. I'm not sure Cal will react any better than Bethany if Daniel's still here when he shows up.

"Can I . . . ?" He hefts the box, adjusting his grip.

"Oh!" I step aside and let him in. "Sorry."

"I thought you might want your aunt's journals back," he says, setting the box down in the foyer with a thump.

The journals! How could I have forgotten? Then again, the

last several weeks have been a bit of a whirlwind, what with moving in and house repairs, all the while trying not to overdo it as my body is still recovering.

"Thank you," I tell him. "I appreciate you returning those to me."

He nods. "Well . . . my dad's waiting in the car, so . . ."

I accompany him back out to the porch, but instead of heading down the steps, he turns and sighs. "Actually, do you have a minute?"

Should I warn him that Cal's on his way? I don't want to scare him off, though. I can tell from his expression that this is important and probably shouldn't wait.

"Of course."

We both take a seat on the freshly repaired steps.

"How's your head?" he asks.

"Still attached," I tell him. This elicits a humorless chuckle out of him.

"How's your shadow?" I ask.

"Still attached," he says. "But I'm managing it."

"Good." There's a pause while I wait for him to get to whatever it is he wants off his chest.

Finally, he inhales, then lets it out. "I'm coming clean with Graham's parents. They have a right to know what really happened to their son."

My chest thumps. "They might press charges," I say quietly.

"They might," he says. "But I'm not going to hide from what I did anymore. That's what caused this whole mess. You said so yourself. Remember?"

"Vaguely." That's not what I'd meant, though. What I'd meant was it was time to let it go and move on. But deep down, I know he's right. He will never fully be able to move on if he doesn't do this.

He takes another deep breath and stands up. "Anyway, like I said, Dad's waiting. This was just a stop along the way. Can you please tell Bethany for me?"

"Of course."

"Thanks, I appreciate it. I'd tell her myself, but..." He winces. "I don't think it would be a good idea. We passed her while she was walking down Main Street on our way over here. She gave me the finger."

I also stand up, a little too quickly, which causes me to wobble a bit. I still get dizzy easily. Daniel reaches out to steady me, but I politely wave his hands away. No need, I've got this.

I've improved quite a bit within the last month, but the doctors say I still have a long road of healing ahead from the damage my aneurysm caused. My mind feels foggy a lot of the time, and I've been forgetting things—little things, like where I put my shoes. Random words, too—just like Cal. It's frustrating, but he's been helping me get through it.

"I'll talk to her," I promise Daniel.

He shoots me a half smile, then reaches past me to tap the newly minted *Beware of Witch* sign I've hung on the door where a wreath would normally go. "A little early to be decorating for Halloween, isn't it? Or was this Bethany's doing?"

"Pretty sure this house doesn't need any decorating for Halloween," I laugh. "Troy actually made that for me after he and Chris finished cleaning up their graffiti."

"Figures that's how Troy would show his gratitude," Daniel says.

"I asked him to make it."

He nods in approval. "Good. Don't ever hide from who you are. Because we both know how that ends up. I, uh . . . I better get going." He heads down the steps, then turns one last time before reaching the gate. "Oh, and Eva?"

"Yeah?"

"I was totally right, before."

"Right about what?"

"You really are a badass."

He passes through the gate and disappears behind the hedge. Why do I have the feeling he's not coming back? Not for a while, anyway. This felt very much like a goodbye.

I'm still sitting on the porch when I hear the distinctive rumble of Cal's truck approaching. A quick duck inside to grab my keys and lock up, then I'm hurrying down the front path as the truck rolls to a stop on the other side of the hedge.

Cal greets me with a wide grin. "You look like you're feeling better today," he says as I climb into the passenger's side.

I laugh and buckle my seat belt. "You say that every time you see me."

"Well, each time I see you, you seem like you're feeling a little better."

He turns the key, and the radio comes alive with the unmistakable notes of the Cranberries' intro to "Dreams."

"I *am* feeling pretty good today. And you know what?" I lean across the middle seat as far as my seat belt will let me. "I think this is our song."

He takes his hand off the gear shaft without switching it. "It is?"

"Mm-hmm. I was listening to this in the car the day we met. Um, in person."

His eyes grow soft. He sweeps an errant wisp of hair away from my cheek and winds his hand to the nape of my neck. Our foreheads touch as the singer tells us we're a dream to her.

"She's wrong, though," he says, his voice low.

"She is?"

And just before our lips meet, he whispers, "You're so much more than a dream to me."

ACKNOWLEDGMENTS

Where do I even begin? This book has been over six years in the making. And in that time, so many things have shaped and changed it. Good things, bad things, sad things. But the most significant of all was when, like Eva, I lost my dad. And though I would have preferred not to know what that level of grief truly feels like, my own experience is what makes Eva's grief so real. But it also made writing this book extremely difficult at times, so I would especially like to acknowledge those friends and family who were there for me throughout the process.

A HUGE thank you to my husband, Jon, and my kids, Owen and Dashiell, for lifting me up whenever I had doubts, for giving me the time and space needed for deadlines, and for just plain cheering me on for so many years while I worked to become a published author. I love you so, so, so, so much.

Thank you to my mom, Julie, and my dad, Steven, for passing down your creativity, your humor, your empathy, and your love for the written word. You surrounded me with books as a child and always encouraged my ambitions, which made all the difference. And thank you to the rest of my family: Ecih, Matty,

Ethan, and Sonja; Uncle Dave and Aunt Cheryl; Marc and Lauri; Jennifer, Karl, Katelyn, Zachary, and John; James, Vickie, and Thomas; and, of course, my mother and father-in-law, Linda and Russell, who've known me since I was Eva's age—I couldn't ask for a better family and support system. And to my second family: Kathy, Jim, Rebecca, Emily, Daniel, and Ellie. I have so much love for each and every one of you.

I would also like to thank Erin, Dan, Gavin, Vivienne, Michele Deppe, Rachel Sullivan, Cookie Hiponia, Laura Taylor Namey, Lisa Wyzlic, Matthew White, Oliver Creutzner, Spike Cordiner, Eve Jacob, Julie Hutchings, Kai Kiriyama, Cindy Baldwin, Paul Bonnington, Stephanie Allen, L. M. Murphy, and everyone else who contributed in one way or another, whether through beta reads, help with queries and pitches, lending me your expertise when I had research questions, or even your enthusiasm and support.

I'd especially like to thank my good friends and critique partners, Carey Torgesen and Helen Boswell, whose keen insights have helped me through many a character motivation or plot problem and who have encouraged me to keep going through every setback. The same goes for my Writerly group, Mark Benson, Jean Malone, Angi Black, Krista Welch, Jennifer Iacopelli, Sarah Blair, Christian Berkey, Tabitha Martin, Trisha Leigh, Jennifer Ritz, Megan Whitmer, Megan Orsini, Nicole Tersigni, Ashley Leath, Suzanne Brandenburg, Sarah Henning, and again, Carey Torgesen. There's no other group of people I'd rather spend nearly a week holed up in a cabin with, writing in our pj's, playing board games, and having nineties pop sing-alongs. I plotted this book at our very first Writerly Retreat, taking over an entire end of one of the cabin's dining tables with my index cards. You were there from the very start, through my dad's death, and through so many of the ups and downs of my life while writing this book. I hope my future projects will be infused with the Writerly cabin's magic as well.

But you wouldn't be reading any of this if not for my incredible agent, Natascha Morris, whose confidence in me and this book means the absolute world. And to Moe Ferrara, thank you so much for your support in this journey as well. I'd also like to thank my film agent, Addison Duffy, for sharing my enthusiasm for this story and for believing it could be even more.

I have so much gratitude for Camille Kellogg and the team at Imprint for starting my publishing journey with Macmillan, and for my editor Rachel Diebel and Jean Feiwel of Feiwel and Friends for taking me the rest of the way. Rachel, your keen eye and expertise have truly helped me dig deep into this story and bring out my best. Thank you to my production editor, Lelia Mander; my copy editor, Jacqueline Hornberger; jacket designer Rich Deas for such a gorgeous cover; Hana Tzou, whose cover copy skills are "chef's kiss"; and to the rest of the team at Feiwel and Friends. You've been such a fantastic group to work with. And to my authenticity readers, whose insights were so incredibly helpful, I cannot express my gratitude enough.

Of course, I can't close without thanking Annie and Lily, for being the best feline writing partners one could ask for, despite walking across my keyboard once or twice. Though your contributions did not make the final cut, I do appreciate the effort.

And thank you, dear reader, for being here, and for being you.

Thank you for reading this Feiwel & Friends book.
The friends who made *Dream to Me* possible are:

Jean Feiwel, Publisher
Liz Szabla, VP, Associate Publisher
Rich Deas, Senior Creative Director
Holly West, Senior Editor
Anna Roberto, Senior Editor
Kat Brzozowski, Senior Editor
Dawn Ryan, Executive Managing Editor
Kim Waymer, Senior Production Manager
Emily Settle, Editor
Rachel Diebel, Editor
Foyinsi Adegbonmire, Associate Editor
Brittany Groves, Assistant Editor
Kathleen Breitenfeld, Jacket Designer
Maithili Joshi and Michelle Gengaro-Kokmen,
Interior Book Designers
Lelia Mander, Production Editor

Follow us on Facebook or visit us online at mackids.com.
Our books are friends for life.